The Beauty and Depth of My Vines

ISBN: 978 1 7336922-0-5

Library of Congress Control Number 2019905741

The Beauty and Depth of My Vines

Stacey Renae

Table of Contents

Dedication

I dedicate this book to my Heavenly Father, as he sent his loving kindness and encouragement over the years—through my family, friends, teachers, professors, colleagues, and fellow authors—to inspire me to keep writing, keep believing in myself and to never stop Dreaming Big.

Author's Note

I truly praise and thank God for how far He has brought me and for blessing me to debut my first book of the written word in poetry. I pray "The Beauty and Depth of My Vines" is a blessing to all who read this book, which has been a labor of love for me over many years.

This book brings to life my love of writing and telling stories on various emotions in a very vivid, descriptive, and endearing manner to engage and inspire the reader.

Enjoy!

The Depth of Passion

Making Love

My body is totally relaxed, and my thoughts are vividly clear.

I am preparing my mind...to receive your loving, my dear.

Softly massage the small of my back with one hand, as you slowly caress my breasts with the other.

Gently, I feel the heat from your mouth, as you impress tender kisses to the nape of my neck.

Your only mission is to satisfy me...to make love to me...

Beyond the passions I have already known, into the depths of pleasures that my soul has uninhibitedly longed for.

Our eyes become interlocked as our bodies intensely overlap.

And, as I gaze into the eyes of my soul mate, my heart begins to melt, for the love between us is truly felt.

We have found our own private paradise in each other. Our destiny is our own ecstasy as our boundless emotions ignite.

I am your waterfall of sheer joy and indulgence, and you are my vintage well of quenched desires that I drink from daily.

Let's surround ourselves in each other, and we shall never be alone.

Passion

We are alone now…

My heart can't keep still, racing…pounding within my chest, as my body clings to yours…

Kisses are slow and succulent,

Tasting every bit of you…

My fingernails dance on the ripples of sweat on your skin.

I can't help but want you…all of you…!

Without limits or fear…but are you "good" for me?

You, who I want to pour myself into.

I cannot begin to explain why this passion is so good and intense…that inflames rims of pleasures and ecstasy that my body and soul has pillowed such sweet dreams of.

What do I do with these desires that live and breathe in the fiery scales of my being?

How do I live with such a burning passion for life, for love and you?

Just Love Me. Set Me Free!

Soul Man

I came to know you when I was very young and impetuous.

You came into my life as I was coming into my own.

I was just starting to absorb and enjoy the fruitfulness of my womanhood.

I was trying to give myself an emotional break from the ups and downs of romance,

But much to my surprise, this was the ordained time for me to meet you—

My Soul Man...

You and I seemed to groove to the same beats, and the things that made you tick made me tick too.

My Soul Man and I loved to cook for each other.

I loved that he would chase me around his place in the nude. We ate and drank from each other.

We were each other's food.

My Soul Man was my sweet thing, and I truly grew to love him like no other.

I could talk to **My Soul Man,** and he would patiently and lovingly listen to my heart.

He encouraged and challenged me as I did him.

We brought out the best in each other, and this is all we cared about at this time in our lives.

I must admit that loving **My Soul Man** grew me up in so many ways. I shall never forget him.

You were the prelude to my God-sent soulmate.

Two of a Kind

We both come from two different worlds, and by some remarkable hand of fate, our paths meet.

We both are in search of love and acceptance and at the same time have diverse ways of achieving the desires of our hearts.

In our attempt to find ourselves, we find each other.

Oh, what wonder and love that we have captured ourselves in?

You are strong where I am weak, and I am your strength when your eyes cannot fight the tears of your fears.

We are now one and the same, for I am you and you are me.

We are inseparable, and yet we are separate spirits.

It is not hard for me to understand,

Why we are together or what brought us together,

 For somewhere far and remote in our minds,

We really knew that we are "two of a kind."

A 90s Romance

So... What's up with this whole R*omance* thing anyway?

Why are we so willing to capture ourselves in it and so openly wanting to become enraptured by it?

Is it just the long-stemmed red roses and chocolate-covered strawberries with all of their oohs and ahhs?

Is it the wining and dining aspect of *romance*? High-priced meals or slow dragging in a mystic, secluded juke joint...to some **real, sweet, and sexy slow jams**?

Or could it be the soft whispers in my ear, with long, intense stares and delicious kisses?

Is it the thrill of the chase to allure me into countless sessions of mystery with hot passions beyond my most wildest and erotic fantasies?

Or can *Romance* be the simplest things?

Like the closeness I feel when you hold my hand. The sharing of **our** intimate thoughts and feelings... Long, endearing walks, and praying together over our meals.

Can the essence of *Romance* just be that I simply like you and I am interested in becoming close to you?

Can my heart be open and willing to let the course of nature and the flow of things to be...just happen naturally?

Can I just give myself to you and you give yourself to me with no questions asked? On the other hand, please do not play games with my mind and emotions... Man! Okay?

But seriously...These things make this whole *Romance* thing sound too complex with so much work to put forth... Maybe not...

Romance is definitely whatever I make of it, and I define my own terms to whatever makes me happy, with the true following of my heart...

Honey, I will tell you from the start, this whole *Romance* thing is so glamorized and quite scary to me... But I am so willing to give this a try, if you are, my love.

The Hunted

You are masculine and chivalrous in your ways, which draws me to you.

Your confidence, along with your strong sense of self, is intoxicating.

You know what you want, and you are wise to know how and when to go after what you want and get it.

Your steps are calculating and strategic as you plan your course for Conquering.

You are a true visionary and play out your wants and desires very descriptively in your mind.

Your affections are openly shown only when you are ready to give them.

You are the Hunter, hunting for a loving and supportive mate.

Someone you can love, protect, provide for and share your life and faith with.

I am **the Hunted**, and I do not need to come to you, for you seek after exactly what you want with no hesitation.

I am **the Hunted**, in high demand but seemingly undervalued.

You are the Hunter...able to handle me with my strong mind, beautiful curvy body, and captivating spirit.

I am **the Hunted,** waiting to indulge in your lovemaking and covering.

As you kiss my pains away. .

You find love, comfort, and tenderness in my arms.

You are the Hunter, and I am **the Hunted.**

I am what you want and need.

Come Get Me.

My Beach Home

A place of soft quietness...draped in white linen sheers...with bay windows slightly cracked, as cool winds enrapture the morning dew.

The marvel of sunrises and sunsets are remarkably similar, vividly clear through the glass ceiling...

Sunrises breathe life on the sleeping and the newly-awakened souls, while Sunsets seal the day with cloudless serenity.

Smooth-textured colors caress each room like individually-wrapped gifts.

The deck overlooks white sands. The waves are plush and reprising.

The fireplace harvests warmth and fills the heart with refined heat...and cuddled rest.

Such a place as this...where my soul lives...

Dance with Me

Dance with me...

Show me the way to your love through your endless, mesmerizing body movements.

Tickle my fancy as we flow together as one moving force of passionate perfection.

You make me nervous with just one touch, as your inner glow takes me in, and I willingly want to be held captive.

Teach me your way...as I follow your lead and walk in your steps.

My heart is free as you dance with me, and I am like a Dove soaring above all my cares and fears.

I feel joy, peace, and uncanny excitement as you swirl me around your world and private space.

Dance with me... Never let me go.

My Music is All I Have

I need something to lean on and something to soothe my analytical mind.

I only have my music, and it is one of a kind.

I write music with poetic lyrics and both together express all that I want to say and what needs to be said.

I sing my music, and my rhythmic tunes seem to come alive. I express my love of music in my instrumental play. The realism of my beats electrifies urban terrains each and every day.

I feel my music is the catalyst used to echo to the world all the love and beauty that is within my heart. For in my music, all my dreams come true and I come alive.

My music lives in me and I live in it.

My Music is me.

To the Beautiful One

To the one who inspired me and never knew it.

Your talent, style, and grace...even your sensuality connected with me consciously at a young age.

I mimicked you in the mirror, as I danced seductively to one of your most unforgettable sensual songs....***Scandalous***.

I wanted to learn to play as many instruments as I thought you did...14 was the magic number made public at the time...

I self-taught and learned how to play the keyboard at the age of 12, and I wanted for myself your white electric guitar that sprayed **Purple Rain** on your adoring audience in your most famous movie.

Your music inspired me to sing, play instruments, and write lyrics to music which was the forerunner to my poetic expression. And I truly wanted to indulge in the **Pop Life** and live **Under the Cherry Moon** with you.

I wanted to love you...and get my kicks with you, while wearing a **Raspberry Beret** with a coat of **Pink Cashmere.**

You are **Purple Rain**, and I am *Orange Rainbow*... You are **Prince,** and I am *Princess.*

Your music truly embodied love, sex, joy, and pain.

On the day you died, I thought of this particular song of yours, sadly... ***"Sometimes it snows in April... All good things, they say never last."***

So let the rain come down 17 days, is not nearly as many tears as I will shed in my lifetime missing you... I love you...

To the last Great Beautiful One... I wish U Heaven.

RIP... My Sweet **Prince.**

The Vines of Love

Love's Echo

When you say "I love you," I feel butterflies dancing in my soul.

You touch my hand and I feel desire, comfort, and peace.

You kiss my ear and I sigh in joy and excitement.

The little things are priceless between us.

When we are apart, I can feel your spirit from across the world as you feel mine.

Nothing and no one can separate us. In **sync**...in love...we are...

Our love is rare...blessed and timeless.

Our hearts truly beat as one.

We are **Love's Echo.**

Especially For You, the One I love

So many people have encountered my life.

Some have haunted my heart then fled like demons.

You have captured me like no one has done before.

Such a wonderful friend I have in you.

Pleasant thoughts fill my mind of you.

Maybe you are an angel in disguise, and I have not realized it up to this point.

Please continue to bring your love and precious gifts to me.

 All that I am trying to say is "I love you," Especially for you the one I love.

Emotion, Emotion

I always seem to become confused about my true emotions in these sought-after affairs. Love Affairs, that is.

My love relationships are never right, for I chose to live my life as the *leading lady* characters in plays, which I have dramatically performed in.

It appears that I steal their paths and embrace them as my own.

At first, I am "Delia," as she had the upper hand of love and deceit over Samson. In the same way as "Cleopatra" had Antony at her feet...

It's easy for men to be taken in by me, but in the end, I am "Juliet" in grieving despair.

I have looked for love in different places. I have played by different rules and drawn to different faces.

But I had to learn the "The Lessons of Love' the real cold, hard way. If love is gone from the eyes, don't fail to realize **it** this day.

If the dream of love is gone, let it fly away!

Stacey Renae

My Beloved

My love, I thank and praise My God and Savior for you.

I love you so much... My God has blessed me with you in my Life.

My husband, you are the Priest and head of my home.

I willingly submit myself unto you.

Our love is beautiful and precious.

We can praise our God together, for He is the center of our love and life.

My Beloved, I love you and accept you as you are with all of your strengths and weaknesses.

Oh, how I have prayed for my Lord to bless me with one of His children to join me as my companion, lover, and friend on this pilgrim's journey.

My Beloved, I pray that the fullness and strength of our love will carry us through the trials and challenges that this life will bring.

May our Almighty God keep His unchanging hands on our lives and love, that we may bear much fruit in His name.

My God answered my prayers by blessing me with you, My Beloved.

Together Forever

You came to me like a new and different season... A blooming sun with much light and shine.

You opened me, this dark gloomy existence, and overwhelmed me with your love.

You were such a refreshing spirit to me, unlike anyone I have ever known.

You simply adored me as I adored you. We were a match made in Heaven.

Then, one day, you left me and went onto the world that you belonged in: Heaven.

Me being the lost child that I am, l left my world to be with you in yours.

The Dream of Love

Looking back, I find myself wandering through my memories of you.

The picture-perfect image that I drew of you... I grew to love you so much without question or doubt.

I wanted you, and I was willing to undergo any feat to keep you.

But this in all was the folly of my fantasy.

You abruptly opened my eyes from the sweetness of my dream to the bitterness of your reality.

Yes, it was I who painted the picture, and I dreamed the dream of love and togetherness.

And you played the part from the start to get my heart and nearly my soul.

Then, you fled far from me, which you knew would make me lose control.

But you did it, for I was just another conquest in the wild oats of your manhood.

Maybe one day, when you wake up from your world of lust and denial—

You will remember the sweetness of my lips and the tenderness of my heart.

Maybe, if you were true and not such a fool, the Dream of Love could have been me and you.

Foolish Love

Thoughtful... Thoughtful of you like spools of endless memories breezing in and out of my mind.

My forsaken love, you left me in a pond of sorrowful tears.

My heart, crushed into countless grains of sand, destined to never love again.

How could I be taken in again by you?

Was I the fool? Or were you my unassuming patsy?

Who was allured into sessions of intrigue, beyond your most secret desires? Hum...

Only to have you callously leave your soulmate in the pursuit of another life...another love.

Now this time...

To have your own heart abandoned and broken...slowly and agonizingly.

All that you are left with are traces of love, lost love which will never return to you.

Oh, my darling, my soul will go on, it has to go on. My heart will mend, it has to mend... But will yours?

To Love

To Look deep inside yourself.

To See what is really there.

To Search for the truth.

To Confront and Conquer your fears.

To Strengthen your weakness.

To Seal your strengths with confidence.

To Secure your unbalanced emotions.

To Meet yourself one to one is to Love!

Love Yourself

My Sister, My Friend

Dedicated to my Sister, Carla

A sister holds a very special place in one's life.

She is your partner-in-crime on this life's journey in your youth, and your precious comforter and confidant as you grow older.

You grow through life with her, at the same speed and pace for most of the way.

A sister can be your memory and recall your most unforgettable childhood tales.

A sister can make you laugh like no other.

She is your surprise cheerleader and your ray of sunshine in somber times.

She makes you look at life from a different perspective, and she brings out the best in you that you don't see.

You are my sister and my kindest friend. I cannot express how much I truly treasure you.

Just remember that you are a special person with countless God-given gifts that you have yet to realize and explore.

May our God continue to bless you richly with the very best of everything this life has to offer.

This world is a much sweeter and gentler place with you in it.

Sister to Sister Love

Friend

Friend...

A word so simple, yet not freely given to others by me.

I value friendship as much as I value the love I have for my Savior and family.

I embrace the "Trio" of God, Family, and Friends very close to my heart.

Many people have breezed and eased in and out of my life,

But only a friend will remain.

I am moody and sometimes spoiled even, but you are still here.

Even when I lost contact with you, I prayed endlessly for your safety and wellbeing.

I am in your corner when you win and when you fall.

I will wipe your tears away, and never lose my respect and admiration for you as a person. You can **bare** your soul and most intimate thoughts with me, and I will never tell them.

These are our secrets and private jokes.

Our long talks filled with indescribable laughter and the sharing of ourselves will live within me forever.

You are my friend... One of the closest persons to my heart.

I am praying for your happiness, success, strength, direction, and salvation.

You are my friend and I love you.

This is what "friend" means to me, and this is what you mean to me.

Always remember, my friend, that I am here for you.

The Beauty of Life

"LIFE"

The Adventure of LIFE is to Learn.

The Purpose of LIFE is to Grow.

The Nature of LIFE is to Change.

The Challenge of LIFE is to Overcome.

The Essence of LIFE is to Care.

The Opportunity of LIFE is to Serve.

The Secret of LIFE is to Dare.

The Spice of LIFE is to Befriend.

The Beauty of LIFE is to Give.

The Joy of LIFE is to Love.

White Cloud, Blue Sky

Blue was your favorite color. Mine too.

I miss you, Daddy, I really do.

I remember all of your light blue jeans and stripy blue shirts that you used to wear too.

Your tennis shoes were always white and blue. Mine are too.

I really never thought about how much we thought alike.

My big plans for success and your dreams of success...

You were proud of me, and I knew this to be true.

You cheered me on in everything positive that you saw me do.

You were not perfect. So no one is, but Jesus...

And I love you anyway...

You looked so handsome in your blue suit and light gold shirt on your

"Home-going Day."

I looked on your face for a long time on that day for I reflected on all that you had been through.

I saw that you were at peace... "You had been in the storm for too long."

It was your time to leave all of your ills and to fly high, so high on a beautiful White cloud, into the deep Blue Sky to rest in God's hands forevermore.

Courage Rain

In the mist of storm clouds and explosive lightening, a still and calm-set moment surfaced.

As I lay in my bed, my mind flushes forward, and I begin pondering on the future...my future. Do I have one?

Will my dreams be realized with a sense of fulfillment, purpose, and truth?

As Courage Rain pours out of my veins, my anticipation grows stronger to savor every morsel of this life.

With my zeal as a Conqueror and Victor in this life, I am determined not to let my life just pass me by.

I must try...take chances and fulfill my Dreams.

Venture out into the unpredictable wilds that this life brings, which I have no control over.

And...keep my Faith.

With Courage Rain within me, treading on dry sands is lighter to bear.

Flowers are still birthed in desert seasons and hazed thirsts are quenched in famine.

Life So Fragile

Life is so short and fragile.

When you are young, you don't have a sense of time.

You just want to be grown and get all the things that you
want and dream of.

Time is slow, and summer days seem to last all year.

Life is short, and people are fragile.

People are human, make mistakes and have regrets.

Some things that happen to you, you do not have control over

And you deal with your pains in youth and in older years.

Life is short, beautiful, and fragile.

No one is young forever, and invincibility is not an option in this
life.

Live life, laugh, smile, dance, and enjoy every joyous moment
possible.

Love the ones that you love and be good to yourself and others.

Life is short and fragile. One day, life will be gone.

Classy Lady

She enters into a room and her presence is felt.

As she breezes by, her sweet fragrance sweeps up the air.

She carries herself with dignity and femininity.

She is smart, strong, and intentional in her actions.

She knows who she is, and openly embraces helping and caring for others.

When you look into her eyes, you can catch a glimpse of her strength, resilience, and kindness.

She is above pettiness but will address it.

She challenges as well as brings out the best in others.

She brings fun, sassiness, and support to those she loves.

Her spirit is radiant, loving, full of joy, and inspires others.

You are proud and Blessed to have her in your corner.

Know My Heart

You again.. A blast from my past...trying to push your way to be a part of my present and yearning to be intertwined with my future.

Sharp-witted, charming even and not hard on the eyes...most would say.

You again...who pops up when you are lonely or in despair, hoping that I will come and rescue you.

You are a wandering yet familiar spirit...that I still love, and you love me.

But you have never been all mine, for I am just too much for you!

You have never taken the time to know my heart, as I know yours...

My heart has ached, been afraid and lonesome, which is all unknown to you.

You have played on my vulnerability. You come around...so you can receive my support, soak up my strength, then suddenly leave again.

To know me is to love me. To love me is to know my heart, which is an ocean of love, strength, purity, and wisdom.

Which you would never want to depart from...if you really knew me

This time, you cannot come back to me. My heart is closed to you. I am not going to let you in.

You again... Not this time or ever again!

God has truly opened my eyes to you.

Find My Way

Find my way to this place.

A place of refined wholesomeness and comfort.

A place where the air is fresh and crisp. The skies are amazingly clear.

A place of safety and warmth that fills my heart with gladness.

A place I am not afraid to lay my head down and rest my eyes.

A place filled with laughter, where purity and holiness reside forever.

A place where I am not discriminated based on my color, race, gender, social class or denomination.

A place where everyone loves everyone with a genuine and sincere heart.

A place where the pains and struggles of this world are cast away forever.

Such a healing place where I can lay burdens down, and they become weightless and float away.

A calming place...where Peace lives and reigns forever.

A place filled with never-ending Praise and Worship.

A place filled with the presence of God, and my Jesus lives there.

Ah...such a glorious and majestic place as this.

Ah, Heaven is this place I will be when my God comes back to take me home.

I must find my way to Heaven.

My Ego Tripping Part 1

The bright, arising sun caresses the powder blue skies with kisses, as the cool winds blow on this hot summer day.

Everyone is outside sitting on their steps, either eating a snowball or playing the neighborhood game "Its.

I quietly stroll through the urban terrains of my neighborhood, and I casually observe that all eyes are on me.

I am the around-the-way girl. I am the neighborhood kid, who goes away to College outside of the inner city.

I am the nerdy girl, who did not get pregnant in the 9th grade. I am neighborhood chick, that some of the boys speak to with admiration and respect.

The rest just turn their heads, because I am the one that they could not get. I am given the "mean-eye" by others, but some of the older ladies speak to me and say "Hi."

I know this is why they watch me so intensely.

I represent their hopes and dreams of success and achievement.

I am their symbol of the past (Inner City Blues), the present (We are moving on up), and the future (Ain't No Stopping Us Now).

I must admit, this attention really tickles me.

I feel when I come home from my educational journey that I have a fan club with an adoring audience waiting my arrival.

They know that the "Star" is home.

CARE

I listen to my heart and sometimes,

My heart is so "Big and Loud".

My inspiration comes from within me...great and loud—

Sounding...echoing with a harmonious "Roar"

All I want is to be heard and received...

My inspiration moves from within me to others—

Compassionate and...intense,

My heart wants to love and protect everyone close to me.

Hear them, love them, inspire them...

Inspire them to live, to be themselves, and to dream, Big and Loud!

Because...sometimes, it is not all about me.

God is trying to tell you something... What?

Be Optimistic

To feel as well as display optimism daily is a struggle for most people.

Trying to focus on the positivity in this life is sometimes inconceivable.

Indeed, it's a challenge (emotionally, mentality, spiritually) to remain positive, sane, and secure.

Sometimes, life is very **unfair**! But, my sweet child, there is hope in Jesus.

There is a shining, glowing, brazen light at the end of this dark tunnel.

Do not allow the Adversary and his presence through others to steal your joy and peace of mind.

First

Count your blessings. Name them one by one, and see what the Lord has already done in your life. Let the Lord (our Creator and Father), through His Holy Spirit, be your counselor and guide. He knows you and your circumstances better than anyone. He may guide you to someone who can further counsel you and/or assist you according to your situation.

Second

Start looking "inside of yourself." Focus on the good that is inside of you. Concentrate on your strengths and your best character traits, knowing and realizing that no one is perfect but Jesus Christ. Our God has blessed you with gifts and talents. Seek His face in discovering His purpose for your life. Write down your goals and aspirations in a realistic manner with timelines—first seeking the Kingdom of God. Know and believe that "You can do all things through Jesus Christ who strengthens you" (Phil. 4:13).

Third

Be good to yourself! No one will treat or love you better than you, beside our God. Indulge yourself in lavish baths of milk and honey. Relax and treat yourself to a good book, a new outfit, a special meal or a trip of a lifetime. Pray and meditate, spending quality time with God. Clear your mind and focus on Him—His will and seek his way for your life.

The Lord loves you, and He calls **all** of His children to live in Victory, Peace, Prosperity, and Love.

Be Positive, Be Optimistic

You Can Win!

Closing Poems

Lifted Hands

Just to Get Here

(There is sunshine at the end of the rain.)

Many tears I have shed, just to get here.

Overcoming multitudes of obstacles, challenges, setbacks

Beyond my own understanding.

Just to get here.

Letting some people go—some family, friends, and revealed foes.

Just to get here.

Pressing forward, in spite of my past, pain, self-limitations, and me...

Just to get here.

Removing the veil of self-doubt from my own eyes and allowing myself to let the Gifts that God has blessed with me to radiantly shine.

God has moved mountains, fought my battles, defeated my enemies, and kept me just so I could get here.

This is how I got here, only by the Grace of God!

Do You Dare to Love?

How deep is your love, my fair maiden, my good man?

Can it climb the highest mountain and overflow into the deepest sea?

Is it unconditional and ever giving and forgiving?

Are you only looking to give love in hopes to just receive it?

Will loving someone empty you of your self-love or drain your own life's purpose and focus?

Is loving someone outside of yourself just too needy to handle, and being alone in your own world is better than nurturing and emotional endurance?

Who dares to love with such demands, without hesitation and is spiritually able to handle this task?

The perfect giver of love is JESUS.

JESUS IS LOVE. His love is patient, kind, powerful, sweet, never-ending, ever giving, unconditional, selfless, and pure.

His love is the true tester of time, for He loved you before you knew and accepted Him into your heart and life.

He is the perfect sacrifice.

The giving of His life gave you and me eternal life. JESUS is the lover of our soul. He is our most precious gift. Who dares to love you?

JESUS does...

Keep Me, My Lord

As I soar into the depth of my spirit, I find a serene, refined place.

Where my thoughts are clear and settled.

This where I come to meet my Lord...

I meet my Lord on the Banks of the River Jordan, where his grace and mercy overflows.

As I surround myself in the beauty of the Holy Presence of my Lord and King, I slowly utter this prayer from my mouth...

Keep me, my Lord, meek and humble as you pour out your abundant blessings upon me.

Never let me forget who I am and most of all, whose I am, for I belong to you.

Protect me, my Lord, from my enemies and all who rise up against me.

Father God, my foes are so many.

This world will hate and despise me as they hated my Savior, your son, Jesus Christ.

I do not delight and embellish myself in the pleasures of this world, for they are only temporary. But the treasures of Heaven are from everlasting to everlasting.

Keep me, my Lord. Be my fortress when I am weak.

Direct my life's paths according to your will and riches in glory.

I am not my own, I belong to you.

Keep me, my Lord, my Mind, Body and Spirit. Humbly, your child and servant...

Amen!

About the Author

Stacey Renae grew up in Maryland and has always loved to sing, dance, write stories, poetry and play instruments. She holds degrees in hospitality and business management and is a true lover of traveling, performance, visual and culinary arts. Stacey Renae is an inspirational writer, poet and has expressed aspirations in writing in several genres including: romantic thrillers, drama, mystery/suspense and fiction that ultimately connect to each other. She hopes to engage, intrigue, inspire and uplift the reader for the wonderful journey ahead still awaits to unfold.

Made in the USA
Columbia, SC
23 May 2022

Alexandra Kollontai
Writings from the Struggle
Selected and translated by Cathy Porter

Alexandra Kollontai: Writings from the Struggle
Selected and translated by Cathy Porter

© Cathy Porter
First published by Bookmarks in 2020
Bookmarks Publications Ltd
c/o 1 Bloomsbury Street,
London WC1B 3QE
www.bookmarksbookshop.co.uk
ISBN 978-1-912926-30-5 paperback
ISBN 978-1-912926-31-2 kindle
ISBN 978-1-912926-32-9 epub
ISBN 978-1-912926-33-6pdf
Typeset by Bookmarks Publications
Cover design by Colm Bryce & Simon Assaf
Printed by Halstan & Co Ltd, Amersham,
Buckinghamshire, England

CONTENTS

Foreword

Alexandra Kollontai was one of the most popular and brilliant writers of the Russian Revolution. She wrote from the front line of the epic struggles of her lifetime, for women's equality and workers' power, and she found a new language to connect these struggles with the revolution in people's relationships, and their feelings about love and sex. I wanted these new translations of her writings a century after October to speak to us in these revolutionary times, with their message of hope, solidarity and women's liberation. Thanks to Colm Bryce at Bookmarks for his encouragement.

About the author

Cathy Porter is a lifelong socialist and activist. She has published books on Russia about women revolutionaries in the 1860s, the art of the 1905 revolution, Moscow in WW2, biographies of Kollontai and the poet and revolutionary Larisa Reisner and over thirty translations, including *The Diaries of Sofia Tolstoy,* Dmitry Bykov's award-winning novel *Living Souls,* and the plays of Maxim Gorky and Karel Capek. A new edition of her Reisner biography will be published this year by Historical Materialism Books, with a volume of translations of Reisner's writings. She is now translating works by the novelist Lydia Seifullina, and working on a biography of Gorky.

Timeline: Key events in the years covered in the book

1861 Emancipation of serfs.

1872 19 March: Alexandra Kollontai born in St Petersburg.

1877 Russia's war in the Balkans with Turkey.

1881 Tsar Alexander II assassinated. Leading terrorists hanged.

1888 Kollontai gains teaching diploma. Has private courses in literature and history.

1893 Marries her cousin Vladimir Kollontai.

1894 Gives birth to their son Misha.
Tsar Nicholas II comes to the throne.

1895 Marxist groups in St Petersburg unite under Lenin as the League of Struggle for the Emancipation of the Working Class.

1896 Kollontai's first visit to a factory.
May-June: huge textile workers' strikes in St Petersburg. She works with the Political Red Cross, smuggling strike leaflets into the factories.

1898 Leaves Vladimir and their son to study Marxist economics in Switzerland.

1899 Ends her marriage. Joins the revolutionary underground and Russia's new Marxist party, the Social Democratic Workers' Party, led by Lenin.

1900-1903 Continues her Marxist studies in France and
Switzerland. Travels frequently to Finland,
publishing articles about Finnish workers' lives.

1903 Works with Bolsheviks and Mensheviks as writer and
agitator. Represents Russian party in Finland. Teaches at
workers' evening classes in St Petersburg.

1904 Joins demonstrations against Russia's war with Japan.
Speaks at factory meetings and student rallies. Joins
Bolsheviks.

1905 Marches in workers' demonstration in January to the
Winter Palace, where two thousand killed by Tsarist
troops. After "Bloody Sunday," writes illegal leaflets
calling for the overthrow of the Tsar. Elected treasurer
of social democrats' central committee in St Petersburg.
Battles socialists and feminist organisations to draw
factory women into the revolutionary movement.

1906 Joins Mensheviks. Organises meetings with women in St
Petersburg's Textileworkers' Union.

1907 Represents Textileworkers' Union at Seventh Congress
of the Socialist International in Stuttgart, and at its
Women's Conference.

1908 Sets up political club for women workers in St Petersburg.
Mobilises them to raise their demands at feminists'
All-Russian Congress of Women. Warrant for her arrest
for calling for an armed uprising, goes underground.
Writes *The Social Basis of the Woman Question*, outlining
the socialist approach to the women's liberation
movement. December: leaves Russia for Germany to
escape arrest. Lives in exile for the next eight years.

1914 Speaks at anti-war meetings in Germany, Sweden, Switzerland, France and Belgium. Works with the Socialist International in Berlin organising women's anti-war demonstrations. August: arrested and jailed three days after war declared. September: leaves Germany for Denmark, then Sweden and Norway.

1915 Rejoins Bolsheviks. Works in Norway for the Bolsheviks' Northern Underground, smuggling Lenin's writings into Russia. Visits America for five-month anti-war speaking tour. Writes her pamphlet for the Bolsheviks *Who Needs the War?*

1916 Her book *Society and Motherhood* published in St Petersburg (now Petrograd).

1917 April: returns to Petrograd two weeks after the revolution that toppled the Tsar. Writes for Bolsheviks' paper *Pravda*. Elected to Executive of the Petrograd Soviet. April-October: the only Bolshevik in the Soviet to speak in support of Lenin's revolutionary *April Theses*. Speaks at meetings calling on workers to support the Bolsheviks. Joins editorial board of Party women's paper *Woman Worker*. July: jailed by Provisional Government as a German spy. Elected in jail to Party central committee.

11 October: attends historic central committee meeting to plan the insurrection. 25 October: delegate at Second All-Russian Congress of Soviets, at which Bolsheviks take power. Elected Commissar of Social Welfare in the first Bolshevik government. Opens communal canteens, orphanages and homes for war veterans. Passes legislation on maternity protection, equal pay, and the protection of women's labour.

1918 March: joins Left Opposition against the Brest-Litovsk Treaty with Germany. Resigns from her Commissariat when Treaty ratified.

Spring — summer: travels to the Volga front of the civil war, calling on people to defend the Revolution against the counter-revolutionary White armies. November: organises All-Russian Congress of Women Workers and Peasants in Moscow. Delivers speech later published as her pamphlet *Communism and the Family*.

1919 Frontline propaganda in Ukraine. Appointed Ukraine's Commissar of Propaganda and Agitation. September: works in Moscow with the new Party women's department, the *Zhenotdel.*

1920 November: appointed Director of the *Zhenotdel*, enforcing women's labour legislation, setting up a commission on prostitution, guiding the new law legalising abortion.

1921 March: censured by Party leaders when she presents the programme of the Workers' Opposition to the Tenth Party Congress.

1922 March: threatened with expulsion from the Party at the Eleventh Congress.

April: Stalin appointed Party General Secretary.

1923 Appointed by Stalin to head Soviet trade delegation in Norway.

Introduction

Alexandra Kollontai was born in 1872 in St Petersburg, capital of the Tsarist Empire, eleven years after Tsar Alexander II issued his Decree on the Emancipation of Russia's Serfs — "Our sacred duty bequeathed to Us by Our ancestors, which Divine providence has called on Us to fulfill". To his ministers, the Tsar said "Better end serfdom from above than wait for them to abolish it from below".

Eighty percent of the population and eighty percent illiterate, Russia's twenty-three million serfs paid a terrible price for their freedom. In the Emancipation's redivision of the land, two-thirds went to the royal family, the landowners and the Church, leaving them with the most unproductive plots, for which they paid crippling taxes. Driven from the countryside by debts and starvation, thousands migrated to the cities to work in atrocious conditions in the new factories, or as servants in the homes of the wealthy.

Like most girls of the aristocracy, Kollontai was raised mainly by nannies and governesses. Living in squalor in a separate wing of the family's house in St Petersburg were the lower paid staff — the cooks, cleaners, maids and coachmen and their families. Her parents held liberal views about Russian society, and were known as exemplary employers. But she saw the grinding poverty of the servants' lives when she defied her mother to play with their children. In her *Autobiographical Essay*, published four years after the Bolshevik Revolution, she wrote: "I didn't know the meaning of privation, but I saw how my playmates were forced to do with out things, and knowing that they suffered when I lived so well grieved me deeply".

"God is too high and the Tsar is too far away," went the peasant saying. The tsars derived their divine authority to rule from the Orthodox Church, and the religious persecution of Muslims and Jews went with the persecution of Poles, Ukrainians, Finns, Germans, and all the other ethnic groups living under Tsarist rule. Muslims were periodically rounded up from their villages and drafted into the army. Jews were driven into the special "Residential Provinces" of the Jewish Pale of Settlement, which by the nineteenth century covered almost a million square kilometres of Russia, from the Baltic to the Black Sea.

Women were associated with every conceivable vice and sin. Under the tsarist marriage law, sanctioned by the Church, they were little better than slaves, unable to work or travel in Russia without their husbands' permission, ordered to be "respectful, loving and submissive at all times, and to show every compliance and affection," and to be beaten regularly to keep them in their place. The peasant woman was legally classified virtually as live stock, with no voice in family or village affairs. Even many noblewomen led lives of constant childbearing and domestic abuse.

The exceptions were married women with property, like Kollontai's mother. Women's inheritance and property rights in Russia were far in advance of those elsewhere in Europe, and she ran a successful timber business, inherited from her father. She had educated herself, read the liberal journals, did charity work with the peasants on her estate, and was a devotee of the "rational dress" movement, which campaigned for comfortable clothing for women, without corsets, and she showed her daughter that women must be self-reliant, hardworking and financially independent.

The end of serfdom had inspired women too to fight for their liberation, and the "woman question" was the burning issue of the 1860s and 1870s. Women from the poorer landowning families bankrupted by the Emancipation were forced to find work as governesses and secretaries in the cities, where groups of aristocrat women were energetically petitioning the Tsar for their access to education. In 1872 he announced the setting up of new girls' secondary schools, but women were still barred from higher education, and the better-off left Russia to study at universities in Switzerland and Germany. They returned as doctors, lawyers and teachers, and many returned as socialists, and joined Russia's first socialist groups, the Populists, who believed the peasants would lead the fight against tsarism. The Populists' programme called for the complete equality of the sexes, and women became leading organisers, travelling with men "to the people," working in the villages as doctors and teachers, preaching peasant revolution.

They were arrested with the men, and sentenced to long terms in Siberia, and revolutionaries still at liberty went underground to form the new People's Will Party, committed to killing Tsar Alexander II. Until then, they believed there could be no political freedom in Russia.

The Tsar's assassination in 1881 cast a shadow over Kollontai's ninth year, and ended any hope of reforms from above. Karl Marx called the new Tsar, Alexander III, "the hated gendarme of European reaction". He blamed the "Jewish plague" for his father's murder, declaring in his Accession Manifesto his "full faith in the power of the Autocracy," and announcing his programme of "counterreforms" — increasing the powers of the secret police, ruthlessly imposing the Russian language and the Orthodox faith on other nationalities and religions, raising school fees to exclude all but the wealthiest, and wiping out the recent advances in women's education.

His reign also saw a spectacular growth in industry, and the birth of Russia's small new merchant capitalist class. But over three-quarters of the new mines, factories and railways were owned by German, Belgian, French or British companies, attracted by Russia's vast natural resources and cheap labour. Workers were generally less badly treated by their foreign employers than by the Russians, but despite all the new Western technology and improved communications, they still lacked the most basic political rights, including the right to vote.

Throughout the 1880s, factory workers' rage against their intolerable conditions exploded into Russia's first major strikes. Peasant women were slower than men to arrive in the factories. Underfed, underpaid and illiterate, their energy drained by the double burden of paid work and caring for their children, they were also slower to strike. But once their anger was roused, they protested with extraordinary courage and often violence. In the country's first textile strikes in the 1880s, they downed tools with the men, destroying so much factory machinery that the government was forced to pass its first factory laws, banning night work for women and the employment of children under twelve, limiting the working hours of those under fifteen to eight a day. The laws were routinely ignored, and strikes continued in an explosive and more or less spontaneous manner throughout the next decade.

In 1894, a year after Kollontai left home to get married, Tsar Alexander's son Nicholas 11 came to the throne, and in May 1896 was crowned Emperor of Russia, and his dominions Poland, Ukraine, and the Grand Duchy of Finland. Three days later, over a thousand of his citizens were trampled to death on Moscow's Khodynka Field, where they had come to receive their promised coronation gifts.

Tsarist policies in the countryside had been brutally exposed in the great famines of 1891 and 1892, which destroyed whole villages, and left three million peasants dead. The new Tsar passed laws restricting their rights to leave the land. He called political rights "alien to the Russian soul," and popular representation "the greatest fraud of our time," and he ordered education to be limited to basic arithmetic and the Orthodox scriptures — "all the rest is superfluous and dangerous". A committed autocrat and rabid anti-Semite, like his father, he forbade Jews to settle in the countryside, and personally sponsored the "Black Hundreds" gangs, which organised savage pogroms in the towns and villages against Jews, workers and students.

Forced by famine to defy his laws, peasants continued to pour into the cities to work in the factories, where economic strikes for better pay and conditions were increasingly turning into political strikes against the autocracy. It was in the 1890s that workers began to create organisations that would support them in their battles, and to look to the new revolutionary groups in the cities, who were finding a new strategy and philosophy of revolution in the works of Marx.

Marx wrote of the historical limits of capitalism, and of the inevitable breakdown of the capitalist order, and he identified class struggle as the engine of history. Revolutions against capitalism would begin as bourgeois ones in their immediate goals, he wrote, but the ruling class would quickly reveal its contradictions, allowing the new revolutionary class, the proletariat, to rise up against its exploitation. "Then will begin the kingdom of socialism, the kingdom of peace, the kingdom of the toilers".

The first Russian translation in 1872 of Marx's *Capital* had been enthusiastically discussed by socialists, more for its philosophical and economic ideas than as a guide to revolutionary action. Capitalism in Russia had been barely developed then. Marx had seen Russia's proletariat, three percent of the population, as still too small to fulfill its historic revolutionary role, and socialism was still defined by the Populists, who saw the peasants as the agents of revolutionary change. But the turmoil in the factories throughout the 1890s seemed to be proving Marx wrong.

By then the working population of Russia had doubled, and socialists in St Petersburg were setting up underground Marxist study groups to put his ideas into action. In 1895, the groups came together as the League of Struggle for the Emancipation of the Working Class, led by Lenin, the first political organisation in Russia to offer tactical support to the strike movement, and recruit members from the factories.

Organisers risked arrest to meet workers and plan strike action, and the summer of 1896 saw a new wave of industrial unrest, mainly in St Petersburg's cotton mills, where anything from a quarter to half the workforce were women. These women would be the inspiration for all Kollontai's later work as a revolutionary, showing her that in striking they were both finding their natural allies in the workers' movement and fighting for their own liberation. She paid her first visit to a factory, studied the works of Marx and Engels, read Lenin's strike leaflets, and was drawn into the revolutionary underground.

In 1898, revolutionaries held the founding conference of Russia's first Marxist party, the Russian Social Democratic Workers' Party, and affiliated to the Socialist International, created by Marx to cut across the national borders thrown up by capitalism to divide workers, and "unite socialists of the world in the fight for peace and social revolution".

The summer of 1898 brought more disastrous harvests in Russia and another famine, and a mass strike at Moscow's giant Gubner cotton mill, with its mainly female workforce. Strikes quickly spread to three hundred factories across Russia, and universities rioted for reforms. Strikers, students and Jews were jailed or fled abroad, and revolutionaries who escaped arrest went underground. In 1899, Kollontai joined the Social Democratic Party, and became part of its network of agents who kept workers in touch with the underground, organising printing presses to put out strike leaf lets, and helping to smuggle them into the factories.

The first year of the new century saw the birth of the new Socialist Revolutionary Party, successor to the People's Will, which called for direct action against the state, and drew mass support from the countryside. Terrorists assassinated hated police-chiefs, government officials and members of the royal family, and peasants looted and burnt the landowners' estates, breaking into the barns to seize the grain.

The social democrats had come into existence to oppose the terror tactics of the Populists with their programme of class war against capitalism, and their message was reaching the factories. The first sparks of revolution in Russia were lit in the summer of 1903, by the economic slump that hit the industrial south. Workers suffered wage cuts, layoffs and deteriorating conditions, and mass strikes across a vast area, from Ukraine to the Caucasus, brought rail ways, factories and oil wells to a halt. Strikes and student riots swept across Russia to Latvia, Poland and Siberia, and local revolutionaries set up strike support groups, and demonstrated with banners saying "Down with the Autocracy!" "Victory to the Democratic Republic!" Entire villages and Jewish communities were massacred in retaliation, and thousands of strikers were arrested or fled abroad.

In August 1903, social democrats from Russia and exile met in Brussels (before reconvening in London) to discuss their tactics in the struggle, and split on how they saw the party needed to lead it. The Menshevik faction wanted a large party, similar to those in Germany and Britain, open to revolutionaries and non-revolutionaries alike, to campaign for social reforms. The Bolsheviks, led by Lenin, argued that legal work was impossible in autocratic Russia, and that without a tightly centralised and largely underground party, the revolution would be smashed. Workers could not wait for the first bourgeois stage of the revolution envisaged by Marx, Lenin said, and instead of begging concessions from capitalism, they should be preparing to seize power directly from the state.

Over the years the differences between the factions would become irreconcilable, culminating in 1914, when a majority of Mensheviks supported Russia's mobilisation in the First World War. In 1903, like many social democrats, Kollontai attached herself to neither faction and offered her services to both, speaking at meetings, raising strike funds, writing leaflets and articles for the underground press.

In January 1904, the Tsar used the time-honoured tactic of liquidating dissent by conscripting men into the army, to fight in Russia's war with Japan. Six months later, most of the Russian fleet was at the bottom of the Tsushima Straits, and the Tsar's imperial ambitions in Asia were in ruins. Month after month, as the war brought fresh agonies of defeat and suffering, the countryside blazed with riots, and the cities were convulsed by strikes, producing a surge of support for the Bolsheviks and the Socialist Revolutionaries. That summer, terrorists assassinated the Minister of the Interior and the Russian Governor-General of Poland, and in the ensuing arrests and pogroms, thousands more escaped into exile.

In December 1904, Kollontai joined the Bolsheviks. During Russia's first revolution of 1905, she helped to smuggle

Bolshevik leaflets into the garrisons and factories, spoke at meetings at factory gates, and organised women's meetings in the capital's workers' clubs, where she began to work out the tactics needed to draw women into the struggle, and make them a powerful force for political change.

The revolution was crushed, and hundreds of her comrades were arrested, and at the end of 1908, with two police warrants for her arrest, she left Russia for exile. For the next eight and a half years, she was based in Germany and Scandinavia, speaking at meetings across Europe and in America, campaigning in the left revolutionary wing of the Socialist International against war and capitalism and for women's liberation.

When Russia entered the war in 1914, she was one of only a small number of revolutionaries who supported Lenin's message to turn the imperialist war into a revolutionary class war against capitalism. She returned to Russia in April 1917, after the revolution that toppled the Tsar, and she was the only Bolshevik in the Petrograd Soviet to speak in support of Lenin's call to overthrow the Provisional Government and stop the war.

By then she was forty-five, a figure of great stature in the Bolshevik Party, a charismatic leader of women, and one of the Party's most gifted and popular public speakers. Over the next six months, she spoke at mass meetings in the factories and on board the battleships of the Baltic Fleet, spreading the Bolsheviks' message of peace, revolution and women's liberation, campaigning in the Party for women's rights to be at the top of its agenda.

When the Bolsheviks came to power in October, she was elected Commissar of Social Welfare in the first Soviet government, its only woman, responsible for reforming the chaotic Tsarist welfare system. She set up new children's nurseries, maternity hospitals and homes for orphans and war veterans, guided much of the Revolution's early legislation on women's maternity rights and working conditions, and helped to draft the Bolsheviks' progressive new Marriage Law of December 1917.

In the spring of 1918, when the massed armies of the

West invaded Russia to bring down the Bolsheviks, backed by the counter-revolutionary White Guards, she travelled to the battlefronts appealing to people to fight to defend the Revolution, and she worked with women on the home front, setting up emergency medical centres, orphanages and canteens.

By the end of 1920, the invaders had been driven out, and against unimaginable odds, the Revolution had survived. With the fighting finally over, women's heroic contribution to victory was rewarded with a new Party women's department, the *Zhenotdel*, headed by Kollontai, which battled male chauvinism to involve them in the fight for their emancipation, and campaigned in the Party for a proper political commitment to tackling their continuing inequality.

Her tenure at the *Zhenotdel* ended in 1922. In the debates about the new economy after the civil war, she wrote the programme of the Workers' Opposition, which attacked the Party for bringing the old capitalist managers back to run the factories, and called for workers' control over industry through the trade unions. The Opposition's leaders were accused of trying to split the Party, and threatened with expulsion. But Kollontai was too valuable to the government, and instead she was sent out of Russia in the autumn of 1922 by the new Party Secretary, Stalin, who appointed her to a diplomatic post in Norway.

She lived abroad for the next twenty-three years, as Soviet ambassador to Norway, then Mexico and Sweden, the world's first woman ambassador. Hundreds of her friends and comrades were shot as enemies of the people, or disappeared into Stalin's camps, but she survived. She gradually lost touch with Russia in those years, and she wrote little. But she was greatly admired there and in the West for her skilful sensitive diplomacy. In 1924, she negotiated full diplomatic and economic relations between the Soviet Union and Norway. In 1940, she represented Moscow in peace talks with Finland to end the Soviet-Finnish War. In 1944, during the brutal four-year Nazi occupation of the

Soviet Union, when Finland was an ally of Hitler, she led the lengthy secret talks with the Finnish and Swedish governments that secured Finland's neutrality.

She was recalled to Moscow the following March, two months before Soviet Victory Day, and she was awarded her second Red Banner of Labour. She was given a flat and a pension, and she worked as an advisor to the Ministry of Foreign Affairs, serving the Party loyally until her death in 1952 at the age of eighty, a year before the death of Stalin.

The ideals she had fought for had been betrayed. But she never lost her faith that a better world was possible, and that future generations would continue the struggle for socialism and women's liberation. In her last diaries, published in 1972, the centenary of her birth, she wrote: "Women and their fate drew me to socialism, and occupied me throughout my life. Let women who come later see we weren't heroes or heroines. Sometimes we were strong, sometimes we were weak, but we believed in our goals, and we pursued them passionately".

Her friend Anna Itkina's engaging and affectionate biography of her, *Revolutionary, Tribune, Diplomat*, published twelve years after her death, at the height of the Cold War, avoids any mention of her murdered comrades, her frequent clashes with the Party, or her more controversial ideas about sexual liberation and workers' power. There are similar gaps in the two otherwise extensive Soviet editions of her works, published in 1972 and 1974, *Selected Articles and Speeches,* and her autobiographical writings *From My Life and Work,* which include large parts of her *Autobiographical Essay.* Most of the writings translated in this book are from these collections. Two of her works on the sexual revolution missing from her *Selected Articles* were translated from versions recently republished online.

These new translations are not the "complete" Kollontai. They are a small selection of her writings from the revolutionary struggle, from her first discovery of Marx in her twenties, when revolutionaries were a tiny underground sect, to her place in the first Bolshevik government, and her fight to defend Soviet power.

In her years as a revolutionary she wrote prolifically, publishing seven books and over two hundred articles, essays and pamphlets — anti-war agitation, government and *Zhenotdel* decrees, reports of meetings and conferences, fiction, book reviews and memoirs, and her writings on women and the family. She was modest about her literary skills. "I don't consider myself a good writer, just average. My style is clear and direct, and I'm good at sketches of people, but my images are pale". Her readers disagreed. She was known as a brilliant polemicist, and for her lively campaigning style, the famous "Kollontai style". After the Revolution her works reached a new mass readership of workers, intellectuals and the newly literate, and the press was filled with requests for more from her and Lenin.

She began to be discovered in the West in the 1970s, when translations of her articles and pamphlets became essential reading for the protest movement. In 1968, her Workers' Opposition pamphlet was translated into English. In 1972, excerpts from her *Autobiographical Essay* were published as *The Autobiography of a Sexually Emancipated Woman*, with an introduction by Germaine Greer, and there were translations of her pamphlets *Communism and the Family* and *Sexual Relations and the Social Struggle*. A year later, there was her pamphlet *Women Workers Struggle for their Rights*. In 1977, the late Alix Holt published her thoughtfully edited and translated *Alexandra Kollontai. Selected Writings,* and there were my translations of her fictional trilogies *Love of Worker Bees* and *Woman At the Turning Point* (the second translated as *A Great Love*). My biography of her was published in 1978 (with a new edition in 2014), and Barbara Evans Clements and Beatrice Farnsworth published biographies of her in America in 1979 and 1980. More recently, Emma Davis makes her life and ideas exciting and relevant now to our struggles in *A Rebel's Guide to Alexandra Kollontai,* published by Bookmarks in 2019.

The ramping up of the new cold war against Russia since the collapse of the Soviet Union has focused attention on Kollontai's diplomatic achievements, particularly in the years before and during the Second World War. In 2017, a bronze memorial plaque was unveiled outside the building on Moscow's Lenin Prospect where she lived before her death. Leading the tributes to her was the Russian Foreign Minister Sergei Lavrov, who spoke of "this legendary politician and statesman, whose outstanding diplomacy saved countless Soviet lives in the Great Patriotic War, and whose famous writings are invaluable historical evidence of her life and era".

A new collection of her memoirs and diaries, *Record of My Life*, was published in 2004. In 2008, there was a new edition of *Love of Worker Bees* and *Woman At the Turning Point*, with a warmly sympathetic introduction. More of her writings have been appearing online, and there is a growing online community of her admirers.

There are also Kollontai hate sites, which call her a criminal, one of Lenin's clique of fanatics who took power in the illegal Bolshevik "coup," forced people to live in communes and hand their children over to the state, then escaped the Stalin terror to live in comfort abroad.

In the West, she is often portrayed as a sort of muddled feminist, with the class politics removed from her vision of women's liberation. But she wrote in the great tradition of Marx and Engels, who saw all women as oppressed by capitalism, but divided by class. She believed working women could only be truly liberated when capitalist property relations had been swept away, and she found a new language to draw them into the struggle of their class for sexual equality and socialism.

Three years after the centenary of the Revolution, it is time we remembered Kollontai again, and what she stood for. She wrote that the bosses are nothing without the workers, and that the fight against them will be nothing without women. She wrote of the humanism and heroism of the Revolution, its drama and romanticism, its mistakes and failures, and "disagreements with the Party on the woman question," and she wrote of its mighty achievements, and paid tribute to those who lived and died for it.

Her writings are the story of how a poor backward country took on the world to create the first workers' state, free of capitalist misery and exploitation. She tells us not to be beaten by the horror show that is destroying our planet, bombing millions of the poorest people in the world and allowing millions of refugees to drown, attacking women's rights, the sick and the disabled, jailing and torturing those who expose the truth about imperialism's crimes. She shows us that hope is possible, and that by organising and relying on each other we can achieve miracles, and we can get rid of an ugly rotten system to make a better one.

Chapter One
"We can't live like this!"

Kollontai's father, General Mikhail Domontovich, was from one of the noblest families of Russia, descended from the thirteenth-century Prince Dovmont of Pskov, posthumously sainted by the Orthodox Church — "loved by the grace of God for his charity to his people, terrible to his enemies". Her mother, Alexandra Masalina, was the daughter of a Finnish serf, who had won his freedom before the Emancipation, and had gone on to run a successful timber business in Finland.

She was married with three children when she and Domontovich fell in love, and she had to divorce her first husband to marry him. It was virtually unheard of in Tsarist Russia for a woman to divorce, and it spoke of her great courage and strength of character. Divorce was under the jurisdiction of the Orthodox Church, and was beyond the means of any but the very wealthy, involving gross police intrusion into people's personal lives, and the couple had to appear before a special session of the Holy Synod to confess the sin of their adultery. Their highly unconventional marriage was considered very scandalous in St Petersburg, and it was also an exceptionally happy one, an inspiring example of love against the odds and across the classes.

She was already pregnant by the time they married, and Domontovich became stepfather to Kollontai's two half-sisters, who were ten and eleven when she was born. Their elder brother stayed with his father, and she grew up virtually as an only child, in St Petersburg and on her mother's estate in Finland, where she ran her timber business.

She was bilingual in Finnish and Russian from birth, and they were adoring and demanding if somewhat distant parents, with progressive views on girls' education. Governesses were hired to teach her science, literature, mathematics and languages, and she was fluent in German and French by the age of seven. Family life was ruled by her mother, and she was a passionate, precociously clever child, unafraid to stand up to her, and acutely sensitive to the injustices of the adult world. In her *Autobiographical Essay*, she described refusing to join her in her charity visits around her estate, taking baskets of food to the starving peasants. "I saw how they lived, when so much was done to make me comfortable and happy, and I rebelled against the many proofs of love surrounding me. I realised at an early age that I couldn't shape my life according to the given model, and I would have to find my own path".

She described learning to read from her father's military manuals, and from the portraits of medalled generals on her nursery walls. "The word war was one of the first to enter my consciousness".

In 1877, the Tsar declared war on Turkey for control of Bulgaria, and her father left with the Russian General Staff for the Bulgarian capital Sofia. Before long a tragic procession of war invalids were arriving at the house, with stories of dead comrades, cholera, frostbite, rotten food and bureaucratic corruption, and she lost her fondness for the generals on her walls.

She was nine when the terrorists assassinated Tsar Alexander II. She was deeply affected by the public hanging of the five main organisers in St Petersburg, and their leader, "iron-willed" Sofia Perovskaya, became her childhood heroine, who she described later as a shining example of women's courage in the fight against tsarism.

Perovskaya too had been the aristocratic daughter of a general, and she was kept at home, safe from "dangerous influences" — "Mother considered I was already rebelliously inclined enough as it was". She longed to go to school, but a new governess, a former village teacher, was hired to teach her history, geography and literature at home. Together they read Darwin's *Origin of Species*, the Russian classics, and the novels of Dickens, Victor Hugo and George Sand, and she passed her school examinations a year early, at the age of sixteen, with the gold medal awarded to top students.

But there could be no talk of her going to university. Jews and women were admitted to higher education only as external students, with the special permission of the authorities, and her parents saw universities as hotbeds of revolutionary ideas. So her education continued at home, and professors from St Petersburg University were employed to take her through the courses in history and Russian literature. (Her favourite writer was the novelist Turgenev).

Despite all the care they took with her education, her parents still saw her future in terms of a safe marriage to a man with enough money to support her, and when she turned eighteen she was brought out into society to find a suitable husband. Instead she set her heart on marrying her second cousin Vladimir Kollontai, a hand some penniless engineering student. Her mother banned him from the house, and to take her mind off him she took her on a trip to Berlin, where she escaped from her to attend a meeting of the German Socialist Party, discovered Berlin's bookshops, and bought a copy of Marx and Engels's *Communist Manifesto*.

She married Vladimir in 1893, at the age of twenty-one, and a year later she gave birth to their son, Misha. "I married partly as an act of defiance against my parents," she wrote in her *Autobiographical Essay*. "But the contented life of a wife and housewife soon became a prison for me. I loved my little boy dearly, and raised him with great care, but mother hood and marriage were never the core of my existence. I loved my husband, but our child was unable to draw us closer". She began to call Vladimir her "tyrant," and to write short stories about women struggling to find their freedom outside the home.

Vladimir had qualified as an engineer, and was working as a government factory inspector. Teams of inspectors had been visiting the factories since the 1880s, and their reports had been too shocking to be published — of toxic air and dangerous machinery, of workers working thirteen-hour shifts for starvation wages, of women sexually abused by their employers, exhausted by endless toil and pregnancies, giving birth in filthy conditions, often beside their workbenches.

She read his factory literature from Germany, France and Britain, where working conditions were incomparably better, and she learned from his engineers about employers' bitter resistance to any reforms. Some were discussing socialist solutions to workers' suffering, and she began to leave the baby with his nanny to explore St Petersburg's bookshops and libraries, and educate herself about socialism.

She discovered the Russian radical journals, and read a German edition of Engels's *Origin of the Family, Private Property and the State,* his Marxist analysis of women in capitalist society, which she described as a revelation.

Engels wrote that women's second-class status under capitalism was produced by the class system and private property, which made them the property of men, and he located the roots of their oppression in capitalism's key institution, the patriarchal family, which turned them into "reproducers". Women in property-owning families reproduced heirs. Working class women reproduced the next generation of labour.

Engels's depiction of working women's lives was filled with compassion, cruelly exploited in the factories, forced to bear the entire burden of the domestic economy in their families. Their liberation was possible only when socialism had removed the economic basis of their oppression, he wrote. He also saw industrial capitalism as a progressive force, which in drawing women into social production, was affecting areas of life far removed from wage labour, and destroying the foundations of the oppressive bourgeois family. And despite the extreme hardships of their lives in the factories, he believed the path to their liberation lay in fighting with men against their shared oppression, outside the narrow confines of the home.

The first Marxist response to the woman question, published six years before *Origin of the Family*, was the hugely popular *Woman and Socialism*, by the German socialist August Bebel, which Kollontai read in an abridged Russian translation.

Like Engels, Bebel analysed women's status from primitive society to the present day, with chapters on prostitution, female labour and equal rights. And like Engels, he denounced the hypocrisy and double standard of the bourgeois ideal of marriage, which distorted people's instincts and emotions. He wrote in detail of women's brutal working conditions in the factories, and he showed how their shared exploitation with men was drawing new fighters into the class struggle. But he insisted that their liberation must be the work of women themselves: "Women cannot expect men to help them out of their condition, just as workers cannot expect help from the bourgeoisie".

Eight years after the Revolution, Kollontai would write the introduction to the first complete Russian translation of *Woman and Socialism,* and she described it as "Women's Bible".

Her reading had a dramatic impact on her marriage. She grew increasingly impatient with Vladimir's liberal faith that his factory inspectors could improve workers' lives. And to prove her wrong, he took her on one of his inspections, at the Krengholm textile factory in the Estonian city of Narva, seventy miles from the capital.

The Krengholm had been built in 1857 by a British company, and was one of the largest cotton mills in the world, employing over twelve thousand workers, almost half of them women. Most of the managers were British, and an earlier team of inspectors had described it as "a little bit of England on Russian soil". In 1872, the entire workforce had come out on strike after sixty workers died in a cholera epidemic, and the army had been sent in to make arrests after the strike turned into a riot. A few improvements had been made, and twenty-four years later, Vladimir and his team were to carry out a major overhaul of the workshops' ventilators. Kollontai's account of her first visit to a factory is from her *Autobiographical Essay*.

"Narva"

It was in March 1896. Vladimir and his engineers had an interesting new project, from a technical point of view, to install a new ventilation system at the Krengholm cotton mill in Narva. They were to spend a week there, and he invited me and my friend Zoya to join them. I was in heaven. I longed to escape from our little flat after the long grey winter, and to see the historic town of Narva, still ruled by the ghosts of the Swedish kings and Peter the Great.

Our happy party left St Petersburg on Saturday, so we could spend Sunday sightseeing, and we took our sledges and skates with us. We visited the fortress, and tobogganed down the fields, captivated by the fantastic snowdrifts covering the pine forests. It was all so happy and magical. That evening, an orchestra played Tchaikovsky melodies and Strauss waltzes in the hotel dining room, as we discussed whether technology could save humanity from its ills, as Vladimir and his engineers claimed. Zoya complained that industry destroyed the beauties of nature. I said we must take the discussion to another level, and that for workers to be free of their misery and exploitation, we had to change the entire economic and social system.

"What do you mean by this freedom you keep talking about?" Vladimir interrupted. "Total freedom means chaos. People need laws. Just laws, but firm ones".

But I was in no mood to quarrel with my husband. In the new surroundings of Narva I had "spread my wings," Zoya said.

Next morning, Vladimir left early for work with his engineers, having arranged for us to be shown round the mill. Its technology, hygiene standards and working conditions were considered extremely advanced for the time, and we couldn't wait to see this model factory.

We were taken first to the "infirmary," where there was no doctor or nurse present, just an elderly retired foreman who performed their duties. "I've seen enough accidents here in my time, I can do any operation better than the surgeons," he said.

In the next room was a small library, with a few tattered volumes of Pushkin and Turgenev on the shelves, but no new books or technical literature. It was clear from the records that almost nobody visited, and the librarian explained that this was because over ninety percent of the workers were illiterate. Next door was the room where evening literacy classes were held. We were told by the teacher that only a dozen pupils attended out of a workforce of twelve thousand, and that they included not a single woman. Hundreds would register every autumn, she said, but they would be too exhausted to study after their long working day, which generally exceeded twelve hours, and numbers would quickly drop. The textbooks were old and out of date, and she had heard of none of the new literacy teaching methods we mentioned. Like the "infirmary," the classes existed only in name.

Our guide took us round the workshops, explaining the workings of the various looms and machines. But seeing that Zoya and I weren't interested, he left us to our own devices. We both had headaches from the hot damp air filled with dust and fibres, and Zoya had to go back to the hotel to rest. I continued to explore the workshops on my own. I wanted to talk to the workers, particularly the women, to find out how they survived in these conditions.

They answered my questions reluctantly, and the older ones were completely silent. But the boys and young men complained bitterly about their slave existence imprisoned behind the factory's walls, allowed out only for church on Sundays. At this the women spoke up, saying they preferred it this way, since it stopped their husbands drinking away their wages. Several of the young men said they longed to study to be engineers, but this was out of the question. The school taught only literacy, and their long hours and terrible working conditions drained them of their energy. Hundreds died of tuberculosis before the age of thirty, they said. "Work here a few years and life isn't so sweet. You become numb to everything, and just wait to be carted off to hospital to die".

Most were housed in the barracks next to the factory — single people, families and children all piled on top of one another. I visited one of their dormitories, crammed with wooden bunks covered in rags and the occasional thin mattress. The windows were tightly sealed, so not a breath of fresh air got through, and the air was heavy with cheap tobacco smoke and the smell of human sweat. On the floor between two bunks, a dozen small children were sleeping, fighting and crying, watched over by a little girl of about six. My eye was drawn to a baby of about my son's age lying very still on the floor. I bent down to him, and realised to my horror that he was dead. The little corpse, lying next to the living playing children.

"Sometimes it happens that they die in the day. Auntie will come at six and take him away," the little nanny explained.

I rushed back to the hotel to share my experiences with Zoya. "We can't live like this, surrounded by human misery! We must fight for workers' rights so they can defend themselves!" I said.

We were still talking that evening when Vladimir burst in, laughing and waving some pink tickets. "We've seats for the new operetta, we must leave immediately."

He stopped, seeing what he called my "stubborn" face. "Why what's the matter Shura? Was someone rude to you at the factory?"

"Nothing's the matter with me," I snapped. "Why must you always think only of me? There are more important things in life, I've seen that now".

I spoke angrily and passionately about the crimes of capitalism. "Dead babies lie on the floor with the living children! Thousands are sentenced to an early death, they live worse than animals!"

Vladimir explained that this was why he had come, to improve their working conditions. "The new ventilators will get rid of the dampness and stuffiness and suck the fibres out of the air".

"It's not about new ventilators, it's about changing the system, so workers have their rights and freedom!" I said.

"Fine," he said, "let the workers have their rights and freedom. You can make a speech about it in the restaurant after the theatre".

"I'm not going to the theatre with you, I don't want to live like you, go on your own!"

After we returned to St Petersburg, I studied the workers' question with new enthusiasm. Zoya and I attended lectures at St Petersburg University on factory conditions and social and economic issues, and I read more about Marxism, and as much illegal revolutionary literature as I could get my hands on. Lenin's *Who Are the "Friends of the People" and Why Are They Fighting the Social Democrats?* made a deep impression on me, and his articles and strike leaflets helped to connect theory with the practical activity in the factories. I stopped writing stories, and zealously

studied Marx's theory of surplus value. The only way
workers could be freed from the hell of their lives was
through revolution. But how was I to find the path to
the revolutionaries, hidden in the underground?

Lenin's name meant little to her when she read his pamphlet
Who Are the "Friends of the People"?, his Marxist response to the
Populists, published illegally in 1894.

Lenin saw capitalism as neither an artificial creation nor
an unmitigated tragedy and source of all evil, as the Populists
claimed, but as an enormous social advance, arguing that it was
not the peasants who would lead the revolution in Russia, but
the workers, capitalism's enemies and grave diggers, once they
had organised themselves and developed their capacity to fight.
He likened the early days of the strike movement in Russia to
the peasant uprisings that had led to the end of serfdom —
"when the serfs were so crushed and stultified they were barely
cap able of anything but sporadic and isolated rebellions, or
rather riots, unenlightened by political consciousness". Just
as the peasants' rage had been interpreted by a small group
of intellectuals bent on killing the Tsar, workers now relied
on organised Marxist intellectuals to give backbone to their
fight, and "to transform their present uncoordinated economic
battles into a conscious class struggle. Then workers will rise
at the head of all democratic forces in Russia to overthrow
absolutism, and lead the proletariat, side by side with the
proletariat of all countries, along the straight road of political
struggle to the victorious communist revolution".

Kollontai made contact with St Petersburg's Political Red
Cross, which had links with Lenin and members of the League
of Struggle, and during the textileworkers' strikes in the
capital in the summer of 1896, she raised strike funds, picked
up revolutionary leaflets to be smuggled into the factories, and
stored them in her flat.

But before committing herself fully to the underground, she
wanted to be better prepared theoretically, and in 1898 she left

Vladimir and their son and travelled to Switzerland, to study Marxist economics at the University of Zurich.

Her Marxist supervisor, Professor Heinrich Herkner, had supervised Rosa Luxemburg, who had finished her doctoral thesis at the university three months earlier, before leaving for Berlin to work with the German Social Democratic Party, and Kollontai devoured her articles for the German socialist press, and the party's women's paper *Die Gleichheit (Equality)*, edited by Clara Zetkin.

Zetkin and Luxemburg both presented the key Marxist arguments in the debates raging in the Socialist International then, between the "Orthodox" Marxists and the "revisionists". Marxists called for a class war against capitalism. The "revisionists" saw revolution as both painful and unnecessary, and believed capitalism could be reformed through legal processes and nego-tiations and economic gains won by the trades unions.

Each of the twenty-two parties affiliated to the International had the right to shape resolutions in the light of its own national conditions, and most declared themselves to be Marxists. But Kollontai was discovering that Marxism meant different things to different parties. The real political power behind this huge federal body was the German party, with its fifty-six deputies to the Reichstag, which already seemed strong enough to lead not only the German working class, but the entire European labour movement. Under pressure to adapt to parliamentary conditions, many socialist deputies were abandoning Marxism for revisionism, and distinguished writers and academics like Kollontai's supervisor published books calling for the class struggle to be taken out of Marxism.

Professor Herkner was highly regarded by moderate socialists in Europe for his book *The Workers' Question*, which had been translated into many languages. He was particularly popular with members of the Fabian Society in England, and to convince her of the revisionists' arguments, he sent her to London to stay with his Fabian friends Beatrice and Sydney Webb. "The result was that the more I listened to them, and the deeper I delved into the laws of economics, the more an 'orthodox' Marxist I became," she wrote in her *Autobiographical Essay*.

On her return to Russia, she ended her five-year marriage to Vladimir and embarked on the long and difficult process of divorcing him. His aspirations had become alien to her, but she would keep his surname for the rest of her life, and she wrote that leaving him caused her much heartbreak: "I am far from being one of those new women who take their experiences with relative lightness, one might even say superficiality, whose feelings and mental energies are directed at all other things in life but the emotions of love. I still belong to that generation of women who grew up at a time in history when love, with its many disappointments, tragedies and eternal demands for happiness, still played a very important part in our lives".

She moved with her son into a cheap flat, paid for by her father, and she joined the Social Democratic Party. She gave literacy classes in the factories, and made frequent trips to the Finnish capital, Helsingfors (now Helsinki), two hundred miles from St Petersburg, representing Russian socialists at meetings of the Finnish Social Democratic Party. She stayed at her mother's estate, travelling around the villages and meeting the peasant loggers and raftsmen, writing articles about their lives for the socialist press. Her book *The Life of the Finnish Proletariat*, published in 1903, was widely compared to Engels's *Conditions of the Working Class in England*, and she became the social democrats' leading authority on Finland, and Lenin wrote to her asking her to write more for the party.

In 1901 she left Russia for Switzerland again, to continue her Marxist studies at the University of Geneva. The town was a popular destination for exiled Russian Marxists, gathered round the revered figure of Georgy Plekhanov, whose writings in the 1880s on Marxism she had read before she joined the underground. In Geneva she had the first of several meetings with Plekhanov, and it was there that she first met Rosa Luxemburg, whose works on imperialism and the mass strike would be a lifelong inspiration to her.

Throughout 1904, as strikes erupted across Russia against the war with Japan, she worked with Bolsheviks and Mensheviks in St Petersburg raising funds for the families of jailed strikers, giving political talks in the workers' clubs in the guise of "geography lessons," and speaking at student demonstrations. The universities were in turmoil. The countryside emptied as men were con scripted, and peasant women rioted, crying out against the landowners' cruelty and the ways the war was hurting them, looting estates and expropriating land. From his place of exile in Switzerland, Lenin saw the upheavals as the start of a new phase in the revolutionary struggle in Russia. "Russia's defeats in the war are a defeat for Russian absolutism and a victory for the workers," he wrote, and he attacked the "economism" of the Mensheviks, which saw the strikes as limited to achieving purely economic gains.

In December 1904 Kollontai joined the Bolsheviks, and became a full-time party activist, and in January 1905 she joined the twenty thousand workers in the capital who marched to the Winter Palace to present the Tsar with their petition for re forms.

They were led there by the charismatic priest Father Gapon, subsequently exposed as a government agent, whose Assembly of Russian Factory Hands was funded by the Ministry of Police. When workers at the Putilov munitions plant began to discuss strike action, Gapon provided them with premises where they could draw up their demands, under the eyes of the secret police. The decision to strike was taken on 3 January, and as the mood became increasingly militant, and Gapon risked losing control of the situation, he was able to convince a majority of strikers to back their demands with a petition to the Tsar. It was signed by 125,000 workers, and read: "We workers, our wives and children, our helpless old people, have suffered terrible things, and we are pushed ever deeper into the abyss of poverty, ignorance and lack of rights. We have come, Lord, to seek Your protection".

Kollontai recorded her memories of the day and those leading up to it in her *Autobiographical Essay.*

"1905"

The scene will be forever in my memory. The bright January sun, the trusting expectant faces, the pools of blood on the snow, the bellowing of the troops, the dead, the wounded, the men, women and children shot.

On the Ninth of January, workers went to the Winter Palace to tell the Tsar of their wretched living conditions, and naively to beg him for freedom of speech and the right to form workers' organisations. Our cunning rulers had decided to use Gapon as a weapon against them, to distract them from socialism and muddle their heads at his bogus "workers' clubs," whose members included police spies and provocateurs. But so great was their desire to fight their exploitation that they joined Gapon's clubs and flooded them, and his Assembly of Russian Factory Hands even included three hundred women.

Russia was bankrupted by its shameful war with Japan, and the countryside seethed with rage. Peasant women were rioting, and men were fighting the Tsar's latest conscription. The industrialists grumbled about his corrupt officials, and working conditions in the factories were desperate. The spark which ignited this rotting nest of universal discontent was the strike at the Putilov works.

By the end of December, the Tsar and his ministers realised they were playing a dangerous game with Gapon. The workers were squeezing him out and continuing on the path of class struggle, forcing the weak priest to come over to their side. Day after day, the first mass workers' resolutions were passed in his clubs. For the first time in Russian history, the organised masses were voicing their demands, and the police were unsure whether to break up the meetings, or continue their game with the provocateur Gapon.

On 5 January, the Putilov's 111,000 workers began their strike. The revolutionary storm spread to every workers' district in the capital, where young people sang the Polish revolutionary song the *Warszawianka*. But Gapon managed to persuade the older factory hands that the Tsar had their interests at heart, and to march to the Palace, break through the wall of his greedy officials and landowners, and tell their "Little Father" about their suffering.

What were the Bolsheviks doing in those days? Lenin was far away in exile, and there was not complete unanimity among those of us in the capital. Some said that it wasn't too late to stop workers bowing their heads to the Tsar, and marching to their deaths. Others that victims were inevitable, but that there was no holding back the tide, and if the workers were on the streets, our place was with them.

On Thursday the sixth, the decision was taken to march to the Palace. Preparations continued over the next two days, and the Tsar was thrown into panic. To avoid receiving Gapon's petition, he fled with his family to his summer palace at Tsarskoe Selo, leaving his most trusted troops at the Palace to answer workers' cry of grief with their bullets.

Sunday was sunny, with a hard frost. From all sides of the city an unending procession of the urban poor, with their elderly relatives and children, converged on the Palace, bearing icons and portraits of the Tsar, and waited for him to appear. Would he receive their petition himself, or send out one of his officials?

People prayed and waited patiently for an hour, two hours, stamping their feet in the snow. The mounted troops guarding the Palace stirred, and the bugle rang out, ominously loud in the frosty air. "Don't worry, it's just the order to line up," a voice reassured the crowd.

More waiting. A dull tense anxiety. Another

signal from the bugle. People waited and smiled and trusted. A third signal, then a sudden volley of rifle shots. What? They're shooting? "Nonsense, the Tsar wouldn't shoot his unarmed people, they must be blanks," someone said. But by then the troops were galloping into the square and the slaughter had started. Bodies fell dead in the snow. Women and children dropped silently over the fences of the Alexandrov Gardens like sparrows.

Over two thousand people were killed that day, with uncountable numbers injured. But what the Tsar did not realise was that he had killed something even greater. He had killed people's superstition, their faith that they could ever get justice from him. Bloody Sunday was the start of a great mass movement against the old bourgeois landowning Russia, and from then on everything was different and new.

The Bolsheviks were fired with new energy. We put out our new underground paper *Petersburg Workers' Week*, and I contributed articles and helped with the technical side of getting it published. I travelled to Finland, keeping our Finnish comrades in touch with the party, and spoke at large demonstrations outside factory gates on Vasilev Island, in Vyborg and Okhta, and in small discussion groups in the workers' clubs. My main concern was to attract more women. They attended the demonstrations in large numbers, but very few came to the meetings, and those who did generally came only once and were never seen again.

Bloody Sunday set off strikes and peasant riots across Russia. The next day, workers at St Petersburg's power stations walked out, and there were general strikes in Moscow, Vilno, Kovno, Riga, Revel and Kiev. Black Hundreds gangs roamed the cities, attacking workers and Jews, and Lenin in exile called on Bolsheviks to form "fighting defence squads".

In February, terrorists assassinated the hated anti-Semitic Governor-General of Moscow, the Tsar's uncle the Grand Duke Sergei. Three months later, workers led a general strike in the Black Sea port of Odessa, supported by a sailors' mutiny on the Battleship *Potemkin*. Universities across Russia were closed by the police, and hundreds of students were arrested. Children as young as twelve were organising Bolshevik "cells" in their schools, and women were striking in vast numbers, often outdoing men in militancy, giving the strike movement unprecedented strength. Kollontai wrote leaflets and pamphlets for the Bolsheviks, including her pamphlet *The Question of the Class Struggle*, which was immediately seized by the police, and in March she was elected treasurer of the social democrats' Bolshevik-led central committee, in charge of managing its strike fund.

Throughout 1905, over 120,000 workers in St Petersburg's shipyards and engineering works came out on strike, and that summer they began to set up workers' councils, or soviets, to keep them in touch with the revolutionary underground. Lev Trotsky had escaped from Siberia to live illegally in the capital and work underground with the soviets, and he saw them as the embryo of a completely new kind of government, with the potential to topple the autocracy. On the tenth of October, thirteen thousand sailors on the fortified island of Kronstadt, Russia's largest naval base, twenty miles from the capital, came out in a mass armed mutiny against their officers. Three days later, Kollontai attended the opening session of the St Petersburg Soviet of Workers' Deputies, chaired by Trotsky — a Jew in Tsarist Russia at the head of the world's first workers' government.

On the seventeenth, the Tsar capitulated, and rallied his citizens to the throne with his "Manifesto," promising freedom of assembly and a free press, and universal male suffrage in elections to Russia's first parliament, his new "consultative" Duma. In the "days of freedom" that followed, new soviets and workers' clubs sprang up, revolutionaries returned from exile and emerged from the underground, and the Soviet under Trotsky's leadership grew to 550 delegates, representing some 275,000 workers.

Unlike Kollontai, most Bolsheviks initially took a very cautious approach to the Soviet, fearing it would go the same way as Gapon's Assembly of Factory Hands. The Mensheviks had meanwhile been building support for the Soviet in the factories, and getting delegates elected. (Trotsky himself had been a Menshevik since 1903, and would join the Bolsheviks only three months before the October Revolution).

The two factions differed on the equally contentious issues of their participation in the Tsar's Duma, and in his rural administrative assembly, the *Zemstvo*. Under liberal pressure, eighteen of the Duma's five hundred seats were being offered to "working men," represented by the social democrats ("persons of the female sex" were barred). The Mensheviks saw the Duma as a useful propaganda platform. A majority of Bolsheviks voted for a total boycott, against a small group of "ultimatists," who were for delivering an uncompromising message against the autocracy, then walking out.

The Bolsheviks were unanimously opposed to any collaboration with liberal landowners in the *Zemstvo*, which they saw as a betrayal of peasants' interests. The Mensheviks had been campaigning in the villages for peasants to use the *Zemstvo* to replace their random expropriations with a more equal redistribution of the land, and Kollontai saw it as a forum where peasant women who had looted and rioted could stand up for their share. Her disagreements with the Bolsheviks on this and the key issues of the Soviet and the Duma led her in early 1906 to join the Mensheviks, while continuing to work with both factions.

It was the upheavals of 1905 and 1906 that drew her to the work for which she would be best known, building a mass movement of working women to fight for their interests, and the organisational framework to connect their liberation struggle to the struggle for socialism.

Women's liberation was central to Marx's writings about class society, and to the social democrats' programme. But their commitment to the woman question was still largely at the level on the issue. Many Bolsheviks feared that campaigning for equal pay and the vote would lead to an autonomous women's movement and divide the working class, and they appealed to women to defer the struggle for their liberation until the revolution had been achieved. The Mensheviks saw the cause of women as best served through an alliance with feminists in the All-Russian Women's League for Equal Rights.

Established in the spring of 1905, the League had been inspired by the Tsar's October Manifesto to petition liberals in the Duma for voting rights for women with property. The organisers had been inviting factory women and domestic servants to their meetings, promising to campaign to improve their working conditions once they had the vote, and women workers made up over half the petition's forty thousand signatures. Kollontai recruited a group of energetic young women from St Petersburg's Textileworkers' Union, Bolsheviks and Mensheviks, to heckle at the League's meetings, appealing to workers not to be duped by the feminists' talk of an all-class alliance of women, and to join the party of their class, the social democrats. But she was doing so without the party's support, and she was banned from the League's meetings, after an organiser tried to strangle her for one of her interventions. She knew the feminists had nothing to offer the thousands of women who were joining the strike movement and fighting on the streets. But as she wrote later in her book *A History of the Women Workers' Movement in Russia,* "I was afraid we would be recruiting them to the party on false pretences, since we didn't yet know how to awaken their class consciousness and encourage their independence".

The day after Bloody Sunday, the Tsar had summoned a group of workers to the Winter Palace and instructed them to elect delegates to his new Shidlovsky Commission, which was to deal with some of their grievances. The Bolsheviks urged them not to waste their time. But they went ahead and elected delegates, and they included several women. When they were refused seats, on the grounds that they had no political rights they held a series of angry demonstrations in St Petersburg, "in the name of all working women in the capital," which were joined by large numbers of men. Workers soon lost interest in the Commission, which collapsed a few weeks later, but the demonstrations showed Kollontai that men's prejudices could come tumbling down when challenged.

Women now made up almost forty percent of the workforce in Russia, generally in the least skilled jobs, where their pay was less than a third of men's, allowing employers to hire three for the price of one man. Excluded from the social life of the strike movement by their family responsibilities, they were cut off from the political literature flooding into the factories by their near total illiteracy, and Kollontai reported that not a single woman attended her workers' literacy classes. She saw factory women's lives intersecting with work and politics quite differently from men's. Denied for centuries any access to knowledge or power, they were now taking paths women had never travelled before, and she believed a completely new strategy was needed to draw them into the strike movement.

In the "days of freedom" after October, she and her factory friends organised women's meetings in the capital's workers' clubs, where they could share their experiences without fear of being ridiculed by men. The clubs' memberships had been exclusively male, and many refused to share their premises. But growing numbers opened their doors to the meetings, at which she called on women to abandon the Equal Rights League and join the social democrats.

Now she had to convince the party that the strike movement had no chance of succeeding without women. *A History of the Women Workers' Movement in Russia,* published in 1920, is the story of how they defied their oppression, and forced social democrats in the years before the Revolution to find new ways of working with them.

Below is an abridged translation of the first chapter of the book, covering the years from the 1870s to the 1905 revolution.

From *A History of the Women Workers' Movement in Russia*

When can we date the beginnings of the women workers' movement in Russia? As members of the proletariat who sell their labour, factory women have joined men in all the strikes and riots against tsarism. Thus the movement's beginnings can be traced back to the very first stirrings of class consciousness in Russia, and the proletariat's earliest struggles, through strikes, walkouts and mass action, to achieve a more tolerable existence.

In 1872, women joined the strike at the Krengholm textile mill. Five years later, they were active in the strikes at Moscow's Lazarev Mill and St Petersburg's New Cotton Spinning Mill. In 1885, they were at the forefront of the famous weavers' riots in Orekhovo-Zuevo near Moscow, wrecking buildings and machinery, forcing the Tsarist government to rush through its factory laws banning night work for women and children.

Significantly, the strikes shaking Russia throughout the 1870s and early 1880s occurred mainly in the textile industry, where most of the workforce consisted of cheap female labour. The unrest in those years was mainly of an economic character, produced by the crisis in the cotton industry, which led to layoffs, falling wages and mass unemployment. And how wonderful it was to see the politically naive factory girl, hopelessly bowed down by her unbearably harsh working conditions, despised by one and all, even by the female half of the urban bourgeoisie, from whom she differed only in her firm attachment to the old peasant customs, now in the vanguard, fighting for the rights of her class. The conditions of her life had drawn her into the struggle against her enslavement by capital, and in fighting for her class she was also fighting the inequality of her working conditions, and for the liberation of her sex from the special chains that have created her subordinate status, even within the working class itself.

Women joined the next wave of strikes in the 1890s. They played a leading role in the economic strikes in St Petersburg in 1894, and in the Yaroslavl weavers' strikes the following spring, the "April riots". In St Petersburg's historic textile workers' strikes in the summer of 1896, they courageously downed tools with the men and joined them in a walkout. Hungry children waited at home for their mothers, and hundreds were arrested and thrown into jail. But above all their personal suffering, all their family cares and maternal feelings, was their loyalty to the common cause of their class.

In these periods of industrial unrest, the timid oppressed factory woman, politically "backward" and without rights, drew herself up to her full height and became an equal fighter and comrade. And this transformation drew her to the path of the workers' movement, which was leading her to her liberation.

The late 1890s brought a fresh wave of strikes and riots in factories employing mainly women, notably at St Petersburg's Maxwell spinning and weaving mills and the Shanshal tobacco factories. And as the strike movement gained strength, so too did the class resistance of the female proletariat.

Political ideas had to be smuggled into the factories in a disguised form, and until the great year of 1905, the strike movement was primarily of an economic nature. A healthy class instinct led women to join the strikes, and they were often in the vanguard as leaders and organisers. But as soon as the struggles died down and they returned to work, in victory or defeat, they became isolated again, still lacking the consciousness or channels of communication to stay in comradely contact with the workers' movement. It was rare to see a factory woman in the illegal organisations in those years. Proletarian women had not yet embraced the broad objectives of the socialist workers' party, and were unresponsive to general political slogans.

For Russia's six million women factory workers, life was an unending round of poverty, hunger and degradation, working twelve-hour shifts for starvation wages, sexually abused by their employers, forced to leave their children to fend for themselves on the streets, with any time off for pregnancy, sickness or childbirth leading to the loss of their jobs. They were housed in cramped insanitary barracks, often sharing bunks with workers on alternate shifts, and they were savagely punished for any attempt to set up self-help support groups. This was the reality of their lives. Their backs were too bent under the weight of their cruel oppression to join the fight against tsarism and the power of capital. Their souls were too crushed by poverty to see a brighter future.

Nevertheless, by the end of the 1890s working women were beginning to join the revolutionary struggle. Our movement can take pride in the many inspiring women whose courage and self-sacrifice helped to establish Russia's first underground political organisations in the 1860s, which led to the revolutionary upheavals a decade later. But none of these women, from the early socialists of the 1870s, with their great personal charm and inner strength, to the iron-willed Sofia Perovskaya in the 1880s, were from the proletariat. These were the women Turgenev celebrated in his poem "At the Threshold," who atoned for the sins of their fathers by breaking with their aristocratic families to fight social injustice and go "to the people," taking their revolutionary message to the peasants.

Even in the first years of the new century, when Marxism was firmly established in the workers' movement, there were still only a handful of women workers in the political underground. Activists were primarily intellectuals — students, doctors, teachers and writers. It was hard to persuade factory women to attend illegal meetings or workers' evening classes, where the ideas of scientific socialism were discussed under the legal guise of arithmetic or geography lessons. Working women were still avoiding life and the struggle, and saw their destiny as the oven, the washtub and the cradle.

The picture changed dramatically when the red spectre of revolution gripped Russia in its fiery wings. The revolutionary years of 1905 and 1906 sent shockwaves through the ruling class, and for the first time workers became conscious of their strength, and that they bore the nation's future on their shoulders. Thou sands of women joined the struggle against tsarism. They were everywhere. To record the facts of their participation in the strikes, riots and demonstrations of those years, to pay tribute to their innumerable acts of heroism and their loyalty to the ideals of socialism would involve reconstructing the entire story of the revolution scene by scene.

Many have memories of the illiterate downtrodden woman factory worker coming to life, attending packed meetings charged with electricity, gazing at the speakers with eager hopeful eyes. And they were out in force in January 1905. Hundreds joined that solemn silent procession to the Winter Palace, and the sun was bright on their faces, which glowed with triumph and determination.

They paid dearly for their naive illusions, and hundreds lost their lives when the Tsar's troops opened fire. But as calls for a General Strike flew across Russia, from factory to factory, from workshop to workshop, women who until then had been isolated from the struggle were often the first to walk out. In October 1905, exhausted by their inhuman working conditions, close to starvation, hundreds left their machines, bravely denying themselves and their children their last crust of bread in the name of the common cause. They become public speakers, and in simple moving words they called on their male comrades to join them, giving heart to those on strike, encouraging those who wavered.

They struggled, protested and sacrificed themselves, and the more active they became, the more clearly they came to see the cause of their suffering in the injustices of the capitalist system.

At the same time, working men were beginning to speak up not only for the general demands of their class, but for the rights of women. When the woman elected by St Petersburg's Sampson Textile Mill as one of its seven delegates to the Tsar's Shidlovsky Commission was refused permission to stand, women reacted with fury. The hardships they had endured with men had brought them closer to their male comrades, and it seemed particularly cruel to emphasise their second-class status at a time when they had proved themselves such worthy fighters and citizens. Women from St Petersburg's mills and factories organised protest demonstrations, which were joined by hundreds of men, and in February they delivered the following petition to the Commission's Chairman:

Under your chairmanship, delegates representing working women have been refused admission. This decision is cruel and unjust. We women outnumber men in St. Petersburg's spinning and weaving mills, and our numbers in the textile industry grow larger each year, as men move to factories where the wages are better. Our powerlessness and lack of rights are exploited, and we bear a heavier burden than men. When the Commission was announced, our hearts filled with hope. At last the time had come, we thought, when we could speak in the name of our sisters to the whole of Russia about our oppression and suffering, about which men know nothing. Then when we had already elected our delegates, we were told that only men would be admitted. Our interests are no different from those of our male comrades, and we demand that the Commission changes this decision.

Factory women who had borne the burdens of the struggle on their shoulders saw their exclusion from the Commission as a blatant injustice, and in the election campaign to the Duma a year later, they attended meetings to protest against being denied a voice in the important matter of electing deputies.

Clear evidence that working women were no longer indifferent to their political rights was that they made up most of the forty thousand signatures to the feminists' suffrage petition to the Duma. Their initial support for the feminists showed that their political awakening was still in its early stages, and had stopped half way. Those who had begun to see their inequality in terms of their sex were not ready to connect this with the wider struggle of their class. They had yet to find the path that would lead them to their liberation, and they naively accepted the hand the feminists held out to them. And the feminists did all in their power to draw them into their "non-class" organisations — which of course were bourgeois through and through.

Fortunately, factory women's healthy class instinct and distrust of the "ladies" put an end to any lasting alliance between them. Throughout 1905 and 1906, the feminists held hundreds of meetings, which working women were invited to attend. They listened attentively and in silence to what the speakers had to say, and heard nothing from them about how the lives of those enslaved by capital were to be improved. Nothing about how they were to be freed from hunger and insecurity and their cruel working conditions. Nothing about their demands for a shorter working day, higher pay, better treatment from their employers, and freedom from police harassment. Such concerns were alien to the feminists, with their narrow exclusively "female" aspirations; they had no understanding of the class nature of the newly emerging socialist women's movement.

Domestic servants were a particular disappointment to them. Servants at first responded positively to their calls to "organise," and in 1905 the League held several well-attended meetings in St Petersburg and Moscow for cooks, cleaners and housemaids. But to the feminists' dismay, when they tried to recruit them into an idyllic alliance with their lady employers, they abandoned them to transfer their allegiance to the party of their class. And in Moscow and several other cities, including Vladimir, Penza and Kharkov, they even organised their own trade unions.

Another organisation even further to the right of the League, the Women's Progressive Party, suffered the same fate. When its leaders too tried to mobilise women workers under the watchful eye of their mistresses, they overstepped the line set by the feminists. Looking at the newspapers from 1905, we see reports of cooks, laundresses and maids in the capital striking and demonstrating on the streets, demanding an end to their mistreatment by their employers, a minimum wage, the eight-hour day, improved accommodation in the factories, and separate dormitories for women. The protests spread like wildfire across Russia, even to the remote provinces. And women's political awakening was not confined to the urban poor. For the first time in Russian history, women in the villages were beginning to speak up for themselves.

From late 1904 until the last months of 1905, the war with Japan sparked an explosion of peasant women's riots across Russia. The horrors and hardships of that disastrous war impacted particularly harshly on the peasant woman. When the men were conscripted, it was yet another burden on her shoulders. Peasant wives and mothers, previously so docile and unaware of any thing beyond their immediate domestic circle, came face to face with unknown hostile forces, and were forced to drain to the last drop the bitter cup of their undeserved inferiority. For the first time in their lives, they left their villages, their passivity and their ignorance behind, and they hurried to the cities, visiting government offices for news of a son, a husband or a father, demanding their widows' pensions, fighting for their rights. There they saw for themselves the ugly reality of the Tsarist system, the lies and injustice and the peasants' lack of rights, and they returned home in a sober hardened mood, carrying in their hearts an inexhaustible supply of bitterness.

The upheavals in the villages culminated in the summer of 1905 in an eruption of peasant women's riots across southern Russia. With an anger and courage never seen before, they armed them selves with rakes, pitchforks and brooms, driving the soldiers from their villages, raiding the barracks to take their conscripted husbands home. They were arrested of course, and sentenced to long terms in jail. But peasant women's protests against the intolerable burdens of the war continued, and in these protests they were fighting both for peasant interests as a whole and for their own interests as women, and the two were so closely connected that it was impossible to separate them.

Following these "political" demonstrations, peasant women were active in the upsurge of economic agricultural strikes across the countryside in 1906, often initiating them and drawing the men after them. And if they failed to do so, they would march to the landlords' estates on their own, armed with whatever came to hand, meeting head on the detachments of Cossacks sent in to punish them.

The downtrodden peasant woman, crushed by centuries of oppression, was suddenly a vital player in the unfolding political drama. During the entire period of the 1905 revolution, women fought with men to defend peasant interests, referring rarely and with enormous restraint to their own interests as women, and doing so only when it would not damage the common peasant cause. This did not mean they were indifferent to their inequality, far from it, and their growing involvement in the political struggle opened their eyes to the causes of their oppression, and showed them new ways of fighting it.

In November 1905, women in Voronezh province sent two delegates to a conference of the Peasants' Union to demand their "political rights on an equal basis with men". There was the historic letter women in the Tver and Voronezh provinces sent to the Duma in 1906, demanding their right to vote in its elections. And there was the telegram to the Duma, addressed to Menshevik deputy Aladin, signed by seventy-five women in the village of Nogatkina in the Urals:

At this great moment in the struggle between might and right, we peasant women from

Nogatkina village support socialist deputies to the Duma who expressed their lack of confidence in ministers by demanding their resignations. We call on deputies elected by the people to give the land to the peasants, and to open the doors of the prisons to release those who fought for our happiness and freedom. We appeal to deputies to fight not only for their own political rights, but for those of women too, who have no rights or freedom, even in our families. Remember, a slave cannot be the mother of a free citizen.

Peasant women in the Caucasus were especially militant. At meetings in Kutaisi province in Georgia, women from the village of Guria passed resolutions demanding their political equality with men. At rural and urban meetings held in Tbilisi province to discuss the introduction of the *Zemstvo* into Transcaucasia, delegates included several Georgian women who spoke to demand their legal and economic equality, arguing that the proposed reallocation of the landowners' land affected them just as much as it affected men. In some regions, peasant women who had rioted and seized the land lost their enthusiasm for the expropriations when it seemed they would be excluded in the redistributions. "At least now we can earn a few kopecks from our extra land," they said. "If it all goes to the men we'll just be working for them, and that way we'll face real slavery".

But their fears proved groundless. Simple economic necessity forced men to demand land for the "female souls". The interests of the peasantry, male and female, were so closely connected that in fighting to free themselves from their bondage to the landowners, men were inevitably standing up for their wives and daughters too.

In fighting for the economic and political rights of the peasantry as a whole, women were learning to voice their own demands. And the same was happening in the cities, where women factory workers' heroic role in the liberation struggle did even more to prepare public opinion to accept the principle of their equality — a principle brought to life in the thunder of 1905, which stirred women to join the fight for their liberation, united with their comrades in the ranks of their class.

Chapter Two
Feminists and Marxists

Strikes and riots continued across Russia until the end of 1905, but with less intensity than before. In December, Trotsky and the other leaders of the St Petersburg Soviet were arrested and jailed. The Moscow Soviet led workers in a mass armed rising in solidarity with them, and three hundred were killed when troops were sent in to crush them.

The "days of freedom" were followed by years of reaction and state brutality. The Duma opened in April 1906, and was dissolved by the Tsar three months later, with all its proposed reforms rejected, and the arrests of all eighteen social democrat deputies. The party returned to the underground, and hundreds of Kollontai's comrades were jailed or fled abroad.

In the months before the Duma opened, she represented social democrats at meetings of the Finnish party in Helsingfors, keeping them in touch with socialist deputies to the Finnish parliament, and a collection of her articles from Finland were published by the party as a pamphlet, *Finland and Socialism*, in which she called on workers to "rise up with arms against the state".

As the party's treasurer, in charge of its strike fund, she invited Bolsheviks and Mensheviks to work together that spring on an ambitious new writing project, the *Workers'*

Annual. At this low point in the struggle, she wanted the *Annual* not only to raise badly needed money, but to entertain and educate workers with political sketches and poems, biographies of socialist leaders, and lively non-sectarian pieces on the strike movement. The piece below appeared in the *Annual's* first and only issue in May 1906, before it was closed by the police, and a year later the Bolsheviks published it as a pamphlet. It was republished after the March 1917 revolution, and in 1918, copies were shipped to America to be read by Russians living in San Francisco and New York.

"Who Are the Social Democrats and What Do They Want?"

An Unjust System

There are so many political groups and parties in Russia now, each with their programme, each promising something to workers and peasants, it is often hard to know who is a friend or an enemy or a wolf in sheep's clothing. So let us explain who the social democrats are, and what we stand for.

Each year, life for those who live by their labour becomes harder, while unimaginable wealth goes to the few who own the capital. Shops are crammed with goods, but the worker who produces them is forced to go without boots or a warm coat in winter. The woodsheds of the wealthy are piled with logs, but the worker hasn't a stick to burn on his fire. The grain is rotting in the warehouses, but the peasant has no flour to bake bread with, and the villages are dying of hunger.

The longer it goes on, the worse it gets. Thousands die from work that is beyond their strength, while the bosses stuff their bellies. However hard workers strain themselves, however much wealth they produce with their hands, it goes straight into the capitalists' pockets.

And now the economy is in crisis. Factories are closing, shops are going bankrupt, small traders are ruined. For the major capitalists, these crises are not so terrible, they have spare capital. They are the mighty oaks of the forest, which grow stronger in the storm, and when it passes, the smaller trees have been swept away. Those who suffer most are the workers and peasants and small artisans, who lose what little they had, and are thrown into the ranks of the unemployed.

These economic crises are inevitable so long as the present capitalist system exists. Each capitalist produces only for him self, indifferent to the needs of society, driven by the desire to accumulate more capital than his rivals. The price of a commodity rises, and factories produce more. If there are no purchasers, prices fall, and there is slump and stagnation. Markets are flooded with certain cheap goods, while others become more expensive, which the workers impoverished by the same capitalists cannot afford to buy.

Despite the capitalists' best efforts, these human crises will end only when the economy is run by society to respond to the needs of all its members. Until then, the sole purpose of the economy is to increase the employers' profits — the "surplus value" they ex tract from the labour workers expend to keep themselves alive.

What Do We Demand?

The imperfections of the present system are plain for all to see, and people have looked for various ways to make a better one. Some called for the wealth to be removed from the exploiters and redistributed among the poor. But with so many more of the poor, it became clear this redistribution wouldn't work, and that each would get only a tiny part of the wealth. One would get half a factory chimney, another a plough or a bit of land. People would trade and try to get the best price for their share, and before long there would be the same inequality again. The sharper business brains would end up with the wealth, leaving the rest with nothing but their workers' hands.

Others put their faith in the proper administration of the country, through democracy and the rule of law. Democratic governments can improve workers' lives, and may seem the way to a better future. But as long as society is divided between the classes of the haves and have-nots — the bourgeoisie and the proletariat — laws on their own, however good they are, cannot rid us of the evils that rule us.

The social democrats correctly see the root of these evils in private property, which has created the class system. The social democrats believe that for poverty and wealth to disappear, so that no one grows rich at another's expense, the whole country and its accumulated wealth — its mines, factories, forests and land — must be the property of each and every one of us. When the workers and peasants take the factories from the bosses and the estates from the landowners, the wealthy will no longer grow fat on the labour of others, and humanity will be spared hunger, crises and unemployment.

Under the existing class system, the privileged few own the capital, the rest have only their labour power. Workers go to the master to sell their hands for just enough not to die of hunger. The master buys their labour for kopecks, and they produce goods for him worth millions of roubles. And the longer and harder he makes them work for him, the greater his profits. There are always those who will fight their exploitation. But he can sack as many troublemakers as he likes, he has thousands more fighting for their jobs.

These injustices are the result of private property.

To change people's lives for the better, the capital and the land must pass from the capitalists and the landowners to the workers and peasants. There is no other option for the new society. The private economy must be replaced by the people's economy, based on comradely collective labour. When the wealth is collectively owned and managed, workers will no longer be slaves of capital, but free citizens, who labour for themselves and run the country in their interests. Only then, in this new communist or socialist world, will we see an end to poverty and famine, which are caused not by a scarcity of foodstuffs, but by a system that exploits the poor to generate more profits — such as when grain supplies are deliberately withheld from the hungry towns and villages in poor harvests to push up prices.

These cycles of crisis and unemployment, which are so devastating for working people, will end only with the disappearance of the capitalist economy, which serves to enrich the few. Each capitalist strives solely for himself, not for society, hence the enmity and competition between them. In the communist economy, there will be no place for this competition. There will be work for all, so workers will no longer have to tear the bread from another's mouth to survive. Some of the goods produced by this new collective labour will be used to cover the needs of society, the rest will be shared by its citizens, calculated by common consent. Work will be made as safe and healthy as possible, and largely mechanised, so each will have to work less. Those who work will be fed and clothed, and able to enjoy all the pleasures and benefits of life presently available only to the wealthy few. And as society grows wealthier, living standards will rise. With the disappearance of private property, society will no longer be divided into classes. People will be respected not because their grandfather was famous or their father was rich, but for their services to their comrades and society.

Can We Change The World?

However correct the ideas of those proposing this social transformation, however alluringly they depict life in the new communist society, many see it as an empty dream. Can we really turn the world upside down, and change the relations between people? How do we do that?

For a long time there was no answer to this question. There were those who believed capitalism could be "tamed," by softening the capitalists' hard hearts with stories of workers' suffering, and some employers were moved to give part of their fortunes to charity. But greed and exploitation continued, and life went on as before. Workers laboured and suffered and lived in poverty, creating the capitalists' surplus value, while the capitalists lived in luxury on the fruits of their labour. The new society imagined and de scribed so passionately by the early socialists seemed to many a fantasy, a longed-for but unattainable dream.

Then the voice of the mighty Karl Marx rang out, showing workers the path that would lead them to the kingdom of comradely labour, unity and equality. Socialism is not a fantasy, Marx wrote. Human societies have their laws, like the laws of nature. It is not enough simply to want a new social order. Establishing it in practice is possible only if the conditions exist to make the transition to the new society not only desirable but inevitable. And Marx showed that these conditions already exist in capitalist societies.

Our rulers like to tell us that the capitalist system is ordained for eternity, and cannot be changed, and those who have known nothing else may see no alternative for humanity. But on the contrary, social systems are extremely changeable, particularly economic systems. Human behaviour is equally flexible, and when modes of economic production change, morality and belief systems change too. Modes of production define human relations, determine government policies, and are codified in law. Under the present mode of production, the law exists to allow the rich to grow richer on the backs of the poor. In the socialist economy, the law will give to each what they earn, and exploitation and inequality will disappear.

Societies had passed through various different systems before the bourgeoisie overthrew feudalism to become the dominant class, and working people had known slavery and serfdom. But never have they suffered such poverty, degradation and lack of rights as under the cruel wage labour of capital ism. Each day, more are cast into the ranks of the proletariat who live from the sale of their hands. Artisans and small traders — shoemakers, carpenters, bookbinders, tailors and dressmakers — go out of business and are forced to find work in the factories. The shopkeeper struggles to survive beside the new department store, with its mounds of goods in the windows. But finally he goes bankrupt, and with hatred in his heart, he applies for a job in the store. The peasant, unable to feed his family from his scrap of land, used to eke out his income by making handicrafts. But now the factories are flooding the market with cheap goods, and he is forced to abandon his land and find work in the town.

The countryside empties, the peasants are starving, there is famine after famine. In the towns, thousands of the unemployed fight for jobs, lowering the price of their hands. This state of affairs suits the capitalists and their shareholders perfectly. The lower workers' wages, the greater their profits. And the more wealth they accumulate, the more powerful they become.

What Is The Answer?

As society divides ever more sharply into the two antagonistic classes, the greater the anger in workers' hearts. Won't this system which enriches the few destroy the whole of humanity? No, Marx said. The capitalist order is terrible and unjust, but capitalism also fulfills a positive role, and in a short space of time has developed the productive forces necessary for the transition to socialism.

An essential precondition for this transition is the collective organisation of labour, which already exists in every branch of industry. In the old economy, the spinner and weaver worked alone at home or in small workshops. This cottage economy has now been replaced by the mass production of the factory system, which has turned the old craftsmen into mill hands. And as mechanised industry expands, this new collective labour is connecting the factory worker with the farm worker, the cities with the villages.

To make the best use of its resources, the new socialist economy must be managed centrally. And here again capitalism serves our purpose, as ever more industrial enterprises are concentrated in the capitalists' hands. The national wealth and the means of production are now managed by the exploiters, and this is our grief. Yet in this concentration of wealth, we can already see the beginnings of the new system.

That is the beauty of the socialist system, Marx wrote. We haven't invented it, it hasn't suddenly sprung from nowhere on god's earth. These new forms of life have been evolving for decades, and flow naturally from existing social conditions. Marx's great service was to show that capitalism contains the seeds of the new system that will lead to its destruction, and that life itself, the social needs of humanity, will inevitably lead us to socialism.

To achieve socialism, we must first destroy the private ownership of the land and the instruments of production. But social democrats do not only speak of socialism, we welcome every social change that prepares the ground for the new society. An instance of this was when the Tsar was forced by the recent economic crisis to pass laws partly nationalising hospitals and schools, the postal services and the railway system. A few years ago, this would have been unthinkable — hospitals, schools and the railways were private business. At present the economy is still run to profit the wealthy. But when state power passes to the workers, the system will already be in place for public services to be taken into public control to serve the needs of society.

Capitalism Is Digging Its Own Grave

Under the capitalist system, factories produce ever greater quantities of goods in the fight for profits. Then as industries gain new world markets, nations are drawn into wars with each other to steal more colonies from which to extract unimaginable wealth. Each major capitalist power seeks a world monopoly for its goods. Imperialist wars for markets and colonies will continue so long as the capitalist system exists. And the deadlier these wars are, the more clearly workers will see that they must take the economy into their hands if humanity is to survive. The day is fast approaching when these capitalist crises and imperialist wars will force us to choose whether we perish, or we overthrow the bourgeoisie to step over the threshold into socialism.

Marx shows us that industrial capitalism, built on competition, requiring enormous resources and spare capital, has called into existence its own gravediggers — a powerful united workforce, which will eventually destroy it. Capital ism is also destroying the intermediate class that used to stand between the two camps — small farmers, traders, shopkeepers and the self-employed — and throwing them into the factories. And however painful the process is for them, this too is hastening the transition to socialism.

As the proletariat grows larger, industry is run by ever fewer capitalists. Most workers have never so much as glimpsed their employers. Modern production methods are making the gentlemen entrepreneurs' role in the factories increasingly irrelevant, and most are run now by foremen, managers and engineers. The less spiders there are, the easier to destroy their webs. If the bosses should all drop dead one fine day, the world would barely notice. Whereas when workers decide to strike, life comes to a stop, as happened in 1905, when strikers brought the autocracy to its knees.

The Future Is In Workers' Hands

Thus capitalism itself is leading us inevitably to socialism. But this upheaval won't take place by itself, someone must work to rebuild society. Who then? The workers, robbed of their political rights, who sacrifice their youth, health and energy to create the wealth that keeps the system going?

Unheard of wealth and poverty are growing. But workers are no longer merely victims, and their exploitation feeds their hatred for the bloodsuckers. They long to enjoy the fruits of their labour, to throw off their shackles and work for themselves, and they are strong because life has educated them in feelings of comradeship and solidarity, standing always and everywhere one for all, condemning themselves and their families to more hunger and sacrifices when they strike for the common cause.

We should not deceive ourselves that the path to the new society will be easy. The capitalists will do all in their power to defend their interests — with threats and violence, or with sweet words, throwing scraps to the workers to divert them from their goals. We see how free they are with their promises as soon as they feel threatened. Comrades, don't fall into their trap! Take the offers rashly thrown to you in moments of weakness, but don't let them buy you off!

Who Are The Social Democrats?

The answer is that the social democrats are you, the workers. They are comrades who have thought deeply about Marx's ideas, and have joined the great workers' liberation movement which unites proletarians of all countries, fighting shoulder to shoulder to overthrow capitalism and establish the new socialist society.

What Do The Social Democrats Demand?

The social democrats believe it is in the interests of all who are oppressed by capital to fight collectively in a powerful organised revolutionary workers' party for this better socialist future. But on our path to our great goal, we do not neglect the immediate needs of those who work in the mines and factories, on the farms and railways, and in domestic service. We demand the eight-hour day, an end to the employment of children under sixteen and heavy work for adolescents; the protection of women's labour, the provision of children's nurseries in workplaces, and proper benefits for the unemployed, the sick, the old and the disabled. We demand the right to strike, freedom of speech and assembly, freedom of worship and a free press.

Realising these demands will depend on our

strength and organisation. Social democrats call on all working men and women to organise under the banner of revolutionary socialism. A hard road lies ahead before we break the bourgeoisie's resistance. But our consolation will be knowing that we are fighting not only for our own liberation, but for the liberation and happiness of future generations. Working people have nothing to lose but their chains, and a whole world to gain. Workers of all countries unite and fight! Victory is on our side!

Throughout 1906, Kollontai narrowly avoided arrest. She smuggled leaflets into St Petersburg's garrisons and factories, appealing to soldiers and workers to set up revolutionary fighting cells, and she spoke at meetings. At a factory meeting on women in the strike movement, the police arrived after she called for an armed rising against the Tsar, and she managed to escape from the hall in disguise.

Increasing numbers of factory women were abandoning the Equal Rights League for the workers' clubs, where she and her textileworker friends were giving talks on topics such as factory hygiene and maternity care, quickly developing the themes of oppression and revolution in the last few minutes, relying on a single word to make their point if police spies in the audience seemed particularly vigilant.

They agreed that they needed a new women's organisation in the party to coordinate their work, and she began the uphill task of explaining the necessity of this to the party central committee. The idea was instantly rejected by the Bolshevik majority as a "dangerous deviation to feminism," and it was several weeks before women were provided with premises for an organising meeting. Then when they arrived at the hall they found it locked, with a note on the door saying "Women-only meeting cancelled. Men-only meeting tomorrow".

It had its intended effect. The women decided they lacked the power or numbers to organise themselves, and when Kollontai asked the central committee to back her work with them, she was told they would neither oppose nor endorse it.

She saw the party failing not only the working women who had signed the feminists' suffrage petition, but also large numbers of students and intellectuals. She was arguing virtually alone against the entire St Petersburg organisation, and criticisms of her were often painfully personal. She was one of only a small number of women activists in the party, most of whose main allegiance was to the male majority, and her struggle was a lonely and difficult one, isolated in the movement as a woman and a mother, and fighting on two fronts, against the feminists and her comrades' chauvinism.

She found new solidarity and ways of working at the two women's conferences of the Socialist International, in 1907 and 1910, where resolutions were passed on equal pay, universal suffrage and laws to safeguard women's labour, which were presented to the main congresses of the International to become part of its programme.

The conferences were organised by women in the German socialist party, led by Clara Zetkin, editor of its women's paper, *Die Gleichheit*, which spoke for a powerful confident socialist women's movement, and firmly rejected revisionist attempts to depoliticise its articles.

Between 1878 and 1890, the party had been driven under ground by Bismarck's Anti-Socialist Laws, and in those years, when calling for universal suffrage was an arrestable offence, women were especially harshly punished for being politically active. To get round the laws, underground discussion circles were set up, in which they learnt new organisational skills, and when the laws were repealed, they emerged from the underground as the most consistent voices of the party's revolutionary left, with the structure already in place for its new women's sections. Centrally directed by Zetkin, the sections used the pages of *Die Gleichheit* to turn the fundamental Marxist principles of women's equality into a programme for all the socialist parties in the International.

Kollontai was the only Russian to attend the first planning meeting in 1906 in Mannheim, and the two conferences in Stuttgart and Copenhagen, representing women in St Petersburg's Textileworkers' Union. Her book *The International Conferences of Socialist Women,* published in 1918, is a record of their debates, in which members of the different parties in the International expressed their views on the woman question — from the small moderate minority, who called for higher wages for men, allowing women to stay at home, to the overwhelming Marxist majority, led by the Germans, who saw women in the factories as a powerful new force in the fight for socialism.

Below is the second chapter of the book, on the 1907 confer-ence in Stuttgart, at which Kollontai spoke in German in support of the Germans' resolution on women's suffrage, arguing that Marxism had nothing in common with compromise, and women had nothing to gain from making concessions on the issue. The chapter was originally published in 1910 as an article in the socialist journal *Our Dawn.*

"The Stuttgart International Socialist Women's Conference"

A new danger is threatening the bourgeoisie — women workers are boldly taking the path of the international class organisations. The downtrodden slaves, humbly bowing before the god of capital, have lifted their heads to defend the interests of their class and their interests as women.

When only the male half of the proletariat was infected by the "poison" of socialism, the capitalists could breathe easily. They still had an inexhaustible supply of compliant female workers, ready to sacrifice themselves to enrich the owners of the instruments of production. The bourgeoisie happily availed itself of this state of affairs, which turned women into men's rivals, setting one half of the proletariat against the other and sapping its class solidarity. And the more isolated from the strike movement women were, the less chance it had of succeeding.

Yet once their class consciousness was raised, they took the hand of friendship offered by their male comrades, and joined the struggle as fighters and organisers. This spread panic in the ruling class. The ground was disappearing from under its feet. Women's growing involvement in the class struggle threatened to remove capitalism's last defenceless victims from exploitation, and the light of the approaching social revolution shone more brightly.

The bourgeoisie listened with ill-concealed horror to the harmonious voices ringing out from the International Congress at Stuttgart. But even more horrifying was the Women's Conference that preceded it. In the past, however radical men's speeches were, whatever "wild" resolutions they passed, employers could always draw comfort from the one sure tactic available to them to break the hotheads' spirit — to replace them with meek submissive women. But what a surprise! From all corners of the world, women from the socialist parties of fourteen countries came together at Stuttgart to sharpen their weapons against the enemies of the proletariat. Could a more dreadful spectacle be imagined! The ridicule the press rained down on them could not disguise their anxiety.

No wonder there is so much hostility to any display of female resistance, any attempt by women to defend their interests. Even the most progressive democratic countries will stop at nothing to prevent working women gaining equal rights with men. This would put a dangerous new weapon in the hands of the proletariat, doubling the ranks of the opposition. They are not so stupid as to agree to such an arrangement!

The organised proletariat has now given the gentlemen of capital something new to worry about. If only recently they could rely on women's isolation in the workforce, that sweet hope was dashed at Stuttgart. Delegate after delegate spelled out women's organisational achievements in the different countries. Germany boasts an impressive 120,000 women trade union members, despite constant police harassment, with 10,500 in the German Social Democratic Party, and 70,000 subscribers to *Die Gleichheit*. England has the largest number of organised women workers, with 150,000 in the unions, and 30,000 politically active in the Social Democratic Federation or the Independent Labour Party. In Austria, there are 42,000 women in the unions. Finland has 18,600 women in the Social Democratic Party. In Belgium and Hungary respectively, there are 14,000 and 15,000 women trade union members.

Women's high level of activism in these countries has brought new solidarity and cooperation. Our main objectives at Stuttgart were to establish permanent contacts between the parties' women's organisations, and to work out the basis for a common strategy on women's voting rights.

Women's suffrage was the main issue discussed. The resolution drafted by the German delegates, presented two days later to the main Congress, was framed to define the tactics of Social Democracy in the campaign, and move these tactics from theory to a practical programme for the International. Working women have been led by their basic material needs to an acute awareness of their lack of political rights, and they see these rights not merely as a "policy decision" for the International, but as a vital and urgent necessity.

In recent years, workers of all countries in the International have addressed the issue of universal suffrage, and it might have seemed that its four-point election formula, supplemented by its fifth clause, stipulating "without distinction of sex," would have left no room for doubt on the issue. But it proved otherwise. A year ago, when the socialist parties were polled on votes for women, although most responded positively, several did so grudgingly and with reservations. Not only men but many women too vacillated on the fifth clause, showing that the principle of sexual equality, so fundamental to the working class, has yet to enter the bloodstream of the socialist movement. One after another, women from Austria, Belgium and Sweden called for political rights for women workers to be dropped from the socialist agenda in favour of a weak compromise formula for electoral reform. Even many staunch socialists were won over by their arguments, and presented them in their countries as models of action. Women themselves are not to blame for this. But the male half of the proletariat, whose class consciousness and fighting spirit have been tempered in battle, should not have allowed itself to be drawn onto this opportunist path. There are principles the working class cannot in its interests afford to sacrifice, slogans the proletariat cannot change, merely to achieve short-term results.

"Without distinction of sex" has yet to become an integral part of the socialist suffrage campaign. It is only comparatively recently that women have begun to work outside the home and play their part in the workers' movement. Proletarian class consciousness is still clouded by ideological survivals of the past, which have blurred the outlines of a truth that should be indisputable: that equal political rights for all members of the socialist proletarian family are in the interests of the working class as a whole.

The resolution presented to the main Congress of the International demanded an unequivocal commitment to the fifth clause, as of equal importance to the other four. But our resolution was not passed unopposed. Two trends emerged in the socialist women's movement: the orthodox Marxists, represented by the Germans, and the revisionists, represented by the Austrians, the Belgians and the English. The German resolution was intended to draw a clear line between the proletarian women's movement and the equal-rights feminists. And this was a sore point for the English, many of whom are working closely with the suffragettes, and in the heat of the suffragettes' selfless and inspiring battle for the vote, class distinctions are often forgotten. British delegates from the Fabian Society and the Independent Labour Party spoke in favour of limited electoral rights for working women, and defended this unforgivable betrayal of workers' class interests before the entire socialist world. The only English delegate to support universal voting rights for both sexes was from the Marxist Social Democratic Federation.

These disagreements showed the need for a common socialist strategy on the issue. But this was not what most of the English wanted, and with the seven Austrians, they called for each party to have the right to determine the question independently, according to the different conditions in their countries. The German resolution forced them to do some hard thinking. Were they defending women workers in their struggle to survive, suffering untold adversities today in the expectation of great triumphs tomorrow? Or were they fighting for more privileges for those who neither toil nor spin?

The Austrians spoke for a powerful women workers' movement, which calls on women not to break the laws banning them from attending meetings and campaigning for the vote. With suffrage for working men in Austria now a real possibility, they argued that women's demand for the vote was "untimely," and that social democrats' "stubbornness" on the issue was preventing the male proletariat from achieving major political gains. Fierce enemies of the liberal feminists, who they refuse to work with, the Austrians nonetheless fell into the same error as the British, claiming that in certain circumstances it is acceptable to put aside the interests of one section of the proletariat — in this case women — to win practical gains for another. This view also received a measure of support from delegates from Catholic France, Belgium and Italy, who argued that campaigning for the vote risked strengthening the power of the Church, leading to new parliamentary groupings hostile to the proletariat.

The ruling class, skilled in the strategy of divide and rule, presents women workers' interests as antagonistic to those of men of their class. While the liberal feminists try to seduce them into losing their living link with their male comrades by putting the "common cause" of women above the cause of their class. Whenever the tactics of Social Democracy are disputed, we must return to tried and tested methods of resolving them, patiently investigating to what extent a given demand is essential for the working class to achieve its objectives. There can be no place for compromise on the suffrage issue, however many immediate benefits compromise may seem to offer. What would become of the class objectives of the proletariat if we abandoned our basic beliefs whenever we hoped to gain some practical advantage? What would distinguish us then from the bourgeoisie?

Workers are strong when they stay true to the teachings of Marxism. Social democrats' commitment to women's political equality is beyond dispute. The compromisers' gradualist "step by step" tactics seek a completely different approach. The proletariat knows from experience that our enemies would see such tactics as proof of our weakness, and that the more "reasonable" our demands, the more paltry their concessions. This is a well-known truth, which must be repeated whenever the core beliefs of Social Democracy are at stake.

The effect of the Austrians' timid compliance would not only have postponed voting rights for working women, it would have destroyed socialism's commitment to defending the unity of the working class as the guarantee of victory. Fortunately however the mood of the conference was unsympathetic to these views, which paled before the indisputable fact that women are the most oppressed and exploited members of the proletariat. It is these pariahs of society, these exhausted slaves of capital, who their comrades in suffering reach out to in the struggle for a better future.

Our resolution called on the International to confirm Social Democracy's principled position on women's suffrage as inseparable from the class struggle, arguing that any deviation from this would damage the entire workers' cause. "We demand the vote not as a right attached to the possession of property, but for all women," Clara Zetkin said, addressing the commission on women's suffrage at the main Congress. "We are not so naive as to expect socialist parties everywhere and in all circumstances to make this campaign the cornerstone of their work. That will depend on the level of historical development in the different countries. What we reject is any attempt to remove women's demand for the vote from our socialist programme".

The atmosphere at our conference was charged with excitement, quite unlike the somewhat lifeless efficiency of the Congress that followed. Its massive organisational structure, the presence of almost nine hundred delegates from twenty-four socialist parties, and the need to observe a whole range of formalities, had the effect of dampening speakers' enthusiasm. Masters of the spoken word crossed swords, experienced in all the fine points of parliamentary debate, and it was only rarely that they captured the audience's hearts.

At the women's conference, the living pulse of faith beat with the confidence of an organisation that was still young and not set in its ways. Our suffrage resolution was passed by forty-seven votes to eleven, and was placed before the Congress, proving yet again that despite the bourgeoisie's claims about the "death of Marxism," the spirit of scientific socialism was alive, inspiring millions to join the international socialist movement.

Second on our agenda was the Germans' proposal to set up a new Women's Bureau of the International, to keep women's organisations in all the countries in touch with each other, and coordinate information about our campaigns. This purely organisational question produced an equally lively exchange of views. The Austrians again revealed their fear of being labelled "feminists," insisting that such a Bureau was unnecessary, calling instead for women's organisations in each country to appoint women to report back on their work.

The Germans argued that an independent grouping of proletarian women would have clear organisational advantages, focusing parties' attention on mobilising the less active members of the female proletariat, whose need to become politically involved grows more urgent by the day. The most exploited members of the proletarian family, oppressed everywhere by special laws, lacking their basic political rights, even in the democratic countries, they desperately need proper representation. But this is not yet fully recognised by the broad masses of the proletariat. A new Women's Bureau could put pressure on parties to take up the cudgels on women's behalf, and educate our male comrades on how best to defend their interests. And when parties pay proper attention to their needs, this will bring new female forces into the army of the proletariat. In Germany, it was the threat of arrest under the Anti-Socialist Laws that led to the party's separate work with women. But these ways of working have already been adopted in countries with far freer regimes.

At Stuttgart, victory on the issue again went to the Left. By a large majority, the conference voted for an independent Women's Bureau of the International, with *Die Gleichheit* as its mouthpiece, and the official voice of the international socialist women's movement.

These decisions on tactics and organisation will determine Social Democracy's approach to the women's suffrage campaign, and will have a hugely positive effect in winning working women to social ism. In the war between the two classes, the outcome will be decided by the balance of forces. Only when women are firmly united, and united with their male comrades in the common class struggle, can they march confidently forward together to the noble proletarian goal of a better socialist future.

The issues of women's voting rights and organisation were discussed at the main Congress at the end of a crowded agenda that reflected delegates' preoccupation with the current crisis in Morocco, where Spain and France were carving out their spheres of influence. Britain was supporting France, and the German Kaiser had declared his support for the Sultan of Morocco against them, and a united resolution on the new arms race bet ween Britain and Germany took first place on the programme. Women's suffrage followed discussions of the colonial question, and the closely connected topic of immigration.

Clara Zetkin in *Die Gleichheit* had consistently attacked the growing military power of the Reich, arguing that the imperialist conflicts ranging France, Britain, Russia, Spain and Italy against Germany and Austria were leading to world war. Zetkin spoke in the main debate on German militarism, and she was sup ported by a majority of the 63-strong Russian delegation, including Trotsky and Lenin. Rosa Luxemburg had not attended the women's conference, and she spoke at the Congress for the Polish party and for Lenin's supporters in the Russian party, since he believed she could present his views better than he could himself, using her genius for argument to compose the statement that was finally adopted: "Agitation must be aimed not only at averting war, but at hastening the general collapse of class rule". She repeated this message at packed workers' rallies in the town, at which she called for mass strike action against the threat of war, and Kollontai shared a platform with her, speaking about the strike movement in Russia.

When she returned to St Petersburg in late September, there was a police warrant for her arrest for her pamphlet *Finland and Social ism*. "Legal proceedings against me held the grim prospect of spending many years in jail, and I was forced to disappear immediately," she wrote. "My son was taken in by good friends, my small household was 'liquidated,' and I became an 'illegal,' and was never to see my home again".

During the next nine months, she emerged from the underground in a variety of disguises, speaking at over fifty women's meetings in the capital's workers' clubs, advertised as sewing circles or lectures on childcare, to avoid police attention. In the spring of 1908, she won the party's backing for a new legal women workers' club, run entirely by women, the innocuously named Working Women's Mutual Aid Society, which organised lectures and discussions, set up a library and cheap canteen, and even planned a summer camp for women and their children. But meetings were soon being disrupted by Bolsheviks who saw the club as the thin end of a "feminist wedge" in the party. Kollontai attempted unsuccessfully to make peace, and the club was soon closed by the police. She then embarked on another scheme to involve women in politics.

That spring, St Petersburg's feminist organisations announced plans for their All-Russian Congress of Women, to be held in the capital in December, and she was determined that social democrats should use the congress to publicise their position on women. The party and trade unions eventually agreed that she could organise a group of factory women to make interventions. The Bolsheviks were now participating in the Tsar's new Duma, a majority of them "ultimatists," and they wanted women to give the congress the "ultimatist" treatment, demanding "the overthrow of the capitalist system which exploits and oppresses us," then walking out. Kollontai rejected this tactic, and embarked on the work of preparing forty-five factory women, the "Labour Group," to deliver speeches on women's suffrage and working conditions and women in the political parties.

They rehearsed their speeches over pies and herrings at meetings advertised as nameday parties, and she described hundreds of women who had never been to meetings before — domestic servants, women from the textile, cardboard, rubber, tobacco and footwear factories — being drawn into a campaign of mounting intensity to "shock the feminists".

The congress organisers called her a criminal and a "hooligan," and she had more narrow escapes from the police. By the summer there was a second warrant for her arrest, and she went into deep hiding. It was then that she started work on her book *The Social Basis of the Woman Question*, her fierce and lengthy polemic against the feminists, intended to arm the Labour Group with the arguments they would need at the congress.

Writing in a passionate and sometimes convoluted style, born of three years of thwarted work, she insisted that women could win their equality only by fighting for socialism. Her vision of the freer more equal family life possible was both utopian and deeply practical — "when the individual household will be replaced by cooperative enterprises, which will provide dozens of separate families with communal laundries, dining rooms and kitchens". And she saw the working-class family as "an infinitely better basis for the new family and the new sexual psychology than that of the bourgeoisie". "It is working women who will prepare the ground for the free and equal woman of the future," she wrote. "The path to her liberation in this new world of labour will be fraught with danger and suffering. But it is only there that she will learn to discard the slave mentality that has clung to her for centuries, and to transform herself step by step into an independent personality, free to love and marry on her own terms".

She took as her inspiration the young peasant woman newly arrived in the city to work in a factory, "who does not hesitate to follow the first call of love, the first heartbeat". She wrote of "free love" not as loveless promiscuity, but as an ideal to be aspired to, and she denounced the abuse that went on in its name — "the gentlemen running the industrial enterprises who force their workers and secretaries to submit to their sexual demands, threatening to sack them if they resist. The masters of households who rape their servants and throw them onto the streets when they become pregnant".

She was also sensitive to the dilemmas faced by middle-class women who had left the feminist organisations but had nowhere to go. "Surely they cannot fail to see how little the feminists have done for working women, how unable they are to improve their living conditions. The future of humanity must seem bleak and uncertain to those fighting for their equality who have no faith in the possibility of a better social system. While capitalism remains intact, their liberation must seem partial and incomplete. What despair must grip the more sensitive and thoughtful of them".

Below is an abridged translation of her introduction to the book, in which she outlined socialism's approach to the woman question, arguing that working women would gain their equality not through feminist charity, but by fighting for the new society that would end the material basis of their oppression.

From *The Social Basis of the Woman Question*

The year 1908 is an important one in the history of the feminist movement in Russia. In December, the Women's Mutual Philanthropic Society and the Women's Equal Rights League will review their work at the All-Russian Congress of Women, and will pass resolutions on their future course of action in the women's emancipation campaign.

As a result of recent events in Russia, complex social and political problems which until recently belonged in the realm of abstract theory are now issues requiring urgent practical solutions, and at the forefront of these is the woman question. With every day that passes, growing numbers of working women are being forced to seek answers to three questions: Which way should we go? Who should we believe? How can we be sure that we will share the fruits of the long and painful struggle for the new social order? The congress is being held to give comprehensive answers to these questions.

Its programme is extremely broad. The first section will cover women's activities in the various professions. The second will discuss their working conditions in industry and domestic service, with a special sub-section on questions relating to the family, marriage and prostitution. The third will assess the present civil and political position of women, and the measures needed to achieve their legal equality. The fourth will discuss the issue of women's education.

This new expanded version of the programme is a distinct improvement on the first draft, published in 1907, which totally omitted any mention of working women's economic position and the legal protection of their labour. Was this is an accident, an oversight? If so, it was a characteristic one. Omitting the economic aspect of women's liberation is the sort of "oversight" that would have immediately determined the nature of the congress, excluding those for whom the woman question is inextricably bound up with the general economic issues of the day. Fortunately, the second part of the programme has now corrected this omission.

It is worth commenting on, since it is characteristic of the organisers' lack of clarity about their goals. For a long time they couldn't decide whether the congress should be a philanthropic gathering, engaged in moral and charitable activities, or should attempt to break through working women's indifference to their fate, and draw them into the ranks of those fighting for their emancipation. At their first meetings, leading lights in the feminist world stood up to demand that the congress avoid "propaganda" on women's working conditions, and focus instead on charity work and the anti-alcohol and anti-prostitution campaigns. Thanks to the more clear-sighted feminists of the Equal Rights League, the opposing tendency won the day.

The congress is to be held under the slogan "The women's movement is a movement of all women in the struggle for their rights". The organisers' servants have been invited to attend, and it has been a spur to the feminist organisations. The female anthill is stirring. At meeting after meeting, the feminists Pokrovskaya, Kalmanovich, Vakhtina and others deliver speeches with the traditional feminist rallying cry "Women of all classes unite!"

However tempting this may sound, however much it may seem to offer to the feminists' "poor sisters," it forces us to examine more closely the aims of the congress, in terms of working women's goals and aspirations. Crucially, the question is whether they should accept the feminists' invitation to join their campaign for the vote, or should remain loyal to their class, to use other means to free not only women but the whole of humanity from the slavery and oppression of the capitalist way of life.

But before discussing whether or not they should participate, and if so how, let us first state the social democrats' approach to the woman question. We may leave our learned friends the bourgeois scholars to weigh brains to calculate the different mental capacities of the sexes, and demonstrate the superiority of one over the other. The materialist Marxist view of human relations fully recognises the naturally existing differences between the sexes, but wants every individual, man and woman, to have the real chance to develop their natural talents and achieve their potential. The historical materialists deny the existence of innately "female" issues, separate from the general issues of society. Specific economic factors have led to woman's inferior status; her natural characteristics have played a secondary role in this. Only the disappearance of the economic forces that have led to her subordination can bring about a real change in her social position. Women can only be truly free and equal in a new transformed world, based on new social and economic principles.

This does not mean that women's lives cannot be partly improved within the existing system, or that campaigns to improve their working conditions should be seen as a brake on the wider class struggle. Quite the contrary. Each new gain won by the proletariat hastens the new society of equality and freedom. Each new right won by working women brings them closer to their goal of total emancipation. However a genuinely radical solution to the woman question is possible only when capitalism has been swept away in the revolution to socialise production.

For the social democrats, this is not merely a

dream, it is inevitable. Economic conditions are forcing women out of their centuries-old enslavement in the home. Throughout Europe, they are now working alongside men in almost every branch of industry. In Germany, Austria, England, France and Italy, of the eighty-nine million workers employed in industry, twenty-seven million are women, approximately a third of them self-supporting. In Russia, only ten percent of women are self-supporting, but this number is still fairly large. Eight million women in Russia, an eighth of the population, now live in the cities, two million of them living by their own labour, and in rural areas the figure is four million.

It should be remembered that it is only comparatively recently that Russia moved to large-scale capitalist industry. But as capitalist production expands, ever larger numbers of women are being drawn into the workforce. The greatest concentration of female labour now is in the textile and clothing industries, in every area of which they outnumber men. They are also employed in large numbers in the food industry, particularly in baking, in the chemical industry, particularly in cosmetics factories, and in glass, china, tile and brick factories. Their numbers are small only in the iron and steel industries and in the mines.

In general what is happening is not the replacement of male by female labour, but new regroupings according to profession. Some industries employ mainly men, others are increasingly employing women. And this is undoubtedly due partly to the fall in child labour since the recent laws raising the age at which children can be employed in the factories to sixteen, for which we must be grateful.

So the idea that women are men's most dangerous rivals in the workplace is one we must tackle head on. The capitalist world is happy to encourage this rivalry, and to use women as a counter weight to the more united and class-conscious sections of the male proletariat. In the proletarian world, women become men's rivals only when they are cut off from the common class struggle, lowering wages and destroying the gains of the organised fight against capital. The moment they join the fighters for the workers' cause, they cease to be men's rivals, and the organised proletariat closes ranks with its comrades of both sexes.

Working women's desire for their emancipation is inextricably linked to recent economic trends in society. As for what must be done to defend their rights and interests, the bourgeois feminists' message, to organise and unite against their male oppressors, has not fallen on stony ground.

The abolition of serfdom four decades ago fundamentally altered economic and social relations in Russia, and threw a hitherto unknown type of woman onto the labour market, struggling like her male counterpart to earn her daily bread. Post-reform Russia brought the woman question to the fore, and in the decades that followed, feminist organisations sprang up all over Russia. The largest of these, the Women's Mutual Philanthropic Society, was established in 1893 to lobby the Tsar for equal educational opportunities for women. Ever since the birth of the woman question in the 1860s, the main focus of the women's emancipation movement has been to improve and expand women's education, primarily higher education, without which the professions remained closed to them. And having completed their higher education, they then demanded their access to state and private employment.

The feminists' education campaigns have been largely successful, allowing women of the bourgeoisie to enter the professions and gain their economic independence. And employers have been quick to see the advantages of employing this cheaper and more amenable workforce. There could be no question of women demanding their political equality, since even most men in Russia still lack their basic political rights. Women's property rights have never been a feminist campaigning issue, since these compare quite favourably with those in Western Europe; a woman property-owner in Russia is considered fully competent in law on reaching adulthood, and is entitled to dispose of her property and undertake civil actions in her own name.

It goes without saying that the women's movement under discussion here is exclusively bourgeois in nature, and involves only a very narrow circle of women, mainly from the nobility, with a few members of the new middle class. Each year, thousands more women in Russia are employed in industry, yet no socialist ideas find their way into the feminists' programmes, and between the emancipated woman of the intelligentsia and the factory woman with calloused hands, there is such an unbridgeable gulf that there can be no point of contact between them.

Women from the two camps were first tentatively brought together in the 1890s, through the activities of the Mutual Philanthropic Society, and philanthropy has been at the heart of the feminist movement in Russia from its very first days. This is not to accuse women of indifference to social and political issues. And can any other country boast such a host of truly noble and charming heroines, who sacrificed their youth and strength, and often their lives, in the struggle for social justice and political liberation? What can history offer to rival the inner strength and beauty of the "repentant noblewoman" of the 1870s, who put aside her privileges and her finery to repay her debts to society by "going to the people"?

Later, when Tsarist repression turned any protest into a struggle to the death against the autocracy, countless new heroines emerged. The repentant noblewoman, with her selflessness and limitless dedication to the people, was followed by a generation of fearless martyrs in the factories, fighting for the emancipation of their class. The list is constantly being filled with new heroines, and future historians will bow their heads in respect for their courage.

As for Russia's feminists, until recently their aspirations were extremely limited, confined to charity work and education campaigns. The picture changed dramatically after the mighty events of 1905. The revolutionary upsurge at every level of society forced the feminists to see that a new state system in Russia was necessary for their emancipation. Women's circles expanded their modest ambitions and became more active. Bold speeches and demands were heard. Declarations, resolutions and petitions were dispatched to rural and urban soviets. Meetings and conferences passed radical motions. In 1905, it seemed there was no corner of Russia where women weren't reminding society of their existence, making their voices heard, demanding their political rights.

The feminists have now abandoned their previous limited demands, and have adopted a new course of political action. This has not happened without discord. Among the new members flooding into their organisations, two distinct tendencies have emerged: those on the right, faithful to the old traditions, who oppose bringing "politics" into their narrow feminist concerns, and those more to the left, committed to campaigning for women's political rights and equality. The right-wingers continue to group themselves around the Mutual Philanthropic Society, with its programme of politically neutral feminism. The

Equal Rights League, established in 1905 by the more "left-wing" elements, was the first women's organisation to adopt a political platform, and has even gone so far as to advocate a Constituent Assembly in Russia.

Throughout 1905, the League set up branches across the country, and by the spring of 1906 had an estimated membership of around eight thousand. Its leaders aimed to recruit women from all social classes on the basis of their vague slogans, and just as liberals in the Duma claimed to speak in the name of all the people, the League claimed to speak for all women.

But growing class antagonisms in the feminist movement led to new regroupings, and in early 1906 the St Petersburg branch of the League split between the "left-wingers," whose politics were often close to the socialists, and the right-wingers, who established the new Women's Progressive Party, launching its activities by setting up new women's clubs, some with a more or less democratic programme, others of an entirely bourgeois nature, with limited memberships and high fees.

Equal-rights feminists of every hue continue to proclaim the need for women's unity, and for a broad-based movement to achieve this. Yet women are inevitably being drawn to the political banners of their respective social classes. The Women's Progressive Party, which claims to speak for all women, without distinction of politics or class, represents the class of the wealthy bourgeoisie. While the Equal Rights League represents women of the liberal opposition, mainly from the intelligentsia and the new bourgeoisie.

By the spring of 1906, there were four clubs for factory women in the working-class districts of St Petersburg, which won the support of the more progressive feminists. Our club in the capital was the first political club for working women. But its political objectives were muddled by the feminists' attempts to form a women's bloc in the Duma, and it was quickly closed by the police. Despite distancing themselves from the more right-wing feminists, members were unable to decide whose class interests the club represented, or what their goals were. Whether they should defend the interests of proletarian and peasant women, or all women. Whether they should pursue the wider goals of the class struggle, or exclusively feminist goals. The club's entire short-lived existence was marked by this indecision, so that when members discussed the feminists' campaign for an all-class women's grouping in the Duma, and their petition for the vote — a petition signed predominantly by working women — they found them selves unable to decide which party they were closest to in spirit.

Meanwhile the realities of life were exposing the delusion of the feminists' campaign. Women's organisations, like men's, were undergoing a rapid process of class differentiation. The champions of women's unity could do nothing to stop women joining feminist groups tinged with varying degrees of political radicalism, and their call for a women's bloc in the Duma soon fizzled out.

Their petition to the Duma would have only had any meaning if any of the parties they approached had included the demand for women's political rights in their programmes. In arming themselves against men's hostility, they appealed only to the various representatives of bourgeois liberalism, ignoring the existence of the one political party with a coherent strategy on the issue, which goes further than even the most fervent suffragists: the Social Democratic Party.

Ever since Marx published his *Communist Manifesto* in 1848, Social Democracy has always defended the interests of women. The *Manifesto* identified the close links between the workers' movement and the woman question, and the process whereby in drawing women into the workforce, capitalism was involving them in the great struggles waged by the proletariat against their exploitation. The social democrats are the only party in Russia to include equal political rights for women in their programme, and to demand in leaflets and articles an end to their second-class status as workers, wives and mothers. Social democrats defend women's interests not only in theory but in practice, and it was their pressure on the other parties that forced the Duma to propose its recent factory reforms for women.

So what prevents our equal-rights campaigners from standing under the banner of this powerful and experienced party? While the right-wing feminists denounce social democrats' "extremism," members of the Equal Rights League should find our position on women perfectly to their taste. But there lies the catch! For all their radicalism, the feminists remain loyal to the aspirations of their class.

The ruling class needs political liberty if capitalism is to thrive. Without new freedoms, the bourgeoisie's economic prosperity will prove to be built on sand. And these freedoms can only be won through its participation in government. The "freedom to work" slogan of the early feminists is no longer enough for them. Winning political rights is now on the agenda. Only their direct involvement in state affairs can bring about an improvement in their status, hence their passionate desire to gain access to the ballot-box.

Yet like their sisters abroad, they go no further than to demand their political equality within the framework of the existing system, without encroaching in any way on its class basis. The bigger picture of the world the social democrats have opened up is alien and incomprehensible to them.

This is not to blame the feminists for their unwitting sins, which are an inevitable consequence of their class position. Nor should we deny their successes in raising their sisters' consciousness. But the female proletariat would be well advised not to attach themselves to their narrow political goals. When they call women workers into their ranks, we social democrats cannot remain silent. We cannot stand by and watch this pointless waste of proletarian energy. We must ask what working women have to gain from joining forces with them, and what they could achieve instead through their own class organisations.

The world of women, like the world of men, is divided into two camps. Women of both camps are fighting under the slogan of women's emancipation, but on the basis of their opposing class interests: their tactics and objectives are completely different.

It may be possible for an individual woman to rise above the interests of her bourgeois class in the name of the proletariat. But a united women's organisation reflecting the interests of the two antagonistic classes is a fantasy. However progressive the feminists' demands, their class position precludes them from campaigning for the fundamental social changes working women need to achieve their emancipation. The aspirations of the two classes may occasionally coincide, but their ultimate goals are irreconcilable.

For the feminists, political equality means equality under the present capitalist system. Political rights, access to the ballot-box, mean seats in the Tsar's Duma. How can this free the working woman from the abyss of suffering which oppresses her as a woman and a human being?

The goal of the feminists is to achieve equal rights with men in capitalist society. They see men as the enemy, who have seized all the rights and privileges, leaving them in bondage and obligation; with each new gain the feminists make, men must forfeit more of their power to the "fair sex".

The proletarian woman has a completely different view of her position. For the proletariat, the liberation struggle necessarily includes the liberation of women; working women's struggle for their rights is part of the struggle of their class. Men are not only women's enemies and oppressors, they are first and foremost their comrades in arms in the fight for a better future. Both are enslaved by the same social relations, the same hateful bonds of capital, which sap their will and rob them of the pleasures of life. The conditions of wage labour weigh especially heavily on women, and may sometimes turn a woman worker and comrade into men's rival. But working people know who is to blame for this. The woman worker, no less than her brother in suffering, hates the insatiable monster with the gilded maw, which falls on men, women and children alike, to suck them dry and grow fat at the cost of millions of lives.

The woman worker is bound to her male comrades by countless invisible threads. The aims of the bourgeois woman are alien to her. They offer no comfort to her suffering proletarian soul, no vision of the brighter future on which the whole of exploited humanity has fixed its hopes. The feminists stretch out their hands to their working-class sisters, and the "ungrateful creatures" listen distrustfully to their talk of class unity, and leave to join the proletarian organisations that are closer to their hearts.

The more class-conscious woman knows that the woman question cannot be solved under capitalism. That while women are forced to bear the burdens of capital, they cannot be free and autonomous members of society, wives able to choose their husbands according to the dictates of their heart, mothers able to look to the future without fear for their children. The goal of working women is to destroy the old class-based world and to create a better one, in which one class can no longer oppress and exploit another.

For women workers, political equality with men means no more than their shared inequality. They know they can be equal only in a world of socialised labour, harmony and justice. And this is not what the feminists want. They are fighting for their political equality with men, so they can prosper in the world of slavery, oppression and tears. Bourgeois women see the vote opening the door to unheard of new rights and privileges, hitherto avail able only to male members of the bourgeoisie. They have a vested interest in promoting the lie that capitalism can substantially improve working women's lives. And each new victory they achieve puts another instrument in their hands to oppress their sisters, deepening the gulf between them. Their interests and aspirations clash ever more sharply, and become ever more antagonistic.

So what is this "universal woman question" the feminists speak of? What do they mean by the "unity" of their objectives? A sober examination of their congress's programme shows this unity to be meaningless. In vain they try to tell themselves that the woman question is not a matter of parties or politics; hard reality refutes this fiction.

It would be pointless trying to convince them that women's cause will be victorious only with the victory of the working class. But to those who are able to abandon their narrow short term objectives to take a broader view of women's destiny, we say — do not call your proletarian sisters into your ranks, they are strangers to you! Abandon your fine phrases and humbly learn the lessons of history. Defend your class rights and privileges, and leave working women to defend theirs, finding their own path and their own methods in the fight for their freedom and happiness. Whose path is shorter will be decided by life itself.

She finished the book in October, and it was published the following January, a month after the congress ended, by the writer Maxim Gorky's *Znanie* (Knowledge) publishing house in St Petersburg. At four hundred pages, it was too long to have served its original purpose at the congress, and she described her Menshevik comrades urging her to water down her attacks on the feminists — "it was not to everyone's taste".

She braved the police to attend the opening of the congress, and sat at the back of the hall as the first speaker on the platform was heckled by a Bolshevik member of the Labour Group. As each issue on the agenda was discussed, the women's confidence grew, and their statement on sickness benefits produced uproar. "What do you know of our lives, bowling along in your carriages splashing us in mud?" a member of the group shouted, to which an organiser replied that it was because they didn't have to endure their wretched lives that they were best qualified to represent them.

Unable to contain herself, Kollontai jumped up to speak, and by the time the police arrived to close the meeting and arrest her, she had escaped and was on the train to Germany and her new life in exile.

Chapter Three
Exile

From the end of 1908 until the outbreak of war in 1914, Kollontai was based in Berlin, the main centre of the Russian revolutionary diaspora in Europe. She immediately joined the German socialist party, and offered her services as a full-time activist. "A.M. Kollontai is one of the most prominent and active members of the Russian Social Democratic Party in Germany," the Tsarist police chief in Berlin was soon cabling back to St Petersburg.

Her book *Around Workers' Europe*, published in Russia in 1912, is a vivid account of her travels across Germany, and her frequent trips abroad — to Belgium, France, Italy, Switzerland, Denmark and England. She spoke in German at meetings in grand party headquarters and in shabby workers' halls, to local youth groups and women's sections, to farmers in the Rhineland and strikers in "Red Saxony". She spoke in English at two workers' rallies in London, and in French at a women's food riot in Paris, and to striking miners in Belgium. "My years in exile turned me into a convinced internationalist, with an unshakeable faith in the creative capacities of the working class," she wrote.

Russia's 1905 revolution had galvanised workers' movement in Europe and America. Over a million workers in Germany came out on strike in 1908, on the docks and railways and in the mines and factories, and she saw the socialist leaders putting pressure on the trade unions to curb the unrest, fearful of the effects of the revolution at home. In *Around Workers' Europe* she was sharply critical of the party's rightward shift since 1905, and its growing conservatism, nationalism and bureaucracy. Her allies were in its left revolutionary wing, led by Luxemburg, Zetkin and the Reichstag deputy Karl Liebknecht, and Liebknecht and his Russian wife became her closest friends in Germany. But she wrote that she was shunned by many in the party as a Russian. "Let Russians with such a superabundance of revolutionary energy go back to preach revolution from their summer dachas, instead of propagating discussions in Germany about the general strike," one official said, and she was told to keep off the subject of Russia at her meetings. "Where is the contact with the centre, the comradely leadership?" she wrote, and the book made her new enemies in the German party when it was published.

Socialism in Russia too was in crisis. The Bolsheviks, the only party that had seemed capable of leading the revolution, were in jail or exile or operating deep in the underground, driven into a particularly hard-line politics which saw any discussion of personal politics and women's liberation as a distraction from the class struggle. *The Social Basis of the Woman Question* was largely ignored by Kollontai's comrades when it was published in Russia a month after she left, and her idealistic vision of the freer sexual relationships possible under socialism became identified with the mass-produced pornography flooding the country in the wake of the defeated revolution.

Sickened by the chaos and violence of the revolution, many socialists abandoned socialism to join the bourgeois liberal parties, which they saw as the only alternative to the autocracy. Others became "mystical anarchists," or were caught up in new-age religions. Kollontai was drawn to the "seeking Marxists," who were discovering revolutionary new insights into human behaviour in the works of Freud.

Psychoanalysis was studied seriously in Russia long before it became popular in the West. Russians were travelling to Vienna to meet Freud and train as analysts, and Kollontai saw his theories of sexuality and the unconscious as the key to a new Marxist understanding of the bourgeois family, and people's feelings about love and sex.

Effective birth control was available in Russia only to the wealthy few. In Germany, large numbers of workers had had access to basic affordable contraception since the turn of the century, and she opened up the subject for discussion in Russia with a thoughtful essay in the socialist journal *Life*, "The Fate of Humanity and the Population Question," about the politics of reproduction, and the liberating new control contraception gave women over their bodies and who they slept with.

She was also corresponding with women in St Petersburg about their campaigning work with prostitutes. Teams of philanthropic feminists in the capital, led by two princesses, had been organising missions to rescue them from the brothels. Socialist women were organising demonstrations with them on the streets, to demand the jobs, maternity services and proper housing they needed. They were also writing to Kollontai about their male comrades' distaste for their work and reluctance to support them, and in her article "Two Truths," she reminded them of Marxism's views on the issue.

Marx, Engels and August Bebel had all written of prostitutes as the ultimate victims of capitalist exploitation. Marx called sex work "a particular expression of the general prostitution of the labourer," a direct result of women's low pay and lack of education — the "complement" to bourgeois marriage, which was itself a form of prostitution. Bebel, in his book *Woman and Socialism*, described prostitution as "a necessary institution in the capitalist world, as necessary as the police, the church, and wage slavery". Kollontai linked the dramatic rise in prostitution in Russia to the economic crisis in the years before and after the 1905 revolution. She wrote of "the horror and helplessness of women's lives, resulting from capitalism's exploitation of their labour," and she paid tribute to the women who were battling male bigotry and hypocrisy to fight with them on the streets.

In the summer of 1910, with Trotsky and the "seeking

Marxist" Anatoly Lunacharsky, she was invited by Maxim Gorky to teach at his training school in Italy for Russian workers. Trotsky gave classes on the techniques of illegal publishing and underground propaganda, Lunacharsky lectured in philosophy and Italian art, Kollontai gave lectures on women's liberation and the sexual revolution.

She developed these ideas in two articles published the following year in Russia in the socialist journal *New Life*, in which she set out the terms for a new discussion in the socialist movement about sexual relations and the family. She found the language for her first article, "On An Old Theme," in the book *The Sexual Crisis,* by the Austrian socialist and feminist Grete Meisel-Hess, who had read widely about psychoanalysis, and whose insights she saw as of fundamental importance to the socialist movement — the "thread of Ariadne," showing a way out of the hypocrisy and jealous dramas of the bourgeois family.

The old form of the family could no longer fulfill people's emotional needs or the needs of society, Meisel-Hess wrote. Bourgeois monogamous marriage exhausted the tenderness between couples, and the conventional outlet for this sexual incompatibility was prostitution — which according to Kollontai, "reinforces men's selfishness, allowing them with shocking naivety to deprive women of sexual satisfaction, reducing one of the most serious moments of human life, this ultimate accord of complex spiritual feelings, to something pallid, coarse and shameful, leaving feelings of spiritual hunger on both sides".

People's longing for more fulfilling sexual relationships could only be realised when they were free from the alienation born of capitalist property relations — "as we sit in the cold with our loneliness, dreaming of better times when we are warmed by the rays of the sun". With the abolition of private property, women would be released from the bonds of the patriarchal family which made them the property of men. The state would take responsibility for the material welfare of mothers and their children, and "in the process a new kind of marriage partnership will develop, based on equality and respect, requiring attentiveness, sensitivity, and a profound awareness of the other's soul. The human psyche will become increasingly complex and sensitive, developing its capacity for unselfishness and generosity, discovering an infinite variety of new emotions. In the socialist future, there is no doubt that love will become the cult of humanity".

"There is no bolt, no defense against sexual conflict," she wrote in her second article, "Sexual Relations and the Social Struggle". "The waves of the sexual crisis are sweeping over the thresholds of workers' homes, creating conflicts every bit as acute and heartfelt as the sufferings in the 'refined' bourgeois world. Yet when we speak of the new sexual morality, we often meet the shallow argument that 'there's no place for it until the economic base has been transformed.' As if the ideology of a class was formed only after the completion of the sudden about-turn in social and economic relations which assures this class of its dominance! The entire experience of history shows us that the ideology and morality of a social class is created precisely in the process of its painful struggle against the social powers hostile to it. The working class is already evolving a radically new morality as another ideological weapon in the class struggle. One of the main tasks confronting the proletariat, as it besieges the beleaguered fortress of the future, is to create healthier more joyful relations between the sexes, based on the creative principles of sharing and friendship, rather than mere blind physical attraction".

She followed these articles with her essay *The New Woman*, published in Russia in 1913 in the journal *Contemporary World,* in which she turned to literature, comparing women portrayed in recent novels and plays with their counterparts in reality. *The New Woman,* "Sexual Relations and the Social Struggle" and "On An Old Theme" were republished together in 1918 as a booklet, *The New Morality of the Working Class,* and translated excerpts of the essay appeared in *The Autobiography of a Sexually Emancipated Woman.* This new abridged translation is from a facsimile of the 1918 edition published online in 2014.

The New Woman

Who is the new woman? We see her in fiction, but does she exist in reality? Look around and she is everywhere, on every rung of the social ladder, from factory workers and secretaries to writers, doctors and scientists.

Yet it is only recently that she has appeared in literature. Over the past decades, the heavy hammer of necessity has forged a completely new kind of woman, with a new psychology and temperament, new aspirations and needs. But writers were still portraying those of the old type, passive, self-sacrificing and dependent.

What shining examples of the new woman there were in Russia in the 1860s and 1870s. But novelists and poets failed to understand her. Turgenev tried to paint her in his novels with his delicate brush, but his heroines were so much paler and less interesting than they were in real life. It was only in his poetry and prose poems to Russian women that he captured their essence, bowing his head before the inspiring image of those who crossed the threshold of the old family to join the revolution.

These first revolutionary heroines were followed by a generation of "faceless" women, who were destroyed like bees in a beehive. The path to their longed-for freedom was strewn with their bodies. Year by year their numbers increased, but writers were blind to them. Poets, trained to see only the conventional picture of woman, were unable to grasp this new image of her and make it their own. Novelists, seeking to explore new colours, new worlds, continued to show them as betrayed, abandoned, suffering — vengeful wives, bewitching *femmes fatales*, innocent character-less creatures, weak "misunderstood" girls.

Tolstoy immersed himself in the psyche of his Anna

Karenina, enslaved by centuries of oppression. But the heroines he revered were his exuberant wifely Natasha Rostova, and his sweet innocent Kitty. At a time when women's options were being dictated by cruel necessity, even the geniuses of nineteenth-century literature did not feel impelled to engage with this new image of them. It was only ten or fifteen years ago that the new woman began to appear in novels — most of them written by women — and to demand her right to be recognised. Now she is no longer a sensation in literature. We meet her in "progressive" novels, addressing urgent issues of the day, and in more modest works of popular fiction. The aspirations of these heroines vary widely of course, depending on their nationality and social class. But despite their differences, they all have things in common that immediately distinguish them from women in the past.

Who are they? They are not "nice" pure girls, who have love affairs that blossom into successful marriages. They are not suffering wives, weeping over their husbands' infidelities, or having affairs themselves. They are not bitter spinsters, mourning the loss of their youth, or "priestesses of love," victims of their depraved natures and wretched living conditions. No, this is a completely new kind of heroine, who fights women's oppression at work and in her family, and stands up for the rights of her sex.

This type of woman is generally single. In the past, she was a wife, the echo of her husband, an appendage. The new single woman does not play this subordinate role. She is self-reliant and independent, with her own interests, her own inner world. Twenty years ago, this type of woman have been unthinkable. There was no place for her, in life or in literature. The conventional female characters in fiction were the young girl, the mother, the mistress, the bluestocking, or the "salon lioness," like Elena Kuragina in *War and Peace*, and any who resembled the modern woman would have been seen as abnormal, psychologically flawed. But life moves on, and the wheel of history has forced writers to expand their vocabulary and change their ideas.

The new women are those in the cities who pour out of the suburbs at the crack of dawn for the long tram ride to work. Drably dressed, young, old, middle-aged, they rent rooms in cheap boarding houses, and get jobs as teachers, shop assistants and factory workers, returning at night to their little rooms, free, alone and independent. They are the girls with fresh hearts and minds, full of bold dreams, hurrying along the streets in search of teaching work. They are in the temples of science, medicine and art, conducting experiments in laboratories, seeing patients in hospitals, burrowing through archives, writing books, joining political groups, making speeches.

How different women in modern fiction are from those in Chekhov or Turgenev, the bewitching heroines of Zola and Maupassant, the somewhat lifeless good-hearted female types in the German and English novels of the 1880s and 1890s. A succession of them pass before us. We see the heroine of Karl Hauptmann's novel *Mathilde*, making her way along the thorny path of life with calm certainty, her gaze fixed firmly on the future. After a series of unhappy experiences, she strikes out on her own and leaves for the city. She knocks at the factory door, young, fresh-faced and healthy, and the brick monster swallows up another victim. But she is unafraid, and steps confidently over the traps fate has mockingly laid for her. She is only a poor factory girl, but she is proud of her independence. The first love affair, tender and radiant as youth. The first timid protest against the loss of her freedom, the first joys of motherhood.

Then the pangs of a new passion, and more hurt, longing and disappointment, and she is alone again. Yet before us is not a crushed "lost" girl, but a proud mother, thoughtful and intelligent, able to stand on her own feet and support herself, whose personality develops with each page of the story.

In contrast to Mathilde is Gorky's Tatyana, in his "Story of a Woman," wandering the countryside in search of work, barefoot and burnt by the sun, "a piece of copper on a rubbish-heap of rusty iron". Today she travels with her comrades to the Don region, tomorrow she is in the Caucasus, bringing in the harvest in Maykop. Free as the wind, lonely as the grass on the steppe, she has no one to protect her, and her life is a constant battle against fate. But like Mathilde, she does not bow under the blows, and deep in her soul, like a clear summer night, she carries her earthly dreams of happiness.

Sometimes, as if to mock her, happiness seems within her grasp. A passing traveller stirs her soul, and she weeps and gives herself to him, simply and straightforwardly, wresting these small joys from life. But she refuses to tie herself to him. "No, it's not for me, I don't want it. Maybe if you were a peasant, but this way makes no sense. It was just for an hour, not a lifetime!" And she smiles at him and goes on her way, alone and lost in her thoughts, dreaming of happiness.

The heroines of this new fiction are of all classes. The woman who works in the factory, forced to struggle for her existence, is inevitably drawn into the wider struggle of her class. The new woman of the bourgeoisie faces different obstacles, and sharper conflicts of interest with her class. But she too is drawn to the new morality the working class is evolving in the collective struggle to adjust to the new economic conditions, and she finds it corresponds very closely to her own.

The passionate clever Olga, in Grete Meisel-Hess's novel *The Intellectuals*, breaks free of her patriarchal Jewish family, overcomes one obstacle after another, and throws herself into life in a great European city. She moves in an elite circle of intellectuals, and struggles to support herself as a writer. And as this centre of culture and capitalism unfolds before her, she learns to assert herself as a woman. Sometimes her path crosses with her lover's. But she is stronger than her chosen one, and building a future with him does not enter her plans. And when passion wanes, they go their separate ways.

Agnes Petrovna, the heroine of Tatyana Shchepkina-Kupernik's novel *One of Them*, is a writer and translator, and "working thinking human being". When an idea takes hold of her, nothing else exists for her. When her lover visits, she can finally acknowledge her needs as a woman, and change out of her work clothes into a dress. But she allows no man to have power over her. It might make some women happy to focus all their energy on a man, and belong to him body and soul. But when her beloved asks her to put their love before her work, the relationship is over.

The young doctor Thérèse, in Colette Yver's novel *Princesses of Science*, strides along the hospital corridors with a sure step, her beautiful head held high. The wards are her temple and her home. Single and independent, severe in dress, she fights to win the respect of her male colleagues, and is proud when they praise her diagnoses as correct. But she firmly resists their attempts to win her in marriage. Her career is too precious to her.

Then just as we are seeing her as a cold "emancipated" woman, we see a different side to her, dressed in bright colourful clothes, on holiday with her lover. She makes no secret of their affair, but she refuses to live with him. She needs to be free for her beloved work.

Rushing past the doctor is another Thérèse, in

Arthur Schnitzler's *Road to the Open*, a socialist agitator, who throws her whole soul into her political work, and has spent time in jail. But when the waves of passion sweep over her, she does not hypocritically don the faded cloak of female virtue, she holds out her hand to her lover, and leaves with him to drink from the cup of happiness. And when it is empty, she parts with him without bitterness or regret, and goes back to work.

Another finely drawn portrait of the new woman is the teacher Vera Nikodimovna in Ignaty Potapenko's novel *The Fog of Life*. She has been raised by her grandmothers in the old traditions, but she has a "past," and this has left a deep scar on her soul. When asked by a friend what drove her into men's embraces, she confesses "none of them knew how little feelings were involved". Torn between the old and the new cultures, surrounded by men who worship her, she becomes a temptress and a drawing-room flirt, luring them on while warding off their advances, claiming her right to be single, free and independent.

The fiery temperamental Maya, in Meisel-Hess's novel *The Voice*, abandons her husband for her Arab lover. Then a second marriage, full of psychological complications, and a new struggle between the old and the new woman in her soul. After another separation, she finally meets the man she has always dreamed of, who gives her the love and freedom she lacked from her husbands, and respects her inner "voice". Her beloved is married, and he knows how to take not only a woman's body but her soul, acting out the comedy of "understanding" her. But the Don Juans come and go, and the husbands stay. So Maya adapts to life with her lover, limiting her claims to happiness to material possessions — he buys her necklaces and earrings, so he must love her. And when the master of her soul becomes violent and despotic, she sees him as entirely within his rights, and with a wounded heart, she must abandon her dreams of happiness with him and put him out of her life.

The new woman does not endure despotism, she demands respect for her personality. And the more self-aware she becomes, the more painfully she realises that male psychology, blunted by centuries of abuse, is often incapable of seeing her as an awakening human being. "I curse my female body. Men can't see there's more to me, something more important," says Anna in Nadezhda Sanchar's story "Anna's Notes". Even Gorky's simple Tatyana protests when men see her merely as an instrument of pleasure. "They could have had me, but I didn't want to, not like that, like cats. What sort of people are they?"

How many episodes there are in these heroines' lives which recall the old days, when they must struggle with their longing to be the shadow of a man, judged only in terms of their relationship with him, with no worth of their own. How hard it is for today's woman to break with this habit, internalised over centuries, of assimilating herself with the man fate has decreed to be her lord and master. How hard she must struggle to convince herself that renouncing herself for the sake of her loved one is wrong.

Twenty years before Flaubert's *Madame Bovary*, the brilliant George Sand was tempted to forsake everything for her lover the poet de Musset. Then the moment came when she realised she was about to lose her freedom with him, that the woman in her, Aurore Dudevant, was suffocating the brave passionate George Sand, and was leading her to her destruction. So she broke with him without regrets, and once the decision was made, no power on earth could break the will of this great human being with the tender feminine soul.

When Aurore Dudevant leaves her estate that

gloomy autumn day for her last farewell with de Musset, we need not fear for her. The experience is over, and we know their encounter won't change her decision; it is merely the last gift of a dying passion bestowed on George Sand by a weeping Aurore.

One of the first of the new heroines was Ibsen's Ellida, in his play "Woman of the Sea". When the sailor she had promised herself to returns to claim her, her husband sets her free to follow him, but she chooses to stay with him, knowing the power her lover has over her soul will destroy her.

The married artist Tanya, in Evdokia Nagrodskaya's novel *Wrath of Dionysus*, faces a similar choice between her marriage and her lover. She lives under the same roof with her husband, without losing any of her independence or her freedom to work. Her world is the world of art, his is the world of scholarship and science. This pure domestic atmosphere is invaded by her blind physical attraction for the handsome Stark. But even as she yields to him, she is too much of a human being to be satisfied by him; he does not feed her soul. Consumed by love, she becomes unable to paint. So she breaks with her lover and returns to her husband, not out of duty or pity for him, but to keep herself alive for her work.

Forced by sharpening economic conditions to struggle for her existence, the new woman must conquer her easily led nature, and learn to be disciplined and resilient. Sometimes we may be repelled by her, and find her alien and "masculine". We peer at her, searching in vain for the familiar agreeable traits of our mothers and grandmothers. Where is the old feminine gentleness and submissiveness, the desire to subordinate herself to her husband?

Women in the past were ruled by their emotions, and this was their main ornament and their main curse. Women's dependence on their emotions often led them to express their jealousy of their love rivals in hideous ways, if not literally by throwing acid at them, then with the poison of abuse. In literature, jealousy and the desire for revenge have been at the heart of almost every tragedy of the female soul. Of course jealousy is a tragedy for the male soul too. But it is significant that Shakespeare did not make his Othello a refined European, but a Moor, ruled by his passions.

The new woman does not demand exclusive possession of her partner, and since she demands freedom for her feelings, she must give the same freedom to her lovers. This means she takes a completely different attitude to the "other woman". Meisel-Hess's Maya in *The Voice*, far from being jealous of her married lover's wife, finds a common language with her, and in many ways the two women share a closer bond than with the man they both love. Maya weeps over the humiliations he inflicts on her rival's soul, treating her as an object and his legal property, without tenderness or kisses, and they are able to go beyond their own narrow feelings to discover that they can be equals and friends.

The old type of woman had no reason to fight for her equality — what would she have done with it? Was there anyone more helpless and pathetic than the abandoned wife? With the loss of her husband, she lost not only her financial support, but the entire focus of her emotional life. The new woman, forced by the scourge of hunger to support herself, no longer builds all her emotions around a man. In the past, the burden was on her to ensure the continuity of the marriage bond. Now she is in no hurry to give her relationships with men any particular fixed form, and she rejects outright or takes an indifferent attitude to marriage. To be sure there are times when love holds her soul prisoner, and her work and interests are pushed aside. But the joys of love are transient states, simply part of the rich store of her experiences.

Shchepkina-Kupernik's Agnes Petrovna is in Italy with her lover, rocked by the waves of a Venetian lagoon. Stars, a gondola ride, love. "Can you imagine living like this forever?" he says, and she shudders. Before her stretches an eternity of kisses, whispering waves and starry harmony, and it horrifies her. "What's the point of living then?" she asks herself. "I'm young and pretty, I'm a woman like any other. Why can't I accept love is everything for a woman? But a lifetime of it would drive me mad!"

Back in St Petersburg, she draws a strict line between her lover and her work. One evening, the two are alone in her flat. Her eyes glow as she embraces him, and he melts with anticipation. But her gaze is not for him, it is for the writing on her desk. "You must go now darling, I have to work or my thoughts will vanish," she tells him.

For centuries, a woman's worth was measured not by her abilities or character, but by the feminine virtues demanded by bourgeois morality, with its strict code of chastity. Women in the past were expected to wear the mask of "purity," even when married, and those who sinned were not forgiven. Romantic writers were careful to save the heroines they loved from "falling". Only those they did not care about were allowed to "sin," as their male heroes did — without being censured for it of course.

The new heroines happily reject this double standard, and neither author nor readers consider them "depraved". We are moved by the humanity of Hauptmann's Mathilde, who sleeps with a series of men, and bears children with her different chosen ones. We love the bold opera singer Magda in Hermann Sudermann's play "Homeland," who after years on the stage and numerous love affairs, returns home to her tyrannical father to claim her right to love who she pleases.

This new moral standard used to be practised in fiction only by "great souls" — writers, actors and artists. "But why should only 'great souls' enjoy this right?" August Bebel correctly asks. "If George Sand had the courage to follow the promptings of her heart, if Goethe's love experiences fill volumes, which are devoured rapturously by readers of both sexes, why not allow the same freedom to others?"

The new women do not deny their feminine natures or the earthly joys of life. They can be mothers without marrying, their lives can be full of adventures, and they no more consider themselves "fallen women" than we do. And perhaps the honesty and freedom of a Mathilde, Maya or Agnes Petrovna are more admirable than the timid morality of Pushkin's Tatyana in *Evgenii Onegin*, or Turgenev's virtuous Liza in his *Nest of Gentlefolk*.

So much literature now is filled with this new type of woman. Born of large-scale capitalist production, she has broken the rusting chains of the old family, and has been thrown onto a new path. And her struggle against the old traditions and expectations strengthens her emotionally and steels her spirit. Political ideas, art, science, her calling — these are the things she lives for, more sacred than the delights of passion, the joys of the heart. The power of centuries still weighs heavily on her. Outlived ideas still hold her prisoner. Atavistic feelings still obstruct her consciousness. But she knows it is through work, not love, that she will learn to assert herself and make her own demands of life, no longer the shadow of a man, naively attempting to reflect the alien nature of her beloved, but a whole and complete human being.

In her years in exile Kollontai published over thirty essays, articles and pamphlets for the Russian and foreign socialist press. She wrote extensively about factory women's lives and working conditions, and in her popular pamphlet *Working Woman and Mother,* she depicted four women's different experiences of pregnancy and childbirth in Russia — a laundress, a dye worker, a factory-owner's wife, and her maid.

In 1912, the Tsar's highly reactionary Third Duma passed its Workers' Insurance Bill, which excluded workers from whole regions of Russia, provided minimal compensation in cases of accident or illness, and no benefits to women in pregnancy and childbirth. She was consulted by socialist deputies on the maternity insurance prgramme they were drawing up to supplement the Bill, and her research resulted in her book *Society and Motherhood,* published in Russia in 1916.

It opens with a survey of recent laws in Germany and Britain which gave workers basic protection against sickness and unemployment, and allowed working women paid maternity leave. She compared these to the "Black Hundreds spirit" of the Russian Bill, and the book grew into a devastating 600-page indictment of the horrors of pregnancy and motherhood for peasant and factory women in Tsarist Russia, filled with statistics on miscarriages, stillbirths, post-natal complications, and infant deaths. Without access to contraception, the average woman gave birth to between six to eight children in her lifetime, a quarter of whom died before the age of four, with one registered midwife for every four thousand mothers, no time off work after giving birth, and no maternity pay. The future socialist society must take full responsibility for working mothers and their children, she wrote, and she called for state maternity benefits to be at the top of the socialist agenda. "After breastfeeding their babies and surrounding their first months with love and tenderness, mothers who wish to return to work should be able to leave them in properly run nurseries, knowing that they will be well cared for, possibly working there part-time themselves, thus extending their maternal feelings to all children in the collective".

She believed that all women should have access to maternity benefits, married or not, and she proposed this in a resolution to the 1910 International Women's Conference in Copenhagen: "Making state benefits available to all mothers, regardless of what form their family lives takes, will help clear the way for the new behaviour and morality already emerging in the working class". (Her resolution was hugely outvoted, on the grounds that it would lead to promiscuity and family breakdown).

She became known in exile as a highly effective public speaker, often compared to the great French socialist orator Jean Jaurès. In *Around Workers' Europe,* she described joining a workers' May Day demonstration in London in 1909, on the first of her three trips to England, marching with fifty thousand people with trade union banners and red flags to Hyde Park, where she addressed the crowds in English about May Day in Russia. Two years later, she spoke with Jaurès himself at a large anti-war May Day demonstration in Paris. ("Me after Jaurès! Dear god!").

The First of May had been declared the official workers' holiday of the Socialist International in 1889 — "a day of demonstrations for the class demands of the international proletariat, for the eight-hour day, and for universal peace". Two years later, thousands across Europe stopped work to take to the streets, and demonstrations in England became mass festivals of workers' resistance. "Today I have seen for the first time in forty years the strength of the English proletariat," Engels wrote from London in 1891.

Lenin's 1896 May Day leaflet, smuggled out of exile, mimeographed and distributed to Russia's factories, called on workers to mark the day with mass protests against the autocracy, and that year saw huge demonstrations in Moscow, which ended in hundreds of arrests. Over the following years there were May Day strikes and demonstrations in Germany, Austria, England, France and Italy, and May Day in Russia was celebrated in 1911 with mass strikes, in which thousands more were arrested and jailed.

The Socialist International, created to build workers'

solidarity in the fight against war and capitalism, and "unite the human race," faced its greatest challenge that summer, when Germany sent a warship to the French-controlled Moroccan port of Agadir. France speedily dispatched fifty thousand troops, and France's ally Spain sent reinforcements. Lenin described this second Moroccan crisis as "among the greatest foreign policy crises of the great powers since 1870," and workers' organisations in Germany, France and Spain declared themselves ready to "oppose with all means at our disposal the cruel machinations of the ruling classes". The Belgian Secretary of the International called an emergency meeting of the socialist leaders, and the French and Belgian parties agreed immediately. Leaders of the German party claimed the government had engineered the crisis to distract attention from the forthcoming Reichstag elections, in which socialists expected to do spectacularly well. According to the party's leading theoretician Karl Kautsky, writing in its paper *Vorwärts*, Germany's arms manufacturers were a "small clique," who could be "brought to heel" at an international meeting of the great powers. There was no meeting of the International.

In *Around Workers' Europe,* Kollontai wrote of her anguish when a majority of socialist deputies to the Reichstag voted for an additional 125 million Marks for the Kaiser's military budget. The party's small left minority, led by Liebknecht, organised anti-conscription meetings in the schools. Luxemburg and Zetkin travelled the country calling for mass industrial action against the threat of war, and factories, docks and railways across Germany were paralysed by strikes.

The following year, the International proved equally ineffectual in its response to Russia's escalation of tensions with Austro-Hungary and Germany in the Balkans. By then Russian foreign policy was in the hands of the Tsar's "holy man," the peasant Rasputin, who urged him to support the Balkan League in the first of two disastrous wars against the Ottoman Empire, which left 123,000 dead, most of them Russians. Strikes, protests and terror attacks exploded across Russia. Students rioted and occupied, all universities were placed under police control, and workers in the capital celebrated May Day in 1912 with mass walkouts.

Some of the largest anti-war May Day strikes and demonstrations since 1905 had been in Sweden. In 1909, 300,000 workers had downed tools in the country's first general strike, and throughout 1912 there were mass protests against the government's proposed new conscription laws. That spring Kollontai was invited by Sweden's socialist leaders to do a three-week speaking tour of the country. Speaking in German through Swedish interpreters, she addressed anti-conscription meetings in factories in Ystad, Varberg, Gothenberg, Lervik, and in the fortress town of Bohus near the Norwegian border, and the conservative press called for her to be arrested and deported. Her trip ended with a May Day rally in Stockholm, where she spoke to a crowd of sixty thousand on the Erde Field. A translation of her speech was published in the paper of the Swedish Socialist Party, *Class Struggle*, and it was republished in Russian in her *Selected Articles and Speeches.*

"The International Proletariat and War"

May Day is our great day, when workers of the world celebrate their solidarity with mass demonstrations. And is it not a sign of this solidarity that I am here today, a visitor from distant Russia, speaking to you in German, a language that is neither yours nor mine, sending you greetings from workers in Russia?

The Russian proletariat, like the proletariat of all countries, is against all wars. The proletariat does not recognise borders between nations, only the borders between the two classes, the exploiters and the exploited. Our rulers tell us, "We must arm ourselves against the threat of war," and they point to their sacred symbols on land and sea and in the sky. They summon up the spectre of war, to hide from the spectre of socialist revolution. And the response of the Socialist International, with one voice, is "Down with War!"

Workers know what is behind the capitalists' threats, burdening them with more taxes so they can produce more weapons to increase their profits. We see the rivalries between the capitalist powers, and how they switch sides and alliances. We remember the recent scandal when French industrialists spread stories in Germany that France's Ministry of War had placed orders for more machine guns and cannon, and the German government, not to be outdone, immediately placed orders for new weaponry and killing machines. It was only later that the stories were shown to have been pure bluff.

In France, workers were told, "Come with us to Morocco! Occupy the Sahara! In the desert you'll find everything you lack at home!" In Sweden, the capitalists repeat their tired old threats about Russia — "we must arm our country against the Russian enemy!"

Yet even if the Tsar and his capitalists dared to attack Sweden, the proletariat would survive. Didn't we survive the Moroccan crisis? And who was it who stopped the crisis developing into full-blown war? It was the workers of Germany, France and Spain, who told their governments, "Not a step further! Here we stand, and if there's war, you'll answer for it with revolution!"

Yes, revolution! The First of May is a holiday for workers in all the capitalist countries, even Russia, to test our readiness for battle.

Revolution is inevitable. The bourgeoisie likes to complain that the capitalist system is "infected with socialism". If that were so, why did two hundred thousand workers in England die of hunger last year in their slums and tenements? Why are there half a million unemployed in France? Why are Europe and America gripped with strikes and lockouts? These strikes are growing increasingly militant, and every strike now is a strike against war.

It all started in Russia in 1905, when people's rage at the Tsar's war with Japan boiled over into revolution. Unfortunately the Tsarist state was too powerful, and the revolution was crushed. But in 1909 the red spectre appeared again in Sweden, with the workers' General Strike against the employers. And despite the hardships and hunger, it was a moral victory for the Swedish working class, and gave the International new confidence in the power of the mass strike. Strikes broke out across France, and a million in England stopped work to defend the demands of their class. Never before in history had British workers come out in such numbers.

We see the proletariat gaining strength year by year. And if the bourgeoisie wants war, we will reply, in the voice of millions of organised workers: "Down with war! Join the socialist revolution for peace!"

At the 1910 Copenhagen Women's Conference, Kollontai was elected to the Executive of its new Women's Bureau, and to the editorial board of its paper, *Die Gleichheit*. Delegates then unanimously voted in support of Clara Zetkin's resolution that the International celebrate women's struggles with a new holiday, subsequently established on the eighth of March.

Kollontai worked at the Bureau's Berlin headquarters coordinating International Women's Day demonstrations throughout Europe against war, low wages and workplace discrimination, and Women's Day in 1911 exceeded all expectations, with over a million women marching and demonstrating in Denmark, Austria, Switzerland and Germany. In her pamphlet *Notes of an Agitator Abroad,* she described addressing a huge rally in Frankfurt, and reported similar meetings in towns and villages across

Germany: "Halls were so packed that women had to ask the men to leave and give up their places to them. Husbands stayed at home with the children for a change, while their wives, the captive housewives, went to meetings and demonstrations. Berlin was a seething mass of women. At one of the largest demonstrations, of eighty thousand women, police tried to seize their banners, but they fought back, and bloodshed was averted only when socialist Reichstag deputies came out to support them. The day set the tradition for a working women's holiday of exceptional militancy".

In November 1912, the International belatedly responded to Russia's war in the Balkans by calling an emergency congress in the Swiss city of Basel, which she attended as a delegate of St Petersburg's Textileworkers' Union. She marched in a ninety thousand strong anti-war demonstration in the city, and she spoke at meetings, and stayed on to work with the Swiss Socialist Party's youth and women's sections, planning the following year's Women's Day demonstrations in Switzerland.

International Women's Day was to be celebrated for the first time in Russia in 1913, supported by the social democrats, and she was writing to women in St Petersburg and Moscow about their plans for the day. The article below was published on 1 March in the party's new daily newspaper, *Pravda* (*Truth*).

"Women's Day"

In 1910, when women in the Socialist International voted to make the Eighth of March a day for women workers in all countries to demonstrate their solidarity, it seemed to us that we had no chance of achieving this in Russia. It was a time of vengeful triumphant reaction. Workers' organisations were smashed. Socialist leaders had fled abroad or were in jail. There was no focus around which to gather our forces, not a single socialist newspaper survived. 1909 and 1910 were joyless difficult years.

But the laws of historical development are more

powerful than the bayonets of the Tsar's bloody satraps, and the intolerable lives of the exploited masses led to a rekindling of the strike movement. Workers faced the choice between suffering in silence, or entering the battle against the double tyranny of tsarism and capital. The Russian proletariat bravely chose the latter course.

Gradually the fight gathered momentum. Throughout 1911 and 1912, Russia was swept with strikes. Some were economic, against layoffs and pay cuts. Others were of a political, anti-capitalist nature, such as the mass May Day strikes in 1912, protesting against the shooting of two hundred striking miners in Siberia.

The two social democratic parties in the capital began to put out their newspapers again, which continued to appear daily over the next two years, with readerships of over fifty thousand. New socialist publications developed their work, and the trade unions came back to life.

The workers' movement in Russia still faces innumerable obstacles. Strikers are punished with jail and exile, and police tyranny knows no bounds. Laws are made for the rich, not the workers! Added to which are the normal daily inconveniences of banned organisations — confiscated presses, constant fines, and the need to keep changing the names of publications and moving premises. Landlords are arrested for renting accommodation to socialist organisations, and finding rooms for meetings and offices is far from easy.

It's a struggle to the death. But fighters' courage has not deserted them, and women are now joining the workers' movement in unprecedented numbers. They are no longer passionate young girls from wealthy families, sacrificing themselves as village teachers. We now see proletarian women fighting with men in the trade unions and in all the organisations of the working class, and we read their appeals and letters in the socialist press.

Ever since the social democrats declared their support for our first International Women's Day in Russia, every political party, all sections of society, have had their say. Some responded with ridicule and contempt. Others accused working women of joining forces with the feminist organisations. So women decided that they must take matters into their own hands to make the day a major political event. They know they will face arrest and jail for this first attempt to voice their demands, but that others will be inspired by their courage and determination, and their sacrifices won't have been in vain.

On the agenda for the day are their demands for the vote and for state maternity protection. The latter is especially close to their hearts. Workers are arrested for demanding proper labour laws, and the socialist amendments to the Duma's Insurance Bill were passed only after angry demonstrations and battles with the police. Even in the Bill's revised version, the protection of working mothers and pregnant women is merely a supplementary clause, and its scope is extremely limited due to its last-minute reworking. It is only working women themselves who will bring about the new laws they need as mothers and workers.

There are still those in Russia who object that Women's Day is a concession to the bourgeois women's organisations, and threatens the unity of the workers' cause. Fortunately these objections are no longer heard abroad. Life itself has supplied the answers.

Women's Day is a link in the long chain of the proletarian women's movement in Europe, which is growing stronger with every year that passes. Twenty years ago, there were only a few women in the trade unions, and scattered brightly here and there in the socialist parties. Now there are over five hundred thousand women trade union members in England, Germany, France and Austria, and twenty thousand in the workers' parties. Working women are organising in Switzerland, Sweden, Norway, Denmark, Italy and Hungary. The socialist women's army is now almost a million strong — a mighty force! And a force to be reckoned with when it comes to discussing the burning practical issues of maternity insurance, rising food prices, child labour, and legislation to safeguard women's working conditions.

There was a time when working men thought they had to bear the burden of the struggle against capital on their own. But as increasing numbers of women enter the ranks of those who sell their labour — driven into the factories by need, or when a husband or father becomes unemployed — men see that leaving them behind damages the socialist cause and holds it back. The more class-conscious fighters there are, the sooner we will be victorious. What consciousness can a women have who stands at the stove, whose life is ordained by her husband or father, with no rights in her family or society and no ideas of her own? Women's "backwardness," their passivity and lack of rights, is of no benefit to the workers' movement, and is indeed harmful to it. But how are they to be drawn into this movement?

Social Democracy did not immediately find the correct answers to this question. The doors of the workers' organisations were open to women, but few joined. Why? Because the working class was at first slow to recognise their double oppression, as workers who sell their labour and as wives and mothers. They did not see that as the most legally and socially deprived members of their class, exploited and intimidated over the centuries, they need a special approach to awaken their hearts and minds.

Working women in the different countries have done a huge amount to ensure that men now understand the need for this work, and the workers' parties have been taking up the fight for women's interests, demanding their political rights and the proper protection of their labour. The more boldly socialists advance these demands, the more women will see us as their allies, and the cause of women as the cause of the entire working class. The challenge facing the parties now is to attract more women as members.

Special committees have been set up to take this work forward, to campaign against rising prices, prostitution and infant mortality, and for new laws to protect pregnant women and nursing mothers. These committees draw women into the common struggle against war and exploitation, while at the same time encouraging them to raise their own specifically female demands.

The social democrats see these demands as fundamental to the entire workers' movement, and they support Women's Day as a day for working women to stand up for their rights. And to those in Russia who still believe this "singling out" of women plays into the hands of the liberal feminists, we say they have completely failed to grasp the diametrically opposed class interests of the two movements.

Bourgeois women want the same privileges and advantages in capitalist society as are presently enjoyed by their husbands and fathers. The proletarian woman wants to abolish all privileges based on birth and class; for her it is a matter of indifference whether her employer is a man or a woman.

Bourgeois women demand equal political rights for women of their class, to allow them to make their way more successfully in a world based on the exploitation of others' labour. The proletarian woman demands political rights for all citizens, male and female, as the first step on the rocky path leading her to the kingdom of socialist labour.

The differences life has put before the mistresses and their servants have proved insurmountable. Working women have seen that the "better society" the feminists dream of has nothing to offer them, and the two movements have long gone their separate ways. Working men have nothing to fear from Women's Day, or from special women's committees, conferences and publications. All these draw women into the ranks of those fighting for a better future. And the slow patient work of building them, far from dividing workers, serves to unite and strengthen the movement.

Proletarian women in Russia face a hard struggle, but they are inspired by the support of their sisters throughout the world. The day is fast approaching when workers of all countries will advance in closed ranks against the capitalists to end the slavery of wage labour. So let us celebrate Women's Day joyfully in Russia, fighting for our emancipation and for the emancipation of the entire working class, bringing the day closer to our goal — the inevitable, longed-for socialist revolution.

On the Eighth of March 1913, five thousand women in St Petersburg occupied the Kalashnikov Stock Exchange, under the guise of a "scientific morning dedicated to the woman question," to demand the vote and their access to higher education, before the police arrived to make hundreds of arrests. There were large Women's Day demonstrations in Moscow and the cities of Tbilisi, Samara and Kiev, and the day was fully covered by the socialist press. *Pravda* put out a special Women's Day issue, with pictures of women fighters, greetings from women abroad, and an article by Kollontai celebrating the demonstrations as "inspiring evidence that the Tsar's gallows and prisons are powerless to kill women's spirit".

The issue produced more letters than *Pravda* could publish, and plans were made to celebrate the day the following year with a new monthly Bolshevik women's paper, *Woman Worker*. Half the editorial board were in exile in Europe, and those still in Russia took on the work of finding writers. The police swooped on the second editorial meeting and threw the editors in jail. But new editors were found, and the first issue of *Woman Worker* appeared in the capital on 8 March 1914. Women organised illegal demonstrations there and in Moscow, and *Pravda* and the Bolshevik papers *The Textileworker, Metalworker* and *Tailors' Gazette* published Women's Day issues. Twelve thousand copies of *Woman Worker* were printed and sold out immediately, and its offices were flooded with letters. The editors did sewing jobs to raise the money for a second and third issue, and thousands of factory women paid their four kopecks for the paper, before it was closed by the police in June, two months before the outbreak of war.

Chapter Four
Who Needs the War?

Throughout the first months of 1914, Kollontai worked with the International Women's Bureau in Berlin, planning anti-war Women's Day demonstrations in Europe, drafting anti-war resolutions for the congress of the International in June that she was to attend as a delegate of St Petersburg's Textileworkers' Union.

In her diaries she recalled the horror and confusion of the months leading up to the war, the rising tide of anti-Russian feelings in Berlin, and the huge patriotic demonstrations the socialist party dared not try to match. In late April, she organised a meeting with a group of women from France, Holland and Scandinavia to plan an international women's peace demonstration in Berlin. But by then there was a police warrant for her arrest, and their plans collapsed. The speech she was to have made was circulated illegally, under the name "Davydova," and she fled to Bavaria, where she stayed for the next three months with her nineteen-year-old son.

In May 1914, street demonstrations in Russia had reached their highest level, with barricades up in the cities. Two months later, the strike movement collapsed in a surge of anti-German feelings.

On 28 June, the Tsar's adventures in the Balkans exploded in Sarajevo with the assassination of the Arch-Duke Ferdinand, heir to the Austro-Hungarian throne. On 28 July, Austria declared war on Serbia, and the Tsar ordered the mobilisation of the Empire's armed forces. On 1 August, Germany invaded Belgium and declared war on Russia. "Russia is ready!" declared Russia's Minister of War.

In newly Russified Petrograd, soldiers marched off to the front singing war songs, and thousands of the Tsar's subjects greeted him on their knees outside the Winter Palace, singing the anthem the *Te Deum*. In Berlin, huge crowds cheered the Kaiser outside the Reichstag, and the Reichstag's largest party, the Social Democratic Party, with a membership of over a million, voted by a huge majority to support his new War Budget, declaring "civil peace" until the war was over, and "the class struggle adjourned".

The following excerpts from Kollontai's diaries were pub-lished in 1924 in the Soviet literary journal *Star,* to mark the tenth anniversary of the outbreak of the war. Ellipses here and in her later diaries are mine, where passages have been omitted.

From "Diaries of 1914"

14 July 1914, evening. Kohlgrub, Bavaria
Several holidymakers here have decided to go home. No one believes there will be war, everyone you speak to says it's madness. Why do my comrades in Petrograd write only of the strikes and barricades and the revolution in the air?

31 July. On the train from Munich to Berlin
I can't wait for news, I need to be close to the centre, to see what the German party is planning. On the way back I pick up a copy of *Vorwärts*. Again that excessively "abstract" tone from Kautsky and the editors. Two days ago, the party organised a small and apparently unsuccessful anti-war demonstration at Unter

den Linden. There are reports of the usual workers' meetings, most of them protesting against the high price of pork. Not a word about building the resistance. When will the party act? "Our country doesn't want war," Kautsky says. Why "our country"? Why not simply say workers of the world won't allow it? According to *Vorwärts*, Russia wants to stay out of the fighting because it's afraid of the inevitable consequences — revolution. The paper warns socialists in Germany not to get mixed up in the fate of "dark Russia," or to assume that the war will automatically lead to the downfall of the Tsar.

1 August, night. Grunewald, Berlin.
Yesterday war felt like a bad dream. Now it's a reality. So much has happened today I can't sleep. When we returned to Berlin this morning, people were still hoping for the best, and there were a few demonstrations. But hope faded with the passing hours, and by evening a new mood had set in, with bawling patriots in the bars baying for blood. "The German people want war!"

The people? The people who yesterday were against the war, who answered the calls to enlist with open hatred of the Kaiser?

As dusk falls, a grey military car travels slowly along the Hubertusallee, scattering leaflets. Germany has declared war on Russia. I feel a pang in my heart, and everything goes black....

I rush to the party headquarters to ask how soon the International can be convened. Haase, leader of the socialist group in the Reichstag, is there on his own. "Are you joking?" he says. "War is inevitable. People have gone mad, there's nothing we can do!"

At the Women's Bureau, I ask Luise Zietz of the party Executive what instructions they have received.

She looks at me coldly and says they have heard nothing, and that Clara Zetkin is preparing a special issue of *Die Gleichheit*. "We've protested and demonstrated, but we must do our duty when our country is in danger," she says, and I look her in the eye, and realise I am no longer a comrade but a Russian....

Jaurès has been murdered by patriots in Paris. It's only now that I grasp the full horror of the war, as if the wheel of history has broken loose and thrown us into the abyss. But the most terrible thing is that despite the tragic loss of this great man, it seems such a small and petty incident against the nightmare of war....

Can't stop trembling. Suffering as for the death of a loved one. So this is war! When we first conceived of it, we imagined the red spectre of revolution instantly springing from its shadow. But this silence from the party, this submissive bewilderment, is enough to drive one mad....

Meanwhile the patriots are busy. Today there was another large demonstration at Unter den Linden to cheer the Kaiser with speeches and ovations, and prayers are being said in all the churches....

2 August, midnight
The Russians are dashing around Berlin cursing the party for not giving the signal for demonstrations. The most pessimistic of us fear the socialists in the Reichstag may abstain in the vote on the War Budget. Not even the wildest pessimist believes they will vote to support it....

The streets are full of army helmets, military battalions, government officials handing out mobilisation leaflets, hundreds of police. People are living in a state of terror, as if before some elemental catastrophe. My heart is suffocating with a sense of complete helplessness. I cannot understand why there has been no statement from the party. It's only in Paris that people are still protesting....

This evening the Russians gathered in my room at the boarding house. We sat in the dark without the light on, as the men from the bakery downstairs were threatening a "pogrom" against us, and the landlady had begged us to keep very quiet.

Now everyone has left, and Misha is asleep. But I cannot sleep. I look out of the window at dear familiar Grunewald, now so malevolent and unwelcoming, and the sky is bright with stars, and all I can hear is shooting, groaning, women sobbing, and I feel these terrible times will never end....

4 August

Yesterday at six in the morning, two police officers arrived and drove us to the police headquarters at Alexanderplatz, where we were placed under arrest and locked in a large empty cell. Through the door I could hear orders being given to search my room, and I cursed myself for not destroying my mandate to the congress of the International.

But that mandate was to be my salvation. This morning, two guards arrived at our cell with a box containing my documents. "Why didn't you tell us you were a socialist?" they said. "If you're a socialist, you can't be a friend of the Tsar and the Russian barbarians — you're free!"

It was yet more evidence of the International's impotence. Those documents, which a week ago would have warranted my arrest, now opened the doors of the Alexanderplatz to me. Misha was driven off to jail, I didn't know where, and I set off with my box to mobilise support for him in the Reichstag....

Kautsky is in the lobby, looking aged and distracted. His two sons have been conscripted into the Austrian army, and his wife is living in Italy. He answers my questions vaguely. "We all have our crosses to bear in these terrible times," he says.

Bear our crosses? Has the old man lost his mind?

The socialist deputy Geyer hurries up, brimming with naive patriotism, and says his two daughters have both volunteered as nurses. "Who would have thought we socialists could be so patriotic! Yes, Germany is dear to our hearts. When she's attacked we must defend her. We'll show you Russians we can die for our country and save you from the Tsar!"

What, with the *Oberkommando* and the sword?

We are joined by the deputy Stadhagen, who anxiously takes me aside to tell me of "shocking, unprecedented" disagreements in the socialist bloc. Last night's meeting had been only half full, he says, with fourteen deputies, led by Liebknecht and Haase, opposed to supporting the War Credits.

I can't believe what I am hearing — support the Credits? "Yes, but the problem was that we couldn't agree on the wording of our statement". The commission drawing it up, consisting of Kautsky, David and someone else, had made it seem weak and equivocal. War is a fact, he says. Opposing it in present circumstances would be "mere childishness". "The workers are for war, and Germany must defend herself. If we vote against the Credits we'll lose all credibility with the masses, and they'll see us as enemies of the people. If a robber attacks my house, I'd be a fool to babble about 'human feelings' instead of shooting him!"

What about workers' solidarity and the International? I ask him. "It's too late for that now, the International is powerless to do any thing".

I feel indescribably sad and isolated. The Reichstag is virtually empty. None of the usual deputies are here, most have enlisted. Frank, David and Wendel appear. "I'm off to fight," Wendel says. "I'm more useful to the army than to *Vorwärts*. If the editors can't see where our duty lies, they should be sent to the mad house!"

Brilliant Wendel, the youngest member of the Reichstag, has turned patriot. Frank too is volunteering. People cluster round to shake his hand. "I've asked to be sent to the front line. How can people sit at home when our comrades are facing the bullets!" he says.

But why oh why let them face the bullets in the first place? Frank's enthusiasm is clearly bogus. But there are many sincere patriots in the party, horrifyingly sincere.

I grab Haase to talk to him about Misha and the other Russian prisoners. I feel embarrassed to be discussing my personal problems with him when the fate of the world and Social Democracy is at stake. But he is friendly and cheerful. "The party is *persona grata* now, I'll have a word with the Chancellor about them," he says.

What has happened? What has changed? Wasn't Haase against the Credits? But there is no time to ask him, as the first session is about to begin. I buy a ticket to the public gallery and go in.

The hall is packed and tense as deputies listen respectfully to a skilful speech from the Chancellor, Bethmann-Hollweg, accusing Russia of throwing down the gauntlet of war. People cheer from the gallery and deputies applaud wildly, including many on the left benches. There are murmurs when he mentions the possibility of Germany invading Belgium (the invasion has in fact already started), then they listen to him again with the same rapt attention.

In the interval I hurry back to the lobby, filled with soldiers and deputies flaunting their army uniforms.

Liebknecht is surrounded by angry deputies who were once his comrades. In the midst of these momentous events, he is still concerned about Misha and the other jailed Russians, and he takes me on a crowded tram ride across the city to the *Oberkommando's* office to demand their release.

The magic title of Reichstag deputy has no effect on the uniformed staff carrying out their instructions like machines, and we are made to wait. He walks across the room to sit down. "Don't take another step!" barks the duty officer. Liebknecht's cheek twitches as it does when he's agitated. "Look, that's where they'll concoct stories about German victories and foreign spies," he says, pointing to the door marked "Press Office". "Next day they'll publish a denial, but in small print so nobody reads it".

We are finally admitted to see an adjutant, who tells us it will take three weeks for the prisoners' identities to be checked, but that I can apply to have my son's belongings returned to me.

We hurry back to the Reichstag for the second session at five o'clock. It is the fateful moment. Part of me still believes the socialists will change their minds and vote against the Credits. Once again the gallery is packed. But unlike the tense atmosphere earlier, people look calm and cheerful, and are even cracking jokes.

The deputies file in. Haase reads the party statement, promising not to abandon the Reich in its hour of need. "For all these reasons, the Social Democrats support the War Credits," he says, to storms of applause from both the conservative and socialist benches.

I think I am going to faint. Liebknecht tries to speak, but is shouted down and walks out. The Reichstag is in uproar. Deputies jump up waving their arms and shouting patriotic slogans, and the Credits are "unanimously" voted through. But there was no vote. The last spark of democracy has been extinguished and replaced with the bullet.

I hurry back to the lobby, where Liebknecht is being mobbed by a group of socialist deputies. "He's a lunatic, throw him in jail!" Wendel shouts. I see the deputy Wurm, who organised my first speaking trip for the party. "What are you doing here? You're Russian, you've no business being in Germany". I hadn't thought of that. I had come to support my comrades, and now realised I had been wrong.

The session closed, and Liebknecht and I left to walk in the Tiergarten. "The working class of the world will never forgive us for this," he said. "But it's not the end. We must act immediately to strip the mask from the party's face and fight for peace. It's only a matter of time before the centre collapses".'

5 August
Chauvinism has infected even the best in the German party. Haase is prevaricating. He knows the insanity of its tactics, but after reading its statement to the Reichstag, his hands are tied. The majority have become patriots, shouting "Long live the Kaiser!"

And what of the German workers, whose courage has inspired the entire International? For so long they waited for a message from the party, besieging its offices to demand a call to action. But since the Reichstag vote their mood has changed sharply. The tension has broken, and has been replaced by a wild patriotism. The party failed to divert this energy into another channel, and now it is too late.

6 August
At 6 this morning, the police came to my room again to question me and check my papers. I showed

them my talisman, my mandate for the International congress. "Ah, so we've arrested you already!" they said, then returned half an hour later saying, "You must leave Germany immediately".

7 August
At dawn there was another knock at the door. But it wasn't the police this time, it was Misha, hungry and exhausted, who had walked all the way from Deberitz jail, the second Russian prisoner to be released. He said they had slept piled on top of each other on the floor, and many had been beaten.

No sooner had I recovered from my joy when the police returned, and ordered us out of Germany....

12 August
We can't leave, we have no money. Every day it's becoming harder to change Marks, and silver has disappeared. The situation is desperate for everyone....

Several lodgers in the boarding house have threatened violence against the Russians. This morning the police arrived to search the room of the two German women next to mine, after someone reported them as Russian spies. Berlin is filled with informers, all in the name of Germany's glory....

13 August, night
Trains leave for the front packed with fresh cannon fodder. Healthy young men crowd the goods compartments and sit on the footboards, singing and waving their caps as if setting off on holiday. The flower of Germany. The carriages are decorated with garlands and posters saying "Catch Russian spies!" Crowds see them off at the stations with kisses and tears. More trains return from the front with the wounded and dying, and there are hundreds of nurses on the streets....

17 August

More news from Belgium, and reports of German victory after victory. "It's like posters for the circus," Liebknecht says sadly. "Every day some new stunt, bigger and more amazing than the last".

It's only with Liebknecht I feel comfortable. Even some in our Russian community have been caught up in the madness....

23 August

In the early days of the war, I was oppressed by the thought that the German party was finished. Now I feel it's better this way. Historically better. Social Democracy was dead. Its creativity had dried up. All its activities were hackneyed, repetitive, congealed. There were no great new leaders, and this too was a sign of its stagnation. All the "promising young men," the Franks and Wendels, like the high priests of a dying culture, used to sit in the Café Josty, gossiping about the party. Gossip and slander and contempt for everything "sacred and infallible". So petty and disdainful and cynical, using the party as a springboard to government power. We need a new Social Democracy, one that doesn't crush the workers' movement of the world with its unbelievably heavy bureaucratic apparatus, and its "model conduct," which was stifling us....

3 September

"German unity" isn't just an empty slogan, and the German party has done more than anyone to promote it, spinning fantasies about the dissolution of all parties in an ecstasy of chauvinism....

Local party branches have been instructed to mobilise workers to "serve their country," and the unions are sending aid to the front. There have been a few small isolated strikes, as if workers weren't sure what they were striking for. *Vorwärts* regurgitates the articles in the bourgeois press, with the only difference that they appear a day late. "The paper is sold at railway stations now!" the editors crow. Not a word of protest, no call to workers to resist the mobilisation. *Vorwärts* has even sunk to publishing a series of inflammatory lies about Russians in Berlin. All this from the party that has expended an unbelievable amount of energy over the years elaborating its "pure inter nationalist principles". Of all the socialist press, only *Die Gleichheit* has stayed true to itself, calling on women to demonstrate against the war and rising food prices, organising poverty relief schemes for mothers and pregnant women, the old and the sick.

5 September

Rosa Luxemburg came to my room this evening to discuss tactics. She sees underground work as premature at present, and believes we must start with small informal meetings. She hasn't lost touch with the workers, and says most are against the war. Her clear-sightedness is heartening, and her merciless sarcasm puts much in its proper place.

6 September

It's all settled. The party has lent the Russians the train fare to neutral Denmark, and first thing tomorrow Misha and I are leaving for Copenhagen, where I can gather my strength to work. I have been on the phone saying goodbye to the dear Liebknechts. Will I ever see them again? I feel hopeful that we can accomplish much with our Scandinavian comrades, and I long for tomorrow, as I used to long for holidays as a child....

It's a sunny autumn morning. Outside the window the leaves on the chestnut trees are turning golden, and I look out at my beloved Grunewald and say goodbye to this part of my life, and to something far bigger. My landlady arrives with a bunch of flowers. Goodbye Berlin, goodbye to the party I once loved, which is now alien to me. I tear myself from the past without tears, and look ahead to the future....

20 October. Stockholm

With Liebknecht's help, I left Denmark for Sweden. At first, some of us still believed we could prevail on parties in the International to oppose the war. But with the bourgeoisie triumphant and socialists divided, we were wandering in the woods.

It was at this time of despair and confusion in the International that Lenin's voice rang out against the whole world, concisely identifying the causes of the war, and more importantly, how to turn it into a social revolution. Soon after arriving in Sweden, I read his *September Theses* in the Bolshevik newspaper *Social Democrat*, and it was as if the wall I had been beating my head against shattered, and I stepped into the light, able to see my way ahead.

I wrote my first letter to Vladimir Ilich, and in his reply he agreed that I should work with my Russian comrade in Stockholm, smuggling Bolshevik literature to socialists in Europe and into Russia.

The International is dead, but new forces are gathering around Lenin to overturn the old social relations and rebuild society on a new basis....

When Lenin first learned of the German vote on the War Credits, he assumed it was a lie put out by the German General Staff to destroy the International. He was living at the time in an area of Poland then under Austro-Hungarian rule, and the day war was declared he was jailed as an enemy alien. He was released a week later, after his Austrian comrades persuaded the authorities that as a revolutionary he was working to overthrow the

Tsar. He then left for the Swiss capital, Berne, where he wrote his *September Theses,* in which he analysed the class interests of the war, as a dynastic struggle for world markets — "launched to divide and decimate the proletariat of all countries, by setting the wage slaves of one state against those of another, to the profit of the bourgeoisie". He appealed to workers and soldiers in the warring countries to strike and desert, and turn the imperialist war into a revolutionary class war against capitalism, and he would repeat this message over the next three years in thousands of pamphlets, letters and articles smuggled out of Switzerland and across Europe into Russia.

Of the sixty-five million soldiers conscripted from the thirty-two warring countries, the largest number, six million, were Russians, mainly workers and peasants, fighting in the hell of the trenches, exposed to the new weapons of tanks and poison gas, gassed to death in their thousands. The Tsarist army suffered its first crippling defeat two weeks after Russia entered the war, when the Russian "Steamroller" was thrown into Eastern Prussia, and was smashed after three weeks of bloody fighting, with the loss of over fifty thousand lives. By the end of the year, Russia's defeat seemed beyond question. The ill-led, ill-equipped Tsarist army was being cut to pieces by the Germans, and patriotism had turned to rage and despair. "Mass slaughter has become the order of the day, and business thrives in the ruins," Rosa Luxemburg wrote.

With the outbreak of war, the International effectively ceased to exist. Luxemburg called it "a stinking corpse," and its leaders "theoreticians of the swamp". Lenin appealed to true internationalists to reclaim its name by building a new communist one to stop the war. He was supported by the small anti-war minority in the German party, led by Luxemburg, Liebknecht and Zetkin, and by members of the French, Serbian, Bulgarian and American socialist parties. But they were marginalised and isolated, and arguing virtually alone.

The war divided parties along national lines, and split the socialist movement — between the majority, "socialist patriots," loyal to their governments; pacifists, who believed the International could still stop the fighting with protests and demonstrations; and the revolutionary left, who called on soldiers at the front to turn their guns on their real enemies, their class enemies at home.

The exiled Trotsky had left the Mensheviks in 1913 to join the social democrats' new anti-war "Interdistrict" faction, which was close to the Bolsheviks. But a majority of Mensheviks allied themselves with patriots in the German party. Kollontai parted company with many of her former Menshevik comrades, and she no longer recognised their leader, the great Plekhanov, who was now an ardent patriot.

Her "Russian comrade" in Stockholm was her lover the Petrograd factory worker Alexander Shlyapnikov, a close friend and comrade of Lenin's, and the architect and main coordinator of the Bolsheviks' "Northern Underground" — the vast chain of communications which was smuggling Lenin's writings from neutral Switzerland across Scandinvia and into Russia.

She worked with Shlyapnikov and his underground Swedish agents organising the transport of thousands of copies of the *September Theses* across the Baltic Sea to Finland, and she translated them at Lenin's request into German, and incorporated many of his ideas into her article "War and Our Immediate Tasks", for the paper of the Swedish socialist party. She had finally found an anti-war programme she could support, committed to internationalism and the class struggle. But she did not immediately move to Lenin's position, as she implied in her diaries; she rejoined the Bolsheviks only in the summer of 1915. In the first months of the war she was a pacifist, and she struggled with Lenin's uncompromising message, that in this crazed epoch of imperialist slaughter there could also be just wars — "of slaves against their masters, and waged workers against capital".

She aired her disagreements with him in a lengthy exchange of letters, in which he discussed Bolshevik strategy with her, and wrote respectfully of her views. "Heartily glad Comrade Kollontai is coming over to our side," he wrote to Shlyapnikov.

A month after she arrived in Sweden, the government ordered a police crackdown on Stockholm's community of Russian exiles, and she was arrested for threatening the security of the Swedish state, and jailed in the remote southern fortress prison of Kungsholmen. Socialists in the Swedish parliament negotiated her release with the King, who ordered her permanent deportation from Sweden, and in February 1915, she left with Shlyapnikov for neutral Norway. Until her return to Russia two years later, she lived with him outside the Norwegian capital Kristiania (now Oslo), which became the new headquarters of the Northern Underground. The following excerpts from her diaries were published posthumously in Russia in 1970 in the journal *Foreign Literature*.

From "Norwegian Diaries"

20 February 1915. Holmenkollen, outside Kristiania

I knew at once that Norway would be right for me. Our Norwegian comrades in Kristiania persuaded us that it would be safer for us to live outside the city in the tourist resort of Holmenkollen, away from the eyes of the police. A half-hour tram ride, followed by a twenty-minute walk through the snow, and we are in this magical kingdom in the forests, overlooking the distant fjords.

Life seems to have stopped here, frozen into immobility like the snow-covered trees. Deep quiet, cleanness, sledges, ringing bells — a world I haven't known for a long time. Strange confused feelings. A mixture of extraordinary peace and pain, that in these nightmarish times we are living in a place of such beauty....

So far the police haven't bothered us. Fru Nissen and I have been planning next month's Women's Day demonstrations in Norway, in solidarity with women in the warring countries, which we will discuss at a meeting this evening.

Our main Northern Underground contacts here are in the Norwegian Transport Union, under its leader old Peter Andersson. I spend many hours with Andersson and his sailors in Kristiania's smoky dockside cafes ....

2 June

Lenin has written to me from Switzerland asking me to write for the Bolsheviks' new paper *Communist*. I like the name. Socialism no longer expresses what we're fighting for. The social democrats have smeared it with blood. I agree to write for the paper, which means joining the revolutionary Leninist wing of the social democrats, with its programme for an international revolution against capitalism. The socialist traitors and chauvinists will be patted on the heads, and we will be hounded and jailed. So be it. The Bolshevik path is the right one....

6 June

Posted my article 'Why Was the German Proletariat Silent During the July Days?' to *Communist*. I am translating Lenin's writings into German and carrying out my assignments for the Bolsheviks, working with our Norwegian comrades who will attend the conference he is organising in Switzerland to lay the basis for a new International. I have started work on a pamphlet for the Bolsheviks against the war. Will it ever be published? Will anyone care?

3 July

"Russia is finally waking up and coming to its senses," a visiting comrade from Petrograd tells us. "Revolution is still a long way off, but it's inevitable".

He reports growing opposition to the Tsar in the new Duma, particularly from Moscow's industrialists.

Of course Lenin is right when he says Russia's defeat in the war is the least of their worries. The internal chaos in all the warring countries makes civil war inevitable. At first I didn't understand the Bolsheviks' civil war slogan, it seemed too abstract. Until recently the pacifists' peace and disarmament slogan seemed the answer to everything. Now I realise it's just opportunism. It's not enough simply to understand the causes of the war and be against it, we need a programme to fight it. It's inevitable that the imperialist war will lead to a revolutionary war against capitalism....

11 July
More stories from Russia about the army. The commanders are all out for themselves, killing each other to advance their careers. Careerism and rivalry are setting officer against officer, which is good in terms of the collapse of the system. But mean while hundreds of thousands of young lives are being destroyed....

28 July
Lyolya Danielsson came today with some letters; we use her ad dress for our postal work. Her husband is an unemployed clock maker and spinner of fantasies, and they have four children, and her material situation is very hard. But the fire still burns in her, and she reaches out to us. I couldn't sleep after she left, wondering what the future holds for women. Will the war hasten this "transitional phase" in our evolution? From all appearances it will. Women are in all fields of work now, their labour power is essential, their value has grown far beyond the confines of their families, and that is a definite plus....

3 August
The anniversary of the vote on the War Credits. The

German advance continues. At a triumphant session in Petrograd of the Duma, Prime Minister Goremykin granted Poland its "independence". Warsaw is doomed....

The heart is frozen by so much blood. Every hour is soaked in this suffering. It's hard to believe we were ever free of this nightmare. As I write, battles are raging, shells are exploding, thousands are suffering, dying....

24 August

We are building links between socialists in Norway and the Bolshevik central committee in Petrograd. We have just had a meeting with our Norwegian and Swedish comrades who will attend the international conference in Switzerland next month. Much discussion of different points of the programme. General unanimity.

27 August

More news of Russian defeats. Kovno, Osovets, Brest-Litovsk....

Whoever wins this war, it will be followed by decades of struggle between the capitalist powers as they vie for world markets. What will happen to Russia? First it will have to develop its productive and technical potential to the level already reached in Germany and America, and objectively speaking, it can achieve this quite quickly. So is another war between Russia and Germany inevitable, with more suffering? Capitalism is spreading across America, and has already reached China and Japan. Can humanity survive? Capitalism may not have reached its highest point yet, but one thing is clear — we are at a turning point in history. We are living through an era similar to the transition from the medieval feudal state, with its knightly warriors and castles.

Capitalism has created the objective conditions for its downfall. Perhaps this is only the first stage in the transition to social ism, the negative, destructive stage. Our revolutionary forces are still weak, and the struggle may last many years. But the war has clearly confirmed the theories of scientific socialism. The mighty conflicts between the capitalist nations confront civilised humanity with the choice between destroying national economies or rebuilding them in a new form, on the basis of socialised labour. Economic crises produced this war, but the struggle has already spread far wider. Now it's the fight for class domination. The historical push will depend on the working class....

7 September
I have been invited by the American Socialist Party to speak at meetings across the United States. It's such incredibly good news I'm afraid to believe it — I'm gasping for joy!

On 5 September 1915, forty socialists from Russia, Germany, France, Britain, Italy, Portugal, Switzerland, the Netherlands, Norway and Sweden met in the Swiss village of Zimmerwald, in the guise of a convention of ornithologists, and unanimously passed their resolution to establish a new International, committed to a class war against capitalism — "taking on ourselves the responsibility for this war, its aims and methods".

Kollontai's invitation to America was from members of the left wing of the Socialist Party, who with the trade unions and the Industrial Workers of the World, the "Wobblies," were waging an energetic campaign against America entering the war. She immediately wired back to accept, and wrote to Lenin, who gave her a long list of tasks to carry out for the Bolsheviks: spreading the Zimmerwald message at meetings, translating his pamphlet *Socialism and War* into English and finding it an

American publisher, raising funds for the party, and keeping him regularly informed on events in America, about which he knew little. "We're pinning so many hopes on your visit," he wrote to her.

She sailed for New York in late September, and used the twelve-day journey to translate his pamphlet. Her diaries of the next four months are a head-spinning account of her travels by train across America, from New York to California, the Midwest and the Deep South. She spoke in English, German and Russian at 230 anti-war meetings in 123 cities — to women activists in Boston and Cincinnati, and Garment Workers' Union members in Philadelphia, to German miners in Illinois, and exiled Russians in San Francisco. In Seattle, she marched in a demonstration mourning the murder of the IWW activist Joe Hill. In Chicago, she spoke at huge peace rallies with the socialist activists Eugene Debs and the IWW leader Bill Haywood. She described schools, churches and the press all banging the drum for war. And when America finally declared war on Germany in April 1917, "to make the world safe for democracy," Debs and Haywood would be among hundreds of socialists and labour activists arrested and sentenced to long terms in jail for treason under the new Espionage Act — resurrected a century later to jail and torture Chelsea Manning and Julian Assange for exposing US war crimes.

Back in New York, she worked with exiled Russian revolutionaries on their anti-war paper *New World*, and she spoke at more packed meetings. New York's Tsarist chief of police sent detailed reports of her activities back to Petrograd, and the American press spread stories that she was a German spy, and an adviser to King Gustav of Sweden (who had ordered her permanent deportation from the country).

She set sail for Norway in March 1916, and described the eventful return journey in an article for the popular Norwegian paper *Saturday Night,* translated into Norwegian.

Immediately Britain entered the war in August 1914, it had imposed a naval blockade of Germany and Austria, to starve them into submission. The North Sea was declared a war zone, foodstuffs were confiscated as "war contraband," and merchant and passenger ships from neutral Scandinavia sailed at their own risk. There was international outrage against the blockade as a war crime, and the resulting hardships in Germany were widely blamed for the mass strikes that led to the Kaiser's abdication four years later.

The Russian version of the article translated here was published in *From My Life and Work.*

"At Sea In the Blockade Zone"

Our peaceful journey back to Norway was interrupted by our encounter with the "sea pirates" of Britain's Royal Naval Fleet. On the positive side, it was a wonderful lesson for us socialists in the arrogance of the major imperialist powers, spitting on the rights of the small neutral states.

Our Norwegian captain had expressed his fears that the British would board our little steamer the *Bergensfjord* and take us prisoner. But what did they care of his fears? Tensions mounted eight days after we left New York, as we entered the North Sea and approached the island of Kirkwall, Britain's naval base in the Orkney Islands. Passengers worried about the mines ahead, and that the recent storms would set them off.

That evening, the shadow of a cruiser appeared on the horizon. Was it British or German? People argued in whispers, and the Americans laid bets. But the ship sailed serenely past and vanished into the distance. The pirates had taken no trophies this time, and we breathed with relief.

The next day passed uneventfully. But as night fell, our fears returned. Suddenly a light flashed in the darkness, then a rhythmic succession of lights, the signals to stop and identify our selves. Our ship responded. Many anxious minutes passed. The engines were switched off, and in the silence we could hear the splashing oars of an approaching boat.

Something interesting had happened on board. The ocean feels like neutral territory, and until then Russians, Germans, British and Americans had all been chatting and socialising together. Suddenly everyone split up into their different national groups. The Germans hoped it was a German submarine, the Russians and English that it was an Allied patrol ship. How alien these groups felt to me, I belonged to none of them. I didn't care who the ship belonged to, they would never be my "allies". I spoke to the young Englishman I had met on the journey out, back from his trip to New York on "war work," with its undreamt of new business opportunities.

A beam of light lit up a launch filled with soldiers, and four British officers boarded the *Bergensfjord* and followed the captain into his cabin. "It's the English!" the Russians said happily, and the Germans looked worried. The officers came out and informed us that we would be searched, then escorted on lifeboats past the minefields to Kirkwall for further inspection. Panicking passengers stampeded the decks, grabbing lifebelts and stuffing their possessions in their pockets. A young American woman clutched her handbag with her makeup and mirror.

Kirkwall's English commander then came on board with the soldiers, who checked our luggage and gave everyone a thorough body search. The women were searched by a uniformed ex-suffragette volunteer, "serving King and country," who went through the formalities with great courtesy. And I thought of Russia, mocked, despised, autocratic Russia, which suddenly seemed a beacon of legality. England's famous *habeas corpus* laws are apparently just an empty phrase now, and the soldiers carrying out the searches looked embarrassed, as if aware of this, and that the laws of war were robbing British citizens too of their rights.

The inspections lasted several hours, and afterwards we were ordered onto the lifeboats for the dangerous journey in rough seas past the mines to Kirkwall, where we were allowed back onto the *Bergensfjord*. The deserted barren island loomed ahead. Eleven centuries ago it had been a Norwegian port. But its old cathedral, built by Norwegian pirates, was all that was left of Norway now in this completely British town, on whose territory we were forbidden to step. Only the captain was allowed to disembark.

After four anxious days, during which the most lurid fears spread on board our ship, we were finally allowed on our way, and twelve hours later we were back in peaceful neutral Norway.

On her return to Norway, Kollontai picked up her Northern Underground work and finished her pamphlet *Who Needs the War?*, addressed to frontline soldiers in the warring countries.

In simple powerful language she humanised the enemy, and spelt out the causes of the war, appealing to soldiers to fraternise and desert and turn their weapons on their enemies at home. Like Marx, she wrote of the patriotic propaganda that sent workers to die in brutal overseas wars for the "homeland," and she was clearly influenced by the lively campaigning language of the IWW's anti-war leaflets written for America's poor immigrant workers, who had no "homeland" to defend.

Who Needs the War? is a classic of anti-war writing, filled with pathos and satire and big ideas, expressed with a directness and simplicity that belied the many months she spent working on it, and the complicated process of getting it published. She posted the manuscript to Lenin in Switzerland, and he sent it to the Tkachev sisters in Petrograd who ran the Bolsheviks' printing press, writing to apologise to her for not consulting her about several changes he had made to the text, explaining it needed to come out quickly. The Tkachevs worked on it day and night for a week on their press in a hut in the Petrograd suburbs, dismantling it as soon as they had finished, and a few days later they were both arrested. But by then the work of translating *Who Needs the War?* into German had begun.

The pamphlet was one of her most enduringly popular works, with an estimated readership of seven million Russian and German soldiers, and its first readers were said to be German soldiers and prisoners of war in Russia.

Who Needs the War?

Heroes

The war isn't over, the end isn't even in sight, but the number of cripples is growing — the blind, the deaf, the lame, those who have lost arms and legs. They left for the front young and healthy, with their lives ahead of them. A month later they were sent back to the hospitals, mutilated and half dead.

Those who started the slaughter, who have thrown people of one country against those of another, worker against worker, call them "heroes". Give the hero a medal, they say, he deserves it, and people will respect him for it.

So what happens to the crippled hero when he returns home with his medal? Instead of love and respect, he is met with fresh humiliation and suffering. His village is full of cripples, some with one medal, some with two, and his family is starving. The men have been conscripted, the livestock has been requisitioned, taxes have to be paid, and there is no one to work the land. The women are exhausted, rushed off their feet and worn out with weeping, and the only "respect" the hero gets is to be seen as a parasite and an extra mouth to feed.

The hero in the town fares no better. His wife smiles and fusses over him for a day or two, and his mother weeps with grief and joy. Her darling boy is alive, she has seen him with her old eyes. But when do working people have time to care for an invalid? Times are hard. Everyone has their work to do and their worries. Food prices have shot up, the children are sick — wars always bring infections and epidemics. His wife must do a hundred things at once, working to support the family "breadwinner". As for his Tsarist pension, it will barely pay for the one boot for his remaining leg.

Wounded officers naturally receive generous pensions commensurate with their rank. But who cares about the ordinary private, the worker and peasant? Power is in the hands of their lords and masters, the landowners, industrialists and government officials. State finances are managed not by the heroes, dying in their millions, but by the same landowners, industrialists and government officials, servants of the Tsar.

While memories of the front are still fresh and the cannon are still pounding, the heroes will be remembered, and the Red Cross and other charitable organisations will come to their aid with miserly handouts. A year passes, then another. Peace comes, and people go back to their old lives, and what becomes of our crippled hero with his medal?

Wounded generals ride around in their motorcars. They took good care of themselves during the war, lining their pockets and stuffing themselves with the soldiers' rations. They won't be joining the heroes begging in the church porch. This is what awaits the saviour of his Motherland, even with ten medals on his chest. The Tsarist government won't give him a second thought. The hearts of the bosses won't grieve for him. What do they care? It's not their brother who is suffering, cursing his fate. He is not a gentleman like them, he is "common folk," born to shed his blood for his masters and die under a fence.

What Are We Fighting For?

Ask a Russian, German, French or English soldier what they are fighting for, and each has been told something different.

The Russians were told that they were fighting to free the Serbs, and to defend Russia against the German invaders. At first the conscripted Russian peasants thought, "We're saving our land from the Germans!" But they soon realised this war isn't about land. What is it about then? It's not only Russians who are fighting in the dark, with no idea why they are shooting, bayonetting and crippling people, spilling the blood of their brothers, workers and peasants of another country. German, French and English soldiers have been told the same lies about the true causes of the war.

The Germans are told: "Russia has attacked us, Cossacks are marching on Berlin! We must defend the Fatherland, and at the same time free Russia from Tsarist barbarity. Russians are too weak to stand up to their enemies at home, we must help them! Let us open the door to their rights and freedom! Let us die for the liberty of the Russian people!"

This is the sweet song the Kaiser sings to his people, and they believe him. Mass editions of the press spread lies about the war, military censorship bans a word of the truth from being published, and the best friends of the working class are thrown in jail. German soldiers have been lied to, just as Russian soldiers were lied to when they were told it was for "land" that they marched into Galicia to be slaughtered.

In France, soldiers were told it was time to take

back the territory of Alsace-Lorraine, captured by Germany in 1870. "Citizens of glorious Republican France! We have won our political rights at home, while our German neighbours are still groaning under the Kaiser's yoke! Let us save them! Let us fight to get rid of the Kaiser and establish a republic for the German people!"

So noble France decided to "liberate" Germany from the Kaiser. Not a bad cause, who needs kaisers? But if we look more closely, we see something else happening. In peacetime, the Tsar and the Kaiser were the best of friends and paid each other visits. In peacetime, the governments of the capitalist countries worked closely with each other to plunder their colonies in Asia and Africa, setting up conglomerates to produce more tanks and dread noughts. And now all of a sudden the tsars and kaisers and capitalists have been seized by the noble desire to "liberate" their neighbours, and introduce them to justice, equality and prosperity!

So the Germans march off to save Russia from the Tsar, and the French to save Germany from the Kaiser. But it can be seen that the Tsar and the Kaiser remain safe and sound, still on their thrones, with their power intact.

As for the British, they were told they were fighting to save Belgium from "German militarism" and the "German war machine". But what has their government done in practice? First of all, it lost no time in helping itself to German colonies and land — needless to say without consulting their populations under whose rule they wished to live, German or British.

The British government waxes indignant about the Kaiser killing the spirit of freedom in the German people, and turning them into a trained obedient herd. And of course that is quite true. The problem is that words and practice don't match. While cursing the "Prussian militarists," the British are learning as much as they can from them. Ever since England entered the war, workers have been fighting plans to replace the existing paid volunteer system with compulsory universal military conscription. The government that claims to be "liberating" Germany from the evils of militarism is so taken with the German example that it has imposed the very same evils on its own people, passing laws to militarise industry and subordinate it to the army, removing workers' right to strike and defend their interests, binding them to the state. All the major capitalist powers have followed Germany in introducing this industrial slavery. Work for a pittance, put up with every kind of insult, or you'll be sent to the front to face the enemy's bullets. Workers in England have been putting up a brave fight against this new attack, this new injustice. But the employers are too fond of the German example to retreat, and they are already beginning to break the resistance.

The capitalists grow richer from the war by the day, while millions of the citizens they were so concerned about litter their countries and foreign countries with their corpses.

This is how matters stand. The evils for which governments have declared war against each other are introduced in their own countries. Germans fighting to liberate Russia from tyranny are suffering the same tyranny at home. The French who have drawn their sword in the name of freedom for Germany are suffering levels of oppression and censorship France hasn't known for centuries. Is there anyone who still believes the lie that the war is being fought to "liberate" a foreign people?

Who Is To Blame?

There are those who say, "Maybe we don't know the reasons for the war, but at least we know who started it, and they must be punished!"

Ask a Russian who this is, and they'll say "The Germans. Germany was the first to declare war". Ask a German, and they'll say "Lies! Germany didn't want war, it wanted to continue the talks. Russia was the first to mobilise, Russia started it!" "Lies!" shout Russia's "allies". "The Tsar only mobilised after Austria's ultimatum to Serbia — Austria started it!" And Austria points to Russia, with Britain at its back.

When we read the governments' red, white and blue war books, with their telegrams, letters and communiqués, it becomes clear that the great powers have been secretly planning this war for decades, competing to rob their colonies in India, China, Persia, Turkey and the countries of Africa. In their diplomatic talks they swore eternal allegiance, but they had just one thing in mind, to deceive and outwit each other — the English the Germans, the Germans the Russians, the Russians the Austrians — and to deceive and outwit their own people. Years were spent preparing for this war, and unimaginable sums of citizens' money. Have nations' resources been spent to meet people's needs for schools and hospitals, for workers' insurance schemes, for affordable housing for the poor? Not a bit of it! National coffers have emptied and taxes have shot up. There are no depths governments won't sink to in meeting their military obligations.

Preparations were being made simultaneously in Germany, Russia, Britain, France and Belgium. And now Britain talks of "poor little Belgium" — when long before the German invasion it was planning to breach its sovereignty with its naval blockade!

Workers are well aware of what their countries'

wealth is being spent on, and that their taxes are being used to build new war machines for the capitalists. And workers in Russia know that half their taxes end up in the pockets of the "builders," who make a profit of 20 to 40 kopecks from every rouble's worth of war supplies, amounting to billions of roubles. Why should we now forget who planned this war? Why should we believe the lie that it is the German and Russian workers and peasants who are to blame, not our murderous governments of tsars, kaisers and capitalists?

They all belong to the same criminal band. They have brought on this bloody disaster with their "foreign policies," sending millions to die for the countries they have betrayed. Die for the glory of the Fatherland! Forget the insults and humiliations. Forget that yesterday you seethed with rage when an officer struck a private. Banish memories of the masters' cruelty, when you cursed your lack of rights. Only yesterday, you would have given short shrift to anyone who counselled you to sacrifice your life for the bosses. You would have laughed in their face if they told you that your employer at the factory was your "brother," and that the German worker or peasant, as oppressed as you, was your worst enemy. Now it's war, and the country must be "united," and you must kill those as ill-fated as you, and sacrifice your life and the life of your comrade from another country to benefit your common enemy. Such is the will of those who created the carnage, the friends and servants of capital.

The Homeland Is In Danger!

But how can we refuse to fight when we have been attacked and our homeland is in danger?

Let those who set off to die for the "homeland"

ask themselves honestly and in all conscience what "homeland" they have. If workers had a "homeland," why would there be this annual flood of refugees into foreign lands, even into Russia itself? Why would hundreds of thousands of the impoverished and dispossessed bravely leave their homes in the hope that another country will prove a more loving stepmother than their own motherland?

The wealthy have a homeland. To the generals, capitalists and landowners, it gives rights and privileges, and it guards their interests. For the French, German and Russian worker, life in the homeland means the struggle for their daily bread against poverty, oppression and injustice. And in Russia it not infrequently means hard labour and exile. This is what the modern homeland gives to its children who create its wealth with their hands, and pay for its military glory with their lives.

Some say, "Even if our country doesn't love her children, who water her earth with our blood and tears, we still love her! We will save the faith of our fathers from the foreign invaders!" But look more closely at who is fighting who. Is it Catholic against Orthodox? Lutheran against Catholic? Christian against Muslim? No, the war has mixed up all the religions. Orthodox Russians shoot Orthodox Bulgarians. French Catholics shoot German Catholics. Muslims fight with Christians to shoot brother Muslims. Pole shoots Pole, Jew shoots Jew.

This war is being waged not between people with different languages and faiths, but between states, the great capitalist powers. Over the past century, each of these powers has seized land from its neighbours to establish new colonies. How many peoples has Britain brought under its imperial rule — in India, Africa and the Caribbean, Australia and Canada?

How many nations have been gobbled up by Tsarist Russia and Habsburg Austria? And Germany hasn't lagged behind, annexing parts of Poland, taking Schleswig-Holstein from the Danes, and Alsace-Lorraine from the French.

The great powers have drawn up new borders, driving the most disparate peoples across these borders, and telling them "This is your country now. Obey our laws in peacetime, and when it's war you must die for the new home we have given you!"

All the powers now at war with each other oppress countless races and religions. Russia oppresses its Muslims, Jews, Finns, Ukrainians and Poles. Germany oppresses its Poles and Danes. England and France oppress the hundreds of millions in their colonies. This war is being fought not to defend people's native customs and languages, or the institutions that serve their interests, but to defend the predators' right to seize as many colonies as possible and steal their resources.

A hideous picture emerges. People of the same nation, the same language, are told to kill each other and destroy each others' lands. The Ukrainian peasant from Russia kills the Ukrainian peasant from Austria. The Polish worker from Russia kills the Polish worker from Germany. Forty-five years ago, the people of Alsace gave their lives for the glory of *la Belle France*. Now they are defending their country under the banner of the German eagle. And who knows, if victory goes to the Allies, perhaps in the next war they will have to die for their new French "homeland".

And what of the millions of Africans and Indians mobilised by the British and French from their colonies? Whose country are they dying for? Their homes are thousands of miles away. The European powers invaded them and put them to the sword, and now they must die for the nations that oppress them.

The "true sons" of Russia, Germany and England have no homeland either. What sort of homeland is it for the millions of wage slaves who work for the capitalists, who have nothing to lose but their chains?

Capitalists of all nations are blood brothers, and in peacetime workers know this. There was a time when people fought to defend their lands from foreign aggression. Now capitalists throughout the world are driven solely by the race for profits, throwing workers of one country against those of another to weaken and divide them.

In peacetime, workers know that their enemies are not workers from another country, but the capitalists on either side of the border. Why, when they are called to the banner of the Kaiser or the Tsar, do they forget everything life has taught them? Why do they take it on faith that the financial interests of the industrialists who happen to be their compatriots are closer to them than the interests of their "enemies" — the Russian and German workers?

The Causes Of The War

Yes, the war is a filthy business which no one would defend. But now that it has started, how can we not fight?

First we must ask why it started. Wars have a variety of causes. Centuries ago, people fought over territory, for the freedom of their native lands. This war was generated by the class system, under which workers sell their labour to the wealthy few who own the capital. As economies expand, capital begins to feel cramped in its own country, and if the capitalists are to increase their profits, they must invest their accumulated wealth in new markets and colonies, destroying entire populations to steal the cheap oil and raw materials they need to produce more goods. Every recent major dispute between the capitalist powers has been over colonial markets. Every nation is driven by the need to bring more markets under its control — whether by diplomatic subterfuge, bribing governments and capitalists in the weak dependent nations, or by force of arms.

To begin with, they hold secret talks to resolve their differences. Even in peacetime, these talks never cease, and if diplomats fail to get their way, governments threaten war. Behind them stand the cannon. There is no stable peace between the capitalist states, only "armed peace," during which preparations for war are intensified. The general population knows nothing of these talks of course. They are not conducted on their behalf, but to serve the imperialist ambitions of the capitalists, who decide whether or not there will be war. All people need to know is that when they are called up, they must go and die.

Naturally the capitalists pursuing these dangerous policies know exactly how their diplomats are faring. The moment they suspect the advantage is going to a rival power, they raise the alarm: "Help! Our country is in danger! Brother workers, forget the past, forget the humiliations, you must die for the glory of your country!"

Governments listen to the capitalists' call. They cannot fail to, since they are made up of the very same capitalists, who serve and guard their interests. To please the capitalists, governments begin to threaten their neighbours, the talks grow more heated, and before we know it there is war.

People must not be told the truth — that they are fighting to make more profits for the capitalists. That would never do, they would never agree to die for such a cause. So instead they are told that their homeland is danger, or they must free their neighbours from the Tsar or the Kaiser, or some such nonsense.

The capitalists at home sit raking in the profits, while the workers die in their millions for them. They are too trusting! They have been misinformed, they haven't seen where their interests lie. And the capitalists take full advantage of this.

The cause of this war is the struggle of national capital for world hegemony. Russian capital is fighting German capital in Russia and Austrian capital in the Balkans. British and French capital is fighting German capital in Africa, Asia and the smaller states. Capital clashes with capital, each seeking to destroy the other and establish its monopoly, robbing the workers who produce the goods, and the consumers who purchase them.

As capitalism spreads across the world and draws more states into its orbit, the deadlier these rivalries become, until war is inevitable. It is pointless trying to console ourselves that this is the war to end all wars. Wars will recur and proliferate so long as the present class system exists, and their aims will be identical to the present one: to make more profits for the capitalists. Have workers come to love their tyrant masters so much that they are prepared to shed their blood to defend their interests? To kill their fellow workers from another country, and destroy their peaceful towns and villages?

What Is To Be Done?

Once the true purposes of the war are understood, the next question is how can we stop the slaughter? How can we be spared new conflicts in the future between the capitalist powers?

Before answering this, we must realise one thing: that wars are inevitable as long as the private ownership of the land and the factories exists, which divides citizens into the classes of the haves and have-nots. Wars are caused by the unjust structure of societies, and will end only when the exploiters have been forced out of power and can no longer drive people into their bloody conflicts. To put an end to wars, the factories must be removed from the capitalists, the land from the landowners, the mines from the private prospectors, the banks from the financiers, and all this private wealth made common property, owned and managed by the people.

To put an end to wars, we need a new more just socialist world. The task now facing the working class of every country is to destroy the capitalist clique that is destroying millions of lives to increase its profits. When the national wealth is con trolled by the workers, people will have no need to kill their neighbours. Their only goal will be their country's peace and prosperity, and the peace and prosperity of other countries. Peaceful nations of free working people will always find a common language!

Yet there still remains the urgent question of how we stop this fratricidal war. The answer is the same in every country. Our governments have set worker against worker, but they share the same interests. The Russian, German, British and Austrian worker all want the same thing, and that is peace.

First we must hold to account the criminals responsible for the catastrophe — the tsars, kings and kaisers and their diplomats and officials, lackeys of capital. Away with these worthless governments of millionaires! State power must belong to the people!

Let all who are weary of this criminal war join the ranks of those who are fighting not the foreign enemy, but their enemies at home. Instead of dying for one's country, wouldn't it be better to win it for the people?

To do away with the tyrants and oppressors who are the cause of the bloodshed? Instead of "liberating" Russians from the Tsar, wouldn't German soldiers be better advised to settle their scores with the Kaiser and his capitalists? Instead of the French aiming their guns at the Germans, wouldn't it be more sensible to aim them at their enemies at home? Instead of giving their lives for the Krestovnikovs, Guchkovs and Morozovs and their honourable fraternity, shouldn't Russians be fighting for their rights and freedom and the victory of the workers' cause?

All that is needed is for each soldier at the front to say "My enemy isn't one like me, robbed of all rights in his country, whose life like mine is crushed by capital and the struggle for bread. No, my enemy is at home, and that enemy is capitalism, which has made slaves of the working class of all countries. Comrade and worker of a foreign army, I know you are not my enemy, so give me your hand, comrade. We are both victims of the same lies, so let us turn our rifles on our real enemy, our enemy at home".

If workers from every country say this, no power on earth will be able to continue the war, and our brave commanders and field marshals and generals will take to their heels in fright! So let us all go to war against our oppressors, and rid our countries of the capitalists, tsars and emperors. And when power is in our hands, we will go over the heads of our defeated enemies to make peace.

To work, comrades! Victory to the socialist brotherhood of nations! Victory to the approaching socialist revolution!

Chapter Five
Back to Russia

A year into the war, the Russian army had suffered such catastrophic losses that the German High Command had effectively discounted the Eastern Front. The Tsar blamed the Jews for Russia's defeats ("nine tenths of Russia's troublemakers are Jews"), and the soldiers blamed "Bloody Nicholas" and the evil Rasputin.

In June 1915, the Tsar was forced by liberals in the Duma to arrest his Minister of War, known as "Rasputin in uniform," and jail him for high treason. He then ordered a massive new conscription drive to replace the dead, starting with first-year university students, appointed himself Supreme Commander of the Russian Army, and set off for the front, leaving Rasputin and the Empress in charge of matters of state.

Over the following year, a million Russian soldiers deserted, commandeering trains and breaking into arsenals on their way home, joining women's hunger riots in the cities and villages, looting shops and warehouses and sacking the landowners' estates. Petrograd filled with stories of Rasputin's orgies in the Winter Palace with the Empress and her ladies-in-waiting, and liberals in the Duma were calling for her to be jailed for treason.

In December, Rasputin was murdered by courtiers of the Tsar, who saw his death as the monarchy's only hope. Shaken by war and rotting from within, the Tsarist regime was drawing new recruits to the revolution.

In Germany, Rosa Luxemburg and Liebknecht spent most of the war years in jail. But in February 1916, in brief breaks in their sentences, they attended the illegal founding conference of the underground Spartacist League, which called on soldiers and workers to desert and strike and turn the nationalist conflict into an international revolution. The world faced the choice between humanism and barbarism, Luxemburg said.

In January, Shlyapnikov returned illegally to Russia to set up the Bolsheviks' new headquarters in the capital. He vividly described the months that followed in his memoirs *On the Eve of 1917*. He was elected secretary of the central committee, and got a job as a lathe-operator in the same engineering plant where he had worked before he left for exile, smuggling Lenin's writings in to the workers. Russia's most militant workers had been the first to be conscripted in 1914. Since they were also generally the most highly skilled, the survivors were now being called back from the front to save Russia's collapsing economy, and Shlyapnikov saw this powerful angry new workforce in Petrograd as the revolution's leaders in the making.

In Norway, Kollontai took over his Northern Underground work, and started on her next pamphlet for the Bolsheviks, calling for the overthrow of the Tsar. It opens with a retelling of the Mark Twain story *The Prince and the Pauper*. Twain had been a passionate supporter of Russia's 1905 revolution, and she used his satire about social inequality to ridicule the Tsar and those who kept him in power. The piece was never finished, and it was published in its incomplete form in March 1917 in Gorky's popular literary anti-war journal *Chronicle*.

"Who Needs the Tsar and Can We Do Without Him?"

There is a story of two boys who were born on the same day, one born into poverty, who knew cold, hunger and exploitation, the other a prince, a little tsar over his people.

They happened to meet one day when the poor boy was loitering outside the palace, and they were astonished by their striking resemblance to each other, and decided to play a trick on the prince's courtiers by switching clothes. Instantly their fates changed. Thrown out of the palace in the poor boy's rags, the prince discovered the powerlessness of the dispossessed, the insults of the rich, the punches of the police. While the poor boy, who had been kicked around like a dog, with no one to protect him, took his place on the throne, dressed in his velvet and ermine, and his courtiers bowed low before him, and his word was law.

What had changed? They were the same people, but the poor boy was now addressed as a god, while the prince was dragged off the streets by the police and thrown in jail.

What does rank mean, the power to rule people? If your rank is Tsar and you wear the crown, there is no limit to your power. The prince in his rags says goodbye to his royal pretensions. He tries to make people on the street bow to him and stand to attention, and they laugh in his face — "the madman thinks he's the Tsar!"

When the giddy new Tsar drives out in his carriage, the police beat back the crowds as they rush to catch a glimpse of him. "The Tsar! The Tsar!"

When the Tsar visits the battlefields — not the front line, perish the thought, that's the place for the soldiers, the cannon fodder — the hearts of many in their grey army coats beat faster, and they long to show off their valour to him.

The Tsar is great! What makes him great? His good deeds? His acts of charity for the poor and needy?

The Tsar is mighty! Why mighty? Because in his kingdom his will is done. The people's deputies to his Duma are powerless, he can issue an Imperial decree to cancel any law he wishes. He is mighty because he has the army's bayonets to protect him, and five hundred thousand police and secret police to punish any who stand against him. He is mighty because he uses the people's money to pay an army of officials to guard his Holy Person, who sniff out peasants protesting against the landowners' cruelty, and workers standing up to their thieving bosses. Off to Siberia with them, you can't be against the Tsar!

This doesn't make the Tsar mighty, it's the authority of brute force. It's how the merchants and landowners ruled their factories and estates in the years of serfdom, using their fists to get their way, and imposing their despotism on their wives and children. Why should such a person be considered fit to rule us?

Is the Tsar respected for his wisdom? Has he written a book, made a scientific discovery, invented a useful machine? Nothing like this has been heard of our Tsar. He despises those cleverer that himself, the talented are a threat to him. He is respected not for his wisdom, but because Nicholas Romanov was destined to be born in a palace, not in a peasant's hovel or a worker's cellar, where he would have suffered the same fate as the prince in the story.

Centuries ago, people chose the bravest and cleverest among them as their leaders. Their chief enemies then were nature and neighbouring tribes, with whom they fought endless battles for gold, cattle and land. There were no judges or written laws, no machine guns or cannon, no High Commands or army headquarters, where generals could sit in safety issuing orders for this or that regiment to be sent to the slaughter. Instead they picked their best warriors to lead them, who had already led them in victory, and had proved they were prepared to give their lives for them. "Let us give him power over us, to hunt down injustice and defend the weak against the strong," they said.

But the favours he granted to his followers went to their heads, and they said: "Let us surround him with a holy aura, so he is seen not just as some Ivan or Peter, but as God's anointed on Earth. Then in his name we can keep his stupid trusting people in a state of fear, squeeze taxes out of them, and pass laws to serve our interests. And any who break our laws will face his wrath".

The Tsar needs the Church to guard his holy image. There has long been a pact between them. "I'll give you gold and jewels for your altars, and land for your monasteries, and in return you must worship me," he says. "Praise my name! Inspire fear and respect for me, and I will protect you!" And the priests swear to serve their "Little Father" faithfully, so long as they can go on robbing people.

When the "Emancipator" Tsar Alexander II freed the serfs and divided up the land — oh how he hated doing so! But everywhere you looked they were raising their hands against the landowners, and it would soon be his turn too — he gave 260 million acres to the Church. 700 million acres went to his family and to the landowners. Russia's peasants were left with the rest, the "paupers' allotments". What great kindness Alexander showed his people, what concern he had for their happiness and welfare.

The Tsar Is A Puppet Of The Nobility

This is well known to all those who benefit from his favours — his priests and capitalists, the commanders and generals in all the divisions of his army, his nobles and landowners.

He has an especially close bond with the landowners, it's a long-standing friendship. In the past, the tsars and boyars had their squabbles over power. The boyars accepted the tsars' authority until they raised their voices and showed their true will, and unruly tsars were quickly dispatched. Paul I was strangled to death by his faithful guards, sons of his princes, and more have been murdered than the fingers on your hand. The tsars decided it was better to live in peace with their nobles, and the nobles decided they could make the tsars their puppets. There's nothing you can't achieve in the Tsar's name, and how well they are paid for praising him!

Sometimes our Tsar quarrels with his nobles and landowners, and tries to go against them to spite them. But he knows he mustn't disobey them, they are his throne's best defence. He needs them to instil fear in his citizens, and he rewards them with titles and land, and millions of roubles in the form of tax exemptions. Not his own money of course, the people's money, from the Imperial Chancery, the Tsar's personal bank. Why the Tsar's? Who gave him the money? No one dares ask his ministers for an explanation of how it is all spent.

As well as his priests and landowners, the Tsar needs his officials in their civilian and military uniforms, who run the country in his name and become little tsars themselves. Every governor-general of a city becomes a little tsar, every police chief, even the constable in his sentry box. All have made their pact with the Tsar. "We will serve you faithfully and defend you against revolutionaries, so long as it benefits us. We will run our own courts and pass our own laws, you only have to sign them. No fuss! The ink is official, the seals to the Chancery are open. Together we are an unbreakable force, and any who stand against us will be crushed".

The Tsar has had to come to this arrangement with his officials; without them he is powerless. Above all he needs his senior officials in the army, his generals and high commanders, sons of the nobility. The soldiers' bayonets guard him like a brick wall. His generals are devoted to him – he has no fears of revolution with them on his side! Many are his close personal friends, and he showers them with ranks and titles, and makes them governors and governor-generals, creating thousands more little tsars in the country. But for this he demands the army's unquestioning obedience. He expects a soldier at his officer's command to shoot his own brother in the Tsar's name. And when his mother joins the other starving women in her village to raid the shop of a wealthy merchant, he is expected to fire at her with a steady hand.

Finally, the Tsar needs the capitalists – his factory-owners, financiers and bankers. They don't have the same blood ties with him as his landowners, but they too need to make him their puppet if business is to thrive. The problem is that the landowners won't let them run the country the way they want.

The landowners would like Russia to be ruled as it was three centuries ago, when the serfs worked the land for them. But now the peasants are leaving the land to work in the towns, and trouble is brewing. They have lost respect for the masters and strayed from the church, and they are entertaining "ideas". When workers get together, revolt is inevitable. And workers' revolts are bad for business, on that the landowners and capitalists are in full agreement.

But the landowner's grief is the capitalist's joy. When the landowner laments the lack of peasants left to rob, the capitalist rejoices at the new workers being thrown onto the labour market — the more wage slaves he has, the bigger his profits. And that is not the only difference between them. The land owners want high prices for bread. The factory-owners are against high bread prices, since they increase the cost of workers' hands and reduce their profits, which doesn't suit the capitalists! They differ too on the issues of customs tariffs and taxes. The capitalists want high tariffs, to limit the foreign goods coming into Russia. The land-owners want low tariffs, and a free market for their exports of grain, meat and raw materials. On taxes, the capitalists would like the main burden to fall on the landowners, while the landowners are currently putting a bill through the Duma to increase the taxes of the capitalists.

The capitalists' fight for their place at the Tsar's throne is particularly bitter at present. They hate the tyranny of the landowners. They need the Tsar as a useful bogey man to frighten the masses, and as a cover for all sorts of business operations carried out in his name. But his powers must be limited, and the powers enjoyed by his landowners, priests and generals shared with the capitalists. With their allies the wealthy peas-ants, they can be an unbreakable force in the Duma against the landowners, passing laws and dictating state policy. "We need a constitutional monarchy!" they say.

Under a constitution, the Tsar would no longer be the pawn of the landowners, but a political football between the constitutional monarchists — the industri-alists and war profiteers Milyukov, Guchkov, Teresh-chenko and Milyukov — and his Black Hundreds poli-ticians Markov, Purishkevich, Bobrinsky and co. "We need the Tsar, he must stay!" they all cry.

Who needs him? The workers and peasants, dying for him in their millions at the front, robbed of their political rights, jailed and persecuted in his name? The Tsar is the enemy of workers and peasants alike.

What Does The Tsar Cost Us?

The Tsar is paid an annual salary of 25 million roubles, plus the income from his mines, mills and factories and the peasants' land. The Tsar is Russia's single greatest capitalist and land owner. His people are starving, and more than 165 million roubles of their money is spent guarding him. There is no money for schools, hospitals or midwives, no money for maternity benefits, as in Austria and Germany, or for old-age pensions, as in England and France. It goes straight into the pockets of the Tsar and his family and vanishes.

What Would Life Be Like Without Him?

Can we really get rid of him, and rebuild society in a new way? The Tsar lives in unimaginable luxury. He has palaces built for him, and armies of guards to protect him. Music plays in his honour when he appears at festivals, and girls bear garlands. His orders are carried out instantly, as if by magic.

Yet the more you think about it, the more you realise there is nothing special about him. He is respected only because he was born in a palace and wears a crown on his head. What has "God's anointed" to do with it? And why should the will of this man be law for 160 million people?

When he goes he won't be missed. And getting rid of him will be only the start. We will have to stop all those hiding behind his throne — his generals, capitalists, landowners and priests — grabbing back power and granting a few crumbs of freedom to people.

The country must be run by the people themselves, through our elected representatives. Ministers and government officials must be our servants, who pass laws to serve our interests.

Fighting for political power won't be enough either. Much, much more will have to be done. But first let's get rid of what we don't need, and we don't need kings, kaisers or tsars. Send them all packing, like Napoleon to Elba! Let us fight together to free Russia from the Tsar, and build our forces for the battles ahead!

Kollontai was still working on "Who Needs the Tsar?" in March 1917, when news of his abdication reached Norway.

By the end of February, hunger riots in Petrograd had gathered unprecedented strength and violence. On 3 March, workers at the Putilov arms factory started another mass strike, which ended in a lockout. Over the next two days, workers across the capital downed tools in solidarity, and the streets filled with demonstrators. Strikers were rounded up and arrested, and the Bolsheviks' offices were raided by the police and their printing press was seized.

Kollontai had been writing to women in the capital about their plans for International Women's Day. But it was celebrated a day early that year. When a group of organisers visited the Bolshevik central committee on 6 March to ask for guidance on their demonstrations, they were told to "show restraint and discipline, and await instructions". But as Shlyapnikov pointed out in his memoirs, no instructions could be issued, as the Party had no printing press. So on the seventh, women took matters into their own hands to make Women's Day a day of civil disorder unparalleled in Russia, wrecking factories and breaking into bakeries, storming the streets with makeshift placards saying "Peace!" "Bread!" "Our Children are Starving!"

On the eighth, women from Petrograd's textile mills came out on strike. Thousands from other factories walked out in solidarity, surging across the Neva bridges connecting the poor suburbs with the centre. They were joined there by women at the Vasilev Island trolleybus terminus, who had earlier visited the nearby barracks of the 180th Infantry Regiment, to win the soldiers' promise not to shoot when they joined the strikers. By the ninth, over half of Petrograd's two million citizens were on the streets, shouting "Stop the War!" and "Down with the Tsar!" Students left their lectures to join them, and women began to invade the soldiers' barracks *en masse*, seizing their weapons. Gathering force and numbers over the next days, they swept through the city in food riots, political strikes and demonstrations, demanding an end to the war and their hunger and suffering.

The police were still mainly loyal to the Tsar, and fired at the crowds from machine guns mounted on rooftops. But soldiers of the Pavlovsky Regiment (to whom Kollontai had smuggled revolutionary leaflets in 1905) fired back at them, then joined the demonstrators, calling on other regiments to refuse orders to shoot. Officers lost the will to lead them, and soviets took control in several workers' districts in Petrograd. By 10 March, the whole city was on strike, without buses, trams or newspapers.

The Bolsheviks appealed helplessly for calm as the demonstrations grew more violent, and several buildings were set on fire, including the Ministry of Justice. As the only party to have called explicitly for an armed rising, they were now called to account by angry workers demanding guns, and Shlyapnikov lost many friends when he refused to arm this sudden spontaneous revolution. Hundreds were rounded up and arrested, including the entire Bolshevik central committee apart from Shlyapnikov, who escaped and went into deep hiding.

The Tsar had been at his military headquarters south of the capital, and relied on his wife to keep him informed of events. "A hooligan campaign," she wrote to him. "A lot of boys and young girls running around shouting that they have no bread, it will surely pass".

He returned to Petrograd on 14 March, expecting a warm welcome from the Duma, and was told that his regime had collapsed, and the country was now being run by a new Provisional Committee of the Duma. A day later, he was forced to sign the abdication papers, bringing an end to three centuries of Romanov rule.

News from Petrograd reached the provinces by telegram, and local authorities across Russia quickly handed over to newly formed soviets. It was only in the second week of March, when over a thousand people had lost their lives in the demonstrations, that the revolution began to make headlines abroad.

The new Provisional Government of the Duma, composed mainly of landowners and businessmen, announced its programme of liberal reforms for the new Russia, and an amnesty for political exiles. But Kollontai agreed with Lenin to delay her departure until she received the first two of his five "Letters from Afar", which she was to deliver to the Bolsheviks' paper *Pravda* in Petrograd — his appeal to workers and peasants to prepare for the seizure of state power through the soviets. "A week of bloody workers' battles, and we get Milyukov, Guchkov and Kerensky," he wrote to her. "So be it. This first stage of the revolution born of the war won't be the last one or a purely Russian affair. Now it's the two classes of the bourgeoisie and the urban proletariat fighting for power. Our slogans are the same: against national defence and the imperialist war. Our tactics: no support for the Provisional Government, no alliance with other parties. Distrust Kerensky above all".

Below are excerpts from Kollontai's diaries of the March revolution, published posthumously in 1967, its fiftieth anniversary, in the journal *Soviet Archives*, as "Back to Russia!" (The ellipses again are mine).

"How We Learnt About the March Revolution"

It was Tuesday the thirteenth of March. I had been unable to buy a newspaper in town, and on the tram back to Holmenkollen I saw the headline on my neighbour's paper: "Revolution in Russia!"

My heart raced. I tried to read over his shoulder, and asked to see it when he had finished. "Don't worry, it's probably just rumours from some Swedish tourist, and tomorrow they'll be denied," he said.

But I knew immediately it wasn't a bluff, and could sense the momentous events behind the sketchy reports. People had risen up, there had been shooting on the streets, the soldiers had joined the demonstrators, this was revolution.

That evening it was hard to write, all I could think of was going home. Next morning there were conflicting reports from two visitors from Petrograd. One said that everything had blown over and the city was now quiet. The other that the shootings and demonstrations were continuing, the soldiers were storming the jails, and revolutionaries had blown up a bridge, breaking communications with Finland.

We devoured the papers, trying to read behind the lines, and one thing was clear: the storm had burst. Who would win? Had the hour of the revolution struck? Workers wanted peace, and in the struggle for peace they would win power.

By Thursday the news was clearer. A new committee of the Duma has been formed to govern the country, and delegates to the Petrograd Soviet — now the Soviet of Workers' and Soldiers' Deputies — have taken their seats in the Tauride Palace.

I stayed at the boarding house all day, working on my pamphlet about the Tsar. Victory is generally still seen in terms of Russia gaining a constitution, and we must start agitating immediately for a socialist republic. The writing flowed, and tiredness set in only as night fell. I decided to leave the last chapter and return to it in the morning with a clear head.

I was woken at dawn by the shop assistant Fru Dundas banging on my door. "The Tsar has abdicated!" she shouted. "The people have won!"

I ran out and we embraced. "We've won, we've won, it's the end of the war!"

Impossible to describe the joy! I rushed into town and met Fru Danielson on the street, and we hurried straight to the offices of the Norwegian party paper *Social Democrat*, to check that the news was true. The editor, stout Vidnes, was elated. "Congratulations! What a victory! Bravo Russia! These are the fruits of all your heroic work and sacrifices!"

He arranged for me to be interviewed immediately for the paper. But my interviewer seemed unable to grasp the significance of what was happening. Far away in Russia there was a "revolution" — how did this affect socialists in little Norway? Vidnes beamed. He is thoroughly "European," and is better informed about international politics than most in the party.

On the stairs my Norwegian comrades showered me with congratulations. What a holiday it was! Ecstatic crowds on the streets were grabbing newspapers and punching the air. The end of the Tsar had finally brought home to people in Norway the reality of the revolution.

I was greeted especially warmly at the offices of the Norwegian Socialist Youth League. The editor of its paper, *Class Struggle*, sweet shy young Arvid Hansen, clasped my hand with great emotion and asked me to write an article.

The evening papers brought more detailed reports from Petrograd. The new Provisional Committee of the Duma is now in power, and working alongside it the Soviet, led by the Menshevik Chkheidze. It reads like a fairytale. A thousand questions jostle for attention, and the most urgent is will there be an amnesty? And if so will it apply to us? Can we go home?

On Saturday morning the Russians held a "soviet" meeting at the boarding house. Even if there was an amnesty, wouldn't it be dangerous to go back? But it was impossible to stay. Young Hansen offered to go first as our emissary. He had to leave no later than Monday, which meant organising his journey today, and he accepted his mission with touching seriousness.

There have been disturbing reports in the press that the monarchists haven't given up and are busy in the provinces. This morning there was the news that the Tsar's brother the Grand Duke Mikhail had been appointed Tsar, and had then abdicated. This evening there were rumours of a possible dictatorship under the Tsar's uncle the Grand Duke Nicholas. The rumours proved groundless, but with no way of verifying anything, we have to treat each piece of news with great attention.

A British journalist reported an interesting scene he witnessed in Petrograd. A crowd of men and women were besieging the main arsenal, guarded by a single elderly soldier, and they didn't have to threaten the old man for the keys, he took off his cap, crossed himself and handed them over, saying "Here, take them brothers, they're yours!"

The papers are filled with eyewitness reports. Much confusion. But little by little, they are adding up to a picture of a completely new Russia.

This evening the Russians met at the boarding house for more discussions. All we can think of is going home. Should we travel to the border and wait for Hansen there, or go back directly? We send cables to our comrades in Russia and to Lenin in Switzerland, asking for his guidance, and we are too happy to eat or sleep.

Everyone in the boarding house is extraordinarily friendly, and strangers stop to talk on the street. A lot of silly questions. But it's clear that people have finally grasped the historic importance of the revolution.

Sunday passed in more feverish discussions. The Provisional Committee of the Duma has formed a new government, led by Prince Lvov and the Constitutional Democrats Guchkov and Milyukov. There are even rumours that women are to get the vote. Fantasies! Miracles!

Hansen is leaving first thing tomorrow. We have given him a mass of instructions based on the conditions of the old regime, when the party was still illegal and working underground. Poor Hansen blinks his pale eyelashes, desperate not to forget anything and fail in his important task. What will our messenger report back to us in ten days? Ten days! In revolutionary time that's ten years!

Next morning I asked Vidnes to organise a public meeting in solidarity with the revolution. But by then he had already had time to digest the great news, and was back to his old officious self. "Yes, yes, of course, a meeting is most necessary, I'll have a word with our Prime Minister about it".

I realised nothing would come of it, and there would be the usual bureaucratic excuses — "it's hard to find premises, we must consult the authorities," and so on. So I organised the meeting instead with the young socialists, who haven't been infected with officialdom.

More encouraging news from Petrograd. The Soviet has elected a new Executive Committee, which has arrested the Tsar's ministers. An English correspondent described the scene as the ministers rushed round the Tauride Palace blaming each other, and the Tsar's advisor Protopopov collapsed on a sofa and threw up his hands. We read the workers' speeches to the Soviet and the soldiers' manifestos, and we are moved to tears by this festival of brotherly hope and solidarity....

A telegram from the Soviet Executive has informed us of the Provisional Government's General Amnesty for political exiles. We can go back to Russia immediately!

But there is another telegram on my desk from Lenin, asking me to wait for his directives to the Party central committee, his "Letters from Afar", which means delaying my return for a week....

Our Swedish comrades have negotiated with the King to lift of my "permanent" ban from the country for the journey across Swedish territory to Finland. But it's hard to trust the Amnesty, and we're all worried about our documents; all of us have false passports. A couple of exiles visited the Russian consulate today for information, and when the officials saw the tall decisive young Russians (everyone in Kristiania knows each other), they were terrified, assuming they had come to arrest them, and told them they had heard nothing.

A group of our Russian comrades from Stockholm and Copenhagen have arrived, to decide who will return, and who will stay to keep communications open between the Party in Russia and Lenin in Switzerland. Happy news that the Bolsheviks are increasing their numbers in the Soviet, and that our paper *Pravda* is being published in Petrograd again....

I argued with Vidnes, who was full of praise for Russia's "democratic" Provisional Government. "You have a responsible parliament now, as in all other civilised countries, what more do you want?"

I presented the Bolshevik case. I said the new government didn't represent the people, and that only workers' power, the dictatorship of the proletariat, could end the war. Getting rid of the Tsar was only the first step. The struggle against the bourgeoisie still lay ahead. "That's why we Bolsheviks are going back, to turn the bourgeois revolution into a socialist one".

Vidnes listened with a patronising smile. "You Russians are incorrigible fantasists! But hats off to you for kicking out the Tsar. Russia will no longer be a bastion of reaction".

After our comrades left for Petrograd, I stayed in Kristiania another week, waiting for Lenin's "Letters". The Norwegian press grappled with the international implications of events in Russia. Much was written about the revolution, but it had ceased to be a sensation, and appeared on the second page with the rest of the foreign news, and the headlines were again war reports and local news. An extraordinary amount of attention was paid to members of the Provisional Government, particularly Milyukov, who was referred to in a deferential, almost ecstatic tone. Journalists stumbled over all the letters of the alphabet with Chkheidze, and wondered exactly what he did, and what the Soviet was. Was it a party? Most of the space was given to sensational sentimental stories about the royal family.

There were no Russian papers. The bourgeois German press was tentative and laconic, as if official Germany couldn't decide how to process the news for German public opinion. *Vorwärts* was dull and anaemic, weighing up events with a sort of artificial restraint. The English papers arrived late, and there were no French ones at all, which was annoying, as I wanted to know how the rest of the world was responding.

The average Norwegian citizen viewed our revolution with some scepticism. I was constantly asked, "Aren't you afraid to go home? Won't the monarchists seize back power?" But by now there could be absolutely no doubt that the victory over tsarism was complete.

Our public meeting on Russia was held the night before I left. I spoke of the revolution's achievements, and said this was only the first stage of our socialist revolution. Once workers and soldiers had organised themselves and increased their numbers in the Soviet, they could take power from the bourgeoisie and make peace between nations to end the war. Then we could begin the work of dismantling the power of capital and building socialism, giving the factories to the workers, and the land to the peasants. The battle would be long and hard and full of sacrifices, but the hour of the proletariat had come.

The normally reserved Norwegian audience was rapt, seized with sympathy and enthusiasm for Russia. "What message shall I give to our Russian comrades?" I asked them. "Shall I tell them you support us in our struggle against the imperialists for socialism and peace?"

"We support you! We support you!" they roared. "Your victory is our victory! Tell Russia we're with you!"

After the chair had finally imposed order, he read the anti-war resolution we had prepared earlier, which was passed unanimously, and the meeting ended with us all singing the *Internationale*. I left to shouts of "Safe journey!" "Hurrah for the Soviet!" and "Greetings to Lenin!"

"Back To Russia!"

Next morning I was on my way home, with Lenin's 'Letters' hidden in my corset, and as I boarded the train I felt my spirits lift.

At the remote Swedish border station of Charlottenburg, eight hundred miles north of Kristiania, a

Swedish policeman in civilian clothes entered my compartment and informed me he would be escorting me across Sweden to the Finnish border. There were crowds of workers at all the stations, but I was forbidden to get out and speak to them.

That evening we changed trains, and I was joined by Comrade Khavkin, a fluent Swedish speaker, sent by our underground comrades in Stockholm to help me if I had problems in Sweden. We stood in the corridor, avoiding my police guard. "Our Stockholm group are going back tomorrow, there's so much to tell you, it's one thing after another!" he said. "Yesterday a courier arrived from Petrograd, Maria Ivanovna, you wouldn't believe the things she said! She was allowed into Sweden with just a factory workers' pass signed by our comrades — the Swedish press has been all over her for interviews!"

He was bubbling over with excitement, and my heart raced with joy. For the first time the reality of the revolution began to sink in. I couldn't hear enough of his secondhand stories from red Petrograd, and we stood talking until late at night.

Next morning, a Russian train arrived from the Finnish station of Tornio, and we raced forward to meet it. The Russians had arrived! Most were former electricians, commandeered to make these infrequent journeys to Sweden, and they greeted us with ecstatic accounts of the new regime. "All upsidedown in one blow! No more Tsar! The people are in charge now! You're not just a worker, you're a citizen!" And with what pride they said the word. Then we all broke into the *Marseillaise* in Russian, and went on singing all the way to the next station.

There two young Swedes boarded the train and entered my compartment, one in civilian clothes, the other in the double-breasted jacket of a Swedish railway official. Were they spies, sent by the Swedish government to arrest me?

"Are you Alexandra Kollontai?" the one in uniform asked.

He was going to arrest me! I looked for Khavkin, to get him to make a phone call or send a cable and kick up a fuss.

"We're so happy to meet you and shake your hand!" he said. "We're from the Youth League of the party. We know you from *Who Needs the War?* Give workers in Russia our greetings. We rejoice with you!"

At the Swedish-Finnish border station of Haparanda, my luggage was removed to be inspected, and I was searched by a woman guard. I was afraid she would find Lenin's "Letters" in my corset, but she was more interested in whether I was concealing guns in my coiffure, and made me remove all my hairpins. Needless to say she found nothing.

When the search was over, we were seated in horse-drawn Finnish sledges, or *veiki*, of the kind I remembered from childhood, in which Finnish peasants used to drive to St Petersburg at Shrove tide. The fast little horses carried us across the broad frozen Tornionjoki River to Tornio, the first station in Finland. Far ahead lay the army barracks of Mother Russia. It was a harsh winter. A deep shroud of snow brightened the gloom of the polar swamps, and there was so much joy in our jingling sledges as we crossed the river. Russia wasn't ours yet, it was still bourgeois. But the government was being pushed aside by the workers and peasants in the Soviet, who were demanding peace and a clean sweep of the old Russia. Before us lay work and struggle, struggle and work, and on that day my soul felt as bright and fresh as the snow and the frosty air around us.

At Tornio, we climbed the steep snowy path to the

customs building, where a sentry with a red armband asked for my passport.

"I'm a political exile," I said.

"Kollontai? The Executive of the Soviet just sent a telegram to let you through. We had to fight to get it. If it wasn't for us you'd still be wandering round Europe!" And there was so much pride in his kind Russian eyes as he said this.

An officer with a bundle of papers checked my name on his long list of political exiles, and the guards quickly checked our luggage. "The soldiers are running things now!" they said.

"So what did you do with the police?" I asked. "Where are they? Did you arrest them?"

"We arrested a few, and some escaped in disguise. When they saw they were finished, most wept and begged our forgiveness, so we let them go".

Then some Russian border guards came up with news of more deaths at the front, and suddenly the mood changed. Before it had been all Russian caps-in-the-air exuberance, now it was all anger and scepticism and bewilderment. But when they spoke of the revolution they became animated again, and their stories flowed.

They said they were just off to a demonstration organised by the Finns to mourn Finnish soldiers who had died at the front, who they called "victims of the Tsar". "We're all friends of the Finns now!" they said.

In Tornio's neat clean station restaurant I threw myself at the Russian newspapers. There were no socialist ones, just the Constitutional Democrats' *Speech* and the *Stock Exchange Gazette*. But I was happy. Russia, the new Russia, wasn't a fantasy. I could see it, sense it, recognise it, and I was dizzy with joy.

The train wound slowly past the snow-covered Finnish forests and little stations packed with people, mainly soldiers, heroes of the day in their red armbands, with their proud smiling faces. I couldn't resist jumping out to make speeches, and our departing train was followed by loud hurrahs for the revolution.

We were back in the new Russia. So many changes, so many victories achieved by this great uprising of the people. And how easily Lenin's "Letters" and my manuscripts had got through!

At the Finnish border station of Beloostrov, the last checkpoint into Russia, a guard rummaged in a pile of papers and waved a red folder at me, with the words "Find and Arrest. " "Do you know what this is? It's your Tsarist arrest warrant, which has been here since 1908. And now I'm destroying it and you're a free citizen," he said, tearing it into pieces. "Welcome to free Russia!"

Chapter Six
Bolshevising the Soviet

The new Provisional Government issued decrees on the economy, education and the land question, free speech and the freedom of the press, and set out to restore morale in the officer class of the army to keep Russia in the war.

But it was the workers and soldiers in the Petrograd Soviet who held the real power now. It was the Soviet that had prevented the Duma from declaring a constitutional monarchy in March to avoid the Tsar's abdication, forcing the Prime Minister, Prince Lvov, to admit publicly, "The Provisional Government has no real powers. Its orders are obeyed only if they happen to fall in with the wishes of the Soviet of Workers' and Soldiers' Deputies".

This was despite the fact that a majority of delegates were Mensheviks or Socialist Revolutionaries (working now with liberal forces in the Soviet), who saw the Provisional Government as the best hope for the bourgeois regime they felt Russia was ready for, and the Soviet's role in this period of "dual power" as merely that of a legal opposition, which could take power only when the government had run out of energy.

Keeping a foot in both the political bodies governing Russia was its Minister of Justice and Vice Chair of the Soviet, the ambitious young lawyer Alexander Kerensky. In 1916, Kerensky had denounced the Tsar and his ministers as "cowards and assassins, guided by the contemptible Rasputin," and as the only minister with the mildest of liberal sympathies, he had been exempted from the Soviet's ban on government members. "Distrust Kerensky above all," Lenin had written to Kollontai in Norway.

Although the Bolsheviks had overcome their resistance to working with the Soviet, their group there was small and divided. Shlyapnikov was one of only a very small number of Lenin's supporters on the Soviet Executive, the Party central committee and the *Pravda* editorial board, who were regularly outvoted by a majority who lacked the confidence to assert themselves against the Provisional Government, or accept the message in Lenin's "Letters from Afar" — to turn the imperialist war into a class war against capitalism.

Pravda took particular exception to his characterisation of the Provisional Government as an "agent of Anglo-French capital, any support of which is an insult to the working class". The Soviet should be putting pressure on ministers to negotiate with Germany for a "just peace," the editors argued, taking them on "only if their actions fail to correspond to the interests of the proletariat".

Lenin believed workers in Russia had more to gain from defeat in the war than from victory, which would consolidate the supremacy of the capitalists. *Pravda* attacked his "revolutionary defeatism" as a betrayal of the German proletariat: "While the German soldier is at his post, the Russian must remain at his, answering bullet with bullet". This provoked fury from readers, and the message was not repeated. But the paper's policy of "revolutionary defencism" led most in the Party to ally themselves with the similarly patriotic Mensheviks.

On 2 April, the morning after Kollontai returned to Petrograd, she delivered Lenin's "Letters" to *Pravda*, which reported, some what unenthusiastically, "the return to Russia of Alexandra Kollontai, noted writer and representative of the Inter-national Social Democratic movement".

Shlyapnikov reported that at a Party central committee meeting held to discuss the 'Letters', after members had had time to digest them, the *Pravda* editors Lev Kamenev and the little known Josef Stalin, both recently returned from Siberian exile, had used their long experience in the underground to argue against them being published. Only the first 'Letter' appeared, on 3 April, with a fifth of the text deleted, surrounded by pieces from the editors advocating qualified support for the Provisional Government, and Stalin's attack on Lenin's ideas as "worthless".

The meeting unanimously approved Shlyapnikov's proposal to elect Kollontai to the Executive of the Soviet, once she had her man date, and she immediately set about getting one. The following article, based on her diaries, was published in March 1927 in the magazine *Red Woodworker*, one of a series of memoirs she published that year to mark the tenth anniversaries of the March and October revolutions.

"My Mandate to the Petrograd Soviet from the Woodworkers' Union"

It was 2 April 1917, my first day back in Petrograd after eight and a half years in exile. It was a completely new Russia I had returned to, without the Tsar, with a new Provisional Government, and sitting parallel to it, sharing power, the Soviet of Workers' and Soldiers' Deputies.

The city was charged with energy, exploding with ideas. On that gusty April morning, it was as if the wind had driven the entire population onto the streets, hurling the last scraps of their patriotism and submission into the gutter. Everywhere crowds of people were demonstrating, arguing, carrying banners. "Bolsheviks," "Mensheviks" were on everyone's lips.

The Soviet had not yet realised its great historic role. Lenin was still in exile, and there were only a handful of Bolshevik delegates. Most were Mensheviks, Socialist Revolutionaries and defencists.

At our Party offices, Comrade Schmidt asked me if I had my man date. "No, I've only just got back," I said.

"We must get you one then, we need to increase our numbers. Let's see which unions haven't elected anyone yet". He rummaged through some papers, and triumphantly produced the address of the Union of Woodworkers. "This one's not affiliated, but they seem friendly to us. Go and talk to them and get them on our side, they're sure to give you their mandate".

So I tramped across the city in the mud to the St Petersburg Side to get my mandate. The office of the Woodworkers' Union was in a damp-smelling basement in a street of workers' tenements, with a long unvarnished wooden table and some benches, and a narrow window letting in a little light. The only person there was a woman in a headscarf sitting on a bench.

"Can I speak to someone from the union committee?" I asked her.

"See for yourself, they're all out," she said.

"When do you expect them back?"

"They'll come when it pleases them. Do you want to see Timofei Ivanych?"

"Who's Timofei Ivanych?"

"You don't know Timofei Ivanych? He's our Chairman. You'd better sit down and wait, he makes everyone wait".

Oh well, so long as he makes everyone wait, I thought. I talked to the woman, the nightwatch-woman, janitor and cleaner, and she complained about the war. Her husband, a woodworker, had been sent off to the front, and she was struggling to survive. "Prices keep going up, you can't believe it, and the queues! You stand for hours for a bit of bread!"

Naturally I tried to "propagandise" her about the

war — who caused it and why, how it was hurting workers far from the front, and so on. She didn't argue, but the expression on her face clearly said "deliver me from idle chatter".

Half an hour went by, an hour. "Do you think they're at a meeting?" I asked her.

"Sometimes there's a meeting. They'll be back by and by. Timofei Ivanych has already been out five times today".

An hour later the door swung open and three men walked in, talking loudly. "Which of them is Timofei Ivanych?" I asked her.

"Them? They're just committee members," she said.

They glanced warily at me, wondering what sort of bird I was, then huddled in a corner, still talking. I heard the words "pay cut" and "layoffs". I went over and asked them when the rest of the committee would be back. "Don't ask us, ask Matryosha," they said.

"I've already told her Timofei Ivanych has been out five times today!" Matryosha said.

When I asked them if they had elected anyone to the Soviet, they became evasive. Who was I? What was I doing here? There was no talking to them.

Another hour passed. I was about to give up and leave, when a sturdy bearded fellow strode through the door, followed by several others. "There, that's Timofei Ivanych!" Matryosha said.

He sized me up with an experienced eye, trained to scrutinise life and detect flaws in a piece of wood. We shook hands, and he asked me if I wanted to place an order through the Soviet.

"No, I've come about something else," I said.

"If you're looking for work we've no office jobs at present, and we don't employ ladies, we can manage as we are".

Since he was Chairman it was him I had to speak to, so I tackled him head on. "Your union must elect someone to the Soviet by tomorrow, it's urgent," I said.

"You were sent by the Soviet?"

"No, by the Party, our Bolshevik central committee".

"The Bolsheviks, eh? What do they want with us?"

"Well you're a Bolshevik union aren't you?"

"Us? No, we're non-Party," he snapped, and he told me to wait, and bustled around giving orders.

His return brought crowds of woodworkers to the office, angrily protesting about their new pay cut. The committee members sat round the table discussing business, then it was my turn. I spoke about the Soviet, and they listened. Timofei Ivanych was for electing someone, but an old man was against it. "What's the use? People say all sorts of things about the Soviet, it won't do us woodworkers any good".

I put my name forward as a delegate.

"Kollontai the Bolshevik? The one in the papers who supports Germany and wants Russia to lose the war? We're honest carpenters, we don't sell our country to the Germans!"

Everyone was shouting, they were all defencists, things were going badly. Timofei Ivanych looked at me thoughtfully in silence, then said "Quiet lads, stop that racket, one at a time, this is important".

It seemed he wasn't so against the Bolsheviks now. He began to speak, and was about to propose something, when a small man in glasses hurried in, clearly not a woodworker, probably a Menshevik. Timofei Ivanych stopped what he was saying, and the man threw up his hands. "Who told you you could talk to the Bolsheviks?" he said, as if he owned him.

Timofei Ivanych stood up and took him aside, and they whispered together for a long time. The Menshevik seemed to be having trouble convincing him. "Tell your Bolshevik committee not to send us any more Soviet delegates off the streets," Timofei Ivanych said at last. "It's the union's business who we elect, we're non-Party".

"That's right! Don't send us Bolsheviks who betray their country!" shouted the committee members.

"Calm down, it's all settled," Timofey Ivanych said, and the Menshevik stuck his hands in his pockets and gloated.

So I left the woodworkers empty-handed, cursing Comrade Schmidt for sending me to this nest of defencists!

Four days later, the Chair of our Bolshevik Military Committee, Comrade Podvoisky, introduced me to a regiment of soldiers as their delegate. At first they said, "It's not right, a woman representing us". But a day later they had recovered from their shock, and given me their mandate.

***

I next met Timofei Ivanych six months later, in the heady days of October. News had just reached us from our first Red Front that we had defeated the Cossacks at Gachina and saved Petrograd, and Kerensky had fled abroad. Our Bolshevik headquarters in the Smolny were a seething cauldron. People packed the halls and corridors — who knew who you would meet. And there I ran into a sturdy bearded Red Guard in a peaked cap with a rifle on his shoulder.

"So you've joined us now, Timofei Ivanych!" I said.

"Something about the Mensheviks didn't suit my proletarian way of thinking," he said. "Our adviser was a learned man, I thought he knew more than we did. Then you came about your mandate, and it set me thinking about the war. I'm just back from the front. We defended Gachina and we'll defend the soviets. Come and see us again. We won't send you away next time, our union is Bolshevik now!"

We parted like old friends, and both went back to work, and in those stormy months I had no time to visit him. But in early 1918 I learned that Timofei Ivanych had been killed fighting the Whites. He died a hero, defending the workers' and peasants' revolution, and the woodworkers continued the work of Great October, ending the world of the exploiters.

The war had re-energised Russia's feminist movement. Aristocrats, intellectuals and former members of the Equal Rights League had thrown themselves into the war effort, hoping to be rewarded with the vote, and the Provisional Government's omission of women's suffrage from its programme had caused huge anger.

On Kollontai's first day back in Petrograd, forty thousand women marched on the Soviet building in a patriotic display of armoured cars, "Amazons" on horseback, and two orchestras. She joined the crowds listening to speeches from the various women's organisations, calling for improved opportunities for professional women, attached to a patriotic programme of fighting the war to victory. When the Chair of the Soviet, the Menshevik Chkheidze, came out to assure them that delegates were working with the Provisional Government to win them their voting rights, she shouted "Stop the war! All power to the soviets!" Angry feminists rushed to attack her, and a group of soldiers carried her off on their shoulders to a small counter-demonstration of soldiers' wives and widows, chanting "Peace!" "Bread for our children!"

A week later, in a demonstration she organised to match that of the feminists, fifteen thousand war widows marched along the Nevsky Prospect to present the Soviet with their demand for an increase in their wretched monthly benefits.

Few Bolsheviks had imagined that the women's demonstrations in March would lead to the overthrow of the Tsar, and articles in *Pravda* paid tribute to their heroic role in the revolution. Thousands of women were being drawn into politics for the first time, joining the Bolsheviks as some of their most militant members, pushing their demands so far to the left that virtually separate organisations of the Party were springing up. Plans were approved to revive the Party women's paper *Woman Worker*, first published in 1914, weekly now instead of monthly, and Kollontai was elected to its editorial board.

But the Bolsheviks' approach to women was as cautious as their tactics for building socialism and ending the war, and she urged the Party to appeal to them more boldly. Activists had been working successfully with their local parties to set up women's committees, and she proposed expanding these into nationwide women's sections, on the German model, which would elect delegates to a central bureau, responsible for organising campaigns for labour reforms and the vote, and writing and distributing leaflets "specifically directed at proletarian women". She emphasised that the sections' work would be subordinate to the Party, and would operate only with its full agreement. But her proposal was overwhelmingly rejected, on the grounds that it would lead to separate women's organisations, and "produce sexual antagonisms in the proletariat".

She was one of just eight women delegates to the Soviet, only four of them Bolsheviks (two from the Textileworkers' Union), and the only woman on its Executive. In her first article for *Pravda* after her return to Petrograd, published on 5 April, she argued that women could make their place in the reorganisation of power only by getting more delegates elected. "It's not only the Provisional Government that wants to settle itself more comfortably in power by opening the door to women with property, excluding the workers and peasants and soldiers' wives who threaten to turn the state on its head. It's the hypocrites with red armbands in the Soviet too. Women will never be handed their rights on a plate! We must take them ourselves and fight for our own interests!"

Five days later, women weavers at Petrograd's Baranov Textile Mill quoted her article in a letter to *Pravda* announcing that they were electing delegates.

Under pressure from Lenin's supporters in the Soviet, led by Shlyapnikov, the Provisional Government had been negotiating with the German authorities for him and thirty-two exiles in Switzerland to return to Russia, in exchange for an equal number of German prisoners of war in Russia, in the special "sealed train" that would take them across German territory.

On 9 April, Lenin and his wife Nadezhda Krupskaya and their party of exiles set off from Switzerland, and a week-long Party conference was held in Petrograd as the Bolsheviks prepared to welcome him back. Supported by the Moscow party and thirteen local organisations, Shlyapnikov and Kollontai spoke for the Leninist minority against Kamenev and Stalin, attacking their claim that the most the Soviet could hope for was to "persuade" the Provisional Government to propose peace to the warring countries. Proceedings were then interrupted by a telegram from Lenin: "Our only guarantee to arm the workers. No alliance with other parties. Last is *sine qua non*. We don't trust Chkheidze". Kollontai and Shlyapnikov proposed a motion in support of his "Letters", calling the Soviet the "embryo of Soviet power," and the March revolution "the point of departure for the revolutionary movement of the entire European proletariat". But they were hugely outvoted by Stalin's resolution, backed by fifty-nine party organisations, calling on Bolsheviks in the Soviet to work constructively with the Provisional Government — "fortifier of the people's conquests, in its great and useful tasks".

Kollontai was the only Bolshevik to speak in support of Lenin's first speech to the Petrograd Soviet in April. In the piece below from her diaries, published posthumously in 1962 in the popular Moscow daily paper the *Literary Gazette,* she describes the impact of his return to Russia on her comrades in the Party and Soviet.

"Lenin's Arrival in Petrograd"

On 16 April, the central committee of the Party sent me with Belenin [Shlyapnikov's underground name] to welcome Lenin back to Russia, with a bunch of flowers and a speech.

At the border station of Beloostrov, we pushed through the crowds jostling for his attention as he and Krupskaya got off the train. I clasped his hand, and Belenin embraced him and pushed me forward, saying "Well if you're not going to make a speech, you can at least kiss Ilich!"

"He's exhausted," Krupskaya said. "Crowds of Finns turned out at all the stations and he made speeches. All he wants is a glass of tea".

On the train back to Petrograd, Belenin, Kamenev and I sat in Lenin's compartment, Krupskaya and their friend Inessa Armand were in the next one. The corridors were packed with his comrades, desperate to speak to him. Throwing off his coat and cap and his tiredness, he questioned them, listening closely to what they said, frowning only when Kamenev raised his objections to his 'Letters'.

Next morning, I set off early to the meeting of our Bolshevik group in the Soviet. I was living at the time with friends on Kirochnaya Street, and if I was lucky I would catch a cab to the Tauride Palace. Generally though I went on foot, and that day I was glad to walk. It was a sunny spring morning, like summer, and after seeing Lenin I was in a buoyant cheerful mood. How joyfully people had welcomed him back. Huge crowds of workers and soldiers gathered to cheer his speeches at the Finland Station, and from the balcony of the Bolsheviks' military headquarters at the Kshesinskaya Palace. What he said was already familiar to me from his articles and letters. But knowing he was here in this new upturned Russia gave me new energy and confidence, and I was happy that our Bolshevik comrades who were still wavering would be called to account.

I hurried to the gallery where our group met, and found them heatedly discussing his ideas. For many of them, these were quite new and unexpected. Those who knew I had been in contact with Ilich in exile drew round with their doubts and questions, and I did my best to explain things. But I couldn't help wondering if his writings we had smuggled into Russia had ever arrived. Had all our postal work in Scandinavia really equipped our comrades at home so poorly? Why did they find it so hard to grasp his great thoughts on turning the bourgeois revolution into a socialist revolution, and ending the war?

The meeting was opened by the worker Paderin, who said Lenin was to speak at a joint plenary session of the Soviet, attended by all the socialist delegates. Several in our group, including Kamenev, objected that this was premature, and that they needed more time to familiarise themselves with his ideas. But it was no time for reflection, it was time for action, and we moved to the circular hall of the Tauride for the joint session of the socialists.

Crowds filled the corridors, shouting and arguing. The Menshevik Martov was telling a group of his supporters that no sane member of the Soviet would accept Lenin's calls for a "Blanquist" insurrection, led by a handful of revolutionaries — "Russians don't like utopias!" I was greeted by soldiers who had heard him speak at yesterday's demonstrations, and when we learnt he was already in the building, we hurried to the hall.

The delegates' benches were packed, and the atmosphere was charged with excitement, the hope that he would say something new, to end the war and put things in their place. He slipped almost unnoticed to the platform, and sat not at the podium but on a chair behind it, with his Bolshevik supporters. "It's Lenin!" the whisper went up. I could see the hostility of most in the audience, the disdainful distrust of the Mensheviks and their bourgeois allies as they prepared to listen to his "utopias". He was greeted by the Bolsheviks with loud cheers and applause. But our left group, sitting on the left side of the hall, was still very small.

Chkheidze presided, and gave Lenin the floor. He didn't speak from the podium, but walked unhurriedly to the edge of the plat form, wanting to be as close to his audience as possible, ad dressing them as he had addressed meetings of political exiles in Geneva, Paris and London. Those on the soldiers' and workers' benches gazed at him with attentive expectant eyes, drinking in his words.

He began in a calm clear voice, speaking extraordinarily quietly and simply, and many said afterwards that it was as if he had put into words what they had been thinking all along. But he was speaking of great and important things — of how to get the revolution running along completely new lines, and how working people, the soldiers, sailors and peasants, could build a new life for themselves through the power of the soviets. The bourgeoisie was too weak to govern Russia, he said. Only the soviets could stop the fighting. It was only when Bolsheviks were in the majority in the Petrograd Soviet that we could begin our socialist revolution, without taking our lead from abroad, or allowing Russia's landowners and capitalists to seize back power, but through our own efforts and determination, relying on the teachings of Marx to build socialism. But first we had to stop the war, in which millions of Russians were being slaughtered for the glory of the Allies.

The audience held its breath, as though under his spell. His voice became more heated as he went on, insisting that any rapprochement with the traitors to the workers' cause was unthinkable. Only the soviets could save Russia from anarchy and collapse, and workers from capitalist exploitation. The hall thundered with applause.

In his speech, later published as his *April Theses*, Lenin de fined the role of our Party in the next socialist stage of the revolution, and the true purpose of the Petrograd Soviet — to give power to the workers and peasants. For many his words were a revelation. Others grappled with his uncompromising message, while the enemies of the revolution struggled to contain their rage.

It was astonishing to see how swiftly people's expressions changed, as the logical chain of his ideas unfolded. The Mensheviks looked at first confused, then distraught and angry. By contrast, the faces of the soldiers and workers cleared, as if a fog had lifted. The great hall of the Soviet was used to hearing empty speeches from the Mensheviks and Socialist Revolutionaries. Now the leader of his people was speaking, about the goals of the revolution that would free them from the power of capital and end the war.

What frightened the appeasers and compromisers most was the clarity with which he developed his brilliant conclusions. He spoke quite differently from orators and phrasemongers like the little lawyer Kerensky or the mellifluous Menshevik Tsereteli. It wasn't a speech, it was a serious political discussion he was having with members of the Soviet, making his points so clearly and sharply that they were grasped by every worker and soldier, as if he was addressing each one of them personally.

"The immediate task of the Soviet of Workers' and Soldiers' Deputies is to prepare for the seizure of power. Only the Soviet can give people peace, bread and freedom," he ended, to more storms of applause.

First to speak against him was the young Menshevik Voitinsky, who accused him of wanting to bring chaos and disunity to the revolution, saying his call to raise the banner of class war was the greatest threat yet to its survival. He was followed by the elderly Menshevik Meshkovsky-Goldenberg, who nominated him to the throne of the anarchist Bakunin. Speaker after speaker stood up to attack him, not only Menshevik and unaffiliated delegates, but several from our benches too.

I was annoyed that our group hadn't prepared a resolution in solidarity with him. We had to show the cowards we supported him, and I decided I would have to speak myself. There were many angry faces in the audience, and my speech was interrupted by catcalls and jeers. But I was so inspired I forgot to be nervous, as I normally am when I speak in public.

Krupskaya and Inessa Armand smiled encouragingly at me from the front row, and after I finished I sat next to Vladimir Ilich, who had taken his seat at the podium. He listened calmly as more delegates spoke against him, and he seemed to be studying them and getting their measure; he was clearly less interested in the individual members of the Soviet than in its general composition. He stopped listening, and beckoned members of our group over to ask who delegates were, and about their politics. When Chkheidze gave the floor to Tsereteli, he faced him and listened intently to what he had to say. But when Tsereteli proposed electing a committee to organise a "unity conference" to patch up our differences, he turned to me with an ironic smile and said, "He's not stupid, but look what the Mensheviks have come to!"

Our rejection of Tsereteli's proposal produced uproar. I had never seen such a commotion in the hall, there was almost a riot. Lenin had rattled the authority of the Mensheviks, forcing many of them to rethink their positions, which was exactly what he wanted. Delegates whispered urgently together, barely following the next part of the proceedings, and Chkheidze had to call repeatedly for order.

But our boycott of the elections was more than just empty words, we meant business, and we left the meeting with a new sense of moral victory. Lenin had spread panic in the capitalist ministers, who wanted to believe the revolution was over. For the Mensheviks, his words were a bombshell, bringing chaos to their ranks, and my speech earned me the hatred of our enemies in the Soviet, who called me the "Valkyrie of the Revolution". But the workers and the rank and file soldiers had grasped his ideas, and it was after this that we began to increase our numbers in the Soviet, gradually crowding out the compromisers who had betrayed the workers, not only in Petrograd but across the whole of Russia. For me it was the start of a new life, agitating for peace and the power of the soviets, and for the liberation and full equality of women.

Shlyapnikov was put in charge of organising the Bolsheviks' new armed workers' militia, the Red Guards, and throughout that spring revolutionaries flocked back to Petrograd. Trotsky returned in May, and assumed leadership of the anti-war 'Interdistrict' group in the Soviet, which voted with the Bolsheviks. Several Menshevik delegates called on the Provisional Government to arrest Lenin as a traitor, and over the next hectic months Kollontai joined the campaign against her old Menshevik allies to "Bolshevise" the Soviet. She became one of the Bolsheviks' most popular and powerful public speakers, taking their message to mass meetings of soldiers and factory workers, calling on women to fight for their rights and an end to their exploitation.

Soldiers' wives and widows in Petrograd had formed their own trade union, and similar unions were springing up across Russia. Petrograd's four thousand laundresses were on strike, and the new restaurant workers' union appealed in the Bolsheviks' *Workers' Paper* for support from "women in the capital's tea rooms". Maids and domestic servants were demonstrating in the streets for better pay and conditions. Women in the bakeries and chocolate and tobacco factories were demanding protection for pregnant women and mothers, and workers at Moscow's Frolic Textile Mill were demanding a hundred percent wage increase for men, and a 125 percent increase for women.

At the end of April, Kollontai attended Russia's first legal trade union conference as a delegate of the Textileworkers' Union. In her article "A Serious Gap", published in *Pravda* a week before the conference opened, she took the organisers to task for excluding women's working conditions and low pay from the agenda. She called for a clearer class strategy from the unions against capitalism, "involving the mass activity of the organised proletariat," and for a proper commitment to involving women in their work and fighting for equal pay. "Every class-conscious worker knows that the value of male labour is dependent on the value of female labour, and that by replacing male workers with cheaper women, the capitalists can undercut men's wages, driving them down to the level of women's. Only a complete lack of understanding could lead one to see equal pay as an exclusively 'women's issue,' and to accuse those demanding it of 'feminism.'" This was the message of the resolution she proposed to the conference, which was passed unanimously.

In preparing the first issue of the resurrected *Woman Worker*, the editors visited women at their workplaces to interview them for their articles, and Kollontai was invited by the leader of the laundresses' strike to speak at their meetings. They had been the first workers in March to come out on strike against their inhuman working conditions — demanding shorter hours, higher wages, the municipalisation and mechanisation of laundries, and the arrest of the managers. Inspired by their courage, she persuaded *Pravda* to devote a page every day to the strike, and the laundresses' demands soon included the Bolshevik slogans against the war and the Provisional Government. They won their main demands in May, and in her *Pravda* article "In the Line of Fire", she celebrated their victory as "a victory for the entire working class, and powerful evidence that workers can take on the bosses and win".

The first issue of *Woman Worker* appeared at the end of May, with her front-page appeal to women to elect Bolshevik delegates to the Soviet, who would fight for their rights and for an end to the war.

"Our Tasks"

A mighty task faces us in Russia, to make a better life for our selves and our children than under Bloody Nicholas.

The Russian proletariat has a special place in the hearts of workers throughout the world. Our great revolution has put us in the front ranks of those fighting to curb the appetites of the exploiters and win state power for the workers and peasants. Now we must use our new freedom, won by the blood of our comrades, to achieve the speediest possible end to the war, which is killing our sons, husbands and brothers. Our women comrades abroad are waiting for us to take the lead.

As we mobilise our forces to build the new democratic Russia, our main task must be to explain to our comrades, women and men, that this war is not our war, it is the capitalists' war, and that it is only the Bolsheviks in the Soviet who are fighting to stop more proletarian blood being shed.

In the struggle to win power for the powerless and build the new social order, much depends on us women. Gone are the days when the victory of the workers' cause depended solely on men. The war has led to huge changes in women's lives, forcing many to take jobs they would never previously have dreamt of. In 1912, there were only forty-five women for every hundred men in the factories. Now it's not uncommon for women to outnumber men by almost a third.

The success of workers' struggle for a better life — for higher wages and the shorter working day, for more hospitals and better schools for our children, for health insurance, unemployment pay and pensions — depends on the thousands of women now entering the ranks of the organised working class. Weren't the women who came onto the streets in March the first to raise the Red Banner of revolution? Let us join them now, in the Soviet of Workers' and Soldiers' Deputies, in the trade unions and in the Bolshevik Party, to end the bloody war between nations, and call to account those in the Soviet who have betrayed the great working class doctrine of solidarity and unity.

The more women who join the struggle, the sooner the exploiters will capitulate. All our hopes lie in organisation. Only when women and men of all countries organise together to defeat the capitalists can we build a better future and a new socialist world, run by the workers themselves.

To win peace, state power must pass from those responsible for the slaughter to our delegates in the Soviet. Comrade women workers, don't stand aside! Join the fight against the war and rising prices. Join our ranks, the ranks of the Bolsheviks in the Soviet. On our own, we are straws any boss can break! United and organised, we are a mighty force no power can destroy!

Between May and October Kollontai published over thirty articles for *Pravda* and *Woman Worker* and for anti-war publications in Germany, France, Finland, Norway and America and Lenin urged her to write more. The first issue of *Woman Worker* sold out immediately. The print run was increased from forty to fifty thousand, and the editors organised mass *Woman Worker* rallies at Petrograd's Cirque Moderne — the "factory of dreams" — where thousands gathered to hear them speak of revolution and women's liberation.

As Soviet delegate for the Bolsheviks' military organisation, Kollontai took this message to packed soldiers' meetings in Petrograd's garrisons, and to sailors' meetings on board the battleships at Helsingfors, the main base of the Imperial Baltic Fleet in the Gulf of Finland. Sailors at the Kronstadt naval base had elected a Bolshevik Revolutionary Committee in March to run their affairs. Bolsheviks at Helsingfors were still in a minority. But the sailors had elected the Bolshevik Pavel Dybenko chair of the new revolutionary Central Committee of the Baltic Fleet, *Tsentrobalt*. Dybenko had persuaded them not to carry out the orders of the Provisional Government unless they were authorised by *Tsentrobalt*, and he had refused to allow Kerensky on the ships, inspiring the story that he had thrown him overboard when he arrived to give one of his speeches. He was popular, charismatic and idealistic, a brilliant organiser and public speaker. Kollontai called him the "Soul of the Fleet, steadfast and totally fearless," and that spring they embarked on a passionate love affair. "It was his powers of feeling, his capacity to experience everything so fully, so ardently, that drew me to him," she wrote. "Our meetings were always a joy beyond measure, our partings full of heartrending anguish".

She was forty-five and an aristocrat, he was fifteen years younger, from a family of illiterate Ukrainian day-labourers, and their affair was considered very scandalous in Party circles. But as she had written six years earlier in her article "Sexual Relations and the Social Struggle," "A professor can marry his young working-class student, or a doctor his cook, and they will be praised for raising her status. But heaven help the woman professor or doctor who sleeps with her young male student or cook — and if he is handsome and has 'physical qualities,' so much the worse!"

Dybenko was one of the main organisers of Petrograd's huge May Day rally, at which an estimated million workers and armed sailors, soldiers and Red Guards assembled on the Field of Mars to mourn the martyrs of the March revolution, bearing banners with the Bolshevik slogans "All Power to the Soviets!" "Victory to the International Solidarity of the Proletariat!" "Peace, Bread and Land!"

Fearing that revolution was imminent, five ministers resigned from the Provisional Government, which then frantically opened negotiations with the Soviet to form a new coalition cabinet, picking Kerensky as its Minister of War. Kerensky committed Russia to fighting to victory, and toured the battlefronts giving patriotic speeches. But when he declared a new offensive in Galicia in June, most of Petrograd's soldiers refused to leave their barracks, and those who did were slaughtered in their thousands when the offensive collapsed three weeks later.

As the Provisional Government slipped into chaos, inflation soared to 400 percent, and bread rations in the capital were cut to 100 grams a day. Soldiers again stormed the jails, releasing four hundred political prisoners, and demonstrators took over the streets, breaking into the bakeries and setting more buildings on fire, calling for workers' power and the end of the war.

On the third of July, workers at the Putilov arms factory started another strike, demanding control over wages and production, the arrest of the bosses, and the immediate transfer of power to the soviets. This rapidly escalated into a general strike in the capital, and strikes spread across Russia. Dybenko and his sailors were besieging Lenin at the Party offices, demanding that the Bolsheviks call an armed rising before it was too late. "Better die for freedom and dignity than live without either!" Dybenko said. Lenin insisted that the Bolsheviks must take power in an orderly fashion, through the Soviet. But as Petrograd's citizens poured onto the streets, the Party changed tack, and decided its place was with them.

On the fourteenth, three machine gun regiments gathered outside the Soviet headquarters at the Tauride Palace, supported by several armoured cars donated by the army, and hundreds of Red Guards and women fighters. By the sixteenth, they had been joined by seven more regiments, twenty thousand sailors from the Helsingfors and Kronstadt garrisons, and half a million demonstrators, carrying Bolshevik placards saying "Down with the Capitalist Ministers in the Soviet!" "Down with the War!" Braving police snipers from the roof, and ignoring Lenin's pleas for calm, Dybenko and his sailors climbed through the windows of the Tauride, demanding to meet the Soviet's leaders, shouting "We trust the Soviet, but not those the Soviet trusts!", before Trotsky ordered them back.

Trotsky and Dybenko were among hundreds arrested and jailed on the spot. The elite Izmailovsky Battalion was recalled from the front to put down the rising, and four hundred were killed in the "July Days" by forces still loyal to Kerensky. Workers selling *Pravda* on the streets were shot, and the Party's offices were raided, and the Bolsheviks were "unmasked" as agents of Germany, which was claimed to have financed and orchestrated the insurrection. Lenin escaped to Finland, and Kollontai was jailed in a mass roundup of Bolsheviks charged with "grave crimes against the state".

Her memoirs of her months in jail were published in 1927 as a pamphlet by the Society of Political Prisoners and Exiles. The ellipses in the excerpts below are again mine.

From *In Kerensky's Prison*

"Shall I let you go? On your own head be it!" said the young officer escorting me to the Vyborg women's prison. How young he was!

The dark prison gates swung open and swallowed up our car. "Make sure you give her a good cell with plenty of light!" I heard him say to the wardress as she checked my papers. "The prison isn't a hotel!" she snapped.

She led me up a metal staircase to a gallery on the right, and stopped at cell 58. The door crashed shut and I was locked inside.

I was inaugurating the prison's new political wing in the new bourgeois republican Russia, freshly decorated for its first intake of women spies. There was a stool and a hard wooden bunk, a shelf with a basin and some washing things, and a high barred window letting in a few dusty beams of light. I fell asleep instantly, and was woken with a cup of hot water and a hunk of black bread; prisoners bought their own tea.

The prison day had begun. My thoughts were racing. How powerful was the reaction? Were our sailors alive? Had our Party survived?

At midday I was visited by the prison director, a fat whiskered garrulous man appointed by the new authorities, who held forth at length about the "baseness" of the Bolsheviks. The "traitors" had all been arrested, he said, and had "repented and confessed".

Confessed to what? I asked.

"Working with the German General Staff. There's powerful evidence against you too. There's your correspondence with the Germans, and your telegram 'Tell Vera can't leave, dentist's appointment.' What does 'dentist's appointment' mean, and who is 'Vera'?"

I was speechless. I didn't yet know of the "case" the Mensheviks had cooked up against us.

I learnt nothing from him about events in the outside world, and my request to buy a newspaper was denied. I was told that due to the "major case" against me, I was under "harsh conditions," forbidden walks, visitors or reading matter.

A long, long prison day. How many more lay ahead? For lunch there was beetroot salad, quite edible for those days. Then the usual bread and hot water, and the light was switched off at nine. Deathly quiet. The white night turned blue at the window. This is how they cut us off from the Party and the world.

Identical empty days in Kerensky's prison. The director visited regularly at noon, and sat on the stool denouncing the Bolsheviks and those who had fallen into their "web". I clearly didn't realise what sort of criminals they were — not regular criminals, political criminals. "What could be worse than betraying your country?"

His favourite topic was "his" prison. He had landed in the perfect job. He took huge pride in its cleanness and its new bathhouse, that the food was better than in town, and that he saved the prison "a few kopecks". "That buckwheat yesterday, so sweet and tasty, I got it cheap, under the counter!"

I wrote my statement. The older wardresses were cold and polite, patriots who had served under the Tsarist regime and hated the Bolsheviks. "When the hooligans let the criminals out onto the streets, they set fire to our new mattresses," one said....

I was finally allowed a food parcel, which I shared with a war dress who looked hungry. I gave her some bread and sugar and a tin of condensed milk, and she put them in her pocket and softened a little. "They're for my cats," she explained. "I've no one, no family, no friends, just my cats. The boys are all tabby and Blacky's kittens are all white, I can't understand it!"

The ice was broken, and from then on she kept me informed of events in the cat world....

Why wasn't I allowed walks? Why had the Soviet done nothing to get me released? Chkheidze clearly took the line that the Bolsheviks must be destroyed. But what of our thousands of "supporters," who applauded us at meetings and voted for our resolutions? Was is too early? How long must we wait? It's one thing waiting when you're busy and active. But the solitude and inactivity filled with endless anxieties....

One morning the director arrived with a corpulent police-chief, who examined me over-familiarly, and glanced round my cell with searching eyes.

The case against the Bolsheviks was extremely serious, he said. Hundreds of my "co-conspirators" had been arrested; there were so many important threads to unravel, it could take months, possibly years, to bring all the facts to light.

"You know you're the only woman we've arrested? You're close friends with Lenin? 'Best friends'?"

"We're comrades, yes".

"Ah, so that's what you call it!"

For a long time I couldn't shake off his vileness. Had the Provisional Government grown so powerful it could hold us indefinitely? Would we face months, years of inactivity?

That evening the director returned, and said "It seems there's a watertight case against you. It's all Lenin's doing. What is he exactly? A businessman? Why is he in hiding? Where is he?"

My heart leapt with joy. Lenin was in hiding! Suddenly things didn't seem so hopeless any more.

Next day my hot water was brought by a pretty young wardress hired by the new regime, her eyes red from weeping.

I asked her what the matter was, and of course it was "him". Her boyfriend was refusing to marry her, and she had given her heart and soul to him, and didn't know if he loved her or was just playing with her. I shared her grief with her, and she forgot that she was forbidden to talk to prisoners, and I was a Bolshevik. "Well if the Bolsheviks think like that they must be good people, and what everyone says about them is all lies!" she said.

After that she often visited in the evenings when the prison was quiet. She was from a worker's family, and it was easy to talk to her and explain what we wanted and what power to the soviets meant. She said my comrades were "neighbours" in the "Crosses" men's jail, and were being held in far better conditions, allowed books, walks and visitors. And it turned out that her boyfriend was one of us too.

A week later, she took me to my first interrogation. An unprepossessing grey-faced prosecutor sat at a table behind a mound of documents, and informed me of the charges against me: assisting Russia's defeat in the war by calling for an armed mutiny in the navy, and leading a "secret mission" to Germany to negotiate loans to fund the insurrection. There were twelve files of prosecution evidence against me, he said, and referred to my telegrams to Lenin in Switzerland, and to ensigns Semashko and Ermoshenko in the Baltic Fleet — neither of whom I knew. "Vital new evidence" was apparently being collected for an even more serious case....

A month after I arrived, I was finally allowed to walk in the yard, and I saw the sky and the racing clouds, and felt the hot August sun.

Next morning I was taken for my walk by one of the older war dresses. She always had a melancholy expression, and as we silently made our three circles of the yard, she kept her eyes on the ground, and I saw she was weeping.

We stopped. "What's wrong, Maria Dmitrevna?" I asked her.

She wiped her eyes, and told me that her son, her precious only son, the joy of her life, had been sent to the front. "He's only a child, and so kind, with such a generous heart!" And from her mother's grief, we passed to the Bolsheviks, and the power of the soviets.

Half an hour passed in a flash, and by the time we got back to my cell we both agreed no one needed the war. But Maria Dmitrevna still locked me in that night, and I was a prisoner of the defencists again....

I had a new neighbour in the next cell, an American dancer arrested as a spy, a noisy quarrelsome woman who complained to the director through an interpreter about the food, and demanded a "prison inspection". The wardresses didn't like her, but were fascinated by her silk underwear and her ballet shoes. "When you go in she's standing on her toes! She says if she doesn't dance her legs go stiff!"

The night she arrived, I was woken by the thunder of boots on the stairs, and women's hysterical shrieks and sobbing. "Help! Get off me, you're killing me!" Then the roar of men's voices and the crashing of prison doors, and more sobbing. "Help! Help! Let go of me, I'm dying!"

Next morning, I was told by a wardress that when the criminal wing was full, criminals would be thrown in the political cells for the night.

Once I was taken for my walk with some "criminals," a gang of robbers. Their leader was a smartly dressed woman in a silk dress with manicured hands, known as "the Baroness". She came over and sized me up. "So this is Kallantaikha the Bolshevik German spy!" she said. Most of her gang were just young girls. "She's a child murderer," the wardress said, pointing to a thin flat-chested little girl. "How old is she?" I asked. "Fourteen," she said....

After five weeks, I began to receive messages smuggled in by the wardresses — greetings from the Baltic sailors, a note from a group of women tram conductors, saying that their spirits weren't broken and the defencists hadn't won....

Day. Night. Day. This morning I woke in an uncontrollably cheerful mood, with a wonderful sense of *joie de vivre*. I tidied my cell and waited for my walk, and outside I plucked up the courage to speak to the young wardress who carries a knout. The little prison yard was used to store firewood, and the smell of the logs was so fresh and resinous that if you closed your eyes you could be in a forest.

When I returned to my cell I had summoned up all my inner strength, and I was resigned. Three years inside, so be it. Five years, so be it. But no, I was sure it wouldn't be that long. The Provisional Government was just marking time. It couldn't respond to people's needs for Soviet power and an end to the war. It didn't understand that history demanded a step forward to a new socialist future...

Kollontai was still in jail in August when the Provisional Government finally bowed to popular pressure and passed its Universal Suffrage Law, giving women the vote. Trotsky had joined the Bolsheviks in July, and the following month he and Kollontai were both elected *in absentia* to the central committee of the underground Party.

In September, her comrades negotiated her release on health grounds. She was then sentenced to a month's house arrest, under permanent police guard. There were more police interrogations, at which she was told of a new case being prepared against her as part of another mass roundup of the Bolsheviks. "But the interrogations were perfunctory," she wrote. "The authorities were clearly out of their depth with all the prosecutions".

In the last week of September, Trotsky and Dybenko led a prisoners' riot at the "Crosses," after which they were both released without charges. Trotsky was then immediately re-elected Chair of the Petrograd Soviet, the post he had held twelve years earlier, reminding cheering dele gates that in 1905 the Soviet had been smashed: "We are stronger now than ever!"

Dybenko returned to Helsingfors, by now a major centre of

Bolshevik power in the navy, like Kronstadt, and on Kollontai's release from house arrest she joined him there, speaking at sailors' meetings on board the ships.

Soldiers at the front faced another brutal winter in the trenches, and the peasants' war in the countryside was past the point of no return. The fuel crisis was forcing hundreds of factories across Russia to close, and the country was swept with more hunger riots. "We have entered the zone of collapse," a Bolshevik delegate told a factory conference in the capital.

The Party central committee had swung dramatically to the left since July, and by the first week of October, the Petrograd Soviet under Trotsky's leadership had a Bolshevik majority. It was the same with the Moscow Soviet, and with soviets in industrial cities across the Volga region, Siberia and Ukraine. The Bolsheviks, led by Lenin and Trotsky, were ready to plan the seizure of power. "We stand on the threshold of the world revolution," Lenin wrote from his hiding place in Finland.

On 11 October, Lenin arrived in Petrograd in heavy disguise to attend the historic secret meeting of the central committee held to plan the Bolshevik seizure of power, at which Kollontai voted with the majority in support of the motion "The armed rising has fully and inevitably matured".

By then the Provisional Government had lost the support of all the main regiments, and its military headquarters had passed to the control of the Soviet. But to give the revolution the appearance of a planned transition, it was decided that the Bolsheviks would take power on 25 October, the opening day of the Second All-Russian Congress of Soviets. Trotsky was elected to lead the new Revolutionary Military Soviet, which was to keep the central committee in touch with the regiments leading the insurrection, and Kollontai was elected to head the commission bringing the Party's programme up to date.

By 23 October, Red Guards had occupied Petrograd's Central Post Office, the main railway stations, the Ministry of Religion and the State Bank, and she moved into the Smolny Institute, the new headquarters of the revolution. The following night,

Lenin cabled the Smolny from his new hiding place in the capital: "Everything now hangs on a thread! The issues before us won't be resolved by speeches or congresses, even by the Congress of Soviets, but by the armed masses. We may lose everything!! We cannot wait!!!"

Cables were then sent to Helsingfors and Kronstadt, ordering "regulations" to be sent to Petrograd. "The sailors will sail at dawn," Dybenko cabled back.

At 2.30 am on 25 October, Lenin appeared at the Smolny to address the central committee. Scattered rifle fire was heard as a group of Tsarist cadets tried to stop workers crossing the Neva bridge from Vyborg. But a detachment of Bolshevik sailors went to defend them, then marched with them to the Smolny, reporting that they were ready to conquer or die.

The promised flotilla was very late, and it was seven in the evening when the Battleship *Aurora,* followed by three torpedo boats, finally sailed down the Neva river into the capital and aimed its cannon at the Winter Palace, where the Provisional Government was in session. That evening the Congress of Soviets opened in the Smolny, and amid muffled blanks from the *Aurora*, Lenin announced that the Bolsheviks were in power. "We shall now proceed to the construction of the new socialist order".

Chapter Seven
Bolshevik Power

In the early hours of 26 October, Lenin appeared before the Congress to ask for its endorsement of the new government, the Commissariat of People's Commissars. He then read the Bolsheviks' Declaration of Peace, "to the peoples of all the warring countries," calling on their governments to agree to an immediate armistice.

Dybenko was elected Commissar of the Navy, and Shlyapnikov was Commissar of Labour. When Lenin proposed Trotsky as the obvious choice for President, or Commissar of People's Commissars, he flatly refused, and Lenin finally took the job himself, with Trotsky elected Commissar of Foreign Affairs.

Kollontai was equally reluctant to accept her post as Commissar of Welfare, the government's only woman. In her diaries of the Revolution, she described "extreme happiness, watchfulness, and an awareness of our responsibilities. One cannot imagine what high demands were made of us, who were complete amateurs in state administration. I was totally lacking in the qualifications needed".

She was the predictable choice to take over this conventionally "feminine" ministry, established by the Provisional Government, which traced its origins back to the numerous charitable institutions funded by Catherine the Great — a ramshackle operation largely subsidised by the revenue from Russia's state-owned playing cards factories. From her predecessor in the Provincial Government, Countess Panina, she inherited responsibility for war veterans' benefits and old-age pensions, homes for the elderly, leper colonies, orthopaedic workshops, mental hospitals, TB sanatoriums, and Russia's wretched orphanages and foundlings' homes, exalted by the names of their royal patrons — the "angel factories". All were crying out for money, which would be avail able only if the managers of the playing cards factories agreed to work with the government.

The day after the Bolsheviks took power, the new Committee to Save the Country paid civil servants in all the commissariats a month's wages to come out on strike and paralyse the new regime. Confident that the Revolution would collapse in a few days, Kerensky appointed himself Supreme Commander of the Armies of the Republic, and left for the Tsar's military headquarters at Gachina, thirty miles south of the capital, to mobilise Tsarist officers to defeat the mutinous rabble. On 26 October, eight thousand officers and Cossacks marched from Gachina on Petrograd. Beating back the regiment of sailors under Dybenko's command guarding the strategic village of Krasnoe Selo, they advanced to the imperial summer palace at Tsarskoe Selo, where the Tsar and his family had taken refuge since his abdication, and were driven back by a hastily assembled army of soldiers and sailors from Petrograd, Kronstadt and Helsingfors. Tens of thousands of men, women and children, armed with rifles, picks, spades and barbed wire, poured through the streets of the capital to dig trenches and build barricades in its encircled suburbs, and hundreds died in the battles to defend the city. But by 31 October red Petrograd had been saved in the Bolsheviks' first military victory.

Kerensky fled to France, and the Tsarist Generals Krasnov, Denikin and Alexeev, Yudenich, Kornilov, Kolchak and Kaledin escaped arrest and fled south to build their new volunteer army of counterrevolutionary White Guards, in close contact with exiled members of the Provisional Government and its supporters abroad.

The Western governments had immediately declared their refusal to recognise the Bolshevik regime, and Britain and France were already discussing joint military action to divide up the most profitable parts of Russia, and replace the soviets with new British- and French-backed governments. Britain, the senior partner in the alliance, claimed the Baltic states and the oil fields of the Caucasus. France was to get the coal and iron of Eastern Ukraine, and the Crimea, with its access to the Black Sea.

The Bolsheviks' first priority was to remove Russia from the war. On 18 November, a delegation from the Commissariat of Foreign Affairs arrived in the town of Brest-Litovsk, on the Polish border, to negotiate a separate peace with the German High Command. By eliminating its Eastern Front, Germany could concentrate its forces against Britain and France, and the armistice was signed on 2 December. A week later, talks started for a permanent peace.

At the same time Bolshevik fraternisation literature was being smuggled to German soldiers at the front, including Kollontai's *Who Needs the War?* The Revolution's survival depended on revolutions spreading to the advanced capitalist countries, which would share their wealth and resources with impoverished Russia, and Germany was to be the first capitalist country to follow the Russian example. "Without revolution in Germany we're finished," Lenin said the day after the Bolsheviks took power.

As the commissars waited for the international revolution that would save them, they embarked on their formidable programme of legislation. Decree followed decree — doing away with Tsarist ranks and titles, nationalising property, reforming labour relations and Russia's collapsing school system, legalising homosexuality and same-sex marriage, abolishing the Jewish Pale. Free health care was promised to all citizens in state-funded hospitals, clinics and maternity homes, and free education to all children between the ages of eight and fifteen in their native languages, including Yiddish. Racial diversity was to be celebrated, and ethnic minorities were to have full educational and occupational equality.

Poverty, war and sabotage and the isolation of the workers' state made much of this early legislation impracticable in the short term — "evidence mainly of our determination to bring about socialism in the future," Kollontai wrote. "Every moment was precious. We were hungry, we rarely got a night's sleep, there were so many dangers and difficulties. But we all worked passionately, for we were in a hurry to build the new Soviet life, and we felt that everything we did today was desperately needed tomorrow, however rough and ready".

It was in this spirit that she issued her Commissariat's first decrees after October, published in *Pravda*, now the official paper of the government, announcing its radical overhaul of the Tsarist orphanages and maternity homes, mental hospitals, TB sanatoriums and old people's homes. As in all government departments, the salaries of her top officials and lowest paid staff were levelled, and she consulted with Lenin on how to abolish the Ministry's old hierarchy and run the Commissariat on Soviet lines. A new five-person management committee was elected, headed by her and her deputy, the mechanic Vanya Egorov, and she appointed panels of experts on education, law and medicine to take over the running of the old departments.

First she had to take over the Ministry. The piece below, based on her diaries of October, was published in 1927 in the monthly art and literature journal *Red Cornfield.*

"The First Grant from the Commissariat of Social Welfare"

October was grey and stormy. Wind gusted through the trees in the grounds of the Smolny, and its endless tangle of corridors and vast bright halls seethed with activity. It was the day after the Bolsheviks had taken power. Workers and soldiers had occupied the Winter

Palace, and Kerensky's government was no more. But we all knew this was only the first step on the difficult path to the first Workers' Republic, and a completely new social order, never before seen in the world.

The central committee was huddled round a table in a small side room, with newspapers taped to the windows. I can't remember now what my question to Ilich was, but he immediately had something more useful for me to do. "Go at once and occupy your Ministry. It's urgent, you mustn't delay". He spoke calmly and cheerfully, and even seemed to be laughing. Then he turned to others who had come to him for instructions or with information.

That damp autumn afternoon will be forever in my memory. I was driven on my own to the Ministry building on Kazanskaya Street, where the doors were opened by an imposing commissionaire, with grey whiskers and braided epaulettes. He looked me up and down, and I said I needed to see his managers.

"Opening hours for claimants are over," he said.

"I'm not a claimant, I've come to speak to your senior officials".

"I've already told you in plain Russian, opening hours for claim ants are between one and three, and it's now four".

I repeated my request, and he repeated his instructions. "We know you, you all say you're not claimants, and if we let you in you go and bother the managers".

"I'm here on government business," I said. "Who's in charge here? Where are their offices?"

It was no use. Opening hours were over, and the stubborn old man had been ordered to let no one in. I tried to push past him, but he blocked me like a wall. So I gave up and went back to a meeting at the Smolny.

Those days were an endless round of meetings, in

the thick of it with the soldiers and the urban proletariat, discussing whether the workers and peasants in their army greatcoats could hold onto power, or we would be defeated by the bourgeoisie.

Next morning at crack of dawn, the doorbell rang at the flat where I had been staying since I was released from Kerensky's jail. It rang again insistently, and I opened the door to a bearded peasant in a sheepskin coat and felt boots. "Does People's Commissar Kollontai live here?" he said. "I've a note for him from his head Bolshevik Lenin".

He showed me a scrap of paper with a scribbled message in Ilich's hand, saying "Give him as much as he needs from Commissariat funds for his horse".

"A horse?" I said.

He then told me the whole story at length. During the war, under the Tsar, his horse had been requisitioned by the army. He had been promised a "fair price" for her, but years passed, and there was no word of compensation. So he set off for Petrograd and spent two months there, visiting all the departments of the Provisional Government. He went from office to office, and left no stone unturned, but nothing came of it. He was running out of money, and was about to give up, when he heard that a new government was in power, which was promising to return to the peasants everything the Tsar had stolen from them in the war. All he needed was a note from its leader. So he tracked Lenin down in his room at the Smolny, woke him at an unearthly hour and got his note, which he showed to me but refused to hand over. "It's staying with me until I get my money, it's safer that way. You can have it when I'm paid," he said.

What was I to do about his horse? The Ministry was still run by officials of the old regime. What a strange time it was. Power was in the hands of the People's

Commissars, but the institutions, like a derailed train, were still running along the lines laid down by the Provisional Government. People grew used to the sight of Red Guards angrily marching striking officials along the streets to be arrested, and disapproving bystanders shaking their fists at them.

How was I to occupy the Ministry? By force? But that would just drive people away and we would have no workers. We decided to call a union meeting of the lower paid staff, those with technical and general jobs in the various departments of the Commissariat — boilermen, cooks, cleaners, mechanics, messenger boys, stenographers and paramedics — as well as workers from the playing cards factories, whose revenue funded the Commissariat. We elected a soviet, and discussed the situation with my deputy, the union steward Vanya Egorov, and next morning we set off to occupy the building.

This time we got past the braided doorman. He had no liking for the Bolsheviks, and hadn't attended our meeting, but he grudgingly let us in, and as we headed up the stairs we were met by a flood of civil servants, bookkeepers, accountants and secretaries, who rushed down without looking at us, and were out of the building before we reached the top. The sabotage of the officials had begun.

Only a few had stayed to work with us. The offices and cashiers' departments had been ransacked, with typewriters thrown on the floors, and piles of documents strewn around. The income and expenses books were missing, and the safe was locked, and we couldn't find the keys. Who had them? How could we work without funds? We were responsible for providing state welfare for a huge range of people and institutions — war orphans and disabled veterans, mental hospitals and old people's homes.

But the keys were nowhere to be found. And my most persistent visitor in those days was the peasant with his note from Lenin. Each morning at first light he would be at my door. "She was a good horse. If she hadn't been good and strong I wouldn't ask so much for her. But I've got my note from your leader and I'm not giving up. It's taken me half a year, but I'll get it". And get it he did.

We summoned all the managers and senior officials and ordered them to hand over the keys, and they claimed not to know where they were, and told us to look for them ourselves. After they left, the tears streamed down my face as I thought of the leader of the strike, who wasn't rich and supported his mother. But telling myself revolutions weren't made with kid gloves, I ordered them to be arrested. And when we finally got the keys, the first grant from the Commissariat of Social Welfare was for the horse, stolen by the Tsarist government by force and deception, for which the determined peasant with his note from Lenin now received full compensation.

Much of Kollontai's early legislation was based on her extensive research into working women's lives in Tsarist Russia for her book *Society and Motherhood*. She worked closely with the Commissariat of Health on new laws to protect pregnant and nursing women and their children, and with the Commissariats of Labour and Justice on the drafting of the first law of the Revolution, the Labour Law of November 1917, which cut the working day to eight hours, banned child labour, raised wages, and introduced equal pay for women. In advance of every other European country, all women, married or not, were to receive sixteen weeks' paid maternity leave, and could have a friend take paid time off work to attend the birth and help with the baby after wards. New mothers were to work no more than four days a week, and factories and offices were instructed to provide properly run crèches and warm rooms where they could feed their babies.

Kollontai also had a major role in the drafting of the Bolshe-viks' next law, the new Marriage Law and Family Code, passed in December by the Commissariat of Justice, which razed to the ground the old Tsarist marriage law. "A large part of my energy and struggles and the example of my life has gone into this victory," she wrote.

Domestic violence, sanctioned by the Church, was classified as a "counterrevolutionary offence," punishable by jail. Women could now choose which surname to use after marriage and on their children's birth certificates, thus removing the old stigma of illegitimacy, and they had the right to initiate divorce, simply by registering the end of their marriage. The power of the Church was further weakened by handing the religious registration of marriages to the civil authorities, and in December she registered her marriage to Dybenko, in one of the Bolsheviks' new state "red wedding" ceremonies.

The law to disestablish the Church was passed only the following February. Lenin stressed the harm that would be done by offending religious feeling, and the groundwork for the new law was being prepared extremely carefully. The workers' state was non-religious, not anti-religious, Lenin insisted, and reli-gion was no bar to Party membership. Although the Bolsheviks were no strangers to expropriating the palaces of the wealthy, monasteries and churches were not to be touched. Instead appeals were issued to monks and priests and their congregations, assuring them that the government had no intention of seizing their buildings, calling on them to share them volun-tarily with the poor and homeless.

Kollontai signed the eviction order for the first monastery to be expropriated by the new regime, in a shambolic operation un authorised by the Party, which left six people dead. Until then the Revolution had been the most bloodless in history, and the incident caused huge anger and shock. For the Bolsheviks' enemies, it was proof that they were unfit to run the country, and she was denounced in the Menshevik press for her ineptitude.

The article below, based on her diaries, was published in 1927 in the popular political magazine *Change*.

"God's Business With the Monks"

Crowds of desperate people packed the stairs and hallways of the Commissariat, shouting, arguing, threatening. People mercilessly trampled under-foot by tsarism, who had received no compensation from Kerensky — soldiers' widows, mothers with babies, orphans and abandoned children living on the streets, the old, the blind, the poor, the homeless cripples of war.

The Commissariat had raised the price of playing cards, but workers at the factories still hadn't been paid. Nurses at the orphanages were threatening to abscond with their babies if they weren't fed, and residents of the old people's homes were setting up soviets and threatening to demonstrate on the streets. The disabled veterans — peasants and workers from all corners of Russia — had organised their own union, and were demanding that the Commissariat find accommodation for them. The imperialist war had thrown them onto the streets as cripples. That's what you get for serving your country as a hero. Curse your country! You long to go back to your village, but no one can feed a cripple there.

Their situation was truly tragic. It's terrible to remember them — angry, hungry, exhausted, their eyes frozen in horror. We had immediately issued a decree raising their pensions, and this helped for a while. But food prices kept going up, and as the weather grew colder, they began camping on the floor of the Commissariat, refusing to leave until they were housed.

Nowhere could be found for them, and the situation was growing dangerous. So on the first of January, the soviet of the Commissariat took the decision to expropriate a suitable building.

A team led by the soviet's secretary, Alyosha Tsvetkov, was sent off to reconnoitre, and returned with news that they had found the perfect place, with small private bedrooms that could comfortably house up to a thousand veterans, warehouses and larders filled with flour, vegetable oil and tinned herrings, and enough firewood to last two years. And where was all this luxury to be found? In one of the largest and holiest shrines of the Orthodox Church, the Alexander Nevsky Monastery.

The Bolsheviks had not yet disestablished the Church, and we discussed the risks, then we sent our team back to make more enquiries. They reported that the monastery was occupied by sixty monks and forty novices, and that the novices had let them in, and had told them of the "class war" between them.

"Comrade novices, what's going on?" our team asked. "Are you exploited by your class enemies the monks?"

"Yes we are, they treat us like slaves!" they said. "They make us work for them for nothing and feed us on bread and water while they stuff their bellies! We've suffered enough from them, we have no life!"

The novices showed them round the building, with its warehouses crammed with provisions, and they parted as friends. One of the younger ones even announced that he was a Bolshevik, and was going to set up a soviet of novices.

After discussing our messengers' reports, we agreed to take the monastery by peaceful means. We issued an appeal to the monks to move to the side wing, leaving the rest of the building to be used as a veterans' hostel. Then we elected a commission to negotiate with the Father Superior.

The novices happily let them in, but the monks immediately went on the offensive. A fat bearded monk told them that under no circumstances could the holy presence of the Father Superior be infected by unknown worldlings without rank or title. "Such a custom does not exist for every passerby to slip in with his petition".

"It's not a petition, it's business, government business," they said. But the monks dug in their heels. Then the novices began to speak, at first quietly, then more loudly. "Stop dragging things out! They haven't come to rob us, they're here on God's business, helping veterans!"

Our commission was finally allowed in to see the Father Superior, a wizened skeletal old man, very deaf, with little understanding of what was going on, who had the answers to their questions murmured to him by a burly monk at his side, with a big cross on his bulging chest. The monks spread stories that the Bolsheviks wanted to desecrate their holy place by turning it over to the common people, and our parliamentarians had their say, but came back with nothing.

When the veterans were told this, there was uproar. "We've shed our blood for Russia! We'll smash up the Commissariat and riot on the streets! It's Bolshevik power, and they let us freeze to death in the snow!"

We spent the whole evening with them, but they were inconsolable, and towards midnight Vice Commissar Egorov, Tsvetkov and I decided we could no longer stand on ceremony with the monks, and I signed the expropriation order.

We arrived early next morning to find the gates

locked, and the monks barricaded inside. We telephoned Dybenko at the Naval Commissariat to send a detachment of sailors, and twenty broad-shouldered fighters arrived, led by a brass band, and marched cheerfully to the monastery. But the monks were well prepared. As the expropriating party swung into sight, the monastery's bells tolled, rousing the faithful from their beds to defend their sacred building, and thousands rushed from all sides, shouting "We won't let the Bolsheviks steal our monastery! We'll die for the Holy Orthodox Faith!" When the monks came out to join them, the sailors were enraged. "What's to stop us taking the building by force if they won't let us in?" some hotheads said.

Such decisions were taken lightly in those days. The idea that operations had to be carefully planned and coordinated was barely understood then — that spur of the minute decisions could bring chaos to the precarious state structure and undermine Soviet power. A moment later, before anyone could tell who started it, there was an exchange of gunshots, which left six people dead, including two sailors and a monk.

The news quickly reached the Smolny. Party officials arrived to stop the expropriation and order the sailors back, and Alyosha Tsvetkov and I were summoned to explain ourselves to Lenin. Vladimir Ilich was unmoved by our accounts of the novices' revolution against the monks. "Commissars have no business acting so irresponsibly in this exceptionally delicate matter," he said. "We will now have to move forward our disestablishment of the Church".

The monks called on worshippers to defend their monasteries against the Bolshevik marauders, and for weeks they held demonstrations on the Nevsky Prospect, trudging through the mud with their icons, dragging Petrograd's citizens with them.

> Another building was soon found for the veterans. But as chief instigators of the scheme to turn the monastery into a socially useful hostel, Tsvetkov and I were anathemised in solemn ceremonies in churches across Russia. "You're in good company, you'll be remembered with Tolstoy," Vladimir Ilich said.

She made light of it, but it was a serious breach of Party discipline, from which her relationship with Lenin never fully recovered. Added to the insurmountable challenges she faced as Commissar, she had failed to impose her authority on Dybenko's sailors, who were disinclined to follow any orders, let alone those from a woman, and she exposed herself to censure and ridicule for entangling her love life with her work. "I can't vouch for the reliability or endurance of women who allow their love affairs to get mixed up with their politics," Lenin said later, in a clear reference to her.

The episode was a major distraction from the Bolsheviks' peace negotiations with Germany. German warships had remained in the Gulf of Finland since the Armistice, German troops were just a hundred miles from Petrograd, and a new German offensive on Ukraine, Belarus and the Baltic countries had been announced, to "wipe out the oriental pestilence of Bolshevism".

On 14 December, the German High Command at Brest-Litovsk issued its predatory peace conditions — for Lithuania, Latvia and Estonia and most of Poland and Ukraine. The talks broke down, and resumed in early January, with the Bolshevik team led now by Trotsky, Commissar of Foreign Affairs, who declared his government's rejection of terms "which carry sorrow, oppression and suffering to millions of people".

Three million Russians had died at the front, and uncountable numbers were crippled. Families had been torn apart, and women who had lost partners toiled in the factories while their children lived on the streets, with thousands of war orphans. Kollontai set up a new Mothers and Babies Department at her Commissariat, led by her colleagues Doctors Korolev and Vera Lebedeva, which drew up plans for new state children's homes, nurseries and maternity hospitals throughout Russia. She also worked with local soviets in Petrograd to open public dining rooms and children's canteens, to make the best use of scarce food supplies.

Communal living was at the heart of her vision of the new socialist family. She saw these hastily thrown together new eating places as an important first step in liberating women from the kitchen, and as a rough and ready example of the new living arrangements possible in the new socialist society, and she took issue with those in the Party who wanted discussions of family life to await better times.

In December, her Commissariat's Mothers and Babies Department announced the opening the following month of the first of its model new maternity hospitals, "Palaces for Mothers and Babies," in a Petrograd "angel factory" formerly funded by Tsarist philanthropy. The countess running it was moved into a side wing with the nurses and babies, and Kollontai and her team of workers and weekend volunteers cleaned and redecorated the building, moving in enough beds and cots to accommodate two hundred of the pregnant women on the Commissariat's waiting list. There was a model surgery, a nursery, a medical laboratory, a dairy and library, and Doctor Lebedeva had organised a Museum of Motherhood, with illustrated posters about infant healthcare and child development. One of these appealed to nursing mothers to share their breastmilk, and the deposed countess used this to confirm the nurses' worst fears — that the Bolsheviks wanted to nationalise women and steal their babies.

For Kollontai, the Palace was to be a shining example of the benefits the Revolution was offering women. Instead, it became a symbol of her battle with their manipulated superstition and ignorance.

The article below was published in 1945 in the Soviet literary magazine *October*.

"The Palace of Motherhood Burns Down"

It was a bitterly cold night at the end of January, the first winter of the Great October Revolution. We had been at the Commissariat until midnight, battling with the obstacles and difficulties thrown up by the Whites' sabotage, and afterwards I had to go straight to the Smolny for a meeting of the Soviet of People's Commissars.

The news was bad. The Germans were advancing in the south, and our front was wavering, sabotaged by officers from the old army. The Red Army barely existed then. Soldiers were deserting, and in many places Tsarist troops units that hadn't been disbanded were hijacking trains and driving them wherever they saw fit. The Mensheviks meanwhile continued their hysterical attacks on us in their newspapers, claiming we had no right to be in power, and would only last another few weeks. "See how they run their ministries! Look at Kollontai, replacing qualified officials in her commissariat with cooks and mechanics!"

Lenin looked unusually anxious that night. He didn't make jokes as he usually did, and after we left, he stayed to check the minutes with his secretary. I went home with a heavy heart. We were all hungry and exhausted, and I worried that our work at the Commissariat wasn't progressing as I wished. So many obstacles and difficulties.

The streets were empty and pitch-black. A gunshot rang out, then another, and were answered by our machine guns. The Revolution was far from over.

"Do you want me to wait, or shall I go home?" my driver asked.

"Go home and rest, Comrade Gusev. Collect me in the morning as usual at ten".

I was living with Zoya and my son in a fifth-floor flat lent to us by a good friend of ours, and as I walked up the stairs, I wondered if there was any food at home. I thought it was no fun being a People's Commissar, and I missed the days when I had been an ordinary party agitator, travelling the world dreaming of revolution. But here the Revolution was, and we were building the new life.

Pulling myself together, I told myself it didn't matter if the flat was unheated, and there was no bread in the cupboard. And Zoya had waited up for me, with the samovar on the table and a few lumps of sugar, even a bread roll, and I soon cheered up. Hot tea and my dearest friend, what more could I want from life?

We discussed the German advance, and whether our front could hold out against this new attack. We would have rebuilt our army before they reached Petrograd — defeat was out of the question! And tomorrow was to be our great day, when the Commissariat's staff, led by the indefatigable Doctor Korolev, would officially open our first Palace for Mothers and Babies.

The Palace was in the old Tsarist Nikolaevsky foundlings' home on the Moika Embankment. That morning I had inspected its nursery, laboratory and library, its exhibition gallery in the circular reception hall, and its large bright wards, each with space for ten beds and babies' cots to begin with. There was still a lot more work to be done of course, but the Palace was to be a model of its kind, and we were confident that it would soon be opening its doors to all the mothers on the long waiting list on my desk. Now I had to sleep. It was already four in the morning, and we all had to learn to sleep briefly but deeply in those days.

I was woken by the telephone. It was Doctor Korolev.

"A fire? Where?"

"At the Palace," he said.

I called Dybenko, who arrived immediately with a detachment of sailors, and we drove through the empty streets, patrolled by Red Guards in their red armbands. There was a red glow over the Moika, and I was frozen with fear. The Palace, my baby, into which we had put all our hopes and dreams, was going up in flames.

By the time we arrived, the fire had engulfed the entire central part of the building. The air was thick with smoke, and my staff were working with the firemen to fight the blaze. But there weren't the crowds of gawpers I had feared — hardly surprising in the middle of the night in a city gripped by revolution.

The sailors set to work with the firemen, and we discussed whether the Palace could be saved. Korolev doubted it. It was clear that the main part of the building, where we had planned to welcome the women later that day, was completely destroyed. The side wing, where we had temporarily moved the nurses and babies from the old foundlings' home, was intact. The fire must have been burning for some time to have spread so widely.

One of our colleagues rushed up choking on the smoke, shouting what we already knew: "It was started in different places, it was sabotage!"

I thought of all our work, all the sleepless nights, all our battles with the old administrators. Just as the Palace was fully equipped and ready to open, the saboteurs had decided to take their revenge.

Korolev led us to one of the wards in the main part of the building. The smoke made it hard to breathe, and there were no lights as the power had been cut, but we could make out the charred remains of the babies' cots. A beam in the ceiling had come down, and the windows were smashed, with shards of glass on the floor. And where was the august countess who used to run the home? Why wasn't she at the scene of the catastrophe?

Suddenly through the swirling smoke, a ghostly procession of nurses appeared in their nightgowns with their hair awry, holding crying babies in their arms. "Get back, it's not safe!" Korolev told them. But egged on by their elderly ringleader, they advanced on me, shrieking "Bolshevik murderer, you started the fire! You wanted to burn Christian souls and kill us with our babies! Just you wait, we'll make you pay!"

The air filled with the women's hysterical cries and their howling babies. I tried to reason with them, but it was no use. "Don't listen to her, she's the Antichrist! She wanted to turn our home into a brothel!" screamed their leader, at which a nurse leapt forward and tried to strangle me. The sailors and firemen intervened, and marched them all back to their rooms with their babies. "They're safe now Comrade Kollontai, we've put guards at the doors," a sailor said, saluting me.

Later that morning, Korolev, Dybenko and my deputy Vanya Egorov and I set up a commission in the undamaged wing of the building to investigate the causes of the fire. We called the countess and the nurses as witnesses. The countess claimed to be ill, and sent her assistant to speak for her, a tall imposing woman filled with hatred for us, who replied to all our questions that she knew nothing. "I was asleep when it started. It was God's punishment to the Bolsheviks for removing the icons".

One of the younger nurses said she had seen her earlier in one of the wards with a can of petrol, but the older ones angrily denied this, claiming it was an electrical fire.

I ordered the countess to appear, and sent two

sailors off to fetch her. She finally arrived, a hand-some grey-haired woman muffled in a grey shawl, with spiteful black eyes blazing with fury. I stood up to shake her hand, and she hid it under her shawl. We stood staring at each other in silence, and she seemed to be smiling, the smile of someone who had finally got her revenge.

She answered our questions briefly, and cast no light on how the fire had started. "It's a great misfor-tune, but was only to be expected in a building without order or discipline. The Bolsheviks have corrupted people. As the new administrators, you know better than anyone how it happened. I expect one of your nurses had a Red sailor staying the night who dropped his cigarette on the floor".

Our sailors were enraged by this, saying "Let's arrest the old witch!" But I told them we only arrested people we found guilty, not just for stupid words.

"God has punished you," she said. "We were merciful and lived by God's laws, and we rescued babies from the streets. Our nurses were kept in order through a strict observance of the Faith, and you stopped us paying money to our priest".

In trying to exonerate herself she had given herself away; she was clearly responsible.

Her interrogation ended, and I turned back to look at the building for the last time. The metal sign we had proudly hung over the door saying "Palace of Mothers and Babies" dangled sadly from a nail. Zoya was there, and she held my hand and said, "Don't cry, it was an old building. The Bolsheviks will build wonderful new palaces for women and achieve mira-cles, you'll see!" And she was right....

Chapter Eight
Blockade and Civil War

In January 1918, two Japanese warships supported by a hundred Royal British Marines landed at the far-eastern port of Vladivostok, Russia's main naval base in the Pacific, gateway to the riches of Siberia, where they were soon joined by five thousand troops of the American Expeditionary Force in Siberia, under Britain's command. Two months later, three hundred and seventy British marines on the battleship *Glory* landed at the strategic Arctic port of Murmansk, and steadily increased their numbers there in the months that followed.

In March, in anticipation of the German invasion of Petrograd, the capital was evacuated 700 miles east to Moscow. Two million people, along with factories, schools and hospitals, were part of this mass resettlement programme, and the government moved into the Kremlin, where the Fourth Congress of Soviets opened on 14 March to debate the Brest-Litovsk Peace Treaty with Germany.

Germany had stepped up its demands to include Finland, large parts of the Caucasus, and the complete demobilisation of the Russian army. Lenin appealed to the Congress to endorse the Treaty, as a "breathing space" for Russia's exhausted people. Kollontai was on the podium as a delegate of the Petrograd Soviet, and she signed the statement of the

Left Communists — the seven members of the Party central committee who opposed "this obscene 'peace,'" under which Russia was to surrender over half its territory to its aggressors. The Treaty would be "a 'breathing space' only for German imperialism," they said. The German demands were a declaration of war, which imposed a duty on revolutionaries to rebuild the army and fight, and they called on workers in Russia and through out the world to rise up and defend the Soviet state.

Lenin argued that to continue the fighting would pass the death sentence on the Revolution. Without a revolution in Germany, delayed but still inevitable, the Bolsheviks would certainly perish, he said. But in the meantime the Revolution must survive, as the best guarantee of international victory. "We'll surrender imperial Petrograd and Holy Moscow, we'll retreat to the Volga, but we'll save the Revolution!"

Kollontai spoke for the Left Communists to denounce Lenin's "breathing space" as unfortunately nonsense, since German troops were already in Ukraine, making it impossible for hundreds of Ukrainian delegates to be present. But she stressed that she joined the group over the issue of Finland.

On coming to power, the Bolsheviks had given all national territories of the Russian Empire the right to secede from Russia, and in December 1917, the Tsarist Grand Duchy of Finland had become an independent state. A month later, German-backed Finnish White Guards fought to overthrow the socialist majority in the Helsingfors parliament, which was defended by Finnish Red Guards. This rapidly escalated into a bloody civil war between Reds and Whites, in which the Bolsheviks provided weapons, and the German army over twenty thousand troops. For Kollontai, it was unthinkable that the Bolsheviks should abandon their Finnish allies to the German invaders who were throwing them into prison camps, and she was one of the 261 delegates who voted against ratifying the Treaty. 784 voted with Lenin, and her vote cost her her seat on the Party central committee. A month later, she resigned from her Commissariat, "on the grounds of total disagreement with current government policy".

Encouraged by Bolshevik disunity over the Treaty, the French and British governments announced their economic blockade of Russia, and a *"cordon sanitaire,"* to stop the Bolshevik infection spreading west. Britain simultaneously eased its blockade of Germany, and opened secret talks with the German government. "The enemy isn't the Boches now, it's the Bolsheviks," said the Chief of the British Imperial Staff, Sir Henry Wilson.

For Britain's Minister of Munitions, Winston Churchill, it was urgent that Germany was reintegrated into Europe in a crusade against "Jewish Bolshevik Russia, a Russia of animal hordes, of typhus-bearing vermin that slay the souls of men and destroy the health and soul of nations. The mob are raised against the middle classes, to murder them, plunder their homes, debauch their wives and kill their children...".

The war had left seventy thousand Czech soldiers and prisoners of war scattered along the Siberian railways, waiting to go home, and it was Churchill who saw that the Czechs could be used as an anti-Bolshevik rather than an anti-German force. In June, British-backed Czech legions in Vladivostok overthrew the soviet and replaced it with a new counterrevolutionary government. This was the first of a series of revolts, in which a hundred thousand Czechs, White Guards and foreign troops were met by forty thousand ill-equipped and largely untrained local Red Guards and volunteers.

From Vladivostok, Czech forces led by the White armies of Admiral Kolchak advanced along the Volga, establishing new governments in Samara, Saratov, Simbirsk and Kazan, the financial base of the counterrevolution. In towns under White occupation, nationalised enterprises were returned to their old owners, Bolsheviks were rounded up and killed in their thousands, and workers suffered ruthless exploitation and starvation wages. They responded with wildcat strikes, and the "White Terror" was matched by the ferocity of the resistance.

The economy was put on a war footing, conscription was

introduced, and the war became a people's war of total mobilisation. Trotsky, now Commissar for War, travelled to thousands of fronts, mobilising the disintegrating Tsarist units into the new Red Army, and teams of activists, journalists and teachers toured the battle fronts on *agit-trains*, equipped with propaganda films, posters and newsreels, exhorting people to fight the Whites.

In late May, as the Intervention against the Revolution struck into the heart of Russia, Kollontai put aside her differences with the Party, and applied to leave for the Volga as a frontline speaker. "I welcome your return to active Party work," Lenin wrote to her.

Over seventy thousand women fought on the front lines of the civil war, in male regiments or in new communist women's detachments, working as saboteurs, taking on dangerous espionage missions behind enemy lines. They were especially valued in propaganda teams like Kollontai's, whose work was centrally coordinated in Moscow by a woman activist named Varya Kasparova. Between May and August, she sailed up and down the Volga with thirty local party activists and Red Guards on the *Red Star agit-steamer*, equipped with medical supplies, literature and *"agitki,"* short propaganda films made for the illiterate. Stopping at the small towns and villages, they went ashore to address meetings in markets and soviet buildings and in people's homes, using slide shows, posters and all their powers of persuasion to convince the communities of Kalmyks, Bashkirs and Tartars to stay and fight the Whites.

She became one of the Bolsheviks' most popular frontline speakers, and turned many of her speeches into pamphlets for the local press. The speech below, from her next tour of the front in Ukraine, was published as a pamphlet in May 1919 by the newspaper of the Kharkov Soviet of Workers' and Peasants' Deputies.

What Are We Fighting For?

This is the question being asked now by every Red Army soldier, worker and peasant. Didn't the Bolsheviks tell us two years ago that we had peace? Why are we being mobilised again and sent back to the front?

Let us look at what has happened in our country since October. The day the workers and peasants took power, they sincerely and openly proposed peace to all nations. But workers in other countries lacked the power to support us, and the imperialists were able to continue the war.

In March 1918, the Soviet Republic was forced to sign the crippling Brest-Litovsk Treaty with Germany, to save some of the peasants' land and the workers' machines. Now a new front has opened up, of the Reds against the Whites, of working people against the foreign imperialists.

The armies of the capitalist states are engineering and financing uprisings against the Workers' Republic. Are we to say "We're against war, we want peace? If we're attacked by the Denikins and Kolchaks we won't pick up our rifles? Let the British, German, French and Russian capitalists bring back the old system and rule us as before, it's all the same to us?"

Obviously no sane peasant, worker or Red Army soldier would say such a thing. The peasants know that with the bourgeoisie back in power, it will be goodbye to their land and freedom. That they'll be doffing their caps to the landowners again, their bellies swollen with hunger, while the granaries swell with the golden harvest.

Workers know that the return of the capitalists means a return to the old lawlessness and exploitation, an end to unemployment pay and the eight-hour day. That they will be driven from their bright new homes back to their damp basements, and the old wage slavery.

The Red soldier remembers the prison life of the Tsarist bar racks, the beatings and humiliations, the rotten meat and the corruption, and his hand reaches instinctively for his gun.

The imperialists have no respect for human life, and working people know this. They know that the question facing us now is whether we will be rulers of our country, or we will allow the capitalists, land-owners and priests to rule us again.

This war is about working people rising up to defend their rights and freedom, their very lives. We are fighting not to occupy new lands, not to enslave other nations, but to defend ourselves against the capi-talists. We are fighting to destroy the power of the pred-ators, so that peasants and their children can peacefully plough their land, and workers can play their part in deciding how the national wealth should be spent in the interests of all citizens, so no single individual takes the lion's share. We are fighting to defend working people's right to run their own country, to protect them from a return to hunger and rising prices, to do away with war, poverty and injustice, and to create a single world republic of workers and peasants.

This new war of the Reds against the Whites is the uprising of the oppressed against the criminals respon-sible for the bloodshed. Our slogans are "Victory to peaceful working people!" "War on War!'

In July, the British Expeditionary Force in the Caucasus estab-lished a government in Baku, capital of Azerbaijan, and took control of its oilfields. In August, fifteen hundred British and French troops staged a coup against the soviet in the northern port of Arkhangelsk, supported by six thousand American troops as backup. British ships patrolled the Caspian Sea and the Arctic coast around Murmansk. The French fleet was in the Black Sea, and the Czechs were still holding the towns along the Volga. Germany had now joined this Allied-Czech-White Russian force to bring down the Bolsheviks, and had set up a puppet government in Ukraine, under the nationalist Hetman Skoropadsky, which was slaughtering Bolsheviks and Jews.

On 30 August, Lenin was shot at point-blank range as he was leaving a factory meeting in Moscow. One bullet penetrated his neck, close to his brain, the other punctured his left lung. The bullets remained in his body, but he was soon back at work in the Kremlin, and he would survive for the next six years, his health increasingly undermined by blackouts, headaches and insomnia.

Kollontai immediately left the Volga for Moscow, where Red Guards were patrolling the streets with orders to deal ruthlessly with the Revolution's enemies. Hundreds of suspected counter-revolutionaries were arrested and shot in the ensuing reprisals. "As the struggle became increasingly bloody, much of what was happening was very alien to me," she wrote in her diaries. "But there was still the unfinished business of women's liberation. Although women now had all their rights on paper, in practice many still lived under the same old yoke, with no authority in their families, enslaved by a thousand menial domestic chores. Many were also single now as a result of the war, and had to bear the responsibility of raising their children on their own".

In Moscow she worked with women on the home front, setting up makeshift kitchens and canteens, applying to the Central Ration ing Committee for increased rations of bread, meat and fish, and appealing to women to eat there with their children. Her work involved many of her old responsibilities as Commissar for mothers and babies, and for Russia's orphans and street children, the most tragic victims of the war and the civil war. Women were widowed and toiled all day in the factories, unable to care for them, and by the end of 1918 there were an estimated two million children living on the streets of the cities, begging and stealing and prostituting themselves for food.

Kollontai's first decrees as Commissar had announced radical improvements to the old Tsarist orphanages and foundlings' homes, and the Bolshevik Family Code she had helped draft had outlined plans for a network of self-governing children's homes across Russia and Ukraine, where their lives would be turned around through kindness, respect and hard work. A few model homes had been set up, but limited resources made the scheme unworkable on a mass scale, and to deal with the crisis, government policy changed to supporting individual adoption and fostering arrangements.

Kollontai campaigned with women's groups in Moscow and the surrounding towns and villages to encourage families to take children into their homes, and her slogan "Be a mother not only to your own child but to everyone's children!" appeared on posters throughout Russia. The main focus of her work with women, spelt out in her article below, published in *Pravda* in September 1918, was to ensure that mothers were no longer forced by hunger and the desperate conditions of their lives to abandon their children.

"The 'Cross of Motherhood' and the Soviet State"

They still visit us "for old times' sake," as they used to visit us at the Commissariat in the early days of the Revolution — hollow-eyed with hunger, at the end of their strength.

There are office and factory workers and party members, many of them widowed or single, independent and self-supporting. But every mother's heart loses its steel and its will to fight in the face of her child's hunger. There are intellectuals — doctors, teachers and students. There are former landowners and capitalists, even a few wives of arrested counter-revolutionaries and saboteurs. All with the same tormented eyes, the same beseeching smiles, the same cries from the heart — "Our children are starving, our innocent babies! Can't the Soviet Republic help us?"

The factory workers generally speak briefly of their plight, ashamed of their tears and weakness. The intellectuals are more voluble and angry. Those who complain most loudly about the cross of motherhood on our poor abandoned country, laid waste by war, are the women of the newly impoverished bourgeoisie. They speak of being driven from their homes, forced to sell their last warm coat to buy milk for a sick child. And listening to their truly terrible stories, you feel both sad and angry. Sad for every suffering mother, whoever she is, and for the present material conditions in our country, the poisonous legacy of capitalism. And angry about the power of class psychology. These mothers who have unexpectedly fallen into the lives of millions of proletarian women weep and curse their fate, stretching out their hands to us, their enemies, to help them. Of course the Soviet Republic won't abandon them in their suffering. But where oh where were they before, living in warmth and comfort behind strong walls, when life for millions of mothers was a daily struggle to survive? The bourgeois mother cared only that her Sashenka or Mashenka had twice as much food as required for their normal development, and grew up surrounded with brightness and joy. For mothers of the oppressed classes, she felt nothing but indifference. What did she care about the poor, the sick and the unemployed?

The picture changed dramatically after the mighty events of October. The Revolution swept the ground from under their feet, and yesterday's millionaires and capitalists were brought face to face for the first time with the forces of hunger and poverty. At first when you listen to these mothers' complaints, you want to brush them off, to ask them what they did, with their sensitive souls and their culture and education, to help working and peasant women with the intolerable burdens of motherhood. They were in power then, their husbands and fathers ruled the country. Why was there no mention in their "progressive enlightened" programmes of the laws needed to protect working mothers and their children? When we boil with rage at the injustices of the capitalist system, we feel like telling them they have only themselves to blame if we don't help them!

But this must not be our response to mothers, whatever social crimes they have committed in the past. We are not vengeful, we create. Let them see that the working class is generous with its enemies, and supports all children who need help from the state. Children are communist Russia's future. If we raise them to be strong and healthy, nothing the enemy throws at them will break them, and victory will be ours!

For the workers' state to survive, we must destroy in all classes the vestiges of the narrow self-centred bourgeois family. The great break with the customs of the past which is taking place before our eyes is opening the way to a more collective form of the family, and a certain amount has been done to establish the material basis for this. But it is too little and too tentative, outside the state structure, in too narrow a framework. In the old days, we became used to taking orders from above, waiting for others to sort things out for us. The Soviet Republic is great because it has opened the way to workers' initiative. Our most urgent task now is to work with mothers to establish the state institutions they need to feed their hungry children.

We see working women crushed by the burdens of motherhood, giving their last crust of bread to their children. We witness the terrible sight of starving children begging for food on the streets of Red Moscow.

It's impossible to hide from these children's eyes. They accuse, implore, cry out. And here we must tell the truth, that we communist women have failed to treat the protection of children with the necessary seriousness. We have been too indirect and inactive. We haven't even carried out a nationwide census of children of school and preschool age. Why are there so few new maternity homes, day nurseries and public dining rooms, which would immeasurably ease the burdens on women? Why have we done so little to encourage them to campaign for the practical measures they need to support them as workers and mothers?

Women in Moscow and the surrounding towns have been working with the soviets to set up communal children's canteens, staffed by volunteers. But these first experiments will be socially significant only when they are rolled out on a mass scale. We must waste no more time in carrying out our programme to set up canteens across the whole of Russia.

Children in Moscow have already been registered, and their ration books issued. The next step is to find suitable premises for the canteens in the towns and villages, and involve women in the work of running them. Food and fuel will be provided by local soviets, which will mean immediate economies for the government. Instead of two hundred stoves, fuel for one central oven. Instead of feeding two hundred hungry children from two hundred separate pots, one collective pot. And what a huge saving of time and energy it will be for mothers. Instead of each standing at her stove, she can take her shift in the communal kitchen once a week, even once a fortnight, knowing her children will be well fed. Or she may prefer to take meals home, whichever is more convenient for her.

The canteens will be a wonderful way to instil the collective spirit in women, showing them that we aren't the monsters of the Whites' and priests' propaganda, and we won't let their children starve. And these must be followed by a whole range of other measures to help working mothers. To work comrades! Let us fight to free women from the daily struggle to feed their children, so they can lift their heads and give their energy to the great task of strengthening the power of the victorious working class!

In September 1917, the editors of *Woman Worker* had written to hundreds of local parties in the Petrograd region inviting women from the towns and villages to a conference in the capital to discuss what they wanted of the Revolution, and ensure that their needs were at the top of its agenda.

The date for the conference, 25 October, was announced before it was chosen as the day the Bolsheviks would take power, and it had to be postponed. A year later, Kollontai and the organisers wrote to parties and soviets across Russia inviting women to Moscow in November for the All-Russian Congress of Women Workers and Peasants.

With postal services barely functioning, they had only a few dozen replies. But over a thousand women came, from Petrograd, Ukraine and Siberia, the Volga and the Caucasus. Hundreds had made long dangerous journeys across war zones, many with children, and volunteers were rounded up to run a nursery. They spoke of fighting at the front, and of working in the factories to support their families, and the organisers gave speeches about working with the commissariats to set up new state day nurseries — which produced anxious cries from the audience of "We won't give up our babies!"

In Kollontai's speech, published two years later in an expanded form as her pamphlet *Communism and the Family*, she began by assuring women that the Bolsheviks had no intention of separating them from their children. Their goal was to relieve them of the more arduous and exhausting aspects of childcare, and radically to improve their lives with better working conditions, equal pay, improved maternity services, and properly run state nurseries in the factories and offices.

She paid tribute to women's heroic role in the civil war, and to the enormous new strength and confidence they had gained in the Revolution, and she discussed at length the huge new economic and emotional demands being made on them, at work and in their families. The Revolution was sweeping away the foundations of the old patriarchal family, and she looked forward to better times after the civil war was over, when the state could build the economic base to achieve communism, and take over the functions of the old domestic economy. Until then, despite all the Bolsheviks' inspiring and progressive legislation, Russia's desperate poverty and economic isolation meant that women's full emancipation still lay in the future, and she called on the Party to make the difficult transition to the new family as painless as possible for them.

Before the Revolution, she had written of the family in terms of capitalist property relations, which "degraded the maternal instinct into the mere instinct to reproduce," and she had celebrated the liberating new technology of birth control. Effective contraception would be widely available in Russia only several decades later, and Russian women were never involved in the birth control campaigns of the 1920s which drew mass support in the rest of Europe and in America. The workers' state was now fighting for its life in a war that made the need for new citizens imperative, and she spoke not of women's reproductive rights, but of mothers' and babies' welfare. New nurseries and crèches, kitchens, clothes-mending centres and laundries would free working mothers to read, go to meetings and concerts and pursue their own interests, and she saw these practical measures to ease their workload as the key to building the new family of the future.

Her speech was warmly applauded by the audience, but was followed by others from women on the platform who did not share her libertarian views on the family, and focused on its more conventional rights and duties.

Lenin then arrived to show his support for the congress, and took the stage to deliver a rousing call to abolish housework: "Despite all the liberating laws we have passed, woman continues to be a domestic slave, because petty housework crushes, strangles, stultifies and degrades her, chains her to the kitchen, and wastes her labour on barbarously unproductive nerve-wracking drudgery. The true emancipation of women, real communism, will begin only when a mass struggle, led by the proletariat in power, is waged against the domestic economy. Do we devote enough attention to this question, which is theoretically indisputable for every communist? Of course not!"

His speech was greeted with storms of applause and the singing of the *Internationale,* and proceedings ended with a resolution to set up nationwide party women's commissions, on the lines of the women's sections Kollontai had proposed the previous spring, responsible for caring for orphans and setting up children's homes at the front, and organising canteens and nurseries in the cities — "to liberate women from the kitchen and the cradle". The Party outlined the commissions' work in its *Pravda* article "Mobilising Women to the Red Front". Factories and villages across Russia were to elect delegates to commissions attached to local parties, who would report back to a Central Commission in Moscow, headed by Kollontai and three others.

She had first discussed the idea of holding the congress with the women she met on her trips that autumn to the textile towns around Moscow, with their mainly female workforce and their long his tory of militancy. Many women were working with their local soviets to set up communal dining rooms and children's canteens, and she was especially impressed by the textile workers in the town of Orekhovo-Zuevo, who had opened several canteens on their own initiative, independently of the soviet. On her first trip they had appealed to her for support from Moscow, and she returned in October with the promise of funds, reporting on her visit in the article below, published that month in *Pravda*.

"The Town of the First 'Rebels'"

The train to Orekhovo-Zuevo, like all trains then, was crammed with passengers travelling to the villages to buy grain — men, women and children, clinging to the buffers, sitting on the roofs. It was just a few days before the decree banning these foraging expeditions, and everyone who hadn't stocked up for the winter was rushing to the countryside.

It was the end of a golden autumn day. The long shadows of the trees, tinged with russet, stole across the fields, luring us into the peaceful mossy depths of the forests. But the train tore on, with no time for its exhausted irritable passengers. Darkness fell, but it was a suburban train, with no lights in the compartments. Dresna. Next stop Orekhovo. Would anyone be there to meet me?

Orekhovo-Zuevo! How many memories precious to every worker and revolutionary are linked to its name! Thirty-three years ago, when Russian workers were still sleeping their heavy nightmarish sleep, angry but silent, crushed, illiterate and submissive, hostile to change and distrustful of anything new, the first "red riot" broke out at Orekhovo's Morozov Cotton Mill, where women rose up in fury against the power of capital. Tsarism did not spare them. Their strike was broken, and thousands were sacked and arrested. But their courage and sacrifices had their effect, forcing the Tsar to hurry through his factory laws, banning night work for women and children in the textile industry. It was Russia's first major strike, and the proletariat's first victory over capitalism, still in its early stages in Russia but ruth less, and working people will forever be indebted to the women of Orekhovo.

A month ago when I visited this historic town, with its 110,000 textile workers, I was struck by the way capitalism makes factory towns the world over identical. Walking down the main street, with its mansions for the senior factory managers, its two-storey homes occupied by the merchants, its squalid barracks housing the workers, and its vast cotton mills, with their glass and metal and noise, I could have been in any of the industrial towns in Saxony or New England, or in the manufacturing area of Belgium near the French border. Capitalism has put its stamp on all these places, wiping out their original national features, shaping people's lives to suit its needs.

The difference in Orekhovo is that the roads are much worse, and there is less food in the shops, and unlike towns in America, Germany or Belgium, there are no welcoming open doors of a public library, no town hall on the main square. Otherwise, workers' lives here differ little from those in the textile towns of Lawrence, Massachusetts, or Roubaix in Northern France, with the same hopes and aspirations.

The soviet took over the mills from the owners the Morozov family in October, and on my last visit it had been too busy fighting its political enemies to have achieved much in the way of practical results. There had been bitter arguments between Mensheviks, Socialist Revolutionaries and anarchists, all vying to win workers to their side, and I wondered how I would find the town this time.

At the station I struggled to push through the hordes of specula tors with their sacks of grain. "Comrade Kollontai?" said a cheerful young voice behind me. "We were afraid you wouldn't come, we'll go straight to the meeting".

We were driven there in a smart carriage formerly owned by the Morozov brothers, drawn by a fat well-fed horse, and I asked my companion about Comrade Katya, who had organised my last trip. She told me she was just back from fighting at the Don front, where she had come under fire from Krasnov's White armies and had barely escaped with her life, and for a moment the bright expression left her face.

The meeting had been postponed until nine, so we went next door to the workers' club, where I met Comrade Katya again, as lively and indefatigable as ever. We were given an excellent meal, such as we had long been unused to in Moscow or Petrograd. But I learnt from the women that Tsar Hunger had already arrived in the town, and they promised to show me their new children's canteens the next day.

We were joined by several women comrades from the neighbouring villages, where the soviets were still fighting to establish themselves, and they had innumerable questions for the Orekhovo activists. How were they to organise canteens with food distribution in its present chaotic state, and convince the soviets of the importance of this work? From the women's replies, it was clear that they had the skill and experience to deal with existing difficulties and anticipate new ones, and that their work was going from strength to strength. The main problem was the distribution of food supplies. "Say what you like, it was a mistake not letting the soviets buy grain and control distribution centrally," Comrade Katya said. "If we'd got rid of the specula tors, we would have had enough to last us until the spring".

Some objected that a strict state monopoly on grain risked antagonising the peasants. But she disagreed. "It's the only way for ward, with no concessions. This is just half measures! You can't feed everyone this way! If our soviet had bought directly it would have encouraged people to trust us, and that's so important!"

There were a fair number of women at the meeting, but unlike my meeting a month ago, the hall was only half full. The subject of my talk was "Working Mothers in the Soviet Republic," and I was told afterwards that meetings on general topics didn't attract big audiences. The women listened attentively, nodding in agreement or shaking their heads. But they asked no questions, as if it was all obvious, and I was annoyed with myself for failing to connect with them, particularly with the mothers. What they needed was concrete practical advice on how to organise life on the new lines, so thousands didn't have to make their pilgrimages to the villages to buy grain.

After the meeting the organisers took me to the hotel the Morozovs had built for their managers when they visited Orekhovo on business, and the gold poured into their pockets. Now it was used for visiting party workers, actors and artists — the great singer Chalyapin himself would stay there when he came to the town for operas and recitals. It was comfort able and tastefully furnished, without excessive luxury, but the elderly housekeeper greeted us without warmth; her loyalty was clearly to her old masters, and she saw us as interlopers, disturbing her peaceful life.

But there was a samovar in my room, and we all sat round it and talked. The women spoke more about their work in the town. The Mensheviks had disappeared or were in hiding, they said, and the grumblers had fallen silent after the attempt on Lenin's life. Those gunshots at the Michaelson Factory were the signal that forced workers to close ranks against this new threat to the Revolution's survival.

Then Comrade Katya spoke of her propaganda work with the Cossacks at the front. "They've been duped by the Whites! They're con scripted peasants, barefoot, in ragged coats, most of them illiterate — it's nonsense that they're all Mensheviks! When you go to villages occupied by Krasnov's armies and tell them the truth, open their eyes to who we are and what the soviets are doing, they immediately come over to our side! The more of us we send there the sooner they'll all be ours, and we can send Krasnov packing!"

She believes deeply, passionately that truth and justice are on the workers' side, and that the Revolution will win. Like Orekhovo's first "rebels," she is a woman of a completely new type, who inspires others to follow her, proud of her young strength and conscious of her rights. A citizen of Soviet Russia.

Chapter Nine
On the Front Line

Germany's socialist leaders had survived the disgrace of 1914, and tightened their grip on the party. But opposition to the war was growing. In 1915, twenty socialist deputies voted with Liebknecht against the Reichstag's new war budget. A year later, thousands tore up their party cards to work underground with him and Rosa Luxemburg in the new Spartacist League for the revolution that would save the Bolsheviks.

Four years into the war, people in Germany were at the end of their strength. Over two million had died in the fighting, and the Allied blockade had produced untold hunger and suffering. The collapse of the Western Front in September 1918 triggered an explosion of soldiers' mutinies and desertions, which set off strikes and riots across the country, culminating on 9 November in a general strike in Berlin, and the Kaiser and his court and government fled to Holland. Liebknecht and Luxemburg were both released from jail, and Liebknecht stood on the balcony of the Kaiser's palace to proclaim the new "free German Socialist Republic:" "The reign of capitalism, which has turned Europe into a swamp of blood, is broken!"

The Chancellor stayed in Berlin, and appointed the Chair of the Socialist Party President of the new Republic. On 11 November, the government signed an armistice with the Allies and opened talks in Versailles for a peace treaty. The First World War was over.

The strikes and riots continued. Luxemburg and Liebknecht spoke at mass factory meetings, and Bolshevik-style workers' and soldiers' soviets took power in several cities, including Berlin. In Russia, headlines in *Pravda* declared this breakdown in the capitalist order to be the start of the international revolution that would save the Bolsheviks. "The head of German imperialism is on the chopping block! The armed fist of the proletarian revolution is raised!"

The new socialist government, backed by its conservative allies in the Reichstag, set out to bring the soviets under its control, and won the trade unions' endorsement for elections to a new parliament, to take its name from the historic cultural centre of Weimar, far from the turmoil in Berlin. The Spartacists were divided on whether to participate in the elections. Although realising they would be a farce, Luxemburg and Liebknecht were in favour of using them as a propaganda platform. But they were hugely outvoted by those who called for a mass armed rising against the state, and for the Spartacists to dissolve themselves into a new communist party to lead it.

Luxemburg and Liebknecht saw this as a huge tactical error, arguing that workers needed more time to develop their solidarity and fighting skills before taking to the barricades. But they supported events as they unfolded, and on 30 December they attended the underground founding conference in Berlin of the German Communist Party. Communists immediately occupied the offices of *Vorwärts*, putting out their own revolutionary issues for two weeks, before police broke in and shot them dead. The government then ordered the far-right paramiltaries of the *Freikorps*, the "bloodhounds of the revolution," to hunt down the "December criminals". Over five hundred communists were ar rested in Berlin. Liebknecht and Luxemburg, the "chief criminals," were arrested on 15 January, dragged from their under ground hiding places and driven off separately, supposedly to jail, and had their skulls smashed in on the way. Four days later, elections opened for the new Weimar Republic.

They were mourned in hundreds of obituaries in Russia, although many were too grief-stricken to write of them until much later. Kollontai's obituary, published in the paper *Workers' World* in February, called for solidarity in grief, and for their struggle to continue.

"Karl Liebknecht and Rosa Luxemburg. Fighters, Martyrs, Heroes"

An unspeakable crime has been committed in Berlin. Karl Liebknecht and Rosa Luxemburg have been murdered by the Social Democrat traitors. Workers' hearts everywhere are united in sorrow.

Why did we love "Comrade Karl," our leader and friend? Why was "red Rosa" our heroine? What made their names symbols of hope and courage for workers throughout the world?

Liebknecht was the son of an old fighter, a founding member of the German Social Democratic Party, and his great father in stilled in him an inextinguishable faith in the victory of communism, and an ardent love and sympathy for all who were oppressed by capital. From his earliest years, he was on the left revolutionary wing of the German party. As a lawyer, he was a friend to workers, ready to rush anywhere to speak for those who had no voice, to fight injustice, state brutality and police violence. And how many invaluable services he performed for exiled comrades in Germany. He had a truly international heart. You're a comrade whether you're Russian, French or German, and the party welcomes you and takes care of you. And the first to welcome every Russian escaping

Tsarist oppression in the land of the Hohenzollerns, where the regime differed little from that in Tsarist Russia, was Karl Liebknecht.

Like Rosa, he spoke out fearlessly against the narrow-minded nationalism and bureaucracy that was blighting the German party and the International. And of all the innumerable activities of this brave fighter for the workers' cause, his main campaign was against militarism. Long before the war, he issued his challenge to the imperialist world, and he suffered for his courage. In 1907, he was arrested for treason after publishing his book *Militarism and Anti-Militarism,* and he was sentenced to eighteen months' hard labour in jail. There he was elected to the Reichstag, and five years later, his name made headlines across the world when he presented the Reichstag with secret documents exposing German arms manufacturers' bribery and embezzlement in the procurement of government war contracts.

He put his faith in the proletarian youth. He organised youth groups in the party to fight war and conscription, and he dreamed of producing brave new fighters for the revolution, the cadres of our future International. But the revolutionary dreams of the young Liebknecht were not to the liking of Germany's socialist leaders, who worked with the police to close his meetings, and did all in their power to obstruct his work.

His greatest service to the proletariat, which earned him their undying devotion and respect, was his unshakeable faith, the moment war was declared, in the international workers' cause. In those days, when almost all the International's leaders were blinded by the call to "defend their country," he declared loudly to the world that the war was a crime, driven by capitalism's need to divide the proletariat and dominate world markets. Alone in the Reichstag, he voted against the War Credits, and he was denied the right to speak. Workers in all countries saw him as the true voice of the International, who spoke for all that was alive in socialism, and he was reviled by the socialist traitors and the imperialist German government, and his former comrades deserted him.

In 1915 he was rearrested at the party's behest, and was conscripted into the army. When he refused to fight, he was made to work burying the dead at the front, and he returned to Berlin in broken health. He was arrested again in the summer of 1916, and was sentenced to four and a half years' hard labour. He was released in the autumn upheavals of 1918, and he returned straight to the battle, his spirit unbroken. When the German Kerenskys came to power in November, sniffing around the bourgeoisie, making their deals and compromises, he called on workers to be done with them. He believed the hour of the revolution had struck, and that the only way forward was for workers of the world to follow the example of the great Russian Revolution, to overthrow capitalism and install the foundations of communism.

True to the working class, he was a living reproach to the socialist traitors, and his great work ended with the bullets to his head.

Beside brave indomitable Liebknecht, with his passionate heart and his clear Marxist mind, was his comrade and ally Rosa Luxemburg. If Liebknecht was the heart of the German revolution, Rosa was its brains. Her path as a revolutionary began in her native Poland, as a founding member of the Polish Social Democratic Party, and for twenty years this brilliant thinker and organiser worked with the German party. Her life's writings, from her first book, *Industrial Development in Poland*, to her master piece on imperialism, *The Accumulation of Capital,* are the works of a deep and enquiring mind, a leading theoretician of scientific socialism, and the distinguished heir to Marx and Engels.

From her earliest years in Poland, she was a fierce critic of the reformist nationalist tendencies in the socialist movement. A thoughtful far-sighted politician and passionate fighter, she was also a witty ironic speaker, merciless with her opponents. As much as she was a theoretician, she was always an activist, at the heart of the revolutionary politics of the German, Russian and Polish parties.

When war was declared, she called on workers and soldiers in all the warring countries to strike and desert, and for this she suffered jail and persecution. A foreigner in her adopted country, she bore the banner of principled internationalism to the end of her life, when she was thrown to the lynch mob of the Black Hundreds reaction, who tortured a sick defenceless woman, broken by her years in jail, and spilt her precious brains on the roadway.

Workers will never forgive this crime against our beloved leaders. But we mourn them not with helpless grief, but with anger. Our heroes have died, but the working class survives. And around their graves, which we cherish so dearly, new fighting workers' battalions are springing up to seize the revolutionary banner the criminals have torn from their hands.

The crushing of the German revolution was a shattering blow to the Bolsheviks' hopes for the international revolution without which they seemed doomed to be annihilated. "We're actually dead, we're just waiting for someone to bury us," Trotsky said in the spring of 1919.

By then Russia and Ukraine were being invaded by the armies of fourteen countries, led by Britain, France and Germany, fighting with their White Guard allies to "strangle the revolution in its cradle," in the words of Winston Churchill. Even deadlier than the fighting were the epidemics of cholera, pneumonia and typhus that killed over five million Russians between 1918 and 1920, stretching the fragile new Soviet health system to breaking point.

Some of the bloodiest battles of the civil war were fought for the precious grain and industrial resources of Ukraine — between Trotsky's small new Red Army, the British- and French-backed White armies of Generals Denikin and Wrangel, the German-backed armies of the Cossacks Kaledin and Shkuro, and the fifty thousand-strong "black armies" of the anarchists.

A succession of governments were set up and overthrown. In December 1917, the Provisional Government of Workers and Peasants was established in Kharkov, Ukraine's second largest city. The following February, the Red Army took the capital, Kiev, and was thrown out a month later by the German army, which established its puppet government under Hetman Skoropadsky. In November 1918, Skoropadsky was ousted by the nationalist Simon Petlyura, Chair of the new Ukrainian People's Republic, who ordered the killing of over fifty thousand Ukrainian Jewish men, women and children. The Red Army gained control of Kiev in February 1919. Six months later, the city was recaptured by Petlyura's forces. In September, it was occupied by Denikin's armies, then in December 1919 by the Red Army again.

Dybenko spent much of the civil war fighting the German occupation forces in his native Ukraine and the Crimea. In May 1918, he was appointed by Trotsky to lead a detachment of sailors on a dangerous mission to organise an underground army against the puppet German government in the Crimean city of Sevastopol. In July, soviets took power in the towns of Kherson and Kerch, supported by his sailors and sailors of the Black Sea Fleet. He was betrayed during the operation by an agent of the Sevastopol government, and was sentenced to death for high treason. Kollontai petitioned the Party in Moscow tirelessly to save his life, and he was released from jail in October, in exchange for ten German prisoners of war in Russia. He then immediately re turned to his activities in the Ukrainian underground, travelling six hundred miles north to raise a detachment to drive Denikin's armies from the industrial city of Ekaterinoslav (now Dnipro).

At the end of October, Kollontai took ten days off organising the Moscow Women's Congress to join him there. She made the dangerous seven-hundred-mile journey south with Podvoisky, now Commissar for War, on his *agit-train*, with its printing press and film crew and teams of actors, who entertained and instructed the peasants in the frontline villages with dramatised scenes of the war with the Whites. She spoke at meetings, and wrote articles for Podvoisky's army paper, *Red Fighter*, which was printed on the spot and distributed to soldiers along the way, and she arrived in Ekaterinoslav two days after Denikin's army was driven out by Dybenko's forces.

She returned to Ukraine in April 1919, travelling to Kharkov with twenty young Moscow party activists she was training in the art of frontline propaganda. She helped to set up and staff Kharkov's first women's commissions, and she spoke at women's meetings, appealing to them to join the Red Army as nurses and fighters. Then in May, she and her team travelled south on an *agit-train* to the mines and factories of the Don Basin — the Donbas — for a century the main centre of heavy industry in the Russian Empire.

"Without the Donbas, the entire construction of socialism is just wishful thinking," Lenin said in 1917. Between the spring of 1919 and the following summer, the entire Donbas was overrun by foreign-backed White armies, led by those of General Denikin, who ordered the massacre of over six thousand Jews in areas under his occupation, and the public hanging of one in ten Bolsheviks. In her diaries, Kollontai described travelling through villages burnt to the ground by Denikin's armies, stopping at stations to show films and give speeches — "meeting communities of anarchists vying with each other for the most democratic slogans, and rich peasants preparing to welcome the Whites, shouting 'death to the communists!'"

She spoke at meetings in the mining communities of Kadievka, Makeevka, Shakhty and Gorlovka, and she went down the mines, "where workers' lives are one long hellish underground struggle, and where the true power of resistance is to be found". In Gorlovka, a meeting she was addressing was interrupted by news that the Whites were approaching, and a train was quickly laid on to take her team back to Kharkov, which was desperately preparing to defend itself against the Whites' arrival.

In June, she was posted from besieged Kharkov to work with the new Soviet government in the besieged Crimean capital, Simferopol. Dybenko was Commissar of the Army and Navy, and she was elected head of its Political Department, in charge of Red Army propaganda. In the weeks before Denikin's armies landed in the Crimea, she ran political courses for soldiers, appealing to them to continue the struggle underground, and worked with local women's commissions setting up emergency orphanages and medical centres.

On 21 June, the night before Denikin's forces arrived in Simferopol, the government fled to join the new Soviet government in Kiev. Dybenko was elected Commissar of the Army, and Kollontai was Commissar of Propaganda and Agitation. With better propaganda opportunities than in the Crimea, she visited the surrounding towns and villages in well-equipped *agit-trains*, setting up new women's commissions, speaking at meetings of Red Army soldiers and peasants, explaining the policies of the Soviet government, and contrasting them with the banditry of the capitalist-backed Whites.

Over a dozen of her speeches in Ukraine were published as pamphlets, including *What Are We Fighting For? Women Workers and Peasants on the Red Front, Crisis in the Countryside, Whose Will the Golden Harvest Be? The War With Tsar Hunger, Be a Firm Fighter!* and *Don't Be a Deserter!* The last two assured soldiers leaving for the front that their families would be cared for, promising eternal glory to those who died for freedom and the power of the soviets, and eternal shame to deserters.

In the pamphlet below, from one of her speeches in Kharkov, published in June 1919 by the newspaper of the Kharkov Soviet, she appealed to peasants and Red soldiers to bring in the harvest together in the midst of looming famine, and called on Kharkov's precarious Soviet government to crack down on speculation and private trade.

The War With Tsar Hunger

When the train arrives in Kharkov from the cold North, the first impression, as in most Ukrainian towns, is of the abundance of food in the markets. The hungry northerners feast their eyes on the mounds of provisions on the stalls. Oh happy town, happy Ukraine, where "everything breathes of abundance, and the rivers are purer than silver!"

Yet when we return with our parcels and count our change, we are astonished to find nothing there. Then we add up the inflated prices of our purchases, and realise the money has gone straight into the pockets of the speculators.

There is hunger in the North, but hunger caused by the lack of food supplies. Hunger is creeping gradually into Ukraine, in the midst of abundance.

The old people here can't remember such a harvest — the golden seas of wheat in fertile Melitopol province, the boundless fields around Kherson, Ekaterinoslav, Poltava and Kiev. Our enemies know that if the harvest is in the hands of Soviet Ukraine, the Revolution will be saved. That if the workers and peasants gather in the crops, we can overcome the pangs of hunger and solve the problems of food distribution, which make up over three-quarters of the problems facing the workers' and peasants' republic.

The Denikins and foreign capitalists are now throwing themselves into a last desperate battle for the fertile South of Ukraine, Russia's granary, launching military operations at harvest time, driving our troops as far north as possible so they can carry away the grain. These are the dreams of the White Guard bands. They know they have no hope of holding onto power in Ukraine for long. They see the soviets here putting down deep roots, which no power on earth can destroy. The only power they have is to destabilise our plans for the new economy, by robbing hungry workers in the North of their bread. In a month or so, the Whites will retreat, but they plan to leave loaded with the harvest of the Soviet Republic.

Will we allow Denikin and the English and French imperialists to carry out their cruel plan? Will we allow the predator bands to steal the bread of the Ukrainian and Russian peasants? At this stage of the civil war, the fight is for bread. All who under stand this and cherish the workers' republic, communists and non-communists alike, must be at their posts, led by our Red officers, to drive the Whites from our fields.

Meanwhile the Kharkov government continues to vacillate on its food policy. The bourgeoisie and the speculators eat well as before. The existing free trade arrangements suit them perfectly, allowing them to screw up prices and line their pockets, and workers are already seeing the looming spectre of hunger in Golden Ukraine.

What is to be done about hunger and rising food prices? For the past year and a half, our Commissariat of Supplies has been grappling with this question. Should we destroy private trade, wage a ruthless war against speculation, set fixed prices, and punish harshly those who raise them? "For goodness sake, then goods would disappear completely from the markets, and we would face real hunger!" some citizens object. Nonetheless, the nationalisation of trade is the only way forward, with the registration of all food supplies, and a sharp crackdown on speculation.

However much hunger there is in the North, food stuffs are registered and distribution has been centralised, so that even when the transport crisis stops supplies getting through, workers receive their rations. And as soon as the situation eases slightly, and there is the next delivery of bread, sugar, meat and fish, these can go straight to the workers.

Speculation has not completely been wiped out in the North. But the centralised purchasing apparatus allows food to be delivered to a network of distribution centres, where with a ration book system, it is handed out to none other than the workers themselves. In Moscow, the centres are generally run as workers' cooperatives, and they offer huge scope for workers' initiative.

These centres have not been set up yet in Ukraine, which is why visitors from Moscow and Petrograd, who breathe in its abundance, feel hungry after a few days. The Kharkov authorities are yielding too much to bourgeois fears that goods will disappear if trade is nationalised. But there is no other option for the new society. Each day they delay strengthens the power of Tsar Hunger.

Of course it would be wrong blindly to follow the example of the first Soviet Republic in the world without learning from its mistakes. The North suffered hunger because we failed to register foodstuffs and set up distribution points before we proceeded to close the speculators' shops and stalls, leading to the temporary disappearance of vital supplies after private trade was abolished.

Workers in Ukraine can learn from our mistakes, as they build cooperatives in every branch of the economy to prepare for the end of private trade, which is turning

> prosperous Ukraine into a place of shameless greed
> and speculation. Workers' initiatives have shown that
> this uncompromising line is the only way to combat
> hunger. A clearer more decisive policy is needed from
> the Kharkov government now, before it is too late, and
> Tsar Hunger arrives in blessed Ukraine.

Russia's churches and monasteries continued to be well
supplied with food after the Revolution, as Kollontai had
discovered as Commissar in her disastrous bungled operation
against the monks. The tragedy had forced the government to
push for-ward its Law on the Separation of Church and State,
which was passed the following February, supplemented by a
decree from her Commissariat, announcing the withdrawal of
state funds for religious ceremonies and the upkeep of religious
buildings, ordering them to be turned into orphanages and
veterans' homes and their contents nationalised, and offering
priests, monks and novices jobs at the Commissariat.

In two articles she published in *Pravda* that December,
"Time To Do Away With the 'Black Nests!'" and 'The Priests Are
Still Busy", she wrote of the power religion still had over
people, and argued that defeating the Church was as vital to the
Revolution's survival as feeding children, fighting illiteracy and
liberating women. Science was central to the materialist
Marxist conception of history. The Bolsheviks had declared on
coming to power their intention to create the world's first
"scientific state," and she called for a new science-based
education programme to free people from the Orthodox Church,
purveyor of the most reactionary ideas of the old regime.

"The Priests Are Still Busy"

> Evening in working Moscow. Crowds of workers at
> the tram stops shiver and stamp their feet in the cold.
> Occasionally, like apparitions from another world,
> a stout warmly clad gentleman slips by, or a lady in

furs, looking embarrassed, as if begging our forgiveness. But looking around us we see more and more of our people. Cars speed by filled with comrades on their way to meetings. Posters announce the Friday lectures. Paperboys shout out the headlines of the *Evening News*, with the latest Red Army victories and world events. Against all expectations, the new life is taking hold. The Revolution is stirring, spreading across the world, and the heart rejoices.

So what is this we hear, taking us back to our not so distant past? The familiar doleful chiming of church bells, summoning the faithful to vespers.

Are there many of the faithful, and who are they? There are more of them than you might think. And it's not only old men and women and naive teenagers, the "backward element," who come to save their souls. There's a bearded worker, a Red Army soldier, a young man who looks like a student, and a quick-witted woman factory worker in a headscarf, whose face appears at all the Friday meetings.

Since state payments were withdrawn from the Church, the whole burden of feeding the "little fathers and mothers" and paying for their services has fallen on their parishioners. Who needs this drain on their resources in these hungry times? The old Moscow church is magnificent and brightly lit, and the priests are dressed in their finest robes. Next door is a communist club, where popular talks and lectures are held. Further off are the offices of the Party and the Soviet, with their lively business like meetings. All this draws people away from religion, and robs the priests of their clients. Faced with this new competition, they must make a special effort to attract new worshippers and show off their wares.

How is it that the churches and monasteries continue to flourish, warm and brightly lit? How is it that a hundred thousand train loads of flour, sugar, butter and eggs arrived for the Church this year from the South? Why does religion still have power over people, taming their will with talk of miracles and a better life in the hereafter, instead of encouraging them to think for themselves and build a new life through their own efforts, struggling against capitalism's cruel legacy of greed, exploitation and egotism?

Next door, the communists are fighting the age-old passivity and ignorance, calling on workers to create heaven on earth and build the new life as quickly as possible, so we can all breathe more easily, and everyone can be fed and clothed and given the chance for an education. No wonder the priests wear their finest robes on weekdays, and the churches are lit up as in Easter week!

It's natural that people exhausted by years of war and suffering and social collapse should seek comfort in this familiar place, and hurry there to pray. And with absolutely no effort on their part, the Lord appears when the priests light the chandeliers. The power of darkness over those oppressed for centuries is still very great. And aren't we communists to blame that the churches are still full? Have we done enough to shake the foundations of the old superstitions?

"For goodness sake, aren't we fighting religion with our debates and lectures on the disestablishment of the Church? What more can we do?" comrades say.

This is vital and necessary work, but propaganda and laws on their own aren't enough. There are no shortcuts in the campaign against religion. We won't eradicate the old slavery with words, or by violently trying to suppress people's faith. Religion holds captive the free flight of the will, the restless criticism of human reason. Religion is damaging to communism, because the new social order can survive and flourish only through the complete freedom of human thought, the mind's indefatigable search in the fields of science, its endless curiosity about Nature's undiscovered depths, still hidden from view.

To weaken the grip of religion on the hearts and minds of mil lions, we must not only agitate against the Church, we must counter it with a programme of education. Carried away by the social struggle and the burning issues of the day, we communists have been guilty of not working out the basis of this programme for our younger comrades and for the future generation.

The workers' state can defeat the old system only if it is firmly based in a scientific materialistic view of the world. To empty the churches, the sciences must be discussed not only behind the walls of the socialist academy, but at our popular lectures and debates on social and political issues, illustrated with slides — on Darwinism and the evolution of life, from inorganic matter and the protozoa to the more complex forms and the invertebrates, on the laws of physics and astronomy, and the latest discoveries in medicine and genetics.

The liberation of human thought: this is the slogan of the class that has defeated its social enemies. Religion is used to hold back science, and prevents the communist state from producing a good harvest. Science frees the spirit of eternal search, and will be victorious in the battle against eternal darkness. When workers' eyes are opened to the mighty horizons of creation in all their logic and beauty, worship and belief in miracles will wither away of themselves. Science shows us that there is no need for religious explanations of the world, and that these explanations are provided by life itself.

At the Eighth Party Congress in March 1919, Kollontai spoke for the Central Women's Commission in the main debate on the Party programme to attack the fierce male resistance to its work. She referred to the hostility to the new commissions she had experienced in Ukraine, and to thousands of letters from local activists begging for support from Moscow, complaining of red tape and high staff turnover, as the best organisers were promoted to work in the commissariats. Political slogans were not enough, she said. To tackle women's continuing inequality, slogans had to be attached to a practical programme to tackle the burdens of family life that robbed them of the time and energy for politics. To remove Party debates from the realms of abstraction, "we must struggle against the conditions that oppress women as workers and mothers. This must be the guiding principle of the Commission's work".

Her speech produced another flood of complaints from local organisers, and in September a decree was issued upgrading the Commission to the status of a Party women's department, the *Zhenotdel.*

The *Zhenotdel* had a similar hierarchy to the Commission, with departments attached to local parties, whose activities were coordinated by the central *Zhenotdel* in Moscow, which had legal powers to issue decrees and represent women's interests in the commissariats, advise them in court cases involving domestic abuse, and enforce existing Soviet legislation on women's labour and the Bolsheviks' declared principles of sexual equality.

Kollontai was the obvious choice as Director. But she had already clashed twice with the Party, first as Commissar, then as a member of the Left Communists, and she was widely felt to be too wayward for a job that involved exhausting meetings with party and union officials "who see women's work as beneath their dignity," she wrote. She was passed over for the more reliable Inessa Armand, and she was appointed to the subordinate post of coordinating work with women in the countryside, addressing women's meetings in the towns and villages around Moscow, and drafting decrees to set up new departments.

Within eighteen months, almost every province in European Russia had its *zhenotdel.* By then she and Armand were collapsing under the strain of their workload, and she came close to death with typhus. Armand succumbed to cholera, from which she never recovered, and after her death in November 1920, she took over from her as Director.

The Allies' economic blockade was still in place, but the Whites had been defeated and the foreign armies had been thrown out of Russia, and with the civil war virtually over, work started to rebuild the shattered economy with a mass mobilisation to the labour front.

Three years after the Revolution, eighty percent of women's work was still classed as unskilled, and as men returned from the fighting to get the factories going, women were complaining to the *Zhenotdel* that the laws on equal pay and the protection of their labour were regularly being flouted. In Kollontai's first decree as Director, she instructed teams of factory inspectors to include at least one woman, to check that the laws were being observed, and that women were properly represented by the trade unions.

Despite Lenin's eloquent speech two years earlier at the Moscow Women's Congress, a survey revealed that women spent an average five hours a day on housework, and she launched a new campaign to socialise the domestic economy, instructing departments across Russia to involve women in the setting up and running of new state nurseries, laundries and canteens.

The most urgent issue discussed at the women's meetings she addressed was the dramatic rise in venereal diseases in the past three years of war and civil war. In those days before penicillin there was still no real medical strategy for tackling the crisis. But in her second *Zhenotdel* decree she announced its new Commission on Women's Sexual Health, which offered free medical treatment in state clinics to prostitutes, and organised jobs and courses of study to get them off the streets. "This is an important revolutionary first step we have taken, worthy of the first workers' republic in the world," she wrote.

Under her directorship, the *Zhenotdel* ran women's literacy classes and political courses, organised exhibitions on childcare and hygiene, supervised the publication of eighteen new women's magazines and newspapers, including the official paper of the *Zhenotdel, Communist Woman,* and established an impressive educational programme with women in the new Soviet republics in Central Asia. Traditionally, the Bolsheviks had seen the best way to reach Muslim women as through their husbands and fathers. Kollontai sent teams of organisers to Azerbaijan, Turkestan, Bashkiria and Abkhazia, the Caucasus and the Crimea, to work with the women themselves, setting up clubs, literacy classes and day nurseries, and generally showing them the benefits the Soviet government was offering to women.

The *Zhenotdel* also played a major part in the drafting of the Law on the Protection of Women's Health, passed by the Commissariat of Health in December 1920, making the Soviet government the first in the world to legalise abortion. The Tsarist law had criminalised those who had abortions and those who performed them, forcing women into dangerous backstreet operations which carried a four percent death rate, and an even greater risk of serious health complications. All women now had the right to free abortions on demand in state hospitals, and it was made illegal for anyone but doctors to perform them, or for doctors to be paid. Given Russia's rudimentary health services, it was still a dangerous procedure, which was performed without anaesthetic. Lenin saw the law as a "necessary evil". Kollontai wrote of women's fundamental democratic right not to have children they were unable to care for, and called the law a "transitional health measure, dictated by the surviving moral standards of the past, and the difficult economic conditions of the present". Local women's departments were instructed to organise meetings in the factories and villages to discuss the new law, and the issue of prostitution, and she saw these meetings as an important way to open up a public debate on the new sexual morality of the Revolution.

In her first statement on taking office, published in November 1920 in *Communist Woman,* she reviewed the *Zhenotdel's* achievements and outlined its future work.

"The Work of the *Zhenotdel*"

Two years ago, the All-Russian Congress of Women Workers and Peasants voted to set up women's commissions, attached to party organisations throughout Russia. These already existed unofficially in Moscow, Petrograd, Kineshma, Samara and elsewhere, and were working successfully with their local parties and soviets. Delegates were now elected by factories and villages to serve on the commissions for a three-month period, and to report back their findings and recommendations to the Central Commission in Moscow, helping us to identify the main goals of our work.

Two years ago, our agitation and propaganda work with women was still haphazard and uncoordinated. We were still "loosening the earth," raising women's consciousness, holding broad-based non-party meetings at which they could discuss their needs. This strategy was largely successful, and in a short space of time thousands of working and peasant women were drawn into our party work, which was stronger and richer for their contribution. The *Zhenotdel* is now taking the commissions' work forward, involving more women in its campaigns, encouraging their creativity and initiative.

Women's meetings to discuss living practical issues have been in valuable in rural areas recently taken by Soviet power, or in areas of Central Asia where our power is not secure, and our work with women has barely started. Elsewhere, these meetings can be used to discuss the issues of prostitution and abortion, and to debate current political events. Special classes have been set up at our Party schools to train new teachers for this work.

There are now women's departments in almost every administrative district in Soviet Russia. Our slogan is

"Through Soviet construction to Communism". Our guiding principle is "Agitation by the Deed".

Women's liberation is fundamental to the entire world socialist revolution. Our main focus is to encourage working women to see that their interests lie in joining the Party, and in campaigning within it for the labour and maternity protection laws they need to lift them out of their oppression. We start from the premise that the goals of working men and women are indivisible, but that women need the freedom to organise to protect their interests, and the health and welfare of the next generation. The *Zhenotdel* does not operate independently of the Party, it supports and supplements its work. There must be no deviation from this principle.

Nor does the *Zhenotdel* exist merely to present the female masses with a popular simplified version of the Party programme, as some comrades at first supposed. Fortunately this view is now dying out, as increasing numbers of women make their presence felt in every sphere of Soviet life. The *Zhenotdel* speaks for them in the commissariats, the soviets and the trade unions. The departments made significant amendments to the Commissariat of Labour's recent decree on the protection of women's working conditions, and we are now working with the unions to ensure that women receive the training they need to progress to more skilled jobs.

As we take on the mighty task of rebuilding the economy, women are being drawn into production on a vast scale. The instability and social disruption of the present transitional period places an especially heavy burden on women, and they have everything to gain from the Soviet Republic raising its productive forces as quickly possible, so we can move to the new communist system. But mobilising them to the workforce is unthinkable unless the laws protecting their labour and the health of their children are strictly observed. It is vital that local departments explain the importance of this to their parties and soviets.

The *Zhenotdel* is drawing women into its campaign against the old domestic slavery, replacing the system of individual consumption with new public canteens, and setting up new communal living spaces in the cities to help ease the housing crisis. In the countryside, we often find it easier to win peasant women to communism than men, by boldly showing them, from their own experiences of the oppressive individual household, that their liberation lies in a more collective form of family life.

We are also involving professional women in the work of building the new society. We have already won over the more progressive elements of the intelligentsia. Those who are indifferent or hostile to us have a pernicious effect on our work. But we must take account of the upheavals in their lives under Soviet power, and adopt a sensitive tactful approach to this class of woman, encouraging her to see that the communist worldview can help to free her from her old painful unresolved feelings of inferiority.

The *Zhenotdel* is training teams of organisers to work with women in the Central Asian republics, and we will discuss how this work should proceed at the First Congress of Women of the Eastern Nations in Moscow next spring. Women's heroic role as fighters in the civil war has destroyed the last prejudices against their equality, and our future activities will involve working with the Red Army to set up new women's military training schemes, and courses in communications and administration.

Key to all our work is strengthening our ties with the international women's movement, and at the International Congress of Working Women in Moscow next summer, we will be sharing our experiences with women from the bourgeois countries, as they build their forces to overthrow capitalism and fight for workers' power.

We now see women in every area of Party life, enriching its work with their initiatives. And the more of these initiatives there are, the more our future communist society will have to gain. The *Zhenotdel* is working with women to build this new society, which will finally and irrevocably liberate them from the vestiges of their age-old oppression and their present hardships to realise their great goal: their complete emancipation and equality.

Chapter Ten
Love in the Revolution

Bolshevik victory had come at a terrible cost. In six and a half uninterrupted years of war, civil war and foreign intervention, sixteen million had died in battle, or from hunger and epidemics. Families were scattered, thousands trekked across the country in search of lost loved ones, and millions of orphans lived on the streets. Industry, farming and transport barely functioned, railway lines were wrecked, mines were flooded, factories were deserted. In the villages, wealthy peasants hoarded and speculated and refused to sell their grain for worthless paper money. In the cities, workers seethed with anger at the privileges of the highly paid "specialists" — the managers and engineers and senior civil servants trained under the old regime who were being brought back to run industry in a desperate bid to raise production.

In the winter of 1920, hopes suppressed by the civil war surfaced at mass meetings across the country about every aspect of life in the new Russia. Crucially the debates centred on workers' role in the new economy, and their relationship with the trade unions. Lenin saw the unions as "schools of communism," with autonomy and the right to strike, but responsible for "educating workers on the lines laid down by the Party". Several anti-Leninist Party platforms emerged on the issue. Trotsky believed the workers' state had made the unions largely redundant, and that they needed "shaking up," and he called for their work to be integrated into the state machinery. The former Left Communist Nikolai Bukharin dreamed of their "disappearance under full communism". Kollontai wrote the programme for the only platform with mass support in the factories, the Workers' Opposition, which demanded the removal of the capitalist managers and bureaucrats, and workers' collective management of the economy through their elected trade union representatives.

Lenin rounded on all of them. Trotsky's "sorry excuse for a programme," full of "glaring errors," was based on the "fantasy" that the workers' state had already been achieved in Russia. Bukharin's position was "half-baked and theoretically spurious". The Workers' Opposition was a "syndicalist menace" and a "disgrace," and threatened to split the Party.

"The Workers' Opposition springs from the depths of the industrial proletariat in Soviet Russia," its programme began, "an outgrowth of the unbearable conditions of life and labour in which seven million workers find themselves, and a product of the vacillations, inconsistencies and downright deviations of our Soviet policy from the clearly expressed class principles of our Communist agenda".

"The Workers' Opposition believes, like Marx and Engels long ago in the *Communist Manifesto*, that the builders of Communism must be the toiling masses themselves. Yet we have ceased to rely on the masses, we give no freedom to class activity. This has created the bureaucracy which we consider our main enemy, our main scourge, and the greatest danger yet to our Party's future". "Ilich will ponder, he will lend an ear to the healthy voice of the working masses, then he will turn the Party rudder to us. Ilich will be with us yet".

At the Tenth Party Congress in March 1921, a majority voted to endorse the New Economic Policy (the NEP), designed to deal with the acute labour shortage after the civil war, and to replace the rationing and labour conscription of War Communism with a strategy to "increase at all costs the level of output". In exchange for the West lifting its economic blockade of Russia, Lenin proposed a series of concessions to capitalism, restoring a certain amount of private enterprise, along with workers' efficiency bonuses, fines and layoffs. The Workers' Opposition, speaking now for the powerful Metalworkers' Union, and for thousands of industrial workers in the Moscow region, the Caucasus and Ukraine, attacked the NEP as a betrayal of the Revolution, and a cruel insult to the ideals and sacrifices of those who had fought for the Bolsheviks and brought them to power.

In January 1922, Kollontai was sacked as director of the *Zhenotdel*. Two months later, she spoke at the Eleventh Party Con-gress to defend the Workers' Opposition, and she was threatened with the other leaders with expulsion from the Party. "1922 was a bleak and unfruitful year for me," she wrote in her *Autobiographical Essay*. "My differences of opinion with the Party over its guiding political principles were attacked by many comrades, as were my views on sexual morality and the family".

In April, Stalin was elected to the new post of Party General Secretary, in charge of Party appointments, and Kollontai was one of the first of the troublesome but still valuable old Bolsheviks he sent out of Russia as diplomats. That autumn he appointed her to head the new Soviet diplomatic mission in Norway, where she had lived in exile before the Revolution, and it was in her first months in Oslo that she wrote her two fictional trilogies about women's lives in the Revolution, *Love of Worker Bees* and *Woman At the Turning Point*, published the following year in Russia (and later in my translations).

In her preface to the 1918 edition of her essay *The New Woman*, she had written: "The less harsh reality is romanticised in women's fiction, the more contemporary woman's psy-chology is fully and truthfully presented, with all her migraines and complexities and aspirations, her inner struggles and contradictions, the richer the material for the image of the new woman we will have to study".

Most of the stories were written extremely directly and simply, for those who might not otherwise read fiction, and she was modest about their literary merits. Republished in 2008, they were praised by the editor in his sensitive insightful introduction for their truthfulness and humanity, and he compared the "didactic, simple as a peasant's boot communist prose" of her story "Vasilisa Malygina" to the stories Tolstoy wrote for the peasants. What makes them so vivid and compelling is that they were clearly written from her own experiences, about women she had known and worked with.

Love of Worker Bees is set at the start of the NEP, with its "Nepmen" and "red businessmen," and its privately run bars and casinos and commercial sex, when workers suffered layoffs and wage cuts. "NEP Russia will be Socialist Russia!" Lenin said. In the factories the NEP was known as the "New Exploitation of the Proletariat". Owners of the new commercial enterprises stopped investing in nurseries, canteens and laundries, and hundreds closed, funds to the *Zhenotdel* were cut, and Kollontai showed many of her heroines losing their jobs and childcare and so much of what they had gained in the Revolution, and being forced back into the home or onto the streets.

The stories were hugely popular when they were first published in Russia. But they soon became the target of the new Stalinist sexual puritanism. In 1926, in an article by the journalist Emelyan Lavrov in the magazine *Young Guard*, "Young People and the Sexual Question. Some of the Consequences of Comrade Kollontai's Latest Revela tions," he accused her of condoning "petty bourgeois debauchery". People in the bourgeois countries might "flit from flower to flower, enjoying the love of worker bees". In Soviet Russia, chastity should be seen as the proper norm. Her call for the state to take responsibility for mothers and their children would "encourage every raw adolescent to think he could satisfy his sexual appetites in the manner practised in her fiction". Her views on sex and the family had outlived their usefulness, he wrote, and must be condemned.

The main characters in *Love of Worker Bees* have all met their lovers in the early days of the Revolution, and these relationships are now in crisis. "Three Generations" is about three women, a middle-aged Party worker, Olga Sergeevna, her mother, and her factory worker daughter, Zhenya, and their different and conflicting attitudes to love and marriage. Zhenya sleeps around and has an abortion, and Kollontai's critics claimed that she shared her casual attitude to sex. But nothing in the story suggests this. The Bolsheviks' Marriage Code she had helped to draft had simplified divorce — meaning "sexual relationships no longer have to be seen as a lifetime of conjugal bliss," she wrote — and she had guided the law decriminalising abortion. But she saw the law as a temporary measure, to deal with the aftermath of the civil war and the collapse of the old family, and she looked forward to a time when the state could care properly for mothers and children and make abortions unnecessary.

Fiction allowed her to explore the new sexual morality of the Revolution through her heroines' lives and complicated love affairs. Although she clearly loved the idealism of young women like Zhenya, with their new freedoms and collective living arrangements, her voice in the story is Olga Sergeevna's, dismayed by her daughter's promiscuity, which has nothing in common with the sexual liberation she had fought for. But like Olga Sergeevna, she had been a "new woman" in her time, and rather than simply condemn Zhenya, she wanted to understand this generation of women who grew up in the Revolution, enjoying sex when the opportunity arose, but too busy to fall in love.

This translation of the story is from a new selection of her writings on the sexual revolution, *Freedom and Love,* published online in 2014.

"Three Generations"

One morning, among a pile of business and personal letters on my desk, I came across a thick envelope that caught my attention. Thinking it must be an article, I opened it at once, but it turned out to be a letter, several pages long. I looked for the signature, and was surprised to see that it was from Comrade Olga Sergeevna Veselovskaya. I knew her as a highly competent worker, with a senior administrative job in the upper echelons of Soviet industry. She had never shown any interest in women's work, and I couldn't imagine why she was writing me this long letter. It was only when I glanced at it again that I saw she had written "Strictly Personal" in red pencil on the envelope. For women who write to me, this generally means a family crisis. Could Olga Sergeevna be writing about some personal drama in her life? It didn't seem possible.

I had urgent work to do, and couldn't read the letter immediately. But the image of Olga Sergeevna kept coming into my mind. I thought of her dry businesslike manner, and her famous "masculine" efficiency, and of her partner, Andrei Ryabkov, a former factory worker, a good man, with a pleasant open face, who was universally liked, but was less well thought of than she was. He worked under her in the same department, and was several years her junior, and whenever I saw them together, their relationship seemed an exceptionally happy one. For him, she was the highest authority. I remembered him saying "What are you still arguing for? Didn't you hear Olga Sergeevna's views on the subject?"

I remembered too how at a meeting once, when someone told her he had been taken ill, her face lost its somewhat distant expression and became suddenly warm and human. He had health problems, and possibly it was about this that she was writing to me. But surely it couldn't be the reason for such a long letter.

I was still in my office that evening when I finally had time to read it.

"I'm in a dilemma," it began. "In all my forty-three years I've never been in such a ridiculous position. I simply don't know where to turn. You know me only as a worker, and as a somewhat unemotional person, so it may be hard for you to believe that I at my age am going through a 'woman's crisis.' And a very banal crisis too, which makes it no less painful and humiliating. But I feel it's only banal in its superficial aspects, not in its essence, and that it's all part of the crisis in our relation ships since the Revolution. Along with everything that's new and splendid, there is still much that is mean, petty and oppressive. Sometimes it terrifies me to think that what I'm writing about isn't just an isolated incident. Then I feel that's just the old way of thinking, and that Andrei and my daughter Zhenya are right when they say I'm blowing things out of proportion. I don't know who is right, them or me. If I'm wrong, and I'm just a product of the old bourgeois way of thinking, please help me try to understand things in the light of the new morality".

The letter broke off — it had evidently been written at different times — and continued on the next page in steadier handwriting.

"I'd like to come to the point immediately. But without knowing something of my past life, you'll see only the bare facts, not the deeper cause of my suffering, which is more complex. Please bear with me and read my letter all the way through. I'm writing to you as a friend, asking for your support".

There were a few blots of ink on the letter, which continued on the next page. "Do you remember my mother? Before she died two months ago, she was still working for the Department of Popular Education, running her mobile library in N. province. But I don't need to tell you, you knew her yourself".

Yes, I had known Maria Stepanovna Olshevich,

and remembered her well. Her circle of acquaintances had been large and varied, and her funeral was attended by members of all the local party, soviet and professional organisations. In the 1890s, she had had much authority with liberals as a publisher of popular scientific works and a tireless campaigner for women's and peasants' education. Politically she was close to the Populists, and she gave a great deal of money to the revolutionary underground. But she was never active in politics. Her passion was for books, and she spent her life setting up libraries, museums and literacy schemes in the towns and villages for the workers and peasants.

Tall, slim and erect, with a lovely tilt to her head and a fine expressive face, she inspired great respect, even a little fear. She had a dry, clear voice, and she spoke briefly and to the point, a cigarette always in her mouth. She dressed simply and never followed fashion, but she had the beautiful well cared-for hands of a lady, with a thick gold ring set with a dark ruby on the fourth finger of her left hand.

"What you probably don't realise is that she had her own emotional crisis when she was young," Olga Sergeevna went on. "And afterwards she developed a strict moral code, and condemned anyone who didn't follow it — deep down she despised them. She was a good person, generally progressive in her views, but in matters of love she was implacable. Most of the arguments between us weren't about politics in the narrow sense of the word, but about our different understanding of what was proper and desirable in my emotional life.

"Mother had married a soldier for love, against her parents' wishes, and according to her she was happy for a while as a provincial officer's wife. She bore him two sons and was a model mother, and he worshipped her. But it wasn't long before she felt stifled by her passive comfortable life. You know what inexhaustible energy she had. She had had a good education for those days. She had read widely and travelled abroad — she even corresponded with Tolstoy. I'm sure you can imagine that a regimental officer could hardly satisfy her needs. Then fate decreed that she met the local *Zemstvo* doctor, Sergei Ivanovich, a character straight out of Chekhov, with the same vague idealism, fond of eating and drinking, greatly troubled by evil and injustice. He was tall and handsome, read the same books as Mother, talked emotionally about life in the countryside, grieved for the 'unenlightened peasantry,' and shared her dreams of establishing schools and libraries throughout Russia.

"It all ended as might have been expected. One hot summer evening, when the colonel was away on manoeuvres, Mother found herself in the arms of my future father, with her book *Mobile Libraries in New Zealand* lying beside her in the grass.

"He was reluctant to accept that their idyllic evening required any radical change to his life. He liked his freedom, and he had a housekeeper, a young peasant widow....

"But as I said, Mother had her own moral code. She told me later that she never resisted her feelings for him. She saw their love as something sacred, greater than any marriage obligations. She was incapable of toying with love, she would have considered it beneath her. In Sergei Ivanovich she found everything her heart and soul were seeking — a man she loved passionately, and a comrade she respected, with whom she could embark hand in hand on the great task of spreading enlightenment and popular education.

'It only remained for her to end her marriage to

the colonel. She was untroubled by the scandal of leaving him. All she knew was that she had to make a new life, one she had freely chosen for her self. She asked Sergei Ivanovich to meet her in the lime grove, and against the chirping of the crickets she read him her brief but unequivocal letter to her husband, concealing nothing from him, and asking for a divorce. Sergei Ivanovich was greatly taken aback, and mumbled about the damage to her reputation and her responsibilities to her sons. But although shocked by his response, her mind was made up. And as she was enchantingly pretty, and he was still in the first flush of his passion for her, the discussion ended in more kisses.

"This made her more determined to bring things to a head. But it wasn't easy. The poor colonel was demented with rage and grief, hurling reproaches at her, threatening to kill her, himself and her scoundrel of a doctor, then weeping and imploring her to stay. But her love for her hero with the compatible soul was greater than her pity for her husband, and when she realised that arguing with him was getting her nowhere, she kissed her sons goodbye and left without another word.

"For months the province talked of nothing else. The liberals sided with Mother, and saw her abandoning her soldier husband for her Zemstvo doctor as a protest against the Tsarist regime. A poet dedicated verses to her in the local newspaper, and at a Zemstvo banquet, a toast was proposed to the heroic women who crossed the threshold of conventional marriage to join those toiling for the welfare of the common people.

"She lived openly with Sergei Ivanovich on his estate, and they worked together to realise her cherished dream of establishing a mobile library in the province. It was at the height of the reaction of the

1880s, after the Tsar's assassination, and her work involved a huge amount of risk and struggle. But with her usual persistence she made contacts, took on the local governors and Zemstvo leaders, travelled to St Petersburg, argued her case, and stood her ground. Then just as her dreams were about to be realised, she and poor bewildered Sergei Ivanovich were both arrested and sent into exile — not a very remote place — and it was there that I was born.

"She lost none of her fighting spirit in exile, running literacy classes for the peasants, setting up libraries and self-education groups. My father drank too much and put on weight. But his arrest gained him a reputation as a revolutionary, and after they were released he fell in with radical members of the Zemstvo. Mother returned to her education work in the province, and for the next year their lives seem to be following a settled well defined path.

"It all came to an end when she caught her balding but still attractive husband making a totally unambiguous proposal to a peasant girl on his estate named Arisha. He tried to deny it, but things turned serious when she became pregnant. Mother immediately packed her bags and moved to the district capital with me, leaving him a businesslike note without reproaches or recriminations, insisting only that he cut down on his drinking, and provide for Arisha and her baby.

"She told me all this much later, evidently in the hope that by being honest with me she would encourage me onto the path of duty. I remember her great strength and self-control in bearing her grief. Not once did I see her in tears, even though I know she never stopped loving my father, and was faithful to him to the end of her life.

"She set up a publishing house in her name that published popular science books, and I was always with her. From my earliest childhood I was part of her circle of people involved with revolutionary ideas, and by the time I was a teenager I was familiar with 'illegals' and 'illegal' activities, and was reading the underground press. We lived very modestly, even ascetically. Home life was ruled by an atmosphere of discipline and hard work, with politics always in the air. I was just fifteen when I was first arrested, which made Mother very proud of me. But it was then that our ideological paths began to diverge. She remained a Populist, while I became a Marxist, and joined the revolutionary underground.

"When I was eighteen, I became close to a leading member of the League of Struggle named Konstantin. He was older and more politically experienced than I was, and under his influence I joined the Bolsheviks. We started an affair, although we refused on principle to get married. At first Mother objected that I was too young and should have waited. But she eventually came round, and we moved in with her and continued our political work under her roof. Konstantin was an 'illegal,' and before long the three of us were arrested. Mother's friends managed to secure her release, but Konstantin and I were sent into exile.

"I'm afraid you may be tired of this long preamble, but without it you'll be unable to make sense of my present dilemma. I'm Maria Stepanovna's daughter, and you never forget the lessons you learn as a child! So please have patience and continue reading, for I'm coming to the crisis of the second generation.

"I escaped from exile on my own without Konstantin, and made my way back to St. Petersburg. And to cover my tracks there, my comrades found me a job as a governess in the home of a wealthy engineer named M. The house was opulently furnished, and he and his wife lived in great style. Although he had been a Marxist in his student days, socialism for him now was merely a subject for after-dinner conversation — he and his friends discussed politics the way they discussed the latest play or painting. I was unfamiliar with this world, and found it alien and repellent. On my first evening at his house, he praised the revisionist Marxists Eduard Bernstein and others, and I attacked their views with an anger totally inappropriate to the occasion, then couldn't sleep all night, furious with myself for having lost control of my emotions.

"Something about the man exasperated me the moment I set eyes on him. I was especially infuriated by the ironically tender glances he kept giving me. But even though I hated his liberal politics and thought he was unprincipled and self-serving, I wanted passionately to change him, and convince him we Marxists were right.

"His wife, Lydia Andreevna, was a fragile doll of a woman, dressed in lace and furs, who had somehow borne him five strapping children. She would gaze at him with adoring eyes, laughingly telling everyone that the longer she was married to him the more in love with him she was. I hated their blissful family life, and was driven to distraction by M.'s consideration for his pretty wife, and his constant worries about her health. I would make spiteful remarks about smug liberals, and go out of my way to tell them about the hardships of life in exile, reducing poor nervous Lydia Andreevna to hysterical tears. 'Why do you keep doing that?' M. would ask me afterwards, with a look of tender reproach.

"Sometimes I hated them both so much I imagined putting an end to their family happiness by dropping a 'careless' remark, so the police would come and raid the house. But it was my refuge, and I couldn't leave.

And when I complained to my comrades, they said 'So why have anything to do with them? If that's how you feel, just stay out of their way.'

"But this was impossible. However much I hated M.'s guttural voice and handsome self-satisfied figure, I was in despair if I didn't see him for a day. I was mortified that I was such an insignificant person in his life, and his slightest neglect of me caused me acute pain. Yet whenever we met we would argue, shouting at each other until we were hoarse, and outsiders would have assumed we hated each other.

"Then sometimes in the middle of an argument our eyes would meet, and those glances had their own language, which I was afraid to understand.

"Once I returned to the house late at night after party work kept me out longer than usual, and he opened the door to me. 'At last, I'd lost hope of ever seeing you again!' he said, and next minute I was in his arms. I wasn't surprised, I had been expecting it for so long. And afterwards I went back to my room, and he spent the rest of the night in his study, where he slept when he had to work late.

"Next evening there were guests, and we began arguing, and it was as though we were enemies again. It was in the first white nights of early spring, and after everyone left he invited me take a drive around St. Petersburg's islands with him. His wife laughed and insisted I go — it wouldn't have occurred to her to be jealous, she found it amusing.

"Life soon became very complicated. It was a difficult time for the party, and I was up to my ears in work and political worries. Like a coward, I kept putting off having things out with him, and waited until the summer, when Lydia Andreevna was leaving for the south with the children. And strange as it might seem, I began to think especially fondly of Konstantin, my comrade and lover in exile, and I redoubled my efforts to get him released.

"If you had asked me who I loved then, I would have said without hesitation Konstantin. But if that meant losing M., I would rather have died. M. was alien to me, yet in so many ways we were so similar and well matched. I hated the way he looked at me, I hated his ideas and his lifestyle, but as a person I loved him desperately, for all the qualities so opposed to everything I valued and admired in people. Our love brought neither of us happiness, but neither of us could imagine parting. I'm still amazed he was attracted to me. Even then I wasn't pretty, I was severe and 'unfeminine' and had no idea how to dress. But I knew he loved me in a way he had never loved his pretty adoring wife.

"We spent the summer alone together in the house, a tense agonising summer, full of conflicting emotions for both of us. Neither of us had a moment's happiness, but we weren't afraid to tell each other how unhappy we were, and it just brought us closer. Then at the end of the summer I discovered that I was pregnant. I thought of ending the pregnancy, but neither of us could contemplate this, and I left for my mother's place in the country".

The letter broke off again, and continued in shaky pencilled writing on an office form:

"I immediately told Mother everything — about my guilt and misery, and the feelings tormenting M., torn between his love for me and for his wife. After hearing me out, she sat in silence for a long time, puffing on a cigarette. Then next morning she came into my room, and announced, 'It's clear you love M. You must write at once to Konstantin.'

"'But what should I tell him?'

"'What an absurd question! That you love someone

else of course! It would be quite wrong to try to spare his feelings, it will only create more misery later on.'

"'But I don't want to spare Konstantin's feelings, I love him, I've never stopped loving him.'

"'Nonsense. How can you love him if you're with M.?' she said.

"I tried again to explain to her my conflicting emotions — my love and respect for Konstantin and our emotional rapport, and my wild attraction for M., who I could neither love nor respect as a person. But she didn't understand. 'Well if it's just physical attraction you feel for him, you'd better pull yourself together and stop seeing him!'

"'But that's the problem Mother, it's love too, just a different kind of love. If he was in danger, I'd give my life for him. If I was told to die for Konstantin, I'd refuse. But it's Konstantin I need and love, my life would be empty without him. I don't love M. that way.'

"'What nonsense!' she repeated angrily.

"But she was becoming confused, insisting first that I write to Konstantin and break up with him, then that I leave M. But leaving either of them seemed wrong and dishonest, and for the first time in my life I felt it had been a mistake to confide in her.

"The outcome was that I wrote to Konstantin telling him every thing. At first I had only a brief reply from him, saying he needed more time to take things in. But even those few lines were filled with a warmth that told me that unlike Mother he under stood.

"And he did understand. Far away in exile, he lived through all my doubts and conflicts, and was able to accept me as I was, claiming only that part of me that reached out to him and couldn't live without him. As far as I was concerned, the matter was partly settled. But Mother was horrified that I was writing to both of them, and it was then that she told me about her own 'crisis of the heart,' evidently hoping it would encourage me to choose between them.

"She was mainly distressed by what she saw as my emotional weakness. 'In every other way you're so fearless. I can't understand why love makes you so cowardly, you must have inherited it from your father. And what about M.'s wife? Are you going to tell her everything too, and make her "accept" the situation?'

"'No, she doesn't come into it. M. loved her, and he still does, but he has never been emotionally close to her. His love for me changes nothing between them.'

"At this Mother completely lost her temper, saying that such four-way relation ships might be acceptable in 'decadent Paris,' but that sooner or later I would have to decide.

"In the spring I gave birth to Zhenya. M. came to stay with us, and those weeks with him and our baby were the happiest of my life. Mother immediately had a far closer relationship with him than she had had with Konstantin, and by the time he left, she had decided the choice was obvious — I must be with the father of my child.

"But the more she insisted, the more I missed Konstantin. It was as if he and I were in one camp, and M. and Mother were in the other, just as we differed politically — Konstantin and I who were in the camp of the proletariat, and the liberal and the Populist charity worker who made common cause with the bourgeoisie.

"Then everything was put on hold when I was arrested again and was sentenced to another term in exile. Zhenya stayed with her grand mother, and I went on writing to M. and Konstantin. Finally Konstantin and I had the good fortune to meet in exile, and we began living together again as man and wife, naturally and happily, without dramas or scenes, two people who were emotionally and politically at one.

"It was then that Mother began in her heart to despise me, sending me long reproachful letters reminding me how much I loved M., accusing me of destroying him merely out of pity for Konstantin. M. issued ultimatums, then abruptly broke off contact with me, and I stayed with Konstantin.

"I was released from exile in 1904, and returned to St Peters burg. It was inevitable that M. and I would meet there again, and it was as though we had never parted. It all started again — the joy and the agony, the intensity of our mutual attraction and our feelings of isolation. I feared the power of our emotions all the more now as he had told his wife, and was insisting that we make our liaison public and get married.

"I was aware more than ever of our differences. Russia was in turmoil, people's politics were increasingly polarised, and what had been just theoretical arguments a few years ago were now vital platforms for action. M. was to the right even of the liberal 'Liberation' group. We spoke literally different languages.

"I despised myself when I was with him, and missed him desperately when we were apart. He hated the Bolsheviks and my work for them, and longed to 'possess me forever and always.' I detested his politics, but lacked the strength to tear him from my heart. There was something strangely maternal about my feelings for him. I felt sorry for him, as if he wasn't being true to himself and I had to help him. How could I leave him at the political cross roads?

"This agony went on for several months, until Konstantin arrived unexpectedly in St Petersburg. This time my confession caused him great unhappiness, and he made his jealousy painfully obvious. Nevertheless we began living together again, not as lovers but as friends. This was more than M. could bear. He refused to believe we weren't romantically involved, and demanded that I leave him. Each day brought some new drama. Once he burst into the flat hurling obscenities at Konstantin, saying if I didn't leave with him immediately it was all over between us.

"I didn't leave with him, and we parted as enemies. Konstantin and I struggled on together. He saw how wretched I was, but was too jealous to be able to help me. For the first time in my life — although I'm experiencing something similar now — I was too unhappy to lose myself in my work.

"It was then that Mother arrived in St Petersburg with Zhenya, summoned by M.'s desperate letters, and demanded that I make up my mind and stop prevaricating.

"'But I made up my mind long ago, Mother,' I said.

"'Well in that case stop torturing M. You say you're no longer Konstantin's wife, so why the pretence?'

"'You're wrong, I'm staying with Konstantin.'

"'You love M.,' she repeated stubbornly. 'You should be courageous in love. Love has its own laws, you're just cluttering them up with logic and reason. You can overcome your differences with M., even your political differences. You won't make a Marxist of him, but you're stronger than he is, and he loves you so much he'll do anything for you.'

"But her advice had the opposite effect on me, and I knew joining my life to M.'s would mean my spiritual death. She arranged for us to meet, and tried to bring about a reconciliation. But there was too much misery and resentment between us, and it came to nothing.

"Then Konstantin and I were both caught up in the revolutionary events of 1905, and our personal problems receded into the back ground. I fled to the south to escape arrest, and he went abroad. Mother returned to the country with Zhenya, and M. stayed in the capital to lead one of the new liberal 'Unions.' Revolutionaries worked and struggled and argued, and when the revolution was crushed and the reaction set in, we had even less time to think about our personal lives.

"In 1908 I was living as an 'illegal' in a little factory town in the south, and it was there that I met M. again. He had abandoned his liberal politics by then, and was an important figure in the world of industrial finance, whose visit to the town was noted in the local press. I was determined to avoid him, but knowing he was there troubled me, just as it had in the past. My work suffered, and before long the police were after me. I had some important documents on me, and my comrades told me to find somewhere safe to hide, and it occurred to me I would be in no danger in the factory apartment where M. was staying.

"A footman announced my arrival, and he came out looking genuinely happy to see me. But his look turned to hostility when I told him the reason I had come. We stood staring at each other like enemies, wondering how we had once loved each other so passionately, suffered so intensely, almost died without each other. It was as if a distant relative of his was standing before me, who bore a remote resemblance to the man I had loved, but was now a totally uninteresting stranger. I regretted coming, but decided to go through with it for the sake of my documents. He could be useful to me, and the stress might make him lose some weight! He explained courteously how inconvenient my presence was, and I invoked the claims of our old friendship and pretended not to understand, and he had no option but to let me stay.

"I can imagine how badly he slept that night. I slept

excellently, despite knowing that in the next room was the man whose fleeting glances had induced burning waves of passion in me, whose presence I had been able to sense from the other end of the house.

"Not once had he asked about our little girl, and that night I knew that our love was over. Next morning we parted coldly, without expressing any desire to see each other again. The past was buried and forgotten.

"Then soon afterwards I met Konstantin again. He had returned from exile, but we had been working in different parts of Russia, and it was several months since we had met. And do you know, I felt extraordinarily remote from him too, and began to see him in a new light. It was as if everything we had experienced in the years since the revolution had left its mark, wiping out every trace of our old selves. We disagreed about everything — our understanding of events, our approach to the tasks of the moment, our vision for the future. He had suffered for his politics and had fallen out with the party, and his personal and political problems had left him bitter and resentful. He had lost his old passionate faith in the revolution, and had adopted a position of cautious watchfulness, convinced that there would be a long period of stagnation and retreat. He spoke like a man weary of the battle, who was withdrawing to find a safe refuge for himself, and with an anger coloured by his unhappiness, he pointed to all our mistakes.

"Unlike him, I was filled with new energy. I felt I had matured emotionally in the revolution, and could now put all my energy into my political work. We tried to continue working together, but realised how estranged we had become, and I grabbed the chance to leave Russia illegally and continue my interrupted chemistry studies in Switzerland.

"Konstantin gradually moved away from the

party altogether. When war broke out he became a patriot, and after October 1917 he actively sabotaged the soviets. As far as I know he died fighting with the Whites. M. managed to escape abroad to avoid the 'punishing hand of the proletariat.' But by then their fates no longer concerned me.

"You must be wondering as you read this inordinately long account of my life what my crisis is. It's all in the past now — what's the problem? But to understand my present unhappiness, I felt you should know a little about what kind of person I am. If nothing else, my story will show you that my female instincts are as strong as anyone's, and I have some understanding of the complexities of the human heart. But for all my tolerance, I'm completely unable to deal with this situation now with my daughter.

"As I said, sometimes I console myself with the thought that I don't understand my Zhenya, just as my mother didn't understand me. But I find the whole thing so shabby and sordid that it sometimes makes me despair. Please help me, criticise me if necessary. Perhaps I'm just old-fashioned, and the new times have produced a new psychology unfamiliar to me. I'd like to come and see you if I may. It will be easier to talk to you now you know something of my past. Can you call me to say when is convenient for you? Evenings are best for me.

"Comradely greetings, Olga Sergeevna.'

She came to see me a few days later at the agreed time, late in the evening. I was struck by how drawn she looked, and by the troubled expression in her eyes. But there was an undeniable charm about her, modestly dressed, with her neatly arranged hair and quiet self-possessed manner, and I found myself looking at her with new interest. Even so, as we chatted about various political matters, I found it hard to reconcile the image of this capable industrial organiser with the writer of the letter.

"Now let's discuss my problem shall we?" she said, interrupting herself in that dry clear voice of hers which reminded me of her mother's compelling tone. "It's about Zhenya, I'd like you to have a word with her. Maybe it's just the usual generation clash, but maybe it's something else. I can't help worrying that she's been corrupted by her abnormal upbringing. Even as a little girl she was carted from place to place, living with me or at her grand mother's or with friends. She's twenty now, and she has worked in a factory since she was seventeen. She's active in the Party and in factory politics — everyone in the district speaks highly of her. She's travelled to the front, and joined the new production drive, naturally she's been exposed to things girls of her age in the past would have known nothing about. And perhaps it's inevitable, and I must just accept it. But on the other hand.... Oh, you can't imagine how confused I've been — I don't know what's right or wrong anymore! It used to make me happy that she's so independent, that she faces life so boldly and can get herself out of any scrape. She's tireless and passionate, just like her grandmother, and she's direct and honest to the point of naivety....

"I expect you know that when I was studying in Switzerland I met Comrade Ryabkov, and I nursed him back to health. Since then we've lived together as man and wife. He's much younger than I am, and in many ways you could say he's my pupil. When we returned to Petrograd in 1917, we both worked for the Bolsheviks and the power of the soviets, and for the past five years we've been very happy together. You know what a sunny disposition he has, and I don't need to tell what a fine worker he is — he's a true proletarian and totally uncompromising. There was no cloud in our relationship, and everything was happy and straightforward bet ween us.

"When we settled in Moscow last year, we invited Zhenya to move in with us. You know our housing allocation, just one room for the three of us. But it can't be helped, it's the same for everyone. Besides, we're almost never home, especially me, I'm often out of town visiting factories for days at a time.

"After our long separation, Zhenya immediately grew close to both of us. Her energy and confidence were infectious, and she made me feel young again. I'd worried she and Comrade Ryabkov mightn't get on, but they became the best of friends. He seemed so much more cheerful with her around, and his health improved, and I would send him off to meetings and the theatre with her. The three of us lived happily together, until...".

She broke off, and sat looking over my shoulder out of the window, unable to continue.

"Well, Olga Sergeevna," I said at last. "I suspect what has happened is distressing but inevitable — Zhenya and Comrade Ryabkov have slept together. Come, what's so terrible about that?"

"But it's not just that, not that at all! It was as though I could see into their souls...".

"And what did you see?"

"Nothing. No love, no passion, no wish to understand or end the situation, as if it was all perfectly normal and it was just me who didn't understand. Then I wondered if I was just behind the times, like my mother was. That's what I wanted to talk to you about".

She said that a month ago, Zhenya had asked her for a ten-minute interview at work — "since that's the only way to get hold of you, Mother!" Then very calmly and without preamble, she told her she was pregnant. She couldn't have the baby, she had no time. The new law legalising abortion had just been passed, and she needed her mother's advice on how to get one.

When Olga Sergeevna asked who the father was, she said she didn't know, and she assumed she didn't want to tell her. But she felt devastated. She said nothing to Andrei, seeing it as Zhenya's business to tell him if she wanted to. But something nagged at her. Doubts began to stir, and details of their life together began to take on a new light.

She despised herself for these thoughts, and tried to push them out of her mind. But they persisted, and prevented her from getting on with her work. So much so that one evening she left a meeting early and went home, where she found the two of them in bed together.

"But I was even more shocked by what happened next. Andrei just grabbed his cap and walked out, and when I blurted out to Zhenya 'So why did you say you didn't know who the father was?' she replied calmly, 'Well I don't, it's either him or the other one.'

"'Which other one?'

"'Oh, a few months ago I was sleeping with another one too. No one you know, it's all over now.'

"'But why? Were you really so attracted to them both? You're so young, it's not normal at your age...!'

"'How can I put it, Mother?' she said. 'I've been sleeping with men for ages. I like them, they like me, and it doesn't commit you to anything. I don't see what you're so upset about. It's not as if I'm underage or prostituting myself or being raped, I sleep with them of my own free will. We stay together as long as we like each other, and when it's over we split up and no one gets hurt. I'll lose a week's work because of the abortion, which is a nuisance, but that's my fault, I'll use something next time.'"

When Olga Sergeevna asked her why she slept with men she didn't love, she said she had liked the other one a lot, but he annoyed her by treating her like a child, which was why she had taken up with Andrei, her soulmate and friend.

"And do they know about each other?" Olga Sergeevna asked.

"Of course they do, I've nothing to hide. They can leave if they don't like it, Andrei doesn't care. The other one was upset, but he soon came round. Anyway I've left him now, I lost interest in him".

Olga Sergeevna tried to point out how selfish and irresponsible her behaviour was. But she retorted, "You say I'm selfish, but tell me honestly Mother, would you say that if I was a boy? I don't mean paying prostitutes or abusing little girls, but if I was your twenty-year-old son sleeping with women I liked who liked me too? Admit it, you wouldn't. I'm the same person I've always been. I work hard, I know my responsibilities to the Party. But I don't see what the Party's got to do with who I sleep with. Obviously I can't have a baby with so much work to do, that would be wrong. As for everything else...".

"But what about me, Zhenya?" Olga Sergeevna cried. "Didn't you consider how I would feel?"

"Why should it bother you?" she said. "You were happy to send us to meetings together, you wanted us to be friends. Why can we be friends but not have sex? What are you so afraid of? We're not taking anything from you, Andrei adores you as much as he's always done. You never have sex with him anyway, you're too busy! You're being so unfair. You lived your life when you were young, why can't he live his? Do you want to tie him to your apron strings?

It must be your mother's bourgeois attitudes coming out in you!"

What upset Olga Sergeevna most was that neither of them showed the slightest remorse, as if it was all quite normal and hardly worth discussing, and she was painfully aware that neither Zhenya nor her gentle honest Andrei considered themselves in any way to blame. It was only with the greatest condescension to her, as someone who didn't understand things, that they said they were sorry she was upset, but she was needlessly turning things into a tragedy. Nothing had changed, no one wanted to cause her pain or distress. But if it really mattered so much to her, they would stop sleeping together, although they couldn't see what difference that would make.

Plunged into this chaos of emotions, Olga Sergeevna had decided to ask my advice. Was it nothing more than youthful promiscuity, or was it something new? Was this the new sexual morality of the Revolution? We discussed these questions at length.

"What I find so painful," she said, wearily leaning her cheek on her shapely arm, in a gesture that reminded me of her mother, "is their lack of emotion, like people without inner lives. If they loved each other I could accept it, however unhappy it made me — because I love Andrei very very much — and it wouldn't leave this bad taste in my mouth, this sense of physical nausea. To put it bluntly, I find myself hating them. I can't understand why they've treated me so badly, with so little thought for my feelings. It makes me wonder if they're capable of love at all. They keep saying they love me. But what does love mean when they cause me such pain, and do it so casually?

"Once when I reproached Zhenya, she said, 'Well it's better than you and my father lying to his wife about your affair!' But there's a huge difference there that she can't or won't see. I loved M. passionately, no less than his wife did, possibly more, and I saw the suffering he caused me giving me equal rights to him. But with these two there's nothing, no compassion, no remorse, not even the most basic sensitivity to others' feelings, just claiming their right to grab at happiness wherever they find it — and they call themselves communists!"

I couldn't help laughing at this, and she smiled too, and when we finally said goodbye I agreed to talk to Zhenya.

She worked for the Party in the afternoons and evenings, and she came early the next morning, a tall slender girl with a lively expressive face that reminded me of her grandmother's. She was rather pale, with dark circles under her eyes, and when I shook her hand it was cold and damp; evidently she hadn't fully recovered from her abortion.

She had a direct unaffected manner, and began speaking at once. "I expect Mother's told you I sleep with men I'm not in love with. But I've read enough novels to know you need time to fall in love, and I don't have it! We're rushed off our feet with work these days — but when have we ever had time for love? Our heads are always full of other things. Of course there are times when you're less busy and you realise you like someone. But as for falling in love, as soon as you grow fond of them they're called up to the front or sent off to another town, or you're both so busy you forget about each other. You just have to enjoy the times you can be with someone. The only thing I'm scared of is catching a disease. But if you look them in the eye and ask them straight out, they won't lie. There was one who really liked me, maybe he even loved me, and I could see how hard it was for him. But I would never have forgiven him if I'd slept with him and he hadn't told me".

She had lovely wide open eyes, and gave the impression of complete candour and honesty. "So tell me Comrade Zhenya, why didn't you tell your mother about your affair with Andrei from the start?" I asked her.

"I didn't think it concerned her," she said. "If we'd fallen in love of course I would have told her, and I'd probably have moved out. But there's nothing between us, if it hadn't been me it would have been someone else. She can't stop him seeing other women can she? I don't understand her! She doesn't mind us being friends, or that he talks more to me than he does to her. She's upset that I'm taking him from her, but she has no time for sex! We're closer in age, we've the same interests, it's so natural...".

"But perhaps without knowing it you might be in love with him?" I put in.

She shook her head. "I don't know what you mean by love. For me it means you'd give your life for someone — you think and worry about them, and want to be with them all the time. As for anything serious with Andrei, no thanks! Oh he's a good person, kind and cheerful and brave about his health, as Mother's probably told you. But I get bored when I'm around him too long and start looking for someone else".

She frowned. "What bothers Mother is that I don't love any of them — she says it's immoral. But I think she's wrong. I remember her when I was a child, forever running between my father and Konstantin, eating her heart out and making them all miserable. My grandmother told her to stop being a coward and decide between them. But she couldn't decide. She loved both of them and they both loved her, and they all ended up hating each other. I don't end up hating anyone. When it's over it's over. The minute someone gets jealous, I remember how jealous Konstantin and my father were of each other, and tell myself I'd rather die than go through that. It's simpler and more honest this way. I don't belong to anyone but myself, and they just have to accept that!"

"Do you really mean to say you've never loved anyone?" I asked. "I'm not convinced anyway by your definition of love, it sounds like something you've read in novels!"

"But what makes you think I don't love anyone?" she said in honest amazement.

"So who do you love then?"

"Well my mother, more than anyone in the world. I couldn't live without her, her happiness means more than anything to me...".

"Despite destroying her happiness and breaking her heart?"

"I'd never have done it if I'd thought she would take it this way, I just thought she was above jealousy like Andrei and me. I know now how wrong I was, and I'm so sad, much sadder than she realises...". Her eyes filled with tears. "I'd give my life for her — it isn't just words, it's how I feel about her. I just wish we could all stop being unhappy and go back to being friends again".

She no longer tried to hide the tears pouring down her cheeks and falling onto her frayed black skirt. "The worst thing is how it's affecting her work. But however much I love her, I still think she's terribly wrong and Andrei and I are right. I always thought she was infallible, and it's shaken my faith in her. I don't want to stop trusting her — how can I trust anyone else if I do?"

She said that in a few days she was moving out to live in a hostel with some girlfriends, and she was worried her mother would be unable to cope without her, as she had been in charge of the tedious business of organising their rations. She sighed, and spoke about her in a sober motherly way. "She won't eat properly unless someone's there to push food at her. Sometimes she goes the whole day without eating, and Andrei's just as bad, they're as helpless as children. Of course I'll visit them and do what I can, but I'm busy and it won't be the same. It's much simpler when people live together".

When it was time to say goodbye, I said "What upset her so much was that she saw you as cold and unfeeling. I'm glad I'll be able to tell her how much you love her".

"Yes, she knows that," she smiled. "I'm sure I'll get into more scrapes with men — I'm her daughter and my grandmother's grand daughter! And there are other people I love too, almost as much as her. There's Lenin of course. Don't laugh, I mean it, I love him more than all the men I've slept with, I'd give my life for him. When I'm going to hear him speak I can't sleep for excitement! Then there's our Party secretary, Comrade Gerasim, I love him too. There's a man for you! Even if he's wrong sometimes I always trust him, because I know that deep down his politics are correct. Do you remember when he was in trouble with the Party last year? What a fight we put up for him, I mobilised the whole district to support him. Yes, I definitely love Comrade Gerasim," she said earnestly, as if trying to convince me and vindicate herself.

"Well I must be off. We're buried in work, I've just been elected secretary of our Party cell," she said with pride. "Life would be so good if Mother could just accept things". She sighed again, a deep childish sigh. "Please tell her Andrei is all hers, I need him as much as I need this chair! Do you think she'll understand and still love me? Say what you like though,

I wouldn't want to fall in love the way she did, I'd never have time to work!"

She left the room, and I sat at my desk wondering which of them was right, Olga Sergeevna or her daughter's generation, with their completely new outlook on life.

Outside the door I could hear her youthful laugh, and her cheerful voice saying "Can't stop comrades, I'm late! We've so much work to do!"

The ending captures beautifully this moment in women's lives in the Revolution. And through her three women Kollontai was looking back on her own life as a revolutionary, born into wealth and privilege in the old Russia, fighting with the downtrodden and oppressed to make a new Russia to inspire the world, blazing a trail for the new liberated sexuality of the Revolution. She knew her heroines, and she brought them unforgettably to life, with their courage and idealism and vulnerability, struggling, passionate and human.

Selected Writings
Kollontai's Main Publications 1900 - 1923
(written in Russian, German and Finnish)

1900 "The Workers' Question in Finland".

1901 "Industry and Trade in the Grand Duchy of Finland".

1902 "Raftsmen in Finland". "Finnish Workers' Housing". "The Land Question in Finland".

1903 *The Life of the Finnish Proletariat.*

1905 *The Question of the Class Struggle.* "Feminists and Proletarian Women in the Women's Emancipation Movement".

1906 "The Workers' Movement in Finland". *Finland and Socialism.* "Results of the Mannheim Women's Meeting of the Socialist International".

1907 "The Election Campaign in Finland". "Finland At the Ballot-Box".

1908 "The Woman Worker in Contemporary Society". "What Is Done in Russia to Protect the Labour of Women Textile workers?"

1909 "Organising Women Workers in Russia". *The Social Basis of the Woman Question.*

1910 "The Working Women's Movement in the West". "The Proletariat and the Bourgeoisie in the Struggle against Prostitution". "The Fate of Humanity and the Population Question". "The Stuttgart International Women's Conference".

1911 *Notes of an Agitator Abroad.* "Working Women's Organisations in the West". "The Housewives' Movement in France". " On An Old Theme". "Sexual Relations and the Social Struggle".

1912 "The Lives of Women Textile workers in Belgium". "International Women's Day in Germany and Austria". *Around Workers' Europe.* "The Inter national Proletariat and War". "Women's Fight in the Swedish Parliament for the Vote". "Working Women and War".

1913 *The New Woman.* "Women's Day". "The Protection of Mother hood". "August Bebel. Fighter for Truth and the Freedom of Women". "The Women Workers' Movement and Women's Fight for Freedom".

1914 *Working Woman and Mother.* "Types and Forms of Maternity Insurance". "War and Our Immediate Tasks". "The International Tasks of Women's Day".

1915 "What is to be Done? A Reply to Socialists". "The Socialist Women's International and War". "The Third International". "Why Was the German Proletariat Silent in the July Days?" *Workers' Wives Unite!*

1916 *Society and Motherhood.* "The Workers' Anti-War Movement in America". "Finnish Socialists in America". "Do Internationalists Want a Split?" *Who Needs the War?*

1917 April: "Where Does Revolutionary Defencism Lead?" "Our Memorial to the Fighters for Freedom". "The Demonstration of Soldiers' Wives". "A Serious Gap". May: "Speech to the First All-Russia Congress of Soviets on the Finnish Question". "Women's Battalions". "In the Front Line of Fire". "Our Tasks".

June: "Prisoners of War of the Russian Imperialists".
"Extraordinary Congress of the Finnish Social
Democratic Party". September: "The Bankruptcy
of the 'Civil Peace' Slogan". "When Will the War
End?" October: "Letter to Working Women in
Red Petrograd". November: "From World War
to Women's Voting Rights". "Working Women,
Stand at Your Posts!" December: "Decree from the
Commissariat of Social Welfare on the Protection of
Women and Children".

1918 "Why the Bolsheviks Must Win". *The Woman
Worker in the Year of the Revolution.* "The 'Cross
of Motherhood' and the Soviet State". "The Town
of the First 'Rebels.'" "Working Women on the
Labour Front". "The First All-Russian Congress of
Women Workers and Peasants". *The International
Conferences Of Socialist Women.* "Among the
'Backward.'" "Old Age is not a Curse but a Deserved
Rest". "The Priests Are Still Busy". "Time to Do Away
with the 'Black Nests!'" *The New Morality and the
Working Class.*

1919 "Karl Liebknecht and Rosa Luxemburg. Fighters,
Heroes, Martyrs". "The Work of the People's
Commissariat of Social Welfare". *Working Women
Struggle For Their Rights.* "Working Women and
the Soviets". *Women Workers and Peasants on the
Red Front, Crisis in the Countryside. What Are We
Fighting For? The War With Tsar Hunger. Whose
Will the Golden Harvest Be? Don't Be a Deserter! Be a
Firm Fighter!*

1920 *A History of the Women Workers' Movement
in Russia.* "Working Women in the Economic
Upheaval". "Working Women and the Red Army".

"International Women's Day: Our Festival and Our Tasks". "Another Victory for Communist Women". "Class War and Women". "The Labour Republic and Prostitution". *Communism and the Family*. "The Work of the *Zhenotdel*".

1921 *The Workers' Opposition*. "The Letters of Rosa Luxemburg". "The Conference of Communist Women Organisers in the East". "Working Women and the Trade Unions". "Production and Everyday Life". "Theses on Communist Morality in the Sphere of Marriage Relations". "Woman, the Last Slave". *The Position of Women in the Evolution of the Economy. Autobiographical Essay.*

1922 "The October Revolution and the Masses". "First Letter to Young Workers: What a Communist Should Be Like". "Second Letter to Young Workers: Morality as a Form of Class Struggle and Class Rule". "Soon — In 48 Years' Time".

1923 "Make Way for 'Winged Eros!'" *Love of Worker Bees. Woman At the Turning Point.* "Third Letter to Young Workers: about the 'Dragon' and the 'White Bird.'" "The Work of the *Zhenotdel* in the New Conditions".

Suggested Reading in English

Allen, Barbara, *Alexander Shlyapnikov, 1885-1937: Life of an Old Dolshevik,* Haymarket Books, Chicago, 2016.

Balabanova, Angelica, *My Life as a Rebel,* Harper, New York, 1938.

Beatty, Bessie, *The Red Heart of Russia,* Century Co., New York, 1918.

Bebel, August, *Woman and Socialism* (trans. Daniel de Leon), Schocken Books, New York, 1975.

Bryant, Louise, *Six Red Months in Moscow,* Thomas Selzer, New York, 1923.

Carr, E.H., *The Bolshevik Revolution, 1917-1923,* Pelican Books, London, 1977.

Davis, Emma, *A Rebel's Guide to Alexandra Kollontai,* Bookmarks, London, 2019.

Deutscher, Isaac, *The Prophet Armed. Trotsky 1879-1921,* Oxford Paperbacks, 1970.

Engel, Barbara, and **Rosenthal, Clifford** (trans. and eds.), *Five Sisters. Women Against the Tsar,* Knopf, New York, 1975.

Engels, Friedrich, *Origin of the Family, Private Property and the State* (trans. Alick West), Pathfinder Press, New York, 1972.

Evans Clements, Barbara, *Bolshevik Feminist. The Life of Alexandra Kollontai,* Indiana University Press, 1979.

Farnsworth, Beatrice, *Aleksandra Kollontai: Socialism, Feminism and the Bolshevik Revolution*, Stanford University Press, 1980.

Futrell, Michael, *The Northern Underground*, Faber, London, 1973.

Haupt, George, and **Marie, Jean-Jacques**, *Makers of the Russian Revolution* (trans. and eds. C. Ferdinand and D. Bellos), Allen & Unwin, London, 1974.

Holt, Alix (trans. and ed.), *Alexandra Kollontai. Selected Writings,* Allison & Busby, London, 1977.

Kollontai, Alexandra, *Autobiography of a Sexually Emancipated Woman*, Orbach & Chambers, London, 1972.

Kollontai, Alexandra, *Love of Worker Bees* and *A Great Love* (trans. Cathy Porter), Virago, London, 1989; Chicago Review Press, 2005.

Kollontai, Alexandra, *Women Workers Struggle for Their Rights* (trans. Celia Britton), Bristol, 1973.

Kollontai, Alexandra, *The Workers' Opposition,* Solidarity, London, 1968.

Lenin, V.I., *The Emancipation of Women,* International Publishers, New York, 1966.

Liebman, Marcel, *The Russian Revolution* (trans. Arnold Pomerans), Random House, New York, 1970.

Luxemburg, Rosa, *The Essential Rosa Luxemburg* (ed. Helen Scott), Haymarket Books, 2007.

Makarenko, Anton, *The Collective Family. A Guidebook for Russian Parents* (trans. Robert Daglish), Pathfinder Press, New York, 1967.

Porter, Cathy, *Father and Daughters,* Virago, London, 1976

Porter, Cathy, *Alexandra Kollontai. A Biography,* Merlin Press, London, 2013; Haymarket Books, 2014.

Rabinowitch, Alexander, *The Bolsheviks Come to Power,* Haymarket Books, 2017.

Reed, John, *Ten Days That Shook the World,* Penguin Classics, London, 2016.

Rowbothan, Sheila, *Hidden from History*, Pluto Press, London, 1974.

Serge, Victor, *Memoirs of a Revolutionary* (trans. Peter Sedgwick), Oxford University Press, 1963.

Shlyapnikov, Alexander, *On the Eve of 1917* (trans. Richard Chappell), Allison & Busby, London, 1982.

Stites, Richard, *The Women's Liberation Movement in Russia,* Princeton University Press, 1978.

Trotsky, Lev, *The History of the Russian Revolution,* 3 vols. (trans. Max Eastman), Simon & Schuster, New York, 1932.

Zetkin, Clara, *Selected Writings* (trans. and eds. Philip Foner and Angela Davis), Haymarket Books, 2015.